I WISH YOU WEREN'T MY MUMMY

I WISH YOU WEREN'T MY MUMMY

Carole Patti Clarke

Book Guild Publishing
Sussex, England

First published in Great Britain in 2008 by
The Book Guild
Pavilion View
19 New Road
Brighton, BN1 1UF

Typesetting in Baskerville by
Keyboard Services, Luton, Bedfordshire

Printed in Great Britain by
Cromwell Press, Trowbridge, Wilts

A catalogue record for this book is available from
The British Library

ISBN 978 1 84624 257 1

Dramatis Personae

The Family

Lorne	our heroine, the damaged child
Lily	her eldest sister and protector
Patrick	heroic eldest brother away in the army
Frieda	second eldest sister, Mummy's girl and not Lorne's friend
Teddy	second brother; takes on role of protector when Lily leaves home
Charlie	youngest brother, of whom Lorne in her turn takes care
Mummy	cruel, beautiful, imperious Indian lady, poor and frustrated
Daddy	likes a drink, Irish, uncontrollable temper when provoked by his wife's affairs
Grandfather	also fond of a drop, teller of tall tales but has heart of gold
Nana	dead but visited by Lorne in her dreams

The Friends

Eric	sweet-natured neighbour with learning difficulties

Edward	mop-haired dreamer
Fellwick	helpful but embittered by polio
Harry	handsome newspaper boy and pigeon-fancier
Susie	Lorne's sterling best mate

The Village

Mrs Crowswick	old, kind neighbour and mother of Eric
Mrs Entwhistle	sometime babysitter
Mr Dobson	orchard owner
Mrs Grindle	nasty piece with nasty twin sons
Mrs Hayworth	Edward's mum
Molly	spinster who takes Lorne to her bosom
Mr Ramsbottom	the milkman
Mr Patterson	driven to drink and contemplating suicide because of...
Mrs Patterson	colludes with Mummy
Mr Drake	the gravedigger
The Vicar	well-meaning but doddery
Ruby	the hairdresser

Chapter 1

The flakes of snow gently fell, dropping lightly against the windscreen of the Jaguar. Dusk slowly made its way across the sky and I felt nervous. With a touch of my hand the wiper squeaked from side to side across the windscreen. I peered anxiously over the bonnet, driving with caution on my descent along the steep sloping hill. Snow lay on either side of the narrow pathway and the road glistened with a film of frosty ice. I took in a deep breath. I was at last, after all these years, taking this journey alone, down towards the tiny village where I lived as a child. The gentle hum of the engine and the sound of classical music, backing the touching voice of Andrea Bocelli as his CD played, created a mellow feeling. I glanced over to my left as I drove past the row of cottages that slanted down towards the village. The car swerved just a little when I pressed my foot on the brake, but enough to make my heart skip a beat. I gave a sigh of relief as I regained control of the car and gently reversed, stopped and pulled hard on the handbrake.

Although the main descent of the hill still faced me, how could I possibly not stop outside the home of Mrs Grindle. I took in a deep breath and stared towards her cottage. I knew I was never going to see that grumpy old woman again, unless as a ghost. There would be no more dog ends lying on the three stone steps leading up to the door where she always stood, balancing a loosely rolled cigarette between the side of her thin chapped lips, whilst tying a knot in the same old grubby headscarf underneath her flabby double chin. She would always spit a couple of times, ridding her tongue of loose tobacco before inhaling smoke from her limp cigarette, which would float back out through the hairy nostrils of her bulbous nose like some fierce dragon. You could hear, if close by, the flap of her loose fitting sandals against the cracked heels of her feet as she strode down the hill towards the village, grunting at or even insulting any of the villagers that may pass along her way. I smiled at how I escaped her ruthless tongue. Maybe she liked me... Maybe she did. I took in a deep breath and wondered if there was a heaven... If there really was, she would know if she should be looking down at the little girl she once knew who had finally come back and remembered her.

The snow drops no longer fell as I peered up towards the clear starry sky. With another sigh, my foot touched the accelerator and I slowly drove away but soon stopped just a few yards further down. The straggled frosty branches of the wild orchard to my left, where fruit barely grew, took my attention. I remembered it as a haunted wood, a place, if you dared to enter, with tall stinging nettles and slimy grass snakes rattling around amongst patches of bluebells that blanketed the ground. In between the glisten of bent branches, looking down, there stood from the view above a tall, narrow, whitewashed, two-storey townhouse. Mrs Patterson, I whispered, sighing on now realizing how she used her destructive personality towards me, her constant squawling, her cruel, cruel comments, her teeth large and stained like horses' behind her ruby red lips, showing sarcasm in her smile when she looked down at me, gloating at my sadness. I peered in between the bent branches at the house where she once lived. Now I had become a woman myself who always felt forgiveness in my heart, I wished that I could have just seen a glimpse of her living reflection through the dimly lit window above, instead of imagining the thick piece of rope that she had slipped through a solid hook screwed into the beams of the ceiling, from which her body was found dangling on that terrible lonely night.

My immediate thought was to turn the car around and drive the hell out of there. My attempt failed; the road was far too slippery for speed. I took in a deep breath and continued to drive steadily down. My dear Molly, the kind villager who welcomed me into her home, whispered to me once more; how could I possibly resist? As I neared the bottom of the hill I pulled on the handbrake and stopped outside Primrose Cottage. Her tiny cottage glistened, not with the snow that lay thick and still on the slanted roof, or the frost that painted the two leaded windows, it glistened with kindness and warmth and love and affection I was once so lucky to be given from Molly who took me under her wing so very long ago. A lump appeared inside my throat as I drove steadily away. Was it for the joy of remembering her, or the sadness of knowing that I might never pass this way again, to sit and stare through the twinkling glass of her window?

My drive took me by the one and only public house in the valley of this tiny village. It looked quaint and within its dark walls and low-beamed ceilings, as old as life itself, it had given sanctuary through its open doors to many a drunk. The same old pattern of grey smoke twirled up into the clear starry sky from the cracked dry chimney pot on the roof above, leaving the warmth inside the open grate of the burning coal fire, where publican stood and pensioners leant against the low wooden bar with hot toddies in clear round glasses and conversation, I would imagine, of Christmases past. There was no rusty old bicycle that once would have leaned against the side of its wall as I slowly turned into what was once just dusty old gravel but was now a neatly tarmacked car park. I remembered my childhood friends. Harry, my friend, I spoke out softly, surely not dead, I wondered where his life had taken him. I would no longer see that scruffy, yet handsome, boy who would kneel down against the ground with his bicycle by his side as he rolled loose tobacco into a piece of thin paper, leaving newspapers hanging from his haversack that he strapped over the rusty handlebars of his bike, with broken promises to angry neighbours about delivering them on time.

The vision of Susie as she once was, my chubby cheerful friend, existed now only in my imagination. Considerably older than me, a teenager with an old head on her shoulders, like Harry, she was scared of nothing and no one. And of course, Fellwick, a twenty-year-old scrawny young man, stricken with polio, passing by the barking hounds that were chained to long leads around the bark of tree trunks in Mr Dobson's fruit orchard. The way Fellwick would make his way over the humpback bridge, always cursing the calliper bolted around the wasted muscles of his leg, filled my heart with sadness. This was our meeting place where, if you walked over the gravel, you could listen to pigeons cooing in a green-painted loft that once stood high on wooden stilts hammered down firmly into the hard soil of a wild plot of land. There was no wire fence left standing where Harry would step behind whistling away whilst priding himself on the joy his very own pigeons brought to him. Our meetings here weren't a colony of hardship, but consisted of mischievous laughter and fun, whilst waiting in anticipation as to who would be the first drunk to be thrown out through the red painted doors of the Old Dragon Inn.

As I stood there, I thought how I have always kept hold so tightly of the memories of Eric, my dearest most-loved friend. I try to imagine his vision, his back hunched whilst carrying his plastic-coated shopping bag over the bridge after his daily walk to the village shop. Eric, I whispered, sighing, whilst pressing the tip of my finger against the switch. The inside window next to where I sat moved slowly down. I caught a breath of air and breathed in deeply. The CD was turned down to just a whisper. The tops of partly frozen bulrushes stood tall against the sloping banks of the river. I sat listening to the calm running water of the shallow stream that still flowed in this tiny valley of ghosts.

A teardrop suddenly rolled down my face, and the salty taste touching my lips encouraged me to tilt the rear view mirror. I sat and stared, not at my sorrowful face, but at the reflection through the mirror on the sudden intrusion of Rose Cottage, my childhood home. Rose Cottage, I whispered whilst wiping my tears away. Of course I would have eventually found the courage to turn the steering wheel whilst manoeuvring the car around to face it myself. Such a pretty cottage, with its whitewashed walls and new leaded windows, I would have thought, if I were a stranger driving past. I found myself staring, my eyes fixed on the view through the mirror, staring with curiosity, trying to see beyond the dark leaded glass into the room above, where most of my childhood was spent, locked in by the click of a rusty latch that was screwed on to the old brown-painted wooden door.

My hands felt moist, leaving prints from my fingertips against the glass whilst tilting the mirror for a wider view of my surroundings. The row of cottages, eight in all, most with smoke swirling from their chimneys, and a glow inside from a lamp lit here and there lighting up the tiny windows, with the sound of the stream flowing that faced them, created a picture of an almost peaceful setting, with the exception of one, just one, where no smoke swirled up towards the sky and where no light shone from inside. The weathered street lamp, rusted with age, still held its flicker through mottled glass, standing as proud as it could just yards from the square board that had been nailed on to a stilt, behind a low brick wall, next to the prickly thorns with hidden buds waiting to bloom in the spring that were, once upon a time, Daddy's roses. The square board itself stood stiff in the calm, cold, frosty air displaying in large print that Rose Cottage was up for sale. It was hard to clear my mind of the repressive thoughts that suddenly came back. Was the cottage itself being deliberate in giving me full view? I imagined whispers creeping up the dark entry, beckoning me down and daring me to find the courage to lift the latch on that beaten back door, and enter inside.

My fingers trembled as I turned on the ignition. The engine hummed in full throttle. Andrea Bocelli's CD was turned to a higher volume, accompanying me as I made my exit from the eerie silence of this tiny village. I didn't panic; I mustn't, I thought as I calmly reversed the car. There was no glancing back with the joys of reminiscence. The choice to abandon my visit to the church left me imagining the mossy gravestones next to some of my dearest friends that had been laid to rest. The thick heavy fall of snowflakes fell rapidly down, and amongst the blurry view I saw the ballerina in the music box, our favourite childhood toy, dance on her glass pedestal, the silver key glistening, turning to her tune. Lily, my eldest and dearest sister, appeared, coming towards me, pressing her face against the windscreen, showing the dimple in her cheek with her smile. I could see Mummy walking up the steep pathway, her leopard-skin coat belted tightly and her shapely legs covered by black seamed stockings, struggling as she walked in the tall heels of her stilettos before disappearing through the heavy blizzard of snow. Daddy's hurting cries echoed out of Rose Cottage's walls, crept up from the valley below and roared inside my ears as I continued to drive up the steep hill in total fear, my sweaty hands trembling at the wheel. The brow came unexpectedly and suddenly I was blinded by dazzling headlights and then the sound of hooting horns.

I remember little else of my exit into the wide open road. Only the sound of the monitor bleeping led me to believe I was still alive. With whispering voices around the bed where I lay, I was aware that I was drifting in and out of consciousness. Don't let me go back, I tried to tell them, but no words came from my mouth.

A freckled face peered from under a linen cap... A clock jangled close to her breast.

Aunt Molly's here. I signalled, fighting for glimpses.

Her smiling face ... captured in pockets of floating balloons...

'She's come to collect you,' Mummy's voice whispered. 'Hurry before she pops.'

I didn't want to go back to the brutality. I tried so desperately to fight with the strong force. I fought by blinking to keep my eyes open until there was no other choice but to go with my subconscious mind, wanting the fragments of hairspray that floated in the air to fall on top of my head.

Chapter 2

I ran around the room wanting the fragments of hairspray that floated in the air to fall on top of my head.

'Sit down, you silly girl, sit down now,' said Mummy as the can of spray was thrown down on to the threadbare two-seater settee.

I didn't hesitate. Obeying the order, I perched myself on the edge of the chair.

'You deserve to choke,' I was told as I placed my hand over my mouth, coughing profoundly. 'Sit back on that chair immediately,' which I quickly did.

I couldn't understand why it was Grandfather's favourite chair, with the broken springs hurting my bottom as I sat back. I could faintly smell his whisky and, not daring to get up and look, I wondered which cupboard he had hidden it in this time.

Mummy glanced once more into the mirror, irritated that a film from the spray had settled on the glass. It was a special kind of mirror with pretty roses painted in pink around the oval frame. Special because no one dared go up and look through it. Only Mummy.

'Grandfather dived into the Irish Sea and saved the mirror from drowning. He caught it just in time as it floated on top of the waves and brought it home specially for you, didn't he, Mummy?'

She didn't answer. I sensed she was irritated by the way she rubbed her long fingers hard against the glass.

'Damn this hairspray,' she said.

Jumping up, I offered to get a rag from the polish box, but being ignored once more, I sat back down in the chair. I wish I was taller, I thought, and wondered if I dared stretch up to look through the glass, whether I could see myself smile.

I wished Grandfather would hurry and call to see us again, I thought to myself, remembering that sunny morning when he sailed over the sea on one of his surprise visits to Rose Cottage. Grandfather was a sailor a long time ago, before he got old and frail and his back turned into a hump. He was quite tall with muscles as hard as rock, floppy white hair and a nose that had been broken several times by the flap of the flagship. He told me that he had to hoist it up on stormy days when he sailed the seas. His teeth had fallen out all at once. One by one they fell to the ground when he was punched in the mouth by a pirate who demanded the treasure on his ship. I screwed my face up remembering when he pulled his false teeth out to show me. His gums were pink and raw.

Grandfather wasn't very drunk the last time he called because he didn't hiccup when he spoke. I loved listening to his Irish accent. It was much more jolly than Daddy's. I remember the latch was lifted up on the back kitchen door. Grandfather struggled to get through with that very same mirror that Mummy was looking through, hoisting it underneath one arm. 'It's antique,' he told my Daddy as he rushed over and took it from Grandfather's arm. He left his haversack on the bare asphalt floor, and then rushed over to the tiny window ledge where I stood, took the Windolene and rag from my hands and lifted me high into the air. We followed Daddy through into the front room. It was the best room, opened only for special people who might call.

The mirror was carefully held up against the wall above the mantelpiece. Grandfather and I agreed that that's where it should stay and Daddy, leaning the mirror against the wall, rushed off to find a nail.

'Is all well with you?' Grandfather asked.

'OK,' I said, mimicking his Irish accent.

Daddy rushed back in with an old wooden hammer, a bag of nails and a thick piece of woven string.

'You've not been giving her a load of blarney, have you, pops?' Daddy asked.

'Oh no, the wee child already knows about me adventures,' Grandfather told him.

Daddy winked at me and he and Grandfather held the mirror over the mantel and listened to me as I told them when it sat just right. Daddy held his hand down and I passed him his hammer and the thickest nail I could find. I blinked every time the nail was struck. It was soon knocked in, leaving a jagged hole through the floral wallpaper. Grandfather held the string and fastened it with shaking hands through the metal rung behind the metal frame. My mouth fell wide open in sheer wonder at how pretty it looked when it was finally hung.

I nearly jumped off my chair at the sudden rattle of the letterbox and as it opened I looked towards it. A set of green eyes peeped through.

'Yoo hoo,' she shouted, flickering her thick coated eyelashes, caked in black mascara.

'It's Mrs Patterson,' I told Mummy.

'Open the door instead of sitting there daydreaming,' Mummy told me.

I jumped off the chair and made my way around Mrs Patterson's gaze, as she watched, blinking once then twice as I took each step closer.

'Come on, lass,' she called, trying to speak like the Queen, just in case one of the neighbours might be passing by. 'It's quite nippy out here,' she called. Her bloodshot eyes, all veiny and red, scared me the closer I got, and on my first attempt the latch turned quickly and Mrs Patterson immediately barged through. The awful violet cologne she wore followed her, leaving a whiff in the air which made me sneeze. She slipped off her white plastic mac then pulled the turquoise chiffon scarf down from around her neck before sitting down on the old springy chair. There was no room to place her scarf and mac alongside her, her wide, plump bottom saw to that as she took up the whole width of the seat. I sneezed once more as I was standing closely behind her.

'Bless you,' she said, pressing her fingertips lightly along the back of her yellow bleached hair, backcombed high into a bouffant and as stiff as her neck, as she turned towards me passing over her coat and scarf. There was a dark line of foundation stuck along the inside of the collar. The stale perfume from the chiffon scarf I held made me sneeze again.

I glanced towards the door at the bottom of the stairs. Grandfather must be coming back soon because he hadn't finished fixing the door, I thought. It was still lopsided with an old rusty screw hanging in the hinge. I imagined Grandfather standing there, not that long ago, when he stripped the old brown paint from that very door with a smelly burning machine.

'It's going to have a new lick of paint,' he told me as I watched in fear. The jet of fire leapt out, burning like the tongue of the devil until the paint cracked and fell in flakes to the floor. 'I need to get me energy rolling again,' he said, stopping the machine and then wiping the sweat from his forehead. 'Now, we won't be rolling that wee bit of lino back yet,' he told me as I swept the chippings with the long handled brush from the bare wooden floorboards and on to the shovel.

'Stand back a wee bit and keep an eye out for me,' Grandfather said whilst lifting up the loose floorboard from where I had been standing. 'This'll help get me energy back,' he mumbled as he unscrewed the top from a flat bottle of whisky that was hidden underneath. The whisky gurgled inside the bottle as Grandfather swallowed hard and fast. 'I'll leave that wee bit for later,' he told me, wiping his hand over his mouth before screwing the top back on. He then placed the whisky bottle into the floor space and covered it with the board, hiding it away like treasure where no one could find it.

Mummy hurled her stiletto-heeled shoe towards me. I saw it flying across the room from the corner of my eye. I ducked just in time.

'She's been stood staring at that door ever since you arrived,' Mummy complained to Mrs Patterson.

'Bloody hell, I thought you were aiming for me at first. Anyway, tell me something new,' Mrs Patterson replied. 'I'd've had that coat of mine hung up by now if I were a kid. It's only manners.'

'There's no room,' I whispered.

'Speak up, lass,' Mrs Patterson ordered.

'There's no room left to hang your coat. Grandfather only left one hook on the door and it's full.'

'Here, pass it back,' she said, reaching her arm over with her back still turned.

'Anyway, not to worry,' she told Mummy. 'Morning will be gone if I don't get off. Pub needs cleaning. I'm sick of mopping up stale piss from t'stone floor in t'gent's toilets. Still, it's a job. Keeps me in fags, don't it?' she added as Mummy unzipped her plastic make-up bag and placed her make-up in a line on top of the mantelpiece.

I took a step further back from the chair as Mrs Patterson stood up.

'Where are you off then?' Mrs Patterson asked Mummy.

I saw Mummy's glare through her reflection in the mirror as she parted her lips before painting them bright red.

'Need say no more,' Mrs Patterson said. 'Oh, I forgot to tell you... That son of mine. Well, he's back from borstal in a couple of days,' she said, wrapping her chiffon scarf loosely around her neck. 'Still blame that fat bastard I married. My Brian's a good lad. Only reason he were sent there in t'first place was 'cause he kept breaking into folks' houses. Wouldn't mind but all he stole were a load of junk, then sold it on for next to nothing, just to feed my hubby's addiction to gambling... And 'is as well. Daft buggers both thought they'd get rich. But that don't stop me loving him... Brian, that is. Can see myself out, lass,' she told me, slipping her muscular arms through the sleeves of her mac before tying the belt in a knot around her waist, hiding the grubby nylon overall she wore underneath.

Within seconds the front door slammed. The springs of the chair had sunk down a little on the seat.

'Sit still,' I was told as I tried to rest my bottom into it. Mummy glanced again into the mirror. I could see her reflection and got quite excited when she opened a tiny round jar. It was so clear you could see the bright colour inside. She pressed her finger down into the loose silver powder inside and then glided it over her eyelids as if a gentle fairy was tiptoeing over them and leaving her sparkle behind. My mouth fell wide open at how beautiful she looked. Mummy cursed underneath her breath as a tiny round box slipped out of her hand and dropped to the floor, rolling and rolling over the cracked lino. I leant over the edge of my chair and watched. It rolled up towards the skirting board underneath the pine wood shelf that Daddy had made for a glass cage of white mice to sit on. Then it suddenly stopped. It's Mummy's rouge, I said to myself. Mummy clicked her fingers. I stood in panic and leapt down to the floor, crawling underneath the shelf to try and reach the tiny round box. I stretched my fingers out as far as they would go in my attempt to touch it and give it back to Mummy.

I felt a hard kick against my bottom. 'Aahh,' I screeched. And then another hard kick from the toe of Mummy's stiletto shoe. 'I've got it,' I shouted in case she couldn't hear my voice from underneath the shelf. I turned around, wanting to get back out as quickly as I could. 'I've got it,' I told her, peeping out and struggling back on to my feet. The smell of mice droppings from inside the cage, mingling with the damp sawdust, made me feel quite sick. The sudden rattle of the wheel made me jump. I turned my head sideways and watched the white mice excitedly turning the wheel around with their tiny feet inside the glass case. I wish they didn't live here, I thought. What if one of them escapes and starts to crawl up my leg? I gave a little shiver and deliberately didn't look at them again.

The rouge was suddenly snatched from me. I patted the dust on my hands against my skirt and quickly sat back down, my bottom still stinging from the kick from Mummy's shoe. I twisted and turned my bottom from side to side, wrestling with the broken springs that twanged each time I moved. Unable to sit still any longer, I sat back as comfortably as I could. I swallowed hard, took a deep breath, and tried not to cry. I held the lump tightly inside my throat – it nearly escaped and a tear filled my eyes.

Mummy held the handle of a tiny bristled brush and then spat into a block of mascara. The brush was rubbed hard against it before she swept it along her lashes that flickered up and down with every stroke. Mummy's long black hair shimmered in the peep of sunlight that shone through the glass of the sash window. I wanted to run over and peek out to see if the yellow butterfly I saw on my way home from school yesterday was still fluttering through the air over Daddy's rose bushes in the front garden. A tiny cloud must have sailed across the sun, before another ray of sunshine beamed through, showing the glimmer of blue mascara on Mummy's long black eyelashes as she flicked them admiringly through her reflection in the mirror. Mummy sucked her lips tightly together, blotting any smudge from the bright red lipstick that she'd painted on her lips, before straightening the tight black skirt she wore that had ruffled over the curves of her bottom. She stretched her neck up towards the mirror, undoing the round plastic button on the top of her frilly white lace blouse before smoothing her fingertips along each seam of her black nylon stockings. Her olive skin glistened against the fluffy powder puff she patted over her slim straight nose. I sighed once more at her beauty as she clipped a pair of long diamante earrings on to the thin lobe of her small rounded ears. I stared at their dazzle through the loose curls of her dark hair before sneezing once again. 'Pardon me,' I said out loud whilst Mummy patted the perfume from the round blue jar on to her finger before dabbing it inside the opening of her blouse against her chest. Mummy looked angry when there was no more left to splash. She suddenly threw it over towards the settee. It landed with a clink as it hit against the can of hairspray before resting alongside it on top of the frayed cushion seat. I recognized the shape of the bottle and sniffed its strong smell in the air. I danced inside my mind, remembering the name. *Evening in Paris*, Lily would softly sing whilst dabbing a little on either side of her long slim neck as she sat smiling at me through the speckled mirror that sat on top of the wobbly dresser in her tiny bedroom.

'Shall we go one day?' Lily asked whilst I stood and looked in, 'to Paris, where we can dance the whole evening away. Shall we?'

I nodded with a smile in approval. I remembered then

when Mummy pushed me to one side, shoving my head hard and fast against the wall on the landing. 'I need more board money,' she told Lily, stepping sharply into her room. Lily had started her first job at the bakery over the bridge on the other side of the hill. She was far too pretty always to be covered in flour, except for her long shiny black hair that she rolled up inside the white cap that she had to wear. With her very first wage packet, after paying Mummy, Lily had walked all the way into town and treated herself to that very same bottle. 'I'll take that from you,' I remember Mummy saying, snatching the bottle from Lily's hand. 'Learn to pay your way in life before buying fancy perfume like this,' she had said, sniffing inside whilst reaching over for the silver top. I waited until Mummy disappeared down into the dark, narrow staircase then peeped through into Lily's bedroom. I saw her tears fall from her dark, chocolate eyes, running down over her dusky complexion before they fell in drops on the floral flared skirt she wore. Her toes moved up and down inside the white plimsolls covering her slender feet as she sobbed.

Lily left home shortly afterwards. I waved her goodbye as she slipped out through the bedroom window and tiptoed along the flat roof over the kitchen. 'I'll be back for you one day,' she called before sliding down the drainpipe, escaping through the yard.

I ran along the landing into my room and peered through the window. 'My heart's broken,' I called. 'Come back, Lily, please come back, Lily,' I cried, my tears stinging my eyes as I watched her run over the bridge and finally out of view.

Mummy had ransacked her room that day like some scavenger with my other sister Frieda by her side. 'Clever bitch, that Lily, she's cleared the lot – not even left a pair of stockings.'

'Right, get your coat on,' Mummy said as she placed her make-up in her leopard-skin bag. 'You'd better hurry, or you'll be left here on your own,' she added in a stern voice.

My toes curled in fear. I don't want to be left with those mice, I thought and quickly jumped off the chair to collect my coat from the hook behind the door leading up to the stairs.

'It's back to school tomorrow, young lady,' I was told as she lifted the catch up to open the front door.

I wasn't told where we were going and I knew better, even at such a young age, than to ask. I looked up at her as she held my hand whilst we crossed the road, heading towards the village pub, the sound of her stilettos echoing with each step she took. There's another car slowing down so that the driver can have a look at her, I thought. I was very aware of her beauty and it was obvious that so was everyone else.

I was itching to bend down to collect some of the tops from the beer bottles that lay on the ground as we walked on to the car park adjoining the pub, where a man was getting out of a white van.

'Jenny,' the man called out. His pointed, deep tan winkle-pickers were the first to touch the gravel before he fully stretched his long legs and stood smoothing the cream slacks that were fastened by a narrow leather belt around his slim waist. His black jacket, as casual as his approach, flapped against his open necked shirt, whilst the crunching of his footsteps drew closer.

I looked up at Mummy before she pulled me swiftly by my wrist to greet this rather tall man.

'Get ready to smile,' she muttered.

His deep blue eyes couldn't avoid showing the crow's feet against his fair complexion. The man smiled, as if amused, through plump lips that showed a set of well polished teeth. His pointed nose almost rubbed against Mummy's skin as he kissed her on her cheek. 'And what's your name?' he asked me in a husky voice, ruffling his fingers through his thinning head of floppy fair hair.

I didn't want to tell him but I knew that I had to. 'Lorne,' I whispered.

'She's unfortunately been off school the last couple of days with tummy problems. Can we drop her off at Mrs Entwhistle's? It's only five minutes by car. She'll look after her for a while.'

'No problem,' he said. 'Let's go.'

I watched as he put his arm around Mummy's waist and I wanted to bite his fingers. I couldn't hear what they were talking about as I sat on the floor in the back of his van feeling every bump from the road as we made our way to Mrs Entwhistle's house. I was often sent there when Mummy had a man to meet, but I didn't mind. She was a nice old lady and I would watch her sew on her machine and wait for the cuckoo to come in and out of the clock which hung on the wall in her living room, and at least I could choose any biscuit I liked from Mrs Entwhistle's biscuit tin.

With Mummy's hand pointing towards the house, the

van slowed down and finally stopped. Phew, I can't wait to get out of here, I thought as the door of the van opened. As soon as Mummy stepped out on to the pavement, I scrambled over the seat and ran up the driveway to Mrs Entwhistle's. I wish we had a bell on our front door, I thought as Mummy pressed her long, red-painted fingernail on the buzzer. I started to twiz around with excitement. She's taking a long time to answer, I thought. Maybe she's forgotten where she's left her walking stick.

Stepping on to the stone that sat outside her front door, I stretched up and lifted the oblong letter box to see if I could see her. The smell of moth balls went straight into my nostrils. 'Why does Mrs Entwhistle's house always have that strange smell?' I asked. With my question ignored, I was led back along the driveway.

'Don't mark the seat with your shoes,' Mummy said as I climbed back into the van. 'She's not at home,' she added, to the man.

'What now?' he asked.

At that moment the engine was switched on, and once again I tried, but couldn't hear what was being said. I could see by the expressions on their faces that they were both laughing. I felt cold and I wanted to go to the toilet. On the journey down the long sloping hill, I passed Primrose Cottage and caught sight of Molly, in her favourite floral housecoat, watering the bedding plants from the sprinkly spout of the steel watering can around the tiny square patch of her front garden.

Then there was Mrs Grindle, her woven headscarf tied tightly underneath her saggy double chin, walking down with a rolled up burning cigarette held loosely on the tip of her mouth in between her thin, chapped lips.

Poor Mrs Hayworth, her round, plump face looking drawn, and Edward, her lanky, freckly-faced son with a mop of red, frizzy hair, protected by his Mummy's hand from the fear of the bullying Grindle boys as they stood waiting to cross the road. The Grindle twins, even though they were sixteen years old, always made a habit of spitting at and thumping poor Edward if he dared be out on his own.

I gave a little sigh as they soon passed from view. I spotted Harry, one of my special friends, squinting against the rays of the bright morning sun. His light brown hair flopping in the breeze as he struggled, pedalling his old, rusty bicycle with his haversack strapped over his shoulder, packed with rolled up newspapers ready to deliver.

Smoke filtered out of miniature, round chimney pots, disappearing up towards the scattered clouds trailing along the sky. As I continued looking through either side of the two tiny windows in the back of the van, searching for the sight of any more friends, I could see the red telephone box as we started to enter the valley. That was always a sign that we were only minutes away from home. I moved closer to the window to try and see if my friend the donkey was at the farm gate. He lived in the field a few yards from my home. No, I couldn't see him. I needed to tell him that I had been in this awful van and I never wanted to be in it again. Never mind, I thought, I'll tell him later. My dear simple friend and neighbour, Eric, mustn't feel cold this morning. Maybe he's been sick again and feels too hot. That's probably why Mrs Crowswick, his mother, hasn't lit the fire, noticing the dull, smokeless chimney pot on top of their roof.

I couldn't understand why we had driven past my home, the van turning sharply into the lane nearby, leaving the row of tiny cottages that stretched along the straight length of road at the bottom of the hill behind. There wasn't anything to hold on to. 'Ouch,' I shouted as I slid to the other side, banging my knee and rubbing it fast and hard with my hand to take away the sting. I looked out from the window at the tall trees that swayed their wiry branches and huge, sweeping leaves, leaving a cast of moving shadows over the tiny row of whitewashed cottages on the opposite side. I felt as if we were slowing down and all of a sudden we stopped. Within seconds, the man got out. I jumped with the loud, creaky noise the handle of the double doors at the back of the van made as they were opened.

'Now go and pick some flowers,' Mummy said. 'I won't be long. See how many daisy chains you can make.'

I was then lifted underneath my shoulders out of the van. His horrible big hands hurt me as he carried me towards the stile. Mummy, he's hurting me, I wanted to shout, wishing I had worn my clogs to kick him hard with. I heard the squelch from my plastic sandals as I was lowered down on to the grass. I didn't turn to look back whilst listening to the rattle of the engine as they drove past.

Even though I had played in this field many times before, I found myself giving a big swallow. I mustn't cry, I told myself as I listened to the gentle breeze and watched it make the flowers move to and fro. The sound of the spring water flowing in the stream attracted my attention as I bent down and carefully broke the tiny thin stem of one of the thousands of daisies that covered this huge field. Avoiding the moss, I found an old stone that had embedded itself on the banks and sat myself down. Whilst tickling my chin with the petals of my tiny flower, I watched the current of clear shallow water moving over and in between the pebbles that lay on the bottom of the riverbed.

I'll make Daddy an ashtray, I thought as I spotted lumps of clay lying on the opposite side of the stream, and yes, I'll make Minnie a vase and fill it with flowers. She's such a kind old lady. I wonder if she gets lonely living in that tiny, dark cottage all on her own, I said to myself, nervously stretching over to get hold of as much of the clay as my tiny hands would allow. I might just have to leave it outside her door. She's not been putting her false teeth in recently and she frightens me when she smiles, and I'll make sure Daddy's ashtray is pretty big. I wonder why he smokes so many cigarettes, I thought. It only makes him cough all the time and he can never get those horrible brown stains off his fingers no matter how many times he washes his hands. With a shrug of my shoulders I excitedly started to make my presents; after all, they were for two of my favourite people in the whole wide world.

I jumped in sheer terror. 'Little girl, your Mummy's back,' I heard him shout, his voice echoing all around me. Oh no, I said to myself, I haven't even finished making Minnie's vase. I quickly hid it with the rest of the clay in a hole inside the banks of the stream. Whoops, my heart skipped a beat as it nearly all fell into the water. I quickly wiped my hands on my gathered skirt, stood myself up and walked towards the stile. 'I'll come back later and pick some of you,' I said to the daisies that were still swaying in the breeze.

'I can climb over the stile myself,' I shouted over to the man who stood like a giant staring at me from the opposite side.

'Where are the daisy chains you made?' he asked whilst I struggled, scraping my leg as I climbed over the stile.

'I've left them for the wild animals to wear,' I said as he walked back to his van, ignoring what I was saying. Opening the rear of the van doors again, I climbed in and sat myself down on the cold tin floor.

I wonder what's happened to Mummy's hair; it looks awfully ruffled. Hmm, maybe he's been kissing her too hard. I do wish I had made that ashtray for Daddy, I thought, as we set off once again, hopefully for home. I don't ever want to see you again, I said to myself as I stared at the back of the man's head whilst he drove. And anyway, I thought, you're going bald; Daddy's got much nicer hair than you.

It only took a couple of minutes before the van stopped yet again. Hurray, I'm home. I stood up as much as I could, bending my head so that I wouldn't bang it on the roof.

'Step over my seat,' Mummy said, opening the passenger door and turning sideways.

'Cheerio, little girl,' I heard the man say.

I'm just glad to get out of your van, I thought, as I mumbled bye-bye to him. With orders from Mummy to wait next to the front door, I skipped down along the flagged pathway, past the heavily scented roses that

Grandfather and Daddy had planted in the tiny front garden, and sat down on the step. I started to feel a little restless and was bored with watching the ants enjoying the sunshine as they moved in and out of the cracks on the old flags that Daddy could never afford to replace. I felt my toes curl as I stretched slightly to see what Mummy was doing. I wish my Daddy was a policeman, I thought, as I saw the man kissing Mummy. He'd lock him up straight away. And, anyway, when I grow up I'm going to meet a prince and he'll have to bow to him if he ever comes back.

I heard the familiar sound of Mummy's stilettos walking down the path as she rooted through her bag to find the key to open the door. As I stood up, the man pomped his horn and drove away. I'll write to my fairy godmother when Mummy opens the door and we're inside the house, and tell her what has been going on again.

'What's all that dirt doing on your skirt?' she shouted, placing the key in the lock. I looked up at her. Her lipstick was smudged and I didn't like her. 'Well, you can wear that same dirty skirt for school tomorrow,' she said, stepping into the front room. 'I'm tired,' she said, throwing her bag down on the floor next to Grandfather's chair. 'I'm going to bed for a while so don't make any noise.'

I wish you weren't my Mummy, I said to myself. Mummies are supposed to wear pinnies and bake cakes and give you lots of kisses and cuddles. Oh well, maybe she will tomorrow. I don't know how many times I dreamt that tomorrow would be different, but it never was. The squabbling that would constantly go on when my brothers and sisters returned home from school and work would make me retreat into the corner of the room. It would only usually last for about an hour, but it was something that I could never get used to. It confused me as to how I was always made to feel different from them. But Mummy's got Indian blood in her and Daddy's got Irish. I've just got to be the same – yes, I am the same.

I moved my head from side to side to each creaky tick of the old wooden clock that stood on the mantelpiece underneath Mummy's mirror. Sometimes it frightens me when it strikes and I'm sitting here all alone. My dear, down-to-earth best friend Susie told me that if there really is a fairy living in Daddy's rose bush, she'll only be there to look after me. I wonder if she has forgotten all about me, I thought, creeping over the lino and peeping through the tiny square window. She might have fallen fast asleep when I was put inside that horrible van. I'll write her a letter. The drawer to Mummy's sideboard rattled. I stood still for a moment. There was no creak from upstairs so I took out what I needed and crept as quietly as a mouse to Grandfather's favourite chair.

Dear Fairy Godmother,

I'm very sorry to tell you that I have just stolen from the top drawer of Mummy's sideboard some paper and an envelope and a pen too. But I am going to put the pen back as soon as I have written this letter to you. When I have sent it to you, I will kneel down and pray to ask God to forgive me for stealing. Do you think he will if I promise him that when I grow up and find a job I'll buy Mummy a brand new writing pad with a new packet of envelopes?

I hope I don't get caught writing to you. You see, Mummy says she has never to see me with a pen in my hand. That's because I'm left handed. Mummy says that only idiots write with their left hand so I'm only allowed to write when I am at school.

Fairy Godmother, I wonder if you have another name, like Alice or Rose. I know that you live in the front garden in between the green leaves of Daddy's roses, but don't worry; I have always kept it a secret. Sometimes I see the sparkle from your wand when I look out from the window inside the bedroom I share with my brothers. I get frightened sometimes when I'm alone up there.

If a greenfly bites you, go and find a dock leaf. You will find one in between the weeds where the dandelions grow around the edge of the garden.

I don't want you to sparkle any stardust today. Do you want to know why? If you do, it's because I can't smile. Shall I tell you why? Because I was thrown against the tin walls of this van. Did you see me as he drove past? I tried to press my nose up against the window and search for you to let you know that I was frightened, very frightened, but I was thrown back when he turned his van around the corner. Minnie, who lives in the cottage next to the field would have snarled at him with her raw gums. That's only because she's very old. She forgets to put her teeth back inside her mouth. That's if I'd have knocked on her door and told her that this horrible man had taken my Mummy away. I've heard grown ups say that you can die from a broken heart. Do you think that's what my Daddy will die of? But I won't tell him about today if you think he will. Do you want to know why? Because my Mummy has lots of boyfriends and Daddy's heart will break into tiny little pieces.

Susie, my friend, asked me if I would like to become an orphan. She said that I would be better off if I did. But I'm not very clever at school. Maybe when I grow up and learn a lot more, I think that I will.

Mummy's gone to sleep now. I only jump when I hear her footsteps because the floorboards creak and that tells me that she has woken up. Then I sit up straight and wait for the door at the bottom of the stairs to open.

I'm going to creep out now and leave this letter for you. I won't leave it near the thorn. That is because you'll prickle yourself if I do. So I will bury it under the soil where nothing grows. I'm going to write my name the wrong way round to see if you can guess who it is from.

Lots of love. Just in case you will not be able to guess, it's from me, Lorne.

I quickly folded the letter into as many squares as I could to make sure that it fit into the tiny square envelope. I looked towards the door and made a run for it. 'Please open,' I whispered. The stiff little catch on the black painted door finally opened. I stood still and listened. There were no creaks to be heard from upstairs, giving me the courage to slip off my sandals and jar the door. You can't close on me now, I told it. Creeping down low, the envelope rustled in my hand. I stopped and listened once more. There was no sound from inside the house. Beginning my crawl along the narrow garden path, I stopped still and buried my head low, not wanting to be spotted by chattering women who walked slowly past along the pavement in front of the brick wall that sheltered Daddy's garden. Sparrows chirped whilst flying overhead. 'Shush,' I whispered, leaning my head up towards the sunny sky. I scurried with my hands into the dry soil of Daddy's cabbage patch where no seeds ever grew. 'I have buried my letter here,' I whispered over to the rose bush, hoping that the fairy would hear me and read it. I felt the sting against my grazed knees as I crawled back along the broken flags of the narrow pathway. I quickly brushed my hands against my skirt, slipped on my sandals and then slowly turned the latch until the front door to Rose Cottage closed quietly behind me.

Chapter 3

The snips of potato peelings hissed, as they did every Sunday. 'Saves the coal from burning too quickly,' Daddy once said. The Sunday roast was eaten silently, except for the scrape of knives and forks. Lily's chair, an empty chair, stood facing the table. Oh, how I missed her.

'I'll be leaving for the airport tomorrow,' Patrick, my eldest brother announced.

'Well, make sure you send your mother money home,' Daddy told him without compassion.

'Aye, I will,' Patrick replied, standing and leaving his dinner mostly untouched.

'He's going to war,' Teddy whispered. 'Borneo, a jungle somewhere.'

I gasped in horror. A sting on the back of my neck knocked me forward.

'I told you not to open your mouth when it's full of food, haven't I?' Mummy said in a rage.

'Ouch!' I screamed to another blow.

'I'll be the next to leave,' Teddy shouted, spitting his food out on to his plate whilst yanking me away.

'Aye, well, the sooner you all leave, the better,' Daddy called, on our way into the kitchen.

'He's been drinking,' Teddy told me as I waited with head bowed, tea towel in my hand.

Frieda skipped by, showing off her flared gingham skirt. Mrs Pritchard, her godmother, had called, and off they went for their usual Sunday walk.

'You wouldn't want to be Bible-bashed anyway,' Teddy told me as I peeped up towards the window.

Mummy had dragged me up the hill to Ruby's only yesterday. A wooden shack where you sat on a stool lined with plastic, cracked by huge bottoms. Ruby was the only hairdresser in the village, posh as well. My hair had been cut short, too short. 'Shampoo's so expensive,' Mummy had complained as the locks of my hair fell and lay in big dark curls on the tiled floor. That's how Charlie noticed the mark of Mummy's hand.

'Keep quiet, Charlie,' Teddy snapped, taking a bundle of used cutlery from his hands.

'I'll be leaving shortly, too,' I told him as he passed me a saucepan to dry.

'You haven't a suitcase,' Charlie said, grabbing a tea towel and joining in with interest. 'Anyway, gets dark at night, very dark.'

'You're not frightened of anything, Charlie, not if you really want to go.'

'What, leave Rose Cottage for good? You'll need a map.'

'And a compass, Charlie.'

Charlie burst into tears. 'Come on,' Teddy told him, 'Get drying those knives and forks.'

'Sometimes, Charlie,' I said, straightening his spectacles, 'it's hard to understand things. I'm sad all the time, very sad. And now that Lily's gone...

'Lorne won't be going anywhere, Charlie, she's only eight.'

'I'm going to roam the streets, become an orphan. Someone will take me in.'

'Lorne,' Teddy said sternly as Charlie started to shake. 'Look at him. He loves you, that's why, and I love you too, and one day we'll all leave together.'

Seeing the sadness in Charlie's eyes, I immediately agreed with Teddy.

Patrick left the very next day. Odd socks lay on the bare bedroom floor, a reminder. His ruffled pillow and hollow bed sent a screaming pain to my heart. There had been no goodbyes. He'd left quietly through the front door next to the best room in the house. Teddy kept quiet that night, and so did Charlie, lying there with the moonlight shining through. I just cried myself to sleep.

Mr Ramsbottom's clogs clattering along the stony pathway, the clink of milk bottles and dawn breaking through, brought a new day.

'Your eyes are swollen,' Charlie whispered in a yawn.

'Daddy's alarm, Charlie, did it go off?'

'He's probably not going to work today. Not with all the racket during the night,' Charlie said. 'Where's Teddy?'

'Teddy's gone, Charlie, hasn't he?'

Charlie shrugged. I ran along the landing and leapt down the stairs. Teddy wouldn't go anywhere without his jacket, I thought with a thumping heart. 'Teddy,' I whispered, noticing it still hanging on the nail behind the staircase door.

'Mother's gone to hospital.'

'Again?'

'Yes, Lorne,' Teddy said as I peered into the living room.

'Don't step in, Lorne, there's broken glass everywhere.'

'Have we had a burglar?' I said, noticing Daddy's armchair tipped on its side. Teddy didn't answer. White liquid dripped out of a tiny broken bottle. 'Mummy's nail polish,' I whispered to myself, sneezing at the strong smell that lingered in the air as I sneaked across the room. 'Oh, Mummy's mirror, it's cracked.'

'Father threw his ashtray, that's why, Lorne. Lorne, step back will you.'

'What does it say?' I asked, 'That word written in lipstick.'

'It says "whore, bloody whore",' Teddy yelled before bursting into tears.

I stood and sighed, sighed so deeply before kneeling to collect what was left of Mummy's rollers from the powdered ashes of the fire. In anger Teddy kicked a block of mascara which slid along the lino. A tiny round lid, an open box of rouge. Her make-up was scattered everywhere.

'Father's been arrested during the night,' Teddy spoke whilst wiping his nose on his sleeve. 'Frieda's gone with Mother.'

'Is Mummy going to die?'

'How the hell do I know?' he yelled in another burst of tears.

'Only I saved her rollers. I'll go and rinse them under the tap.'

'The clock's broken, too,' he said quietly to himself in a skip of a breath.

'Lorne,' Teddy called.

'Only a few more to rinse and they'll be as good as new,' I called back.

'Lorne,' Teddy called again, his voice anxious. 'It's Charlie.'

There, Charlie stood shivering in his pyjamas, his pea eyes under thick rimmed spectacles looked on in disbelief.

'Come on, Charlie,' whilst drying my hands against my long nightie. 'I'll take you ... take you...' I paused a second. 'Yeah, to look out through the south wing.'

I left Teddy looking puzzled and gently guided Charlie through into the parlour. 'You see out there, through the window?' The thin bones of his shoulders stiffened as I guided him closer. 'Imagine, far beyond Daddy's roses.' He stared out ahead and I followed his gaze. 'Well, Charlie, it's supposed to be a surprise. You see, when Daddy wins on the football pools, those coupons that he draws crosses on every week, we're going to live in Blackpool. Imagine, Charlie, donkeys and sand, a posh house with its very own wing where we can sit and look at the Tower. Mr Wilde, the headmaster, always goes there for his holidays. He's shown the whole class photographs and told us stories.'

Charlie stood on his tiptoes staring further out. 'Can you hear? Listen, Charlie, the waves splashing against the shore.' Charlie nodded. 'And when the tide goes back out to sea, you can hear the bells on the donkeys jingling. And there's a circus, too, with monkeys and clowns. And Teddy will laugh again.'

Charlie wanted to wee in excitement. I took him out through the back door, down the entry to the lavatory that stunk. 'Hold your nose, Charlie,' I told him, taking a deep breath myself. 'Our lives will change one day, won't they, Charlie,' as I reached high, 'from blocked up toilets and this rusty broken chain, and silly things grown ups do?'

We all helped to clear up that morning, Charlie, Teddy and me. Mummy's make-up lay wiped and clean next to her rollers on the drainer.

'It's no use, Lorne, the tops won't fit back. The brushes are already hard and dry,' Teddy complained. 'Nail polish doesn't last, not now, now the bottle's smashed.' He gently took them from my hands and with a crash, and a shudder from me, threw them to the bottom of the dustbin.

Charlie and I sat and waited with our feet in the air as Teddy swept, and then mopped the living room floor. Teddy gave the nod to Charlie who crawled on his hands and knees, dabbing polish on an old rag from the large round tin. I crawled behind, applauded by Teddy.

'The lino's never shined as much,' he said, encouraging me to roll my duster and rub that little harder.

Satisfied at a job well done, Charlie set out three plastic bowls. Teddy poured the cornflakes and I ran out to collect the milk. 'Better not, Lorne, just a drop in each,' he said as I pressed down the silver top and started to pour.

We all sat and crunched, all with our silent thoughts. Did they wonder, like me... Were they waiting, too, for a thunderous knock to echo through the parlour on a door gently closed to the outside that hid the misery inside these walls?

'Shush,' Teddy said. Charlie and me stopped chewing. 'Footsteps down the entry,' he whispered. He jumped up. 'Blimey, Mother's back and Father's a step behind. Frieda's just about to lift the latch,' he said, peeping as low as the table out through the window towards the back yard. Charlie and me sat still and stiff, as stiff as the dead.

'Let's scarper,' Teddy told us, rushing off with the milk.

Charlie grabbed the spoons; I grabbed the bowls. As we ran through into the parlour, Teddy whispered, 'They'll think the birds have picked it,' piercing his thumb nail through the silver top before placing the bottle back on the step.

Teddy took the lead after we were all closed in behind the door that led up the narrow staircase. 'I know every creak on these stairs,' he whispered whilst pointing out where to step.

'He'd make a good scout, wouldn't he, Charlie?'

Teddy reached out his hand and grabbed the spoons. 'They're rattling too much, Charlie.'

'You're leaving me behind,' I complained, aware of the darkness.

Teddy and Charlie halted whilst I climbed the next stair. 'Don't be dropping those bowls,' Teddy said in a whisper.

'I won't,' I whispered back.

'Come here, Lorne,' Teddy said, stretching out his arms as we reached the landing. 'This panel's loose,' he pointed out as he carried me across. 'Come on, Charlie, you can do it,' I whispered over Teddy's shoulder. Charlie hesitated before suddenly leaping over. Brave Charlie, I thought, smiling down towards him with pride.

'Quick, get those bowls hidden under Patrick's bed,' Teddy instructed after lowering me down and hiding the spoons under the pillow. Then he gave a sigh, the biggest sigh whilst staring out through the bedroom window.

'Cheer up, Teddy, now that we don't have to bury Mummy.'

'We'll all be getting buried,' he turned to say, 'if you don't hurry. We don't want any questions. I reckon you're already late.' Charlie checked his watch that never ticked and agreed. 'Feet in, Lorne,' Teddy said, helping me on with my socks.

Charlie pulled the elastic over his head showing off his new tie. 'Are the stripes still on it?' he asked, pulling it down to inspect. The elastic went *ping*.

'It's snapped,' I told Teddy, 'Charlie's tie.'

'No doubt the rag and bone man will spill his load again. Anyway, Charlie,' Teddy whispered over in anger, 'it'll be full of germs.'

Finally dressed, Charlie and me stood like two soldiers waiting for Teddy's inspection. 'You'll do,' he said, taking his steel comb from deep inside his overalls he'd just stepped into.

'Teddy,' I whispered. 'Your pyjamas, you forgot to take them off.'

'Haven't time, Lorne.'

'Ouch!' Charlie said, as Teddy parted his hair.

'Doesn't need it, Lorne,' as I stood next in line. 'It'll soon grow again,' Teddy sighed, ruffling his hand through my hair.

Coats were handed to us from the nail behind the bedroom door. Teddy huffed at Charlie's attempt to pull the broken zip on an anorak that disguised his tiny frame. 'Your hem's hanging,' Teddy said. I ruffled my long red coat above my ankles to inspect. Teddy seemed impatient. 'Come on, Lorne, hurry.'

'The buttonholes, they're too big,' I tried to explain whilst refastening the row of odd buttons that kept popping out.

'Right,' Teddy said. 'We'll go the same way down as we came up.' He lifted me up and Charlie followed, looking puzzled, behind. The living room door, to Teddy's relief, was firmly closed. His heart beat faster on our short journey through the parlour. 'As quiet as a mouse,' he warned Charlie who crept behind. Teddy lowered me down and turned the latch while Charlie and I held our breath. 'Run,' he whispered, shoving us in front into fresh morning air. Charlie led the way, sprinting over the bridge. 'Hold on tight.'

'I am, Teddy,' I said, holding on to his hand as we sped along in pursuit.

'Charlie, come back!' Teddy called once we were over the hump and out of sight.

'Charlie,' we both called as he galloped ahead. Teddy pressed both his fingers between his lips and let out a shrill whistle and Charlie came to a halt. Teddy, now more relaxed, leant his back against the crumbling stone of the orchard wall, crossed one foot over the other and rooted deep inside his pocket. He took out a Woodbine, and with the fierce strike of a match, inhaled deeply. Charlie returned, catching his breath before inspecting the time through the cracked face of his fingerless watch.

'Just a few more puffs and I'll dock it,' Teddy said.

It was as if a cloud of sadness followed the rest of our journey. A crunch of pebbles grinding under our footsteps was the only sound heard. Teddy kept his head low. I gently squeezed his hand. 'There'll be better days, Lorne.

One day,' he said with a sigh as we reached the top of the brow.

The church steeple seemed to dominate the stretch of road. We passed the graveyard that morning. 'Look straight ahead,' Teddy urged, briskly moving us on. My best mate Susie stood behind the railings, both hands clasped around the iron bars as if some monkey trapped in a cage, watching, waiting in anticipation as Teddy, Charlie and I walked past. 'Listen, Lorne, I know Susie's your best friend but, remember, she's older than you and people gossip, especially on that estate where she lives, so don't be telling her what's gone on. We'll be the laughing stock.'

Teddy left us at the school gates and Charlie skipped his way in. 'Mummy's alive,' Charlie shouted as Susie crossed his path.

'I probably knew before any of you lot,' she told me. 'I don't know why you're keeping your lips so tightly closed. Surprised, are you?' Susie said, seeing the look on my face.

'Me Auntie Dorothy's worked in outpatients years. She's only a cleaner but, anyway, she came galloping in after t'night shift. Me ma's still in her nightie now, sat there in t'kitchen listening to gossip. Would have run to owd Betty's florists,' Susie reminded me, 'that's if your ma, well, had passed away. Roses, red 'uns, a whole bunch...'

'Mummy likes pink, too,' I told Susie who pretended to jump at the sound of my voice while escorting me up the stone steps.

The bell for class rang its last chime. Art would have been my favourite lesson if only I was any good at it, I thought, sitting after the rumble of chairs came to a halt.

Susie went to the front of the class and whispered in Mr Stock's ear. The short plump man slowly raised his head and peered across over half moon spectacles. The scrape of pencils sliding over paper and the mixing of brushes were the only sounds in a fully concentrating class.

A tall, slim, freckle-faced girl with long, red hair tied high in a pony-tail seemed to keep her distance on the narrow back bench we shared. 'Stop staring,' she snapped.

'I didn't mean to, it's just... The chequered ribbon in your hair. It's very pretty.' She checked with her long fingers that the stiff bow was still intact.

'Oh, by the way, Polly's our new girl,' Mr Stock announced, struggling off his seat. She was welcomed with a clap. I clapped the hardest, seeing she was seated next to me. The seats rumbled once more. Mr Stock banged his ruler and work commenced.

Polly's face burned bright with anger after my elbow nudged hers. 'I'm sorry,' I whispered, scurrying under the desk as her paint brush rolled. Polly's patent shoes shone like the sun as her feet tapped up and down. Her socks were as white as snow.

'Sir,' she called. 'Left handers are so clumsy. May I move?' I heard whilst crawling my way out, showing her dislike on the snatch as the long bristled brush was whisked from my hand. She couldn't resist a sly smirk whilst peering down. I peered down too. They were white, my ankle socks, only they got stirred by a long wooden stick in a melting pot of washing, and they've never looked the same. They've only slipped under the arch of my feet because the elastic's frayed, I was going to explain; only her exit was swift.

Polly had, in her finery, made me feel a class apart; a stern lesson, my first in a world outside the walls of Rose Cottage. The knot in my throat gurgled. Mr Stock glared. I swallowed hard and sat myself down, head bowed. After all, concentrating on being a fine artist was, I suppose, more important than hurt feelings. I felt a draught around my feet, signalling the classroom door had opened. Peeping out from the corner of my eye, a tall, dark, willowy shadow wearing a black floating gown approached. I could smell rotted lilies as Mr Applehurst, the vicar, sat down next to me, brushing his hands, in interest, lightly over my drawings.

'They're Daddy's roses. The thorns, they're sharp, but much easier to draw,' I explained. 'She did come home, Mummy. I didn't see her, Teddy did. Teddy lied, didn't he?' I asked, scribbling a huge cloud over the sun that should have shined with bright yellow paint. A tear dropped, hitting like a piece of hailstone against the sketchy petal of Daddy's rose. 'You've taken her, given her to God, haven't you?' sheltering my head low between my elbows as tears fell like rain.

'Lorne, your mother's alive, as alive as you and I are sitting here. It's just that I saw the empty seat beside you and thought it would be nice to have a little chat. I'm sorry I caused you so much despair. Ah,' Mr Applehurst called out, beckoning Susie over.

'Don't see why I should spend t'last couple o'weeks of me school days being t'dog's body around here,' Susie mumbled on her way down, after placing the empty waste bin close to Mr Stock's short, stubby feet with their steel, capped shoes that tapped annoyingly against the wooden floor.

'Lorne and you have been friends ... well, for as long as I can remember.'

'We have, sir. Worry about 'er all t'time.'

'Yes, I'm sure you do.'

Susie chose to ignore my scowl. Had she been whispering in Mr Applehurst's ear, too? Was this the reason for his visit? I wanted reality left behind, not to come following.

'Budge up,' she told me, sitting herself down. 'She ain't got no life, sir, no hopes, no dreams. Ouch!' Susie complained on my nudge.

'We should all have hopes and dreams, Lorne. Susie does.'

'I do, Mr Applehurst, plenty.'

'Yes, they're very important,' he continued. 'Even though there's never a spare minute running the parish, I must admit life wouldn't be much fun without them. Lorne?' There was a silence that seemed to last forever.

'She ain't got no answer, sir, 'cos she's been told all her life there's no hope for 'er. Ouch!' Susie called out again.

'It's only because Mummy's lost the love in her heart. I try to find it for her, sir, and when... Well, when I think I have, I'm sent back searching.'

'Maybe you have an interest, something you yourself would like...'

'To be a bell-ringer,' I blurted.

Mr Applehurst smiled. 'Well, we'll settle for that. When school's finished for the day, to the belfry we'll go.'

This time Susie nudged me. 'Me as well, sir?' she asked as he stood to leave.

'And Charlie,' I whispered to her.

'And Charlie?'

Her request was approved.

'You're smudging,' Susie told me, steadying the brush as my hand shook with excitement.

'We're going up in t'belfrey,' Susie announced at the close of school, making sure Polly heard as she walked along past the rows of desks. Within seconds I was whisked off my seat and pulled along through the hall by the warmth of Susie's chubby hand.

'Can't have dried snot on your cheek, not where we've been invited,' passing me a crumpled hanky whilst grabbing my coat as we rushed through the cloakroom and out into the open air.

'Charlie,' I called.

'Where is he?' Susie asked in a huff.

Charlie was spotted on my determined search at the back of the school. His short grey pants were unable to protect him from the goose pimples covering his thin legs.

'I've weed in my pants,' he whispered, lifting the thick rim of his spectacles to wipe away a tear.

Charlie was a loner, not boisterous like other boys his age. He was a scrawny, yet clever, looking boy, always in shabby clothes. He suffered fun poked at him constantly from a cluster of brats in the school yard, solely for their pleasure. It wasn't the first time Charlie had weed in his pants and it wouldn't be the last.

'There's only a little stain, Charlie,' on my inspection.

'Aye, well, accidents will happen,' Susie said urging us to make a move.

'Anyway, t'breeze will soon dry 'em off,' she remarked as she dragged me along with Charlie in tow.

'We're going up into the belfry and you're invited, too,' I called out to Charlie as we ran.

'Looks haunting, don't it?' Susie shouted, glancing over to the vicarage, set back from the busy main road. 'Archbishop would 'ave called there at some point for afternoon tea.'

'The archbishop,' I whispered, peering back in wonder. Our frantic run ended. 'There it is, t'belfrey,' Susie said proudly.

'Will there be bats up there?' Charlie asked inquisitively.

'Probably,' Susie replied, knowing how keen he was on nature, especially small creatures.

Charlie was allowed to lead the way before Susie, in her excitement, dragged me behind ignoring my stumble down the narrow cobbled steps.

'Hey, got to be smart going up there,' she said, stopping me before the final step. 'Here, foot up. Now t'other,' pulling my socks back over the heels of my feet before Mr Applehurst greeted us.

He turned the iron key in the lock of a rather quaint arched door. Winding stone steps immediately faced us, spiralling up into darkness. Surprisingly, Charlie ran ahead and followed behind the confident steps of Mr Applehurst.

Enclosed within powdery brick walls, the sound of our footsteps echoed down into an eerie darkness as we rose towards the chill.

'Couldn't you dream of being a ballerina?' Susie asked, leaning against the wall whilst coughing profoundly.

'There'll be no more stubs left in the church grounds will there, Susie?' Mr Applehurst called down.

'No, sir, there won't,' Susie called out whilst trying breathlessly to continue the climb.

'The belfry,' Mr Applehurst told us, encouraging with a gesture of his hand for us to step in.

'We'll be stood over th'altar, sir, won't we?' Susie asked, nudging Charlie and me to step over the gaps in the creaky wooden floorboards as a glimmer of light rose up between the cracks from the church below.

'Charlie, look. Jesus sleeps up there,' I whispered, stretching my neck and peering as far as the eye could see in wonder towards the bell tower.

'He'll be deaf if he does,' Susie replied. 'Look at t'strength in those ropes. You'll be stood in t'circle one of these days,' she told me, patting me on my shoulder.

'If it weren't so bleeding cold up here, I'd be joining too.'

'It means practice, Lorne, lots,' Mr Applehurst told me, allowing me to feel the thickness of the rope.

'It ain't going to pull you up there, in t'tower, so hold on properly,' Susie said. 'Hold on to your dream, kid.'

My fingers trembled and my toes curled with excitement. I stared, my eyes fixed above, imagining on my pull, the chime of the bells ringing out to villagers walking merrily past, filling the pews for the Sunday morning prayer.

Mr Applehurst turned my attention by lifting from the stone ledge above a canvas-backed book. He blew off the dust once then twice. 'It's yours,' he said, holding out the offer.

'She's never had a book in her life, never mind a Bible,' Susie told him, encouraging me with a gentle push to step forward.

My heart filled with gratitude. I accepted with open hands. Charlie remained standing in the centre, hands inside his pockets and neck stretched high peering as far as the eye could see up towards the bell tower.

‘’Ee’s looking for bats, sir. Charlie,’ Susie called, ‘they only come out at dead of night.’ Having broken his concentration, our departure was swift. Charlie stepped down into the spiral with ease.

‘You’ll be running up and down these steps when you’re old enough to ring t’bells,’ Susie told me offering me a helping hand as I cautiously trod each step.

‘Keep blinking,’ she said on our sudden exit into the dazzle of sunlight.

‘Charlie,’ I shouted, running up the cobbled steps to where he stood, leaving Susie to go her separate way. ‘A Bible, Charlie! I’ll read to you tonight when the moonlight’s in the sky. We’ll shine your glasses so every word will sparkle,’ I told him as we carefully crossed the main road. ‘We’ll share it, Charlie ... the Bible,’ noticing his inquisitive look before I passed it over.

Charlie walked proud, as proud as I felt as we headed down the brow for home. We giggled at tadpoles shaking their tails as we peered over the humpbacked bridge down towards the stream.

‘Come on, Charlie,’ pulling him away from the amusement, aware that from behind the windows of Rose Cottage, was a fear of being watched. Charlie slipped his hand from mine when we stepped into daylight at the bottom of the dark entry, proud to show me how much he’d grown by lifting the latch to the back kitchen door himself. ‘Hide it, Charlie,’ I whispered, hearing the high pitched sound of Mrs Patterson's voice. Charlie slipped the Bible inside the loose arm of his anorak.

Mummy had left the laughter of Mrs Patterson behind as she stepped into the kitchen. Her eyes looked wicked and cold. 'Been strolling home from school, have you?' she asked, pushing Charlie out of the way. 'You'll get what your father gives me when I'm late.'

'Aye, and that's a bloody good hiding,' Mrs Patterson called from the living room.

A burning scowl, a dried bloody nose. The pain in my chest, almost unbearable, left me no wish for the moon to shine. I'd hoped to die that long, painful night, lying there in my bed with my Bible hidden by my side.

'No school today, Lorne,' Teddy whispered looking over me. I was surprised as I woke with the early morning sun shining through. I looked at him with horror. 'I'll stay with you, promise, until you're better. Remember, Lorne, one day you'll be able to leave Rose Cottage. You'll be able to say goodbye to it.'

'Forever,' I whispered.

'Yes, Lorne, forever.'

Chapter 4

The next couple of years went by slowly. Nothing much had changed except I was a little older and my heart still ached for Lily and my brother, Patrick, had joined the Army. I missed them terribly but at least they were away from the misery that went on at Rose Cottage.

'Lorne, why do you constantly stand staring out of that window at the same view every day? Must get boring,' Teddy yawned, suddenly appearing before lying on his bed complaining of a hard day's work.

'I'm looking out for Lily walking back over the bridge – spotting me up here. I can almost see her, Teddy, her floral flared skirt flowing in the breeze as she quickens her step. Do you think I'll grow up to be just like her? I'll never be as pretty but I'll try and be as kind as she was to everyone.'

'You talk as if she's dead,' Teddy said.

'Life's everlasting, Teddy, so the Bible says. Lily will never die,' I snapped. The beauty of the orchard in full view became a mist.

'Hey,' Teddy said, scurrying towards me. 'There's no need to weep.'

I could feel the beat of Teddy's heart as I leant my head against his chest while he gently patted my back. 'You know how Lily became a mother figure to you? All that love and protection she tried to give, well, don't think for a second she wanted to leave you behind. She had to leave Rose Cottage to try and find a better life…' Teddy paused for a few moments. 'Lorne, Lily gave birth to a baby girl. The baby was stillborn.'

'Dead?' I whispered.

Teddy nodded and swallowed hard. 'Never tell a soul. Ethel, her godmother, me and now you are the only ones in the valley that know. Ethel reckons Lily missed you so much her pregnancy was deliberate. Ethel told me she never left the darkness of the dingy flat she rented. It was a long recovery from her depression. Ethel decided to mislead her, giving shining reports of you, just to see her smile. Without Ethel's care, God only knows. Lily's now got a new job, a telephonist in a really swanky firm. The busier she is, Ethel says, the better. Lily will never come back to live at Rose Cottage, you've got to realize that. But one day, when the time is right, she will come back to see you, so keep watching, Lorne, over the bridge,' Teddy said, turning me to face it. 'And get ready to run as fast as you can to greet her.'

Teddy's words gave me hope and ever after, when I looked out of the window, I always wished that this would be the day Lily came to see me.

Mummy had decided that we should all go on a holiday. It would be our first. She borrowed the money from a lending company and I remember Daddy having a huge row with her about it and throwing her into the pantry. I sat terrified on the chair, unable to stop my legs from shaking as I listened to her cries. Although she wasn't very kind to me, I felt sad and wanted to help her. I wanted to shout 'Bully, bully,' to my Daddy as he paced up and down along the main living room floor, his face screwed up with anger. The cries finally stopped and Daddy helped her up from the floor. Her eye was pretty black and swollen. Ouch, I said quietly to myself. I bet that hurt. They both went up to the bedroom for a while and I quickly stood up from my chair to see if there was any blood in the pantry. No, just a few tins of beans that had rolled along the floor. That's lucky, I thought. She won't have to go to hospital like last time.

Eventually, they came down from their bedroom. Daddy walked through into the narrow, oblong kitchen holding Mummy's hand. He started kissing her whilst rubbing his hand over her bottom. Whoops, I'd better not look, so I pretended to paint my fingernails with an imaginary brush.

'I'll have to let them know at work what the dates are for this holiday,' I heard my Daddy say as he filled the kettle with water to make some tea. I wanted to jump and jump with joy. I wanted to tell the whole world we were going on a holiday.

I was told that I could go and sit on the wall at the front of the garden where the rosebush grew. I hurtled along the kitchen, through the back door and ran up the entry. Lifting myself up on the wall, I heard a voice behind me.

'Hello, have you come out to enjoy the sunshine?'

I turned my head around and there was old Mrs Crowswick who could barely walk, bending her hunched back to pick up some of the weeds in her garden which was next door to Rose Cottage. 'I'm going on holiday,' I said as she tried to stand up as straight as she could to talk to me. 'Mrs Crowswick, I'll ask my Mummy if I can help you. My Daddy has a fork; I'll get if for you. It will be so much easier.'

'No, no, my sweet thing,' she replied. 'I'm only pottering and Eric will be home soon. He promised to plant some bulbs in that spare patch over there. Can you see?' she said, pointing her frail finger in its direction. Eric was her son who looked nearly as old as she did. Every time I would see him he would always be carrying an old plastic bag which was full of cracks, and he always held his head down making strange noises from his mouth, which I don't think he could close properly.

'And where are you going on holiday?' she asked.

'Oh, somewhere very beautiful, Mrs Crowswick,' I replied. 'I've never written on a postcard before. I'll buy one when I'm on holiday and send it to you and Eric, telling you all about it.'

'That will be very nice,' she replied. 'I'll keep it on my mantelpiece, next to Mr Crowswick's photograph.'

I looked over her head towards the dark sash window at the front of her house, imagining his ghost standing staring at us. He must have died a long time ago, probably before I was born. What a shame for Mrs Crowswick, I thought, being on her own all this time with just Eric for company.

My eyes focused on the apple trees in the orchard just over the bridge as I turned my head back around to allow Mrs Crowswick to carry on with her weeding. It won't be long before the boys from the village come and raid them, I thought, noticing that the apples looked pretty large. They're brave, having to climb over that wall and then up the trees. Mr Dobson, who owns the orchard, will definitely catch them one day. He'll have a heart attack soon. Every year he chases them with his stick, then has to stop and lean over the bridge, coughing and spitting. He's far too fat to try and run that fast.

I got used to the wall being my second home. At least I got to speak to everyone who walked past this quiet, quaint village. I tried, but couldn't understand, why my Mummy only rarely allowed me to play with the few children that lived here. I would often watch them jumping under and over the rope as it whipped against the pavement, and listened as they counted numbers out loud as the girls took it in turns to skip.

Oh no! Coming from around the bend at the corner of the road was Monica. I'll start singing until she's walked past me, I thought, looking from the corner of my eye as she pushed her shiny twin pram nearer to me. I wonder if she's going to say sorry to me for saying that my skin is black. I'd argued with her that it isn't black, it's brown. I quietly started to sing 'All Things Bright and Beautiful' and waited as she got closer to see if she would stop and apologize. I felt angry, and my voice started to sing out of tune as she slowly walked past me, deliberately stopping a little further on, sitting her dolls up against the pillows on either side of the pram. I know that you're only showing off, I said to myself, trying to continue to sing. Just because you haven't a pretty face and you're fat and spoiled, and you look like you're fifteen instead of your eleven years, doesn't give you the right to call the colour of my skin black, I thought, as I watched her walk off with her head in the air. And anyway, I'll have a doll's pram one day and I'll buy one black doll and one white. That will make you angry, and I'll never be your friend again until you say you're sorry, I thought, watching her wiggling her bottom as she disappeared from view.

I started to feel pins and needles in my feet and climbed down from the wall into the garden. I spotted a weed near the daffodil standing on its own. I felt a little out of breath after breaking its stem and blowing its seeds. I watched as they floated in the air before eventually scattering over the ground.

I jumped with the banging of the window. 'Lorne,' I heard Mummy shout, 'come and put these clothes through the mangle for your father.'

'I'm coming,' I shouted, making my way back along the entry. I could smell the soapy, boiling water. 'I'm here, Daddy,' I said, knocking on the bathroom door and opening it. The room was full of steam. 'I can't breathe properly in here, shall I reach up and open the window?'

'No, I'll do that,' he said, turning the last bolts of the mangle which fitted in between either side of the bath. 'You just run the cold water.'

Why do I always get this job?, I thought, as I placed the plug in the bath allowing the water to run in. One day I'll get my hands trapped between these tight wheels and they'll be as flat as the clothes that come out at the other end. I wonder why we have to have a washing machine stuck in the corner in between the bath and wall. I'm certainly not going to have one in my bathroom when I grow up. It doesn't even work, I thought, as I watched Daddy turning the washing around and then lifting it up and dropping it into the bath with the large wooden stick.

'You're a good little worker,' he said, wiping the sweat off his brow. I kept looking up at him, wanting to ask where we were going to go for a holiday but the words wouldn't come out. The plastic washing basket was practically full, the job nearly done. Yuk, my fingers looked just like Mrs Crowswick's, old and wrinkly, I thought, as I dipped them back into the cold water, collecting the remaining socks that were floating around.

After finishing the rest of the jobs that I had to do around the home, I was finally told that we were all going to a Butlins Holiday Camp for a week and it was in Wales. The excitement seemed too much to bear. I knew from being taught at school that Wales had lots and lots of mountains. At last I'll be able to see one for real, I thought, looking down towards my feet at my plastic sandals. I wonder if the polish I use to shine the lino will make them sparkle. They'll need to be shiny if I'm going on holiday. I'll try it when Mummy's not around.

I counted each day that went by, excited when the postman, over the next few weeks, would knock on the door with another parcel of clothes that Mummy had ordered from Mrs White's catalogue. I always crossed my fingers that there might be a pretty dress in one of them for me. Maybe there'll be one in the next parcel.

'Don't you tell your father about this,' Mummy snapped as she saw me watching her try on another new dress in front of the long mirror which hung on the pantry door. I wondered why she hid everything that was in the parcels all over the house. I hope he doesn't find any of them. Maybe she'll buy him a new shirt, then he might not shout at her. I hate it when they fight, which hasn't been for a while, because Mr and Mrs Marsden who live next door haven't banged on the wall recently to tell them to be quiet.

Chapter 5

My journeys from school to home took me longer than they used to as I purposely took each step as slowly as possible. I dreaded walking down the entry and in through the back door to the list of jobs that would be waiting for me. My first was always to empty the ashes from the grate and light the fire. The house held such a cold, unloving atmosphere. Maybe one of my dreams would come true one day and I would come home and Mummy would be sitting on the chair next to a roaring fire with her arms stretched out for me to be hugged.

'Yuk,' I said out loud as I opened the back door and walked into the kitchen. 'Mrs Patterson has been again.' I could smell her stale perfume. I could always tell when she had been to Rose Cottage. Anyway, she smells as common as she looks, I thought, whilst leaning over the pot sink to open the window. There were very few people I disliked in the village, but I certainly didn't like Mrs Patterson. She was Mummy's best friend and would constantly come to the house so that Mummy could teach her how to apply make-up to her face. She insisted that she wanted her make-up to look exactly the same as Mummy's, especially on her eyes, and she must also have a beauty spot painted on the top of her cheek, just where Mummy painted hers. I wish Rose Cottage had lots of rooms, I thought quietly to myself as I reached out for the shovel behind the back of the door to clean out the fireplace, then I wouldn't have to look at Mrs Patterson's reflection as she admires herself through the mirror, her eyes heavily painted with black eyeliner. Anyway, she's old enough to know how to put lipstick on her lips; even I know how to do that. I've had lots of practice whilst Mummy's been at work.

My Daddy started to return home from work much later in the evenings. The oily smell on his overalls was much stronger than usual. I missed looking out through the window, waiting and watching for him to walk over the bridge so I could run up to him, take his haversack from his shoulder and carry it for him. It pleased Mummy that he was working overtime. I missed the little chats I was lucky enough to have with him in the evenings and couldn't understand why Mummy would always shout when he fell asleep in the chair. I started to look forward to the end of the week when he would hand his wage packet over to her. There was no shouting then and Daddy would be allowed to sleep as long as he wanted.

I overheard Mummy saying to my sister, Frieda, that she had decided to work an extra couple of days until the holidays, packing glasses at the factory. Frieda had a big smile on her face when Mummy told her that she was the one in charge. Oh no, I thought, she'll boss me around all through the school holidays.

'Lorne's only allowed out twice a week, and only after she's done her jobs,' I heard Mummy say. 'I want you to inspect what she's done and if it hasn't been done properly, she stays in.'

Frieda was Mummy's favourite and could do no wrong. I had not really noticed before how thin her lips were as I watched her reassuring Mummy that she had nothing to worry about.

Frieda made it very clear to me that she was five years my senior. I remember when a group of the neighbours walked past Rose Cottage. I was collecting the petals that had fallen from the roses in the garden when one of them said, 'How's the prettiest girl in the village?' as they all looked at me from over the wall. My sister wasn't far away and heard what had been said. From then on she always bore a grudge against me. I had to close my teeth together very tightly whilst watching her as she smirked, listening to Mummy rhyming off the list of jobs whilst she wrote them down on a pad. I desperately wanted to pull my tongue out at her. You are a mean, mean sister, I said to myself. I hope that you hurry up and get married so that I don't have to live here with you any more and, anyway, when I have a boyfriend he won't have spots all over his face like yours has.

The last day of school before the break for the summer holidays had actually arrived. We were told by Mr Wilde, the headmaster, to empty our desks and take what was in them home. I could see Rose Cottage in the distance and, as I got closer, I noticed Eric sitting on the bench in his garden. 'Hello,' I said, looking over at him as I walked along the pavement towards the entry. The sunlight must have been blinding him as he tried to look up, holding his hand on his forehead to protect his eyes. 'Can I come and sit next to you for a while?' I asked. 'I've got some paintings that I've done at school.' I could see that he was trying to smile so I confidently walked over and sat on the bench next to him. 'I've only got a few minutes, Eric, then I'll have to go. I'm not the best painter in my class but do you like this daffodil I painted? It's my favourite. I like flowers, Eric, do you? Your mother said that you're going to plant some bulbs over there,' I said, pointing over to remind him. 'Eric, I'm allowed out twice a week whilst I'm on school holidays. Can I help you? Why don't we plant some daffodils? Here, you can keep this picture of the one I painted to remind you how pretty they are.'

He moved his arm up to his mouth to remove the saliva that was just about to drip down his chin. Most people were scared of Eric, but I wasn't. I placed my tiny fingers around his huge hand and squeezed it as hard as I could. 'I'll have to go now, Eric,' I said, standing up and letting go of his hand as gently as I could. 'I'll sit my painting next to you.' I said, bending down to pick up a tiny broken slate I had spotted. 'I'm putting this slate on top of it, Eric, so it won't blow away,' I told him, aware of the slight breeze.

'My Daddy's going to be very surprised when he opens his haversack today,' I said, holding up my last two paintings for Eric to look at. 'I tried to paint that rose exactly the same colour, like the one he planted in the garden. It's not quite the same colour, but nearly. I'd like to give this painting to your mother, Eric, but my Daddy likes red roses, and I smudged the yellow paint on the other so I can't really give it to anyone. Sometimes Daddy goes to work without taking anything to eat because he hasn't had enough time to make any sandwiches, so when I hear his alarm clock ring to wake him up, I jump out of bed and go downstairs to make the sandwiches for him. He must like them, Eric, because he eats them all up, so when I made them this morning, I folded one of my paintings and placed it on the top before wrapping them in one of the empty bread packets that I save.'

'I'll call for you soon, Eric,' I promised as I gave him a little wave. 'We'll need a spade. I'll borrow Daddy's and I'll stick your picture that I painted on your bedroom wall if I can find some Sellotape.' I gave him a final wave whilst reluctantly making my way towards the entry for home. I wonder where I can hide Daddy's new picture, I thought, as I opened the back door and stood in the kitchen looking around for a hiding place. Yes, I've found it. I'll fold it now before putting it in Mummy's sewing box on top of the kitchenette.

I felt quite hot after carrying the wooden chair I needed to stand on to reach for the box. I hope there are no spiders up here, I thought, feeling the dusty surface on my fingers. I gave a sigh as I struggled to open the lid. 'No one will ever find you up here,' I said, finally placing it in the box. Then, with a quick rub of my hands, I stepped down and lifted the chair back to its usual place. Oh no, where's my picture of the yellow rose I painted? I put my hand on my heart as I spotted it lying on the floor. I'm really going to have to hurry, I thought, bending down to pick it up. I've not even cleaned out the ashes from the fireplace. I rushed over and picked up the shovel. I'll pretend that the Queen's coming. That will make me do my jobs a lot quicker.

I wish we could have a real tablecloth, I thought, as I

struggled to unfold the plastic one that had stuck together with the heat from the sun that was shining through the living room window. I placed it over the table. And anyway, it's a good job that I'm only pretending that the Queen's coming. I don't think she'd like to eat her tea with us. I wished I could throw it away in the dustbin. The stale smell of vinegar that was coming from it made me sneeze a couple of times. One day I might get some spending money and I'll save up and buy Mummy a new one. Yes, and it will be made of lace just like the one Mrs Entwhistle has on her table.

With the knives and forks finally set (making sure that Daddy had the shiniest), I decided to place my painting of the yellow rose in between the salt and pepper pots. That looks better, I thought, standing back to have a better look. I know, I'll find the scissors and cut it out so that it looks like a real flower, and anyway, no one will ever know that I've smudged it. I wonder what I can use as a vase. My eyes started to wander around the room searching for anything that would be suitable. Uh oh, I hope there won't be any shouting tonight, I thought, as I noticed the strip of wallpaper partly hanging down from the wall in the corner of the room. Daddy and Mummy always shout at each other when that happens. I know, I'll ask the fairy that lives in the garden if she'll grant me a wish that we can all live in a house that doesn't have damp walls. I bet I won't be able to go out and play now, I said to myself, deciding to collect one of the milk bottles from the back yard to put my rose in.

Quick, quick, pick up the cuttings from the floor, I told myself as I put the rose in the bottle and placed it in the middle of the table. I wish I could look forward to Mummy coming home from work. I spotted her in the yard feeling if the washing on the line was dry. I'll try not to frown this time when she walks in. I'll cross my fingers and ask her as soon as she does if I can go out to play after tea.

'Why hasn't the washing been brought in?' were her first words as she slipped off her mac from over her shoulders. I ran straight over to collect it before hanging it on the usual hook behind the door. I walked silently past her whilst she ripped open the envelopes that the postman had posted through the letterbox. I wonder why she's hiding what he's sent inside her bra. It will only fall out when she takes it off, I thought, shrugging my shoulders as I made my way back along the kitchen to the yard.

'I've folded the washing and put it on top of the chair ready for ironing,' I called over to Mummy. 'Please may I go out and play after tea?' I asked, standing still in the kitchen, wanting to keep my distance from the living room where she was sitting in case she got cross with me.

'There's half a crown. Go and get five pounds of potatoes from the Dobsons,' Mummy said, opening her purse and taking it out, once again ignoring my question.

Oh well, at least I can have a little walk, and I might be lucky and find a penny by the roadside. I liked the apples Mr Dobson sold. I smiled as I skipped along the pathway, just managing to look over the wall where the orchard was. There were Mr Dobson's Alsatians tied with long pieces of rope around his favourite apple tree. My heart skipped a beat when they both spotted me. They ran towards me, stopping sharply with a jerk. Oh no, I hope that Mr Dobson has tied that rope tight enough. I watched them scrape their paws against the bricks of the wall. If that rope had been just a little longer, they might have nearly reached me. 'I'm not going to pinch Mr Dobson's apples,' I said to them, taking two paces back when they both looked up at me with snarls on their faces. 'See, I've got half a crown,' I said, holding it out with my hands as I continued to walk along to the end of the wall turning into Mr Dobson's drive. I wanted to run as fast as I could to the farmhouse door, but I'd always been told that if you run away from a dog it will chase you and bite a big hole in your bottom, so I walked slowly over the gravel towards Mr Dobson's. I'm glad that I showed them my money, I thought, aware of them watching me through the open spaces of the trees in the orchard. They probably think I'm rich. Rich enough to buy every apple that Mr Dobson has grown. That's why they've stopped barking at me, I thought, slightly turning my head around to check if they were still tied to the tree.

All of a sudden I felt myself falling. I could feel the palms of my hands stinging as they pressed against the tiny pebbles. 'Ouch,' I shouted as I hit the ground. I felt tears immediately fill my eyes. 'Where's my money? Where's my half a crown gone?' I cried, standing up slowly whilst holding on to my grazed elbow. I moved my feet around in the gravel trying to find it. 'Please God,' I said, looking up to the sky, 'please help me find it. I won't be able to go home if I don't, and I haven't got anywhere else to live. I don't care if the dogs bite me now. At least I'll be able to stay at the hospital,' I said, wiping my nose on my sleeve.

'Why are you crying?' I heard a voice say, jumping once

again with the sudden sound of a tyre skidding. There was Harry, delivering his papers, pressing his hands tightly on the brakes and stopping his bicycle right in front of me. 'You've only slightly grazed it,' he said, looking curiously at my elbow.

'I've lost my money,' I replied, losing a breath in between words.

'How much?' he asked, pulling out a newspaper from his canvas bag.

'Half a crown,' I cried.

'Here, hold on to this,' he said, pulling the strap off his shoulders and handing me the bag. 'Where did you fall?' he asked as he got off his bicycle, allowing it to drop with a thud to the ground.

'Just here,' was my reply, watching him on his hands and knees searching through the gravel.

'What are you going to do if I can't find it?' he shouted, moving further away from me.

'I'll have to run away. Can I stay in your pigeon loft?'

'You won't like it,' he said. 'They're far too noisy, and anyway, I haven't cleaned it out this week so it's really smelly.'

'I can hold my breath,' I called over to him.

'You won't have to,' he said, standing up and brushing his hands over his knees to get rid of the dust. 'I'll make you a bargain,' he said with a smile on his face.

'Where have I left that newspaper?' he asked, walking towards me.

'It's next to the wheel of your bicycle,' I said, pointing in its direction.

'Right, if you take this newspaper for me and give it

to Mr Dobson, I'll give you this half a crown that I've just found. Now hold on tight to it,' he said, placing the money into the palm of my hand before picking up the newspaper and folding it.

'Here, now don't make any creases in it. Mr Dobson looks forward to his evening paper.'

'I won't, Harry. You might be in it one day for saving my life,' I said.

'Well, maybe if my pigeons win a race I'll probably be in. I'll have to go now or I'll be the one who's going to be in trouble. I've got all those deliveries to do,' he said, getting hold of his bag and placing the strap over his shoulder.

'You're the best paper-boy in the land,' I called out as I watched him ride away on his rusted bicycle, waving his hand before disappearing on to the road.

'Thank you, God for sending Harry to help me,' I said quietly as I climbed up the steps to Mr Dobson's front door. 'Mr Dobson, your newspaper's here,' I said, holding it out to where he was sitting on his rocking chair next to the boxes of fruit and vegetables.

'Is the lad too scared to bring it himself?' he grunted, reaching for it with his grubby hands. 'I told him that I was going to chop his fingers off.'

'Please may I have five pounds of potatoes,' I kindly interrupted, holding my money out to him.

He turned towards the kitchen. 'Christine,' he shouted. 'Christine,' he called again.

'Yes, Dad,' I heard her reply.

'Get a bag of potatoes from the yard,' he told her, repeatedly tapping his dirty fingernails on the tin box where he kept his money. 'Just caught him in time,' he said, beckoning to me to pass my half a crown to him.

'Who?' I asked.

'The lad who delivers my papers. Caught him red-handed, the bloody thief. Don't mind the odd piece of fruit, but the skinny bastard had his hands in my cash box.'

Hurry up, Christine, I thought, as I watched the flies crawling all over Mr Dobson's display. I'll bet Harry's pigeon loft smells better than Mr Dobson's home, I thought, noticing the dried up food stuck to the plates on his table. Poor Christine, she's nearly as fat as Mr Dobson. I wonder why she looks more like a boy than a girl. I watched her shuffle towards her father and pass him the potatoes. I wouldn't want to be fat if I was twenty like she is, I thought, feeling quite sorry for her. I wish I had a ribbon that I could give to her. It would look pretty in her hair; then maybe the boys in the village wouldn't make fun of her any more.

'Here, love, take the change,' Mr Dobson grunted once more, handing it to me and passing over the bag of potatoes. I wonder if Mr Dobson will really chop Harry's fingers off. But no one will get a newspaper if he does because he won't be able to ride on his bicycle. I'll tell Harry how much danger he's in, and anyway, he can always write a note to say that he's sorry. He's always writing things and strapping them around the pigeons' feet. He could send his letter by pigeon if he's too frightened to go and give it to Mr Dobson himself.

I made my legs walk as fast as they could towards home, having to stop for a few seconds to swap the bag of potatoes from one hand to the other. I expected to be shouted at for being late as I placed the spuds on the wooden shelf in the kitchen.

'Get them peeled and chipped thinly,' was all Mummy said from the living room where she was standing looking through the mirror that hung on the wall over the top of the fireplace. Uh oh, I wonder where she's going tonight, I thought, noticing the piece of steak lying in the frying pan on top of the cooker. 'Have you taken any of my hairgrips?' I heard her shout.

I glanced from the kitchen into the living room.

'Don't backchat me with "maybe Frieda has",' she shouted, placing her rollers in her hair.

I quickly turned away not wanting to aggravate her any more. I really hate you, Mummy, I said to myself. I really hate you for always making me feel so unhappy. I could feel a lump in my throat whilst searching through the drawer for the potato peeler. Daddy always gets steak for his tea when she wants to go out. It's his favourite. I wonder if she's going dancing with Mrs Patterson. I don't know why my Daddy always says yes to her, and then shouts at her when she comes home. I'm glad that I'm in bed when that happens. At least I can take a deep breath and put the blanket over my head until all the shouting has finished.

'May I go and sit on the wall?' I asked, drying my hands on the tea towel. 'I've finished peeling the potatoes.'

'Take that damn milk bottle off the table on your way out, and if I want a bloody rose I'll cut one from the garden myself,' she replied.

Whoops, here comes another lump in my throat, as I

walked over to the table to collect it. 'Never mind my yellow rose,' I said, picking up the bottle and lifting it out. 'I think you're beautiful, too beautiful to sit on top of a smelly tablecloth.'

I could hear the grinding of the nail file as Mummy sat there filing her nails. One of these days I'm going to pull a face at you, and it will be the most horrible face I will ever pull, I thought, looking over at her. I quickly walked back through into the kitchen. I wasn't going to allow her to see the tears rolling down my cheeks. 'Never mind,' I said, looking down at my rose whilst bending down to place the milk bottle next to the back door. 'I'll post you through Mrs Crowswick's letterbox. You're lucky you don't need watering. Mrs Crowswick's far too old to keep getting up and down to check if you're thirsty. At least you won't be thrown away and I'll be able to come and see you when I help Eric in his garden.'

Mrs Crowswick mustn't get many letters, I thought, as I stood on my tiptoes to open the creaky, oblong letterbox and carefully push my rose through. I'll stop crying now, now that I know that my rose is safe. What a nice surprise Mrs Crowswick will have when she finds it.

I could smell fried onions coming from the kitchen up along the entry. Daddy must be due home. He loves onions with his steak. I was right. As I looked over, there he was walking over the bridge. 'Daddy,' I shouted, waving my hand. I stopped at the edge of the kerb and looked left and right before running across the road to meet him. 'It was my last day at school today. I don't go back for a whole six weeks,' I told him, reaching out to his shoulder, taking hold of the strap and pulling it over his arm to carry his haversack. 'Did you eat all of your sandwiches?' I asked, looking up at him for his reply whilst holding on to the cuff of his jacket as we made our way to Rose Cottage.

'I nearly ate the loveliest painting I've ever seen,' he replied, looking down at me.

'Oh,' I gasped, 'did you really?'

'Nearly,' he said with a wink in his eye.

'Daddy, don't tease me,' I said, imagining that he'd at least taken one bite of it.

'I stuck it on the side of my machine and all the men wanted to take it home to give to their wives.'

'Did they really?' I asked, chuckling with embarrassment.

'Hmm, something smells good,' he said, taking back his haversack as we reached the top of the entry.

'I'm sitting on the wall for a while,' I said, letting go of his jacket to allow him to walk the short distance to the kitchen where mother was cooking. If there is any shouting tonight, I thought, at least Daddy will be happy when he finds another rose in his sandwiches tomorrow.

Chapter 6

It seemed longer than usual before I heard the knock on the window with Mummy standing there signalling me to come in. I ran down the entry and into the kitchen, collecting a plate from the shelf before standing in a queue for something to eat. Wow, you're lucky you didn't get a slap, I thought, looking down at the floor as my brother bent down trying to pick up the fried egg that had slipped from his plate. Whoops, there go his chips, too. I listened to Mummy cursing under her breath as he frantically picked them up. My body started to shake with laughter. I couldn't hold my plate still as it moved up and down with me.

'Who's that giggling?' I heard her shout as she ordered my brother to throw what remained of his egg into the bin. Ugh, I hope he's not going to eat them, I thought, looking at him standing there with just chips that he had picked up off the floor on his plate. I tried to be as quiet as I could but my laughter got the better of me. I had no control.

'Right, you little bitch, get up those stairs. You'll soon stop laughing when you realize you're not going to get anything to eat.'

I promptly placed my plate back on the shelf. 'Butterfingers,' I whispered to my brother as I walked past him, making my way through the living room towards the stairs.

Umm. I wish I had Frieda's bedroom, I thought, giving a quick peek in. She's certainly got a lot of pretty things on her dressing table. I couldn't resist temptation as I tiptoed over the floorboards, stepping over her slippers to have a closer look. Wow, just look at that musical box! Finding it hard, but resisting turning the key to see if the ballerina inside it would dance, I perched on the edge of the stool and picked up the bristle hairbrush. I imagined Frieda's reflection standing at the door staring at me with anger as I looked through the mirror. I'd better go before she catches me, I thought, quickly brushing my hair, then making sure that the brush was put back in the exact place where I found it before tiptoeing back out towards the room where I slept. Frieda must feel like a princess having a beautiful hairbrush like that and a ballerina that dances for her whenever she turns the key.

I do hate this room; it frightens me, I thought, sitting myself down on the corner of my bed. I wished I didn't have to sleep in the same room as my brothers, glancing around at their empty beds. Oh well, I sighed, at least my bed's next to the window and I can see everyone that walks by. I knelt down next to it and rested my elbows on the ledge.

'Susie,' I shouted, surprised to see her making her way along the path towards the front door. 'Susie, I'm up here,' I shouted again, knocking on the window to get her attention.

'Open the window,' she called, looking up at me as I stood up.

'It's stuck,' I replied. Susie was a lot stronger than me.

'Push harder,' she shouted, 'I bet I could open it with one hand.'

'I've not been allowed anything to eat, so I'm weaker than normal,' I called back. With one huge groan it was finally open.

'You ought to get the same windows that my dad put in at our house. Do you want to come and have a look?'

'I can't, Susie, I have to stay in my bedroom. Are they pretty?'

'Well, they're better than the sash windows that you've got. Dad's just finishing putting the bathroom one in, so I've pinched two fags out of his cigarette case. Can't you come out? I'll teach you how to smoke.'

'Sshh,' I said, 'I'll really be in big trouble if Mummy hears what you've just said. Do you know that Mr Dobson's going to chop Harry's fingers off?' I said. 'He tried to pinch some money out of his cash box. I really hope he doesn't.'

'Lorne, you silly thing. Mr Dobson's only trying to frighten him. He'd go to jail for ever if he did that.'

'Would he really?' I replied.

'Look, I'll knock on your door and ask your mum if you can come out. We only need some matches and I've found a great place to hide.'

'Won't I cough like Daddy does when he smokes?' I asked.

'Well yes, but after a few drags you'll be all right,' she said, walking towards the front door and knocking on it twice.

I couldn't actually hear what was being said when the

door was finally opened, but within seconds it was closed again and Susie reappeared, shaking her head.

'Have you got to stay up there all night?' she asked.

'I don't know,' I replied. 'Mummy's going out so I might be allowed back down. I think she's going dancing. I suppose the answer was no,' I said looking down at her with disappointment on my face.

'Never mind. I'll pinch some more fags when Dad's had a few beers. He normally gets drunk on a Friday evening, so he won't notice that any are missing. Don't forget that there's a jumble sale at the Church Hall on Friday. I'll meet you there at three o'clock,' she shouted as she started to walk away.

'But I haven't got any money to buy anything, and Mummy might not let me go,' I called out.

'I'll lend you a shilling. I'm babysitting tomorrow for my sister. She's staying out later than she normally does so I'll be paid extra. See you then. Don't be late.'

'I won't, Susie. I'm quite excited. I'll pay you back when I get a babysitting job.'

'Okay,' she said, waving to me before disappearing out of view.

I quickly turned my head towards the bedroom door at the sound of the catch being lifted. It opened and there was my brother, Teddy.

'Quick,' he said, putting his hand underneath his jumper and pulling out some bread. 'I've managed to sneak this up for you to eat,'

'Has it got margarine on?' I asked, walking over to him.

'Don't be stupid,' he replied. 'It's been dangerous enough.' He passed the two slices of dry bread over to me.

'You're very brave. I hate being in this room on my own,' I said, biting off a corner of the bread.

'Well, you shouldn't have laughed at me,' he replied. 'You know what Mother's like if you laugh.'

'I wasn't laughing at you, Teddy, I honestly wasn't. I was laughing at your fried egg lying on the floor. Didn't Mummy make you another?'

'Yes,' he grunted, closing the door and leaving me on my own once more. Poor Teddy, I thought, still chewing on the bread. I was grateful, even though it was dry, that he'd brought me something to eat. I'll buy him a chocolate cake from the refreshments stall at the jumble sale. Maybe he'll grow a little more. Even though there was only eleven months between our ages, I knew how conscious he was of his tiny build. I'm glad I chose him to be my favourite brother, I thought, perching myself again on the edge of my bed.

Uh oh, here she comes. I was right, Mummy was going dancing. I watched Mrs Patterson walking slowly towards Rose Cottage. I wondered why her hair looked like a bird's nest as she came closer into view. Maybe she's put a whole can of spray on it. That must be why it never moves when she turns her head. I'll bet even if there was a hurricane it would still stay in the same position on top of her head, I thought, giving a little giggle, crouching low so that she wouldn't see me watching her through the window. My knees began to feel sore as they rested against the floorboards. I could feel the tiredness in my eyes whilst gently rubbing them. 'Ouch,' I said, placing my hands on the ledge and lifting myself up. I could hear the buzz of conversation downstairs as I walked around the room. Next time I'll lean on a pillow, I thought, rubbing my legs to ease the cramp.

At the sound of the front door closing, I walked as quickly as I could towards the window. There was Mummy and Mrs Patterson, arms linked, walking with an air of confidence across the road and over the bridge. Mummy must have lent Mrs Patterson her leopard-skin bag, I thought, watching it move to and fro as she held it against her hip, waddling her bottom with each step she took.

'They've gone out to play bingo,' Teddy shouted up to me as he struggled to put his arm into the sleeve of his jacket.

They look far too dressed up just to go and have a game of bingo, I thought. 'Oh well, Mummy might win some money,' I shouted back to him. 'Where are you going?' I asked as he finally zipped up his jacket. 'You look nice. Have you put some Brylcreem on your hair?'

'Sshh, I borrowed some of Father's. He's fast asleep in the chair. I'd have brought you a drink up but I'm late.'

'I know, you've got a girlfriend, haven't you?' I said, looking down and smiling at him. 'That's why you've used Daddy's Brylcreem.' With a wink in his eye, placing his hands inside his pockets, he slowly disappeared out of view.

I felt restless as I sat back on the edge of the bed, the springs wriggling underneath my bottom as I moved up and down. I'm so thirsty. I'll go and ask Daddy if I can have a glass of water. I moved along the dark landing, glancing up at the bare light bulb hanging from the ceiling. I wish I was more clever at school, I thought, then I could get a good job and surprise Mummy with a beautiful chandelier. My heart skipped a beat. 'Whoops, that was lucky,' I said out loud, clinging on to the bannister and saving myself from falling down the stairs. I could have broken my legs and then I wouldn't have been able to go to the jumble sale, I thought, looking at the loose carpet and wishing that Daddy would nail it down properly.

I pulled my face at the creaking of the living room door as I pressed down on the handle and opened it. Daddy's snores echoed around the tiny room. He must be so exhausted, I thought, noticing his legs fully stretched out. I wonder why he wears those worn out slippers. They must be too small for his feet. That must be why his big toe sticks out through the hole in them.

I started to tiptoe towards the back of the chair where he was sleeping. I slowly stretched out my arm and placed my hand gently on his shoulder. 'Daddy,' I said gently, giving him a little shake. 'Daddy, may I have a glass of water?' There was no response as I slowly walked around his chair, not taking my eyes off him for a second. 'I'm going to have a glass of water. I didn't try really hard to wake you,' I told him in between his snores, 'but I'm sure you won't mind.' I felt quite nervous as I walked towards the kitchen. What if Mummy comes home early and catches me? I quickly looked over my shoulder to check that she wasn't there.

Ooh, I said to myself, reaching for a glass. I wish it was as shiny as Grandfather's medal that he shows me every time he comes to stay. I turned on the tap and filled it. If only I was grown up. I could have my own tap and a shiny glass and I could fill it with as much water as I liked, but I would miss Grandfather because he'd be dead by then. I wonder why he tells lies. If his medal was really worth one million pounds, surely he would sell it and buy Mummy a big house and Daddy a pair of slippers that fit him. I wonder if he really did have tea with the Queen when she presented it to him. I'll bet she sat a long way from him. He always smells far too much of whisky. I wonder why he always has a glass of it for breakfast. Maybe he doesn't like drinking tea out of the plastic cups that Mummy buys. They do smell when you put your nose near them, I thought, drinking the water as fast as I could and avoiding placing my lips on the bits of the glass that were missing.

I gave a sigh of relief as I drank the last drop. I glanced over to Daddy and wished I could sit on the couch next to him. Whoops, I'd better go, I thought, as I noticed the movement of his toes curling up inside his slippers. Anyway, he'd only get into trouble if he allowed me to stay down with him. I'll get into bed and dream about all the beautiful things there will be at the jumble sale, I thought, whilst creeping past Daddy. It's so kind of Susie to lend me a shilling. I wish I could buy her the biggest box of matches made so that she can smoke her cigarettes. I'm still scared of coughing though when she gives me one, I thought, as I pulled down the blanket and got into bed. I could hear the chattering of people walking by as I placed my head on the pillow. Don't feel lonely, I said to myself as the sound of their voices disappeared into the distance. Anyway, I've far too much to dream about.

Chapter 7

I couldn't believe that it was morning when I opened my eyes and listened to the clatter of the empty milk bottles that Mr Ramsbottom, the milkman, had just collected. I jumped out of bed and gave a gentle knock on the window. 'Morning,' he shouted, turning his head and looking up at me. I gave him a little wave whilst watching him place the empty bottles in a crate. I could see the muscles on the top of his arms as he lifted it and stacked it high on to his milk float. I wonder what tune he's whistling, I thought, as I watched him hoist himself into the driver's seat. 'Bye, Mr Ramsbottom,' I whispered as he slowly drove away. I wonder why his milk float doesn't have doors on it. He must fall out of it when he drives around corners. That's probably why he walks with a limp.

I could hear the crackling sound of the radio coming from downstairs as I took off my nightie and reached for my dress that I always left hanging over the landing. If Frieda hurries up and gets married, I'll be able to have her wardrobe. If I'm allowed, I'll ask Mrs Entwhistle, who would sometimes babysit me when Mummy was busy, if she would be so kind as to make me some clothes on her sewing machine. I'll pick some daisies from the field whilst I'm on school holidays and make her a necklace and a bracelet, too. She'll be really surprised. She'll probably place them with her diamonds that she keeps locked away in her jewellery box. Here goes, I said to myself, holding my nose for a few seconds whilst looking down at the chamber pot which was sitting on the landing floor nearly full to the top with everyone's urine. 'One, two, three,' I said, letting go of my nose and bending down to pick up the handle, trying to keep the pot as steady as I could with my other hand. I took each step down the stairs as carefully as I could, not being able to avoid the odd spill that I hoped nobody would notice.

'Can someone open the door?' I shouted. 'Open the door, I'm going to drop it,' I shouted again. At last the handle of the door was pushed down and opened. I wish I could throw this right over your head, I thought, as Frieda stood holding the door open with a big smirk on her face, watching me struggle as I tried to keep the chamber pot balanced. Anyway, I'll never make her a daisy chain so that she can look pretty when she goes out, I thought, as I made my way towards the bathroom to dispose of it.

'Go and ask Mrs Crowswick if I can borrow a cup of sugar,' Mummy shouted from the living room, 'and wash your hands.' I didn't even look over to her as I turned on the tap. 'Take one of the old cups,' she said as I struggled to place my feet into my sandals. My knuckles hurt me slightly as I knocked as hard as I could. Please hurry, Mrs Crowswick. Mummy has to go to work soon and she can't drink tea without any sugar in.

'Oh, Eric, you scared me then,' I said as he suddenly opened the door. 'Please may I borrow some sugar?' I asked, handing the cup over to him. 'I'll come and help you in your garden this afternoon. It will look so pretty when we've planted all the bulbs,' I said, pointing in the direction where Mrs Crowswick wanted them planted. I wonder where Mrs Crowswick has put my yellow rose, I thought, trying not to stare into her living room whilst Eric was in the kitchen. 'Thank you so much, Eric. I'll bring you some back when Mummy has been shopping,' I said, reaching out and taking the cup from his hand. 'I'll call for you at three o'clock if it doesn't start to rain,' I told him, looking up towards the grey clouds that filled most of the sky. I wonder why the jacket of his pyjamas has got so many different buttons on, I thought, shrugging my shoulders. Maybe Mrs Crowswick can't see very well when she's sewing, but they still look nice. 'Bye, Eric. I'm going to make Mummy a cup of tea now,' I said, reaching over and touching his hand.

I filled the kettle with water as soon as I arrived back in the kitchen. I know, I'll pinch some of these matches for Susie, I thought, whilst striking one to light the gas ring on top of the cooker. I wish I could sit and have a conversation with Mummy, I thought, aware of the sound of her voice as she spoke to Frieda. I've so much I want to talk to her about. I'll make her the best cup of tea I can. As I watched the steam blowing out from the spout of the kettle, I wondered if she would give me permission to go to the jumble sale tomorrow. I carried the tea to her, aware of the odd tea-leaf floating on top. I didn't have time to place it on the mantelpiece as Mummy took it immediately from my hands. 'Keep out of the way,' she said, 'I'm late as it is.'

I quickly went and sat on the old wooden chair next

to the window. I looked out to see if my friend the robin had returned to the yard. 'I haven't left you any crusts of bread from Daddy's sandwiches,' I whispered, hoping he could somehow hear me. 'I didn't wake up in time to make him any.'

'Who are you talking to now?' Mummy said with a sarcastic tone in her voice.

'It will be one of her stupid friends that she imagines she's got,' Frieda laughed. 'She's always talking to herself, Mother.'

'It's a sign of madness,' Mummy snapped.

Well, how come all the daisies in the field are my friends? There must be at least three hundred. I wonder if I will go mad. I hope not, at least not until I've grown up into a lady. I wonder if Mummy will save me all her pretty dresses. I'll ask her when she's not in so much of a rush. 'Shall I pass you your coat?' I asked, rising from the chair.

'I'll be bringing some pies back at lunch-time,' I heard her say whilst I was standing on my tiptoes reaching for the hook her coat was hanging on. 'Make sure the table's laid and the bread is buttered,' I was told as she took the coat from my hand.

'I'm helping Eric plant some bulbs in his garden this afternoon for Mrs Crowswick,' I quickly said.

'You're helping in this house first. The stairs need sweeping; in fact, sweep them twice. I'll inspect them when I get home.'

At least she didn't say I couldn't. I gave a sigh of relief as I watched her walk towards the front door. 'Bye, Mummy.' There was no reply as the door was slammed behind her.

I jumped up and down with excitement. I'll give Eric a spoon, I thought, so that he can dig the hole. His feet might slip when he's digging if I let him use Daddy's spade. My heart skipped a beat as the letter-box was opened. 'That scared me,' I said out loud, watching the envelopes fall to the floor. I ran straight over and tapped on the window. He's got a nice uniform to wear, I thought, as I waved over to him. 'See, even the postman's my friend,' I whispered, watching him stretch out his arm and wave back. I walked over to the door, bent down and picked up the envelopes, reading the names they were addressed to. Mummy's lucky having three letters sent to her in one day, I thought as I placed them on top of the gas meter so that she could see them as soon as she opened the door.

'Hello, hello,' I heard a voice shout. 'Hello,' she shouted again. All of a sudden the door into the living room partly opened. There was Mrs Patterson struggling to get through whilst carrying a suitcase in each hand.

'Are you going on holiday?' I asked, holding the door open for her.

'If that bastard of a husband of mine didn't spend all his time and money in the pub, I probably would be. Never get married, young girl, they're all the same.'

'Who are?' I asked.

'Men.'

'Don't you like Mr Patterson?'

'I've hated him for years,' she replied, lifting the suitcases and placing them on top of each other on the settee.

'But I'm going to marry a prince when I grow up.'

'Ha, that's what we all say. They're all bloody princes until we marry them.'

I wonder what those marks are on her neck, I thought, as she looked through the mirror admiring herself. 'Are you coming to live here?' I asked, looking over in the direction of the suitcases.

'The bastard will have to drop dead in his chair before he lets me live anywhere,' she quickly replied.

Oh dear, poor Mrs Patterson. I actually feel quite sorry for you now, even though I don't like you very much. 'Shall I give Mummy a message?'

'No, I'll see her later. At least you can all pack for your holidays.'

'When are we going?' I asked.

'Huh, you mean you don't know when you're going on holiday?'

'I've forgotten.'

'You've forgotten!' she said, looking down at me.

'I knew that we were going on holiday but I didn't know when. Mummy has probably been too busy to tell me.'

'It's Saturday you go, that's why I've brought the suitcases,' she replied, shaking her head whilst walking back towards the door. 'Dear me, fancy not knowing when you're going on holiday.'

This has got to be one of the best days of my life, I thought, rushing over to the suitcases as soon as Mrs Patterson had left, pulling down the zip and opening one of them. 'Wow, look at all that space,' I said out loud, holding on to the lid and looking inside.

'What are you doing, touching someone else's property?' I quickly let go of the lid and turned around. There was Frieda pointing her finger directly at me. 'You can forget about going to help Eric this afternoon when Mother finds out about this. Have you swept the stairs yet?'

I didn't answer her whilst walking over to the fireplace to collect the wooden hand brush that was leaning against the hearth. I could feel a lump in my throat and a sharp pain in my tummy. I know, I'll talk to Jesus, I thought, wiping the tears from my eyes with the bottom of my dress as I made my way to the top of the narrow stairs.

'Dear Jesus, I hope you don't mind me talking to you whilst I'm working. There's a lot of stairs to sweep and I have to sweep them twice. I might cough a little whilst I'm speaking to you, but that's because a lot of dust comes up from the carpet. I'm going to stop crying now so that I can talk to you. You see, I'm in trouble again. I opened one of Mrs Patterson's suitcases. I know it doesn't belong to me but I'm going on a holiday to Wales on Saturday. I got so excited I just unzipped it and had a look inside. I promised to plant some bulbs with Eric this afternoon so that Mrs Crowswick's garden would look pretty. Did you know that I am Eric's best friend? He'll be very sad if I let him down. Friends aren't supposed to let each other down, are they? I was even going to ask Mummy if I could make some sandwiches so that when all the digging and planting had been done I could sit on the bench in his garden and have a picnic while we watch the flowers grow, but I can't now because Frieda's going to tell Mummy what I've done. I don't like to ask but I need your help. Is there anything that you can do to make Mummy forgive me? You're very kind because you forgive everybody. Excuse me sniffing, there isn't any more toilet roll left to blow my nose on. Is it the same time in heaven as it is here? If it is, Mummy will be home in two hours. She's bringing some pies back. They're really nice. I'll find out the recipe because I'll probably die when I'm an old lady so I'll bake you one in heaven. I should be a good cook by then. Thank you very much for listening to me, Jesus. I'll let you go now so you can have some time to think.'

'You've left some dust in the corner,' Frieda said, once again pointing her finger to where it was lying as I swept what I thought was all of it into a heap ready to go on to the shovel. 'Tell you what; I'll make a bargain with you. You clean my bedroom until it gleams and I won't tell Mother what you did,' she said, looking down at me as I knelt on the floor.

What if she's playing a trick on me just because she wants her bedroom cleaning, and what if I do make it gleam and she still tells Mother?

'Well, come on, give me an answer,' she said impatiently.

'Will you swear on the holy Bible?' I asked, standing up to shake off the dust that had settled on my dress.

'Swear on the Bible?' she laughed, turning to walk away. 'Okay, I swear on the holy Bible.'

Right, I'd better hurry, I thought, walking as fast as I could towards the kitchen to collect the shovel. I'll clean Frieda's bedroom so well her eyes will sparkle when she sees it.

'There's a box of chocolates under my bed,' she said, passing me part of an old shirt that was used for a duster. 'I've counted how many are left so don't even think of taking one of them or I'll break my promise and tell Mother that you're a thief as well as opening Mrs Patterson's suitcase.'

'Are you going to eat them all by yourself?' I asked.

'Why?' she asked.

'Because you'll get fat if you do,' I said, taking the duster from her hand.

'I'll never get fat, and anyway if I did it's better than being skinny like you are.'

You're so rude and mean, I thought, as I made my way upstairs to her bedroom. I immediately crouched down on the floor to look underneath her bed. Wow, just look at the size of that box, I thought, not daring to touch it. I wonder if I asked would she give me the ribbon that's hanging off it. I could take it to Mr Dobson's and give it to Christine for her hair. I'll bet she hasn't got any ribbons, especially a green one.

This room's dirtier than the stairs. I stood up to inspect Frieda's dressing table and noticed the dust in the air as the sun shone through the window. I scratched my head quickly at the thought of it dropping on to my hair. 'You scared me,' I shouted, turning around to place the fluffy slippers neatly against the wall.

'I've only come to check that you're not rooting through any of my belongings. Don't forget to take that rug down into the yard. I want it banged against the wall at least six times,' she said, before disappearing down the stairs.

Oh no, I'm going to get dustier than ever. Bending down, I began to roll up the rug. It was heavier than I imagined as I lifted it up and placed it under my arm. I could feel my cheeks burning whilst struggling to hang on to it. 'Keep out of the way everyone,' I shouted as I ran through the living room, clinging on to as much of the rug as I could before dropping it on the floor against the back door.

'There's no one else in, only me,' Frieda said. 'Have you finished?'

'Nearly,' I replied. 'There's just this rug.'

'Remember, beat it at least six times. That's the only way you'll get the dirt out.

I deserve one of her chocolates for doing this, I thought. I wonder how many flavours there are in that box. I'll ask Father Christmas, when it's nearer the time, if I can have some in my stocking, but with a red ribbon wrapped around so if Frieda lets me have the green ribbon I can give them both to Christine. Then the boys will certainly whistle at her with two ribbons tied in her hair.

I wish Susie was here. She's so much stronger than me. I struggled back up the stairs, gripping on to the rug as much as I possibly could.

'Yes, you've done a good job,' Frieda said as I walked back into her bedroom.

I'm never going to clean your room again, I said to myself as I lay it down on the floor watching her as she sat on her stool filing her nails, pretending to be like Mummy. 'When you get married, this will be my room, won't it?' I asked.

'You'd ruin my mattress,' she quickly answered.

I wondered if she really was a witch. No, she can't be. She hasn't got long hair, but it's the right colour.

'Why are you staring at me?' she asked crossly.

'I'm just wondering what you would look like with long hair.'

'Prettier than you,' she said, turning around to look at herself through the mirror.

'Do you ever watch the ballerina dance?' I asked, hoping that she would turn the key at the side of the box. 'Does she dance to music?'

'Haven't you got anything better to do than to ask me stupid questions?'

I gave a sigh of disappointment and turned to walk away. Whoops, I haven't set the table. I hope it isn't lunch time yet. I rushed down the stairs and ran straight over to the clock to check the time. I picked it up to check what numbers the fingers rested on. That's lucky. I've just enough time before Mummy comes home. I wish we had a cuckoo that lived inside you. I placed it next to my ear and listened to it faintly ticking. But you're far too tiny, aren't you? I'd better put you back just in case I drop you. I'll come back and wind you up later, I said, standing on my tiptoes to place it carefully back on top of the mantelpiece.

'Mother will be here in a few minutes,' Teddy shouted through the living room window.

'What are you doing with that?' I asked, pointing at the tyre he was holding.

'It's got a puncture. I'm going to fix it for Harry,' he said, throwing it down in the yard. 'She'll just about be walking over the bridge,' he said, wiping his hands on each side of his overalls.

I was glad Daddy had given them to him to wear, even though they were far too big. I'll cut the material on the legs later, I thought; then he doesn't have to keep rolling them up all the time.

With a quick glance to check that the table was set properly, I ran through into the room and over to the window. Isn't she beautiful? I thought, whilst leaning on the chair and stretching as much as I could to get a better view. I imagined running over to her as she walked over the bridge, her arms stretched out fully so that I could run into them and be given the best hug ever. One day she might let me do that when she's not so busy. I'll have to stop at the edge of the kerb when I do so that I won't get knocked down and killed, I thought, as a car sped past.

'Here, take this,' Mummy said, passing me the plastic shopping bag as I opened the door to welcome her.

Ooh, it's heavier than I thought. I struggled to grip on to the handle with both hands. I could feel the heat from the hot pies against my legs as I made my way into the kitchen.

'Hurry, before they go cold,' I heard Mummy say in the background. 'Frieda,' she shouted from the bottom of the stairs, 'come and serve lunch out. I've only got about twenty minutes left. What time did Mrs Patterson call with the suitcases?' I heard her shout up to her again.

'I don't know,' Frieda replied. I could hear the sound of her footsteps as she rushed down the stairs. 'Lorne does, don't you, Lorne?' she said looking at me with a grin on her face.

Don't you dare break your promise and tell Mummy what I've done when I've cleaned your bedroom for you, I said to myself, trying to give the same evil grin back to her.

'What are you pulling your face for? Get the plates

down from the cupboard and, Frieda, you serve,' Mummy said, pulling her coat from her shoulders and resting it over the back of the armchair.

I'll never get used to the awful silent atmosphere at meal times. It was there again as we were all sitting around the kitchen table for lunch. I wish Teddy would close his mouth whilst he's eating, I thought, as I watched the meat and potato from the pie churn around in his mouth. The only sound was the scraping of the odd knife and fork against the plates as everyone ate.

'Please may I leave the table?' I asked. 'I've just left a little pastry on my plate. I can't eat any more.'

'Scrape it on to mine,' Teddy said, reaching over for the sauce.

'No, you can sit there and wait until everyone else has finished,' was Mummy's reply. I wondered why Frieda was allowed to leave without permission, watching her stand up, once again pulling another face at me.

'Right, clear the table' Mummy said, standing up from her chair. 'Did you hear me?' she shouted, looking straight towards me.

'I've got to get back to work,' Teddy said, pressing his fork into the last crust of pastry.

'Will you start your own business when you grow up?' I asked, reaching over for the salt and pepper.

'Doing what?'

'Mending tyres.'

'I might do,' he replied, passing me his plate whilst wiping his hand across his mouth.

'Don't use too much washing-up liquid,' Mummy said as I passed her, holding the plates as steady as I could.

I could see the plate on top of the pile beginning to slip. Whoops, that was lucky. I rushed towards the sink and placed them in the bowl.

The loud beat of music made me look up towards the ceiling. It was a sign that Mummy had left to go back to work. Frieda would never dare turn it up that loud if she was at home. I could hear the pounding of her feet against the floor. Maybe she's learning that silly dance again.

Chapter 8

With the dishes finally washed, I excitedly dried my hands on the tea towel and, checking there wasn't anyone watching me, I rooted through the cutlery drawer and picked up the biggest spoon I could find. I immediately left the kitchen to collect Daddy's spade that leant against the wall in the yard.

'Isn't that too heavy for you to carry?' Teddy called over, noticing my face going bright red.

'It is a little, but I'll get used to it. There's lots of work to be done,' I replied before disappearing along the entry to call for Eric.

Giving a sigh of relief, I rested the spade against the wall at the front of Mrs Crowswick's house and gave a quick knock on her door. 'Eric, you're still in your pyjamas,' I said with disappointment in my voice as he finally opened the door. 'I've brought Daddy's spade and here's a spoon for you. It's the biggest that I could find,' I said, passing it over to him. 'Are you going to get dressed? You'll get soil on your pyjamas if you don't.'

'Come in,' he replied slowly, turning around and leaving the door open for me.

'Good afternoon, Mrs Crowswick,' I said, raising my voice slightly, aware that she was a little deaf. 'You don't look very comfortable. Shall I put another cushion behind your back?' I asked, walking towards the chair she was sitting in.

'No, no, I'm quite all right,' she replied, stretching out her arm so that I could hold her hand.

'I'm going to the jumble sale at the church hall tomorrow. Would you like me to bring you a coat back?'

'Don't worry about me, my dear, you just have a nice time. Will you pass me my purse?' she asked, pointing to the mantelpiece. 'It's lying next to Mr Crowswick's picture.'

I stood up on my tiptoes to reach for it. 'Mr Crowswick looks very kind,' I said, staring at his smiling face.

'I talk to him every day, you know,' I heard Mrs Crowswick say. I quickly looked all around the room before placing the purse in her hand. I was right, his ghost must live here.

'Yes, he was very kind. The kindest man you could ever wish to meet,' she replied. Oh, Eric, hurry, hurry. I'm a little bit scared, I said to myself.

'Would you buy me a small loaf when you and Eric go to buy the bulbs?' she asked, passing me one shilling. 'Don't let him sell you yesterday's, he's a rogue is that Ronnie. He's only staying in business because it's the only shop around. And here's a penny to spend at the jumble sale. Eric,' she shouted, making me jump, 'where are you?'

'Thank you very much, Mrs Crowswick,' I said, bending down and kissing her on the forehead.

'Now don't lose it. Put it somewhere safe,' she said with a smile.

'You look nice, Eric,' I said as he slowly walked into the living room. 'I like your woolly jumper. Won't you be too hot?'

'I can t-take it off if I am,' he replied with a stutter.

'We'll leave your spoon in the garden next to the spade. Then we can start working as soon as we've been to buy the bulbs.'

'I've got t-two shillings,' Eric said, patting his hand on the pocket of his trousers.

'We'd better go then,' I replied, gently taking the spoon from him.

'Isn't this exciting?' I said as I lifted up his plastic shopping bag from the corner of an old wooden chair that leant against the living room wall. 'Put your hands over your eyes if the sun's too strong,' I told him, noticing he was squinting as he stepped out into the fresh air. 'That's what I do sometimes.'

'Would you like to rest for a while?' I asked, watching Eric struggle with each step he took.

'I don't mind.'

'Uh oh, don't look at him Eric,' I said, squeezing his hand harder as I noticed one of the Grindle boys walking towards us. 'I wonder why he never washes those snakes off his arms. They look horrible.'

'Boo,' he said to Eric as he brushed past him. 'Like your new boyfriend,' Grindle shouted with a strange laugh.

I turned my head around quickly to check that he wasn't standing right behind us. I'm not old enough to have a boyfriend, I thought, and anyway, even if I was I would never have you as one, Grindle. I watched him spit on to the pavement as he carried on walking. At least when Eric wears jeans they don't hang halfway down his bottom like yours do.

'We're nearly there now, Eric,' I said, pointing as we

walked around the corner at Ronnie's shop. As we reached the open door, Eric gave out a little laugh of excitement.

'Good day to you both,' Ronnie said, leaning over the counter. 'What can I do for you?' Eric knew exactly where to go as he let go of my hand and walked slowly over to where Ronnie kept his plants.

'We've come to buy some bulbs to plant in Mrs Crowswick's garden. Have you got any that will grow straight away?' I asked.

'I don't know about that,' he replied, lifting up the counter and quickly closing it behind him. 'Come on, lass, let's see what we can find. How's the family then?'

'All right. We're going to Wales on Saturday on holiday.'

'Hmm, your mother still owes me four shillings. Tell her if she'd like to see me after I've shut shop I'll sort something out.'

'What have you chosen, Eric?' I asked, walking over to him. He was holding a packet of seeds in one hand and searching through his pocket with the other for his money.

'Those bulbs look nice, what are they?'

'Daffodils. You can have the lot for sixpence,' Ronnie said, reaching for a brown paper bag and throwing them in.

'Oh, these are beetroots you're holding,' I said to Eric, stretching up to read the label on the packet. Eric looked at me with a smile on his face. 'But we can still plant them. Shall we, Eric? Shall we have a vegetable plot next to the daffodils we're going to grow?'

'I like b-beetroot,' he replied, once again with his usual stutter.

'I do, too, Eric. Mrs Crowswick would like a small loaf

that's been baked today,' I called over to Ronnie as he made his way back towards the counter. I wondered if his belt was too tight, noticing his tummy hanging over his trousers. It must hurt him if it is.

'How much is it for a bag of broken biscuits?' I asked, handing over the shilling for Mrs Crowswick's loaf.

'The cheapest are plain. Here, I'll throw you some in free,' he said. 'And don't forget to give your mother my message.'

'It's going to be wonderful, isn't it, Eric?'

'Yes, w-wonderful,' he said, opening his shopping bag so that I could put Mrs Crowswick's loaf inside.

'They should grow in no time,' Ronnie said as Eric passed over his money. 'Now, lad, don't be walking away until I've given you your change.'

'Thank you very much for the biscuits,' I said as I placed them with the seeds and bulbs into Eric's bag.

'It's a fine day for planting,' Ronnie said, tapping his fingers on the counter.

'I'll give Mummy your message as soon as she comes home from work.'

'Don't forget, lass.'

'I won't,' I replied, reaching out for Eric's hand. 'Don't you think Ronnie's shop smells?' I asked Eric as we stepped out into the sunshine.

'It's d-damp, the w-walls are damp…' I could tell he hadn't finished what he wanted to say, and then after a few more seconds. 'Y-you could s-smell it in the air,' he said.

'Would you like a biscuit before we start work?' I asked as we walked down the path to Mrs Crowswick's garden.

'Here, sit down on the bench for a while. I'll get them out of your bag. You can be the first to choose. It looks like some have sugar on,' I added, peeping inside before passing them over to him.

'I've got your loaf,' I called to Mrs Crowswick who was moving part of the lace curtain to look out through the window. 'I'll bring it to you now.'

'What did you buy from Ronnie's?' she asked as she opened the door.

'Beetroot and daffodils. I'll put your loaf on the table. It's really fresh, and here's your change from the shilling you gave me.'

'There's some tea in the pot. Would you like some?' she asked, pulling off the woollen tea cosy with her frail hands. 'Did I hear you say beetroot a minute ago?' she asked, pouring the tea.

'Yes, Eric and I are going to make you your very own vegetable plot. Don't you think that's a good idea?'

'A splendid idea,' she said, lifting the sugar on to the spoon before stirring it into the tea. 'Now don't spill it,' she said, opening the door for me. 'It's quite hot.'

'Oh, Eric, you've eaten all the biscuits. We could have dipped them in our tea. You must have been hungry. Be careful when you drink it, it's quite hot, Mrs Crowswick says,' I told him, passing him his cup.

'Right, we'll have to hurry,' I said, looking at my wrist and pretending I wore a watch. 'We'll share the spoon, shall we? Daddy's spade is much too heavy. I might scream if I see a worm,' I said as we both bent down to dig the holes. 'So don't get frightened if I do. I wonder how many times they'll need watering.' I turned to Eric for an answer as I placed a bulb into the hole. 'Right, Eric. You cover that over with soil. Now, what you do next is press it down very gently. Here, I'll show you. Hurray,' I shouted, clapping my hands. 'We've planted our first daffodil. Are you all right, Eric?' I asked, watching him go bright red as he coughed. 'I'll pat your back; that should help. Don't you think that you should rest for a while?' I said as his cough died down. 'It's hard work being a gardener.'

'He always coughs when he gets excited, don't you, Eric?' Mrs Crowswick said, walking towards us with the aid of a stick.

'We've planted our first daffodil,' I said, pointing over to where it was.

'It won't be able to breathe. You should always leave a shoot sticking up from underneath the soil.'

'What's a shoot?' I asked her, feeling confused.

'Pass me the bag with the rest of the bulbs in and I'll show you. You see, that's the shoot,' she said, feeling it with her hands. 'It always sits on top of the bulb, then a beautiful daffodil will suddenly appear.

'Quick, Eric, we'd better dig it up straight away or it will die if it can't breathe.'

Eric quickly began searching in the soil with his hands. 'Got it,' he said holding it up to inspect it.

'Is it dead?' I asked.

'You'll have saved it,' Mrs Crowswick replied. 'Now let me talk you through how to plant it. If I could bend a little more I'd show you myself.' My hands felt a little shaky as Eric and I did exactly as Mrs Crowswick told us. 'See, now you know how to plant a daffodil,' she said, whilst gracefully walking away.

'Fixed it,' Teddy shouted, walking along the pathway with a tyre over his shoulder. 'How's it going?' he asked, looking curiously over the tiny wall to where Eric and I were working.

'We've only the beetroot left to plant,' I replied, placing the last bulb into the soil. 'Eric and I are going to make some sandwiches with them when they've grown. Would you like us to make you one?'

'If the worms don't eat them first,' he said. 'I'm off to Harry's. Catch you later.'

'The worms won't eat them, will they, Eric?' I said, watching him rip open the packet of seeds.

'N-N-No, no,' he answered as he poured the seeds into the large hole he had just dug.

'We could even eat them with some hotpot, couldn't we, Eric? I'll just take these cups inside to Mrs Crowswick. Then shall we sit down on the bench for a while to see if anything has grown?' I asked, bending down to pick up the cups. Uh oh, I'd forgotten that the ghost of Mr Crowswick lives in Eric's house. 'Will you come with me, Eric? Anyway, we need to wash our hands. You carry one cup,' I said, passing it over to him. 'And I'll carry the other.'

The house was silent as we opened the door and walked in. 'Sshh,' I said, placing my finger against my lips.

'She always has a n-nap at this time,' Eric stuttered as we crept into the kitchen.

'Have you ever seen a ghost?' I asked, whilst turning on the tap and passing Eric the bar of soap from the top of the sink. 'Aargh!' I screamed as Eric gave a growl and pulled his face at me. 'You scared me, Eric. Anyway, ghosts don't do that, only monsters do. You won't do it again, will you?' I asked, taking the soap from him. 'And stop making those spooky noises,' I told him, giving him a light slap on his back with my wet hand. 'Let's go and check if anything has grown,' I said, taking hold of his hand and leading him towards the front door. 'Will you please stop making those scary noises; you're frightening me.'

'Okay,' Eric replied giggling like a child.

'We'd better creep so we don't disturb them. No, they've not grown yet, Eric. Let's go and sit down on the bench. It's been one of the loveliest days of my life today. Has it for you, Eric?'

'Yes, l-lovely,' he replied.

'I'll have to go soon. Mummy will be home. I'll check the plots from my bedroom window tonight. Will you do the same?' All of a sudden, Eric raised his foot and then slammed it down on the ground and raised it back.

'Oh, that's horrible. Is it an earwig?'

'It *w-w-was* an earwig,' Eric said.

'You can be funny when you want to be, can't you, Eric? Do you know any jokes? Oh no, Eric, Mummy's here. I should have set the table again for tea. I'll have to go straight away, Eric. Oh no, the spoon! You'll have to hide it somewhere in the garden. Quickly, will you do it now?' I said, bending down to pick it up and placing it in Eric's hand. 'I'll get into trouble if she knows that I've taken it out of the drawer. You see, I never asked her permission. That looks like a good spot over in the corner where all the weeds are. Quickly, Eric, before anyone sees it. I haven't time to give you a real kiss on your cheek,' I said, placing the palm of my hand against my lips, 'but this is a special one.' I blew it in his direction. 'See if you can catch it, Eric.'

I quickly picked up Daddy's spade and crept as quietly as I could along the entry and into the yard. Phew, that's lucky, I thought, as I just caught the spade from falling to the ground whilst leaning it back against the wall. If it had fallen, Mummy would have heard the bang it made and then I really would have been in trouble, and Daddy would never trust me again for taking it without asking him.

Chapter 9

'Look at those filthy hands of yours,' Mummy said, looking down at me as I opened the door and walked into the kitchen. 'You should be made to wash them in the toilet, they're so dirty.'

Yuk, I thought, rushing over to the sink and turning the cold water on to wash them. My arms weren't that long. I'd probably fall inside the bowl trying to reach the water, and I might never be able to get out, unless I screamed as loud as I could for help. 'Eric and I have planted some beautiful daffodils in his garden. Would you like to have a look?'

'So that's where you've been all afternoon, little Miss Muck. You want to try helping in your own garden before anyone else's,' she said. 'And don't even think of using a clean towel to dry those hands,' she added as I reached over ready to take one from the pile.

'Shall I ask Ronnie if he can order some more daffodil bulbs?' I asked, rooting through the washing basket to find a dirty towel. 'I'll plant some in the garden for you, if he can. Ronnie said that you owe him four shillings and could you go and see him when he's closed his shop, and I think he said he would sort it out with you.'

'When did you see Ronnie?' she asked.

'Today. Eric and I went to buy some bulbs. Eric even

bought some beetroot seeds. I'm sure he'll give you some when they've grown.'

'Don't you ever go into that shop again. Did you hear me?' she shouted. 'If I didn't have to feed you little bastards, I wouldn't owe the money, and don't say anything about this to your father.'

'I won't, I promise. You can give me away if you like, I don't mind. I'll still come back, but just to do my jobs, then you might not owe as much money.'

'Ha, ha,' she laughed. 'Who on earth would want a girl that pisses in her bed like only a baby would?' I felt my face burning with embarrassment. 'Now get out of my sight. I'm busy.'

I'm not going to take any notice of what you've just said, I thought, walking past her to make my way up to my bedroom. 'I'm not going to take any notice,' I said out loud, repeating it with every other step I took before I reached the top of the stairs. I ran as fast as I could along the landing, opened the door of the bedroom as quickly as I could and continued to run until I landed on top of my bed. I couldn't wait to bury my face into the pillow. Releasing the knot in my throat, I cried uncontrollably. I felt an ache in my tummy as I clung on to the pillow with my hands. 'Please, God, please find someone to take me away from here. I'd even come and stay with you in heaven, but I'm frightened of dying.' I whispered, tasting the salt from my tears as they dropped down my face and over my lips.

'Would you like to be my secretary?' I heard Teddy say as he placed his hand on my shoulder sitting himself down beside me on the edge of the bed. I didn't look up as I shook my head from side to side. 'No,' he said, 'I'd pay you a good wage. I've two more punctures to fix tomorrow. It looks like I'm in business. Pay you a penny in advance,' he said, squeezing it in between the pillow and my hand. 'And anyway, you need it for that jumble sale you're going to tomorrow. I was bitten by a tarantula today. It's left a big hole in my leg,' he said, letting out a little moan. 'See, I knew you'd sit up. I'm only kidding you. Here, blow your nose on this,' he said as I watched him pull an old rag from his overall pocket.

'Ooh, I'll get oil on my nose if I do,' I replied, trying to catch my breath.

'Use the end of it and then I'll throw it away. I'll be able to buy as many rags as I want with the wages I'll be on,' he said, passing it to me. 'I know Mother's in a bad mood. I can tell by the way she's cooking the bacon and eggs. The kitchen's full of smoke, she's cooking so fast. I've been told to tell you that your tea's ready.'

'I'm not hungry,' I replied, wiping away the tears with my hands.

'Well, you will be later, so you'd better come down with me. I'll sit next to you. Come on, hurry,' he said, pulling up my arms. 'Did you really believe a tarantula had bitten me?' he said as we both walked down the stairs.

'No, I did not,' I replied.

'Then why did you sit up straight away? Come on, tell me the truth,' he said, reaching for my waist and tickling me.

'Okay, okay, I did believe you. Stop tickling me,' I begged, crouching on the stair.

'Tell me you'll take the job as secretary and I'll stop.'

'I will, I will, I'll even work for you for free.'

'That's what I like to hear,' he said, taking his hands away. 'Sshh, stop laughing. Hurry now, tea will be on the table. Sshh,' he said. 'Take a deep breath.'

'That was really funny, Teddy, but please don't tickle me again. I don't like it.'

'Then stop laughing.'

I soon stopped as he opened the door to the living room. The room was silent as I tiptoed towards the table. Carefully pulling my chair out, I sat down.

'Your eyes look swollen. Have you been crying?' Frieda asked, chewing on her bacon.

You wouldn't care if I had, I thought. I picked up my knife and fork and gave her the most horrible look that I could.

'Hurry, everyone. Your father will soon be home,' I heard Mummy shout from inside the kitchen.

'Pick the bacon up with your hands,' Teddy said, watching me struggle with my knife. 'It's too crispy to cut; it will only fly off your plate and fall on to the floor. I'll eat it if it does so that it won't be wasted,' he said, dipping a slice of bread into the yolk of his egg. 'That was a big yawn,' he added as I stretched open my mouth as wide as I could, covering it with my hand.

'I'm not feeling very well,' I whispered. 'I want to go to bed and dream about the jumble sale.'

'Here, I'll take your plate. Have you finished?'

'Yes,' I replied, watching him place the white of the egg that I had left inside his mouth.

'I volunteer to wash all the dishes tonight. Anyway, I need to get rid of all this oil from my fingers.'

'Thank you, Teddy, but Mummy will shout if I don't wash them.'

'Pretend to cough,' he said, which I did straight away. 'See, it's not working.'

'You've only coughed twice, that's why. Why don't you put your fingers down your throat and make yourself sick,' he said. 'She'll believe you then.'

'How horrible. Have you ever done that?' I asked.

'Yes, just before my dentist's appointment, and it worked.'

'What do you mean?'

'Well, I didn't have to go, did I? I don't care if everyone laughs at my crooked teeth.'

'Do they, Teddy?'

'Sometimes,' he replied.

'Will you have them straightened one day?'

'Never,' he said.

'I'll never laugh at your teeth.'

'I know you won't,' he replied. 'Well, come on. We'll wash the dishes together. You'd never make an actress if you can't even pretend that you're ill.'

'I don't want to be an actress,' I told him, lifting myself off the chair. 'I'm going to be a princess.'

'You'll look nice wearing a crown.'

'Will I, Teddy?'

'Yes, very nice. Now, I'll wash and you dry.'

'Your father's tea is in the oven,' Mummy said to Teddy. 'Tell him I won't be long. What are you staring at?' she asked as I watched her slip her arms inside the sleeves of her coat.

'Nothing,' I answered whilst she opened the oven door to check that the temperature was right.

'Then turn around to that sink and stare at all those dishes you should be drying. I'm off,' she said, grabbing the handle of her bag, slightly slamming the door as she left.

'Is the oil coming off your fingers?' I asked Teddy as he splashed them in the water.

'I've just put some more liquid in,' he replied, 'so it should be doing by now.' He lifted his hands up into the air to inspect them.

'Look at all those bubbles you've made,' I said, leaning over to pop some.

'Father's home,' he said, nudging me.

'Where's your mother?' he asked, sniffing the air as he walked into the kitchen.

'She's gone out,' Teddy replied.

'Where to?'

'I don't know, but she said that she wouldn't be long.'

'Your dinner's in the oven. Shall I get it for you?' I asked, watching him look curiously at what was on his plate as I opened the oven door.

'No, turn it off,' he said. 'I'm going up for forty winks.'

'Why does Daddy have to go upstairs to have forty winks, Teddy?' I asked, looking curiously at him for an answer. 'I can wink more than forty times just standing here.'

'It's a saying that some grown-ups use when they want to go to sleep for a little while,' he answered.

'Oh, by the way, Mrs White gave me some wool to give to you. I've hidden the bag she put it in behind some bricks in the yard. Pass me a tea towel,' Teddy said. 'I'll dry my hands and go and get it for you.'

'Are there lots of different colours?'

'How should I know?' he replied, 'I've not looked inside. Boys aren't interested in balls of wool.' The excitement was too much to bear as he left the kitchen to collect it. I ran towards the bathroom.

'Where are you?' he shouted.

'I'm in the bathroom,' I replied. 'I needed the toilet.' I could hear the rustling of the paper bag.

'Hurry,' he said. 'It feels like she's given you loads.'

'Really?' I said, jumping off the toilet seat and pulling down the handle of the chain.

'Here, go and hide it before anyone takes it off you,' Teddy said, passing it to me.

'Teddy, she's even given me these,' I said, looking inside the bag and pulling out two tiny dark green plastic knitting needles. 'Do you think there's enough wool in here to make a patchwork quilt?' I asked, opening the bag as wide as I could. 'Monica has one on top of her bed that her grandmother knitted for her. It looks so beautiful.'

'Doubt it,' Teddy said, looking down into the bag. 'There's probably enough for a scarf.'

'That's what I'll do, Teddy. I'll knit a scarf especially for you.'

'Okay then, I suppose I could do with one. It can be cold when you're fixing those tyres.'

'Can I go and start it now? I might have finished before bedtime, and then you can wear it around your neck in the morning.'

'Yes, there's not much left to do in here and, anyway, Mother might not be long before she's back,' he replied, tipping the basin to one side and pouring the dirty water into the sink. 'I don't know what will happen if she finds out that Mrs White has given you all that wool.'

'Will she throw it all in the fire?' I asked.

'Probably. She did with that material you were given. Do you remember? The living room smelt of it for days.'

'Maybe she forgot that I was going to make her a cushion so that she could rest her back on it after she finished work,' I replied.

'Maybe,' Teddy answered, shrugging his shoulders. 'Now go,' he said, 'And make sure that you knit it long enough so that I can wrap it twice around my neck. It might be very windy tomorrow.'

I crept all the way upstairs and along the landing, not wanting to wake Daddy up. 'Wow, just look at all those colours,' I said out loud as I tipped them out of the bag onto the top of my bed. I'll start with the red one, I thought. 'I'm going to make you into a beautiful scarf,' I said to the six balls of wool whilst placing them in a neat row on top of my pillow. 'It's for my brother. You'll really like him when he puts you around his neck.'

What a busy day I'm having, I thought, picking up the knitting needles and sitting myself down onto the edge of the bed, trying to ignore the sound of the football being kicked, and the shouts to pass it to each other, as the local boys practised playing football. They'll be told to go away soon by one of the neighbours. I wonder which one will tell them off this time. They do cheer loud though when a goal is scored, I thought, casting the stitches on to my knitting needle.

'Don't you dare look,' I said as Teddy popped his head around the bedroom door. 'It's a surprise.'

'I won't,' he said, keeping his eyes closed. 'Why do you always hum that tune?' he asked.

'What tune?'

'You know, "All Things Bright and Beautiful".'

'Because everything should always be bright and beautiful, shouldn't it, Teddy?'

'I suppose so,' he said. 'Anyway, I can't stand here with my eyes closed much longer. I'll be back later. I'm just going to check what work there will be for tomorrow.'

'Will you have lots of tyres to fix?'

'Should have. See you later.'

'Yes, I'll see you later, Teddy.' I stretched up and looked through the window, watching him step off the pavement and cross the road towards the bridge. 'Good luck with your work.' I said out loud before he disappeared out of view. This scarf is going to look so nice, I thought, whilst stretching the few rows of knitting that I had done to make it look longer.

'Oh no, what's happening?' I threw the knitting on top of the bed and stood up immediately. I stood still with fright as I heard something else smash against the wall. It sounds like it's coming from the kitchen, I thought, whilst looking around for somewhere to hide. I grabbed my knitting and quickly made my way to the tiny alcove at the far end of the room. I wish it had a door with a key to it so that I could lock myself in, I thought, pulling the old curtain that was nailed to the top of the wall to one side to get in. 'Oh no, don't hit her again, please don't hit her again,' I cried, sitting myself down on to the floor and burying my head between my legs listening to Mummy's screams.

'You're a fucking whore,' Daddy shouted. That sounds like a plate being smashed. I jumped as I heard it hit the wall. If I had pigeons like Harry has, I could strap a letter around its leg asking for help. I wonder if it would know where the police station is.

'You're a black slut, you dirty bitch,' I heard him shout.

'I'm leaving you, you useless bastard,' Mummy screamed. 'You only shag me on a Sunday, so what do you expect? Get off me, get off me, you bastard,' she shouted.

Uh oh, it sounds as though Daddy's dragging her up the stairs. I could feel the strong beat of my heart as I listened to her being dragged along the landing.

'Get off me,' she shouted.

'Like fuck I will. Get in there.'

I jumped again with the sound of their bedroom door being slammed. 'Please don't hurt her any more,' I whispered to myself, sitting as still as I could.

All of a sudden the shouting stopped. I wonder what Daddy's groaning about. Maybe he's hurt his hand when they were fighting, I thought, lifting myself slowly off the floor. The brightness of the bedroom made my eyes squint as I pulled back the curtain. Holding on to my knitting as tightly as I could, I crept along the floor towards my bed. We won't be going to Wales on Saturday if Mummy is leaving. I felt a huge lump in my throat and told myself not to cry. Anyway, at least I have a scarf to knit, and there's the jumble sale tomorrow. I hope Susie doesn't make me smoke one of her cigarettes, I thought, as I lifted up the mattress to check that my money was still inside Grandfather's old sock. I wish he didn't have to keep going back to Ireland. I wonder if he really did kill that whale when it tried to attack his throat. Fishermen are brave though, so he must have done.

I found it hard to keep my eyes open, rubbing them constantly with my hands, and giving out a big yawn. I'll say a prayer to God now before I get too tired, I thought, kneeling down on the floor and resting my elbows on the bed.

'Dear God, I've been praying to you a lot recently, haven't I? I know that you are busy with all the people that you have to look after in heaven, so I'll be as quick as I can. Thank you for making kind people like Mrs White. She gave my brother some wool to give to me so I'm going to make him a scarf. Do you think Grandmother will one day be able to walk. I heard Grandfather say that he was getting too old to keep pushing her around in her wheelchair. Sorry for yawning. I'm very tired today. You see, Mummy and Daddy have been fighting again and when they do it always makes me feel sleepy. I think Daddy's hurt his hand when he was hitting her. He's been making lots of groaning noises. He's trapped Mummy in the bedroom so she won't go out again. I wonder what a whore is because that's what he called her. Uhm, maybe it's some kind of animal. I was going to surprise you and leave you a postcard in the church to tell you all about our holiday in Wales, but I don't think that we are going now. Mummy said that she was leaving but, God, she hasn't got anywhere to go and she'll get cold and hungry. I know that you can do a lot of wonderful things. Please God, please don't let her leave home. There's hotpot being served at the jumble sale tomorrow – it's my favourite – and there's even orange juice if you want it. I'm so excited. I'll speak to you again tomorrow and tell you all about it.'

Giving one more yawn, and pressing the palms of my hand down on to the bed, I lifted myself up off the floor. I know where I'll hide the wool, I thought, lifting up my pillow and carefully placing it underneath. I felt terribly cold whilst slipping my sandals off. Not daring to step out on to the landing to collect my nightdress, I pulled the blanket to one side and climbed into the bed. I hope Teddy won't mind that I haven't finished knitting his scarf, I thought, whilst resting my head on the pillow. I'll definitely finish it tomorrow.

Chapter 10

I didn't remember falling asleep and was quite surprised when I opened my eyes to see the dawn breaking. I hope they'll sell me a box of matches at the post office. I did promise Susie that I'd get her some. I'm too frightened to take any from Daddy's box. Anyway, I'd be a thief if I did, wouldn't I? I felt underneath the pillow to check that my wool was still there. At least I haven't wet the bed during the night, I realized, as I quickly got up. Hold on, I told myself, placing my hand between my legs and making a quick dash towards the landing. I hope no one wakes up and sees me, aware of the stillness of the house. I gave a little shiver as I sat myself down on top of the cold chamber pot, holding my breath for as long as I could to avoid the smell of everyone's urine. Yuk, I hate having to use this, I said to myself, standing up to inspect how full it was. I wonder if it makes a ring around everyone's bottom like it does to mine.

Wow, that scared me! A bell suddenly started to ring on Daddy's alarm clock. I quickly straightened my nightdress. Hurry and get back into bed, I told myself. The sudden loud noise of his cough made me jump as I crept as quietly as I could towards my bedroom. Phew, that was lucky, aware of the sound of his footsteps on the stairs. I'll miss making his sandwiches for him, but

I'm far too frightened. He might still be angry. I wondered how many more bruises Mummy would have on her body today. Susie told me that people who come from Ireland have very bad tempers. She's very clever.

I'll try and finish Teddy's scarf before he wakes up. I glanced over to where he was sleeping, feeling anxious of any noise I could hear downstairs. I found myself knitting faster than I thought I could. I wonder how long it would take to travel the world. Grandfather's said that he's travelled it and come back home with huge blisters on his feet. I don't believe him though because I saw him wink at Daddy when he was telling me.

I could hear the usual sound of the radio that Mummy always switched on whilst she was getting ready for work. I'd better practise how to ask her if I can go to the jumble sale. Maybe I should tell a lie and say that I've been asked to help on one of the stalls. No, I'd better not. I could say that Mrs Crowswick has given me a shilling and ask if I could go and spend some of it at the Church Hall. No, she'd only take it off me. I'll promise that I'll stay in forever and do all the cleaning if she will let me go. Maybe that might work. Oh, I do hope that she says yes, I thought, placing the wool safely back under my pillow.

I felt quite nervous as I took each step down the stairs. As I reached the bottom, I stood still and stared at the closed living room door. 'Here goes,' I said, crossing my fingers before gently pulling the handle down to open it.

'Get my hairspray from over there,' Mummy said, pointing over to the window ledge before taking out her last roller. Phew, that's lucky. Daddy hasn't left any marks on her face like last time.

'What are you staring at? You're always staring,' Mummy said with the usual snap in her voice. I squinted as she snatched the can of spray from out of my hand.

'What's the matter, did you think you were going to have your face slapped?' she asked, pressing down the nozzle and spraying her hair.

'Would you like me to make you a cup of tea?' I tried not to look at her too much whilst asking.

'Yes, make two, Mrs Patterson likes hers strong.'

I wondered why Mrs Patterson was calling so early in the morning. Perhaps she's coming to collect her suitcases. It looks like we won't be going to Wales now.

'Please don't leave here, Mummy,' I whispered as I filled the kettle with water.

'She's knocking on the door; go and open it,' Mummy shouted from the living room.

I quickly made my way towards the front door. 'I'm here,' I shouted, standing on my tiptoes and stretching up, listening to her continually knocking.

'You could catch your death of cold out here,' she said, rubbing her arms as the door was finally opened.

'Do you take sugar in your tea?' I asked, following behind her as she walked towards the living room.

'No, it rots your teeth and makes you fat,' she replied. 'Jenny, I'm here,' she shouted. 'Uhm, let's have a look at you.' She walked towards Mummy with a sympathetic look on her face.

'Hurry up with that tea,' I was told as I made my way towards the kitchen.

'The bastard. Did he do that?' I quickly turned around. 'This isn't the place for you, child,' Mrs Patterson snapped before sitting down on the edge of the couch. 'Ooh, that's horrible,' she said, catching a glimpse of all the marks on Mummy's back. 'He what ... he raped you?' she snapped again. 'Get me a gun and I'll bloody shoot him,' I heard her say to Mummy.

My hands started to shake as I lifted the kettle on to the top of the cooker. Oh no, she's going to murder Daddy, I thought, switching on the gas to boil the water.

'I'd have kicked him in the balls if he'd done that to me. Anyway, come out to bingo with me tonight. Molly won the jackpot last night, lucky bitch. Mind you, she deserves it. It's not nice when you're a woman and can't have children of your own. She's fostered a few though, but it can't be the same as your own, can it, Jenny?' The sound of water boiling inside the kettle interfered with what else was being said.

I wish I could be Molly's daughter. I'll ask her when I feel brave enough, then I'll be able to sit with all the other girls and wear pretty dresses like they do. It must be nice going to school on a Sunday, especially with Molly being the teacher.

'Where's that tea?' Mrs Patterson called as I poured the boiling water into the pot. 'I'm parched.'

'She'll be day-dreaming again,' I heard Mummy say as I quickly stirred the tea and poured it into the cups.

'Well, I certainly wouldn't throw this holiday away. What about all those competitions you'd planned to enter? And anyway, the bastard isn't worth you giving up a holiday. Mind you don't spill,' Mrs Patterson prompted me as I walked slowly into the living room holding the two cups as steadily as I could. 'Here, pass it to me,' she said with an impatient tone in her voice, reaching out and taking the cup from my hand.

'Put mine on the hearth,' Mummy said.

'Now, Jenny, you ought to drink it straight away while it's hot, otherwise it won't do you any good,' I heard Mrs Patterson say as she slurped on her tea. 'And don't worry about the plates that were smashed, I've got plenty. They might have the odd crack on them, but they'll do.'

'Please may I go to the Church Hall?' I asked. 'There's a jumble sale there this afternoon. And there's even hotpot to eat.'

'You're a skinny wee thing,' Mrs Patterson said, looking at me from top to bottom. 'You'd better go. Maybe a plate of that hotpot won't do you any harm.'

'Can I, Mummy?' I said, turning to her for her approval.

'Might go myself,' Mrs Patterson said as I waited for an answer.

'I'll clean the house every day whilst I'm on school holiday and I won't ask you for another thing, so please can I go?'

'Let the tiny thing go,' Mrs Patterson said to Mummy. 'She'll not get up to any harm in a place like that, not with all those do-gooders that'll be there. The vicar's the one you have to watch. Hmm, wouldn't surprise me if he pocketed some of the takings. He'll be pissed again for a few more days. Always is after a charity event. He was the same after the Christmas Fair. He's fallen off his bicycle a few times, drunk of course. I've heard that he even wears his bicycle clips underneath his gown, never takes them off, you know. Doesn't do many christenings either. Mind you, I'm not surprised.'

'Why?' Mummy asked.

'Well, in case he's had a skin full. I shudder at the thought of him dropping one of those babies. Here, take this cup from me,' Mrs Patterson said, standing up.

'I'll walk to the top of the hill with you, Jenny. The exercise will do me good.'

'Well, can I go?' I asked, looking at Mummy once again.

'I suppose the answer is yes, but don't expect me to give you any money. I'm not paying for other people's junk.'

'I don't mind,' I said, grateful that I was allowed to go and that Teddy and Mrs Crowswick had given me a penny each, not forgetting the shilling Susie was lending me.

'Well, there's not much you could do if you did,' Mummy replied. 'Now go and get my coat.'

'Looks like you won't be getting any hotpot after all,' Mrs Patterson said, 'Unless it's free.'

'It won't do her any harm to do without. She's lucky to even be going,' Mummy told Mrs Patterson. 'Anyway, she'll eat with the rest of us when I get home. Now put that cup down and get my coat.'

'Talking of money,' I heard Mrs Patterson say as they both walked towards the front door. 'I wonder what that Molly will buy with hers. It won't be stockings and suspenders that's for sure,' she laughed as the door closed behind them.

Phew, thank goodness they've gone. I gave a sigh of relief. I wonder what my hair would look like if I clipped my fringe back. I glanced at Mummy's box of rollers left lying on the floor. I quickly bent down and shuffled the rollers from side to side. 'Yes, I've found one,' I said out loud, picking up a large black hairgrip. This is harder than I thought. I struggled to hold my hair back as I slid on the grip. Running as quickly as I could over to the fireplace, I stood on my tiptoes and could just about see my face. I stared at myself. 'What do you think?' I asked the mirror.

'You see, I want to look more grown up. I'm going to a jumble sale with my friend, Susie. She's older than me and I would like to look more her age. It looks quite nice, doesn't it? I've made my mind up. This is how I'll wear it. Susie will be surprised.' I slid the grip out and hid it inside the pocket of my dress.

'Where's that scarf that you've knitted for me?' Teddy asked, popping his head around the door.

'Teddy, I'm truly sorry but I didn't have enough time to finish it. I will tonight.'

'Good job it isn't windy,' he said with a wink.

'There's a couple of holes in it where I've missed the stitches, but I'll sew them up when I've finished.'

'You've had nothing but that jumble sale on your mind for the last couple of days. That's probably why. Can you go?'

'Yes, Teddy, I can. Thank you for the penny.'

'Stick hold of it tight. You won't be able to buy anything if you lose it.'

'Mrs Crowswick gave me a penny, too,' I whispered. 'You won't tell anyone, will you?'

'Better things to do than to tell tales. Listen, I'd better walk with you to the Church Hall. What time does it start?' he asked.

'One o'clock,' I replied.

'Can't have you walking on your own with all that money you'll be carrying.'

'Am I rich, Teddy?'

'Rich enough to go to a jumble sale. And don't go and spend it all in the first five minutes.'

'I'll try not to. Will you call for me before Mummy comes home for her dinner in case she changes her mind and stops me from going?'

'What time?' he asked.

'Before twelve o'clock,' I replied.

'You'll be freezing waiting all that time,' he told me.

'Will you, please will you?' I begged.

'Let me think,' he said, rubbing his hand on his chin. 'I'll probably have to work overtime today if you want me to take you so early. Don't suppose I mind, though.'

'So will you?' I asked.

'I'll be back here just before twelve.'

I felt my toes curl up inside my sandals with excitement. 'I'm lucky to have a brother like you, aren't I, Teddy?'

'I suppose so,' he replied, blushing slightly. 'Well, I'd better make a move, I've a business to run. See you later,' he shouted, walking into the kitchen. 'And make sure you put your coat on,' he called, opening the back door. 'It's nippy out here.'

'I will, Teddy. You won't forget to come back for me, will you?' I called.

'Of course not,' he replied, closing the door behind him.

I'll get my jobs done as quickly as I can, I thought, picking up the shovel to empty the ashes from underneath the fireplace. I'll need plenty of time to get ready, especially if I'm having my hair clipped back.

'Have you just woken up?' I asked Frieda, turning my head slightly around to see her.

'The chamber hasn't been emptied. It smells up there,' she said, rubbing her eyes before sitting herself down on the chair.

'I'll empty it when I've finished doing this,' I told her, bending down to fill the shovel. The tapping of her fingers on the arm of the chair irritated me. I was conscious of her watching me as I held the shovel as steadily as I could.

'You'll never make it to the dustbin without spilling some on the floor,' she said as I carefully walked through the kitchen towards the back door.

Steady, I said to myself, lifting up the latch. 'Made it,' I whispered, shivering a little at the cold air as I stepped out into the yard. I could see her standing there looking at me through the living room window from the corner of my eye. Just pretend she's not there, I said to myself, reaching over for the handle of the dustbin lid. Oh no, it's stuck. Come on, dustbin lid, open for me. She'll only laugh at me if I can't lift you up. I tugged at it once more. 'It's stuck,' I shouted, looking towards her.

'What?' she mimicked.

'The dustbin lid is stuck. Will you help me lift it off?' She had a puzzled look on her face whilst lifting her hands halfway into the air, pretending that she didn't understand me. I'd better put the shovel down and try and open it with two hands, I thought. I bent down and, carefully placing the shovel on to the ground, held the handle with two hands and tugged as hard as I could. This is harder than I thought. I wish Teddy was here.

He'd help me. At last I felt it coming loose. With one last tug the lid was off and in my hands. 'Hurray,' I shouted, looking down inside the bin. Uh oh, just look at all those broken plates. Now we'll definitely have to eat off Mrs Patterson's plates. I felt a little sad when I finally picked up the shovel and threw the ashes over the pretty plates we used to have.

'You scared me,' I shouted, looking once again towards Frieda as she banged on the window.

'You've dropped some,' she laughed.

'What?' I asked, looking down to see a little bit of ash lying on the ground.

'I knew you would,' she laughed again.

'Well, it's only a little bit,' I answered. Before I realized what I was doing I pulled out my tongue as far as it would go at her. Within seconds she appeared in the yard.

'Don't you ever do that to me again, you little shit. Mother's right, you are a little bitch. I want an apology. Hurry,' she said, 'What do you say to me?'

'I'm sorry,' I said, but I don't really mean it, I said to myself.

'You will be when Mother reads it on the report card I'm making about you. I'm going to show it to her at the end of every week. And do you know the first thing I'm going to write on it?' I didn't reply as she moved her tall lanky body closer to me. 'I'm going to write, Lorne was rude to one of her elders – example, pulling her tongue out. In fact, I'm going to make it now,' she said, slamming the back door behind her.

I don't know why she's making such a fuss, I thought, reaching for the tall stiff brush that rested against the wall. I've had people pull their tongues out at me, especially the Grindle brothers, they're always doing it.

'Morning, my dear,' I heard Mrs Crowswick say as she stepped into her garden.

'I like your woolly hat; I bet it keeps your head nice and warm,' I told her.

'On a crisp morning like this, my dear, I need it.'

'Do you need any help, Eric?' I asked, watching him struggle with Mrs Crowswick's wheelchair.

'He always gets it stuck trying to get it through the door,' Mrs Crowswick said.

'Here, I'll lift the front and you lift the back,' I told Eric, going over to him. 'Are you ready, Eric?' I asked as I knelt down. 'On the count of three we'll both pick it up at the same time.' I could feel my cheeks starting to burn. 'Don't let go, Eric,' I told him, lifting it over the step and on to the path outside.

'Don't forget my blanket,' Mrs Crowswick reminded Eric, watching him wipe his brow. 'Would you like to come for a walk with Eric and me?' she asked, sitting herself down on the seat of the chair.

'I'd love to but it's the jumble sale today. I'm going to leave earlier than I should so that I can be first in the queue.'

'Oh, is it today? I'd completely forgotten,' she answered, taking her gloves out of her coat pocket and slipping them on her hands. 'I need my scarf and I've forgotten my handkerchief. It's in the drawer next to the sink,' she told Eric on his return.

I could see the confused look on Eric's face as he scratched his head. 'Shall I help you, Eric?' I asked, taking the blanket from his hand. 'This looks warmer than your woolly hat,' I told Mrs Crowswick as I wrapped it around her legs.

'I've had it donkey's years,' she said as she rubbed her hands over it affectionately. 'I used to cover Mr Crowswick up with it when he was too ill to get up the stairs. Memories,' she said with a tear in her eye.

'I'll go and get your handkerchief,' I said, giving her hand a gentle squeeze.

'My scarf's hanging on the hook of the pantry door,' she told Eric.

'Let's have a race, Eric. You get the scarf and I'll collect the handkerchief from the drawer. See who gets back first.' Within a second he had disappeared into the kitchen. 'Wait for me,' I shouted, running in behind him. 'You're going to win, aren't you, Eric?' I said, watching him run over to the pantry door.

'Y-yes,' he stuttered along with a giggle of excitement.

'You might not though,' I challenged him as I opened the drawer and pulled out one of Mrs Crowswick's handkerchiefs. We both looked at the open door and started to run as fast as we could.

'Beat you,' Eric said, diving out on to the path.

'Only by two steps,' I laughed. 'Wasn't that fun, Eric? It's nice to play games, isn't it?'

'You both have so much fun when you're together, don't you?' I heard Mrs Crowswick say as Eric wrapped the scarf around her neck.

'Are you going for a long walk?' I asked as I placed the handkerchief in Mrs Crowswick's hand.

'Not too long,' she replied. 'Eric and I get tired far too easily these days.'

'Will you be too tired to come to the jumble sale with me?' I asked Eric. 'My friend, Susie, will be there but she won't mind me taking you with me.'

'I'm sure he'd love to,' Mrs Crowswick said. 'Well, Eric, would you like to go?' she asked.

'Y-Y-Yes, yes, yes,' Eric replied, with a huge smile on his face.

'Oh to be young again,' Mrs Crowswick said as Eric turned her wheelchair around.

'We're leaving just before twelve o'clock. You'll be ready, won't you, Eric?'

'I'll be r-r-ready,' he replied.

'Now you're getting too excited,' Mrs Crowswick told him. 'Take it a little slower; you're pushing my chair far too fast. Bye, bye, my dear, we won't be too long.'

I could hear the echo of her voice as I watched Eric carefully manoeuvring her wheelchair in between the two narrow walls as they made their way along the entry. 'Bye, Mrs Crowswick,' I called, giving them a little wave before they disappeared out of view.

Chapter 11

The morning went pretty fast as I ran around the house doing as many jobs as I possibly could, stopping just occasionally while sweeping the stairs to check that my hairgrip was still safely inside the pocket of my dress. It doesn't matter, Frieda, if you don't think that I've swept the stairs properly, I thought, as she brushed me aside whilst inspecting them with a report card in one hand and a pen in the other, because I'm not going to sweep them again. I've got to get myself ready for the jumble sale, I said to myself as I watched her bend down to have a closer look at the carpet, and I'm glad that you're not speaking to me, even though I wanted to ask you if I could put some of your cologne on. Anyway, she'd only say no if I did, I thought, shrugging my shoulders and walking away. I glanced over towards the fireplace at the tiny clock that stood ticking away on the mantelpiece. Uh oh, Teddy will be here for me soon. Hurry, hurry, I told myself, quickly making my way into the kitchen. Wouldn't it be nice if we had hot water, I thought, turning on the tap over the kitchen sink, then I wouldn't have to keep screwing up my face every time I have a wash. Here goes. I caught some of the running water in the palm of my hands and skipped a breath as I splashed it over my cheeks.

'Aren't you ready?' I heard Teddy say. 'You've only minutes before Mother arrives home.'

'Quickly, pass me a towel,' I said. 'I can't see properly for the water in my eyes.'

'All this talk about the jumble sale and you're not even ready,' he said, placing the towel in my hands.

'I'm sorry, I really am,' I replied, patting my eyes dry so I could focus properly.

'Then hurry,' he told me, looking down towards my feet. 'You haven't even got any socks on.'

'Will you help me find some, then I'll be ready much quicker. There's some up there,' I said, pointing towards the rack.

'What, those grey ones?'

'Yes, they're the only ones I've got.'

'They're still damp,' he said, reaching up and feeling them.

'It doesn't matter, I'll still wear them.'

'Are you sure? You might catch a cold.'

'I'm not bothered if I do. Going to the jumble sale is much more important.'

'You won't be saying that if you can't stop coughing,' he answered, jumping up and pulling them down. 'Where's your coat?' he asked, passing me the socks. 'Hurry up, we've got to go. Don't pull them up to your knees; keep them rolled down, at least until they dry.'

'It's hanging over the maiden inside the pantry,' I replied, almost losing my balance as I placed my foot inside one sock.

'It's this red one, isn't it?' He held it out for me to see. It's a good job it comes down to your ankles. At least it will keep those thin legs of yours warm. It's still as nippy out there as it was early this morning,' he told me as he watched me slip my arms inside the sleeves. 'Here, your collar's twisted; let me straighten it for you. Now, we really are running out of time. I'll fasten your coat for you; I'll do it much quicker than you can.'

'Can you get my hairgrip from inside my pocket before you do?'

'Quickly then,' Teddy replied. 'Now, put that hairgrip in as fast as you can,' he told me, lifting me up so that I could see my face in the mirror. 'You're heavier than I thought, so hurry.'

'I've nearly done it, Teddy.' I held on to as much of my fringe as I could before clipping it back. 'You can put me down now.'

'Thank goodness,' he said. 'Yes, you suit it clipped back,' he told me with a smile. 'Now give me your hand; we'll have to run. It's nearly twelve o'clock. We'll go the back way, you know where Harry has his pigeon loft. You'll have to climb up a lot of steps there before we reach the main road, but it's better than passing Mother. She'll definitely be on her way home by now.'

I could feel the slight pressure on my arm as he pulled me along the kitchen.

'I can't keep up with you,' I shouted as we ran along the entry and crossed the road to where Harry's loft was.

'Yes, you can, just hold on tight.'

'I'll have to sit down for a while,' I told him. 'I've got a stitch inside my stomach.'

'You'll have to climb some of these steps until you're out of sight,' he said. 'Then you can sit down.'

'Oh no, Teddy, I've forgotten Eric and my money. What am I going to do?' I asked, nearly tripping over my own feet.

'Harry,' Teddy shouted. He placed his fingers inside his mouth and whistled over to him. 'Harry, quick! I need to borrow your bicycle.'

'Uh oh, he's going to crash straight into us,' I said, watching him pedal as fast as he could in our direction. I could see particles of dust flying off the ground into the air as he turned his bike sideways.

'Good job these brakes work,' he laughed, stopping just inches away from where we were standing. 'What's your problem?' he asked.

'I'll be two minutes,' Teddy replied. 'I need to go back to Rose Cottage, quickly.'

'I've hidden my money in Grandfather's sock underneath my mattress,' I told him as he set off on Harry's bicycle. 'Be careful it doesn't drop out; there's a hole in it.'

'Can't lend me some, can you?' Harry asked.

'You won't forget to call for Eric, will you?' I called, watching Teddy cycle towards the road. I turned to Harry. 'I've saved it to spend at the jumble sale. It starts at one o'clock.'

'So that's why you look so nice; you're going to a jumble sale.'

'How much would you like?' I asked.

'How much have you got?'

'Well, Teddy gave me a penny and so did Mrs Crowswick.'

'So that means you've got tuppence. That would do,' he said.

I won't be able to buy anything at the jumble sale if

I've got to lend it to Harry, I thought, watching him root inside his pockets.

'Well, would you believe it?' he said, pulling his hands out. 'I've just found a sixpence, and I'm going to give it to a very pretty girl.'

'She's lucky, Harry, the girl you're going to give it to.'

'Yes,' he said, 'she's very lucky.'

'What's her name?' I asked.

'Forgotten,' he replied. 'But she wears a long red coat with black buttons, and she wears sandals on her feet.'

I quickly looked down at my feet. 'I'm wearing sandals and a red coat as well,' I said, double checking that the buttons really were black.

'She used to have a fringe but it's fastened back today with a hairgrip.'

I put my hand on top of my forehead to check that my fringe was still clipped back.

'And guess what?' Harry said.

'What?' I asked looking up at him.

'She's standing right next to me.'

I turned around to check that there wasn't another girl with a red coat on standing nearby.

'Here, it's for you,' he said, closing it in the palm of my hand.

'Oh, Harry, is it really for me?'

'Well, I can't see anyone else with a red coat on, can you?'

'No, I can't Harry; oh, thank you.'

'Now put it inside your pocket. I was only teasing about lending your money, you know.'

'Were you, Harry?'

'Course I was.'

'Look, here's Eric crossing the road,' Harry said, pointing to him.

'He's coming to the jumble sale with me. Looks like he's going to buy a lot of things with the size of the bag he's carrying.'

'Poor sod; he's no friends, you know.'

'I'm his friend, Harry.'

'Good job you are,' he replied. 'It must be rotten not to have any friends.'

'Thanks again for the sixpence, Harry. Are you and Mr Dobson friends now?'

'Not a chance,' he replied. 'Gave me a good kick up the backside the other evening. Still sore now.'

'Oh,' I said, putting my hand up to my mouth. 'Did it hurt?'

'What do you think with those filthy clogs he wears? Of course it hurt. Anyway, it's nearly time to raid his orchard. I'll try and take the lot this time.'

'What, every single apple?'

'You're telling me,' he said. 'I'll just have to practise running faster. Don't want another kick like that one.'

'Eric, I'm over here,' I shouted, jumping up and down and waving my hand to get his attention. 'He might not recognize me, Harry, because my fringe is clipped back.'

'Eric,' Harry shouted, making me jump. 'We're over here.'

'I'm sorry I forgot to call for you, Eric, but I remembered just in time, just before Teddy and I were going to climb the steps. I bet we won't be first in the queue now.'

'You've plenty of time; it's only ten past twelve,' Harry said, looking at his watch.

'I l-l-like your hair,' Eric said.

'Do you, Eric? I think it looks a lot better like this.'

'Yes, it's nice,' he replied with his usual big smile on his face.

'Thought you were only going to be a couple of minutes,' Harry bellowed, cupping his hands around his mouth as Teddy started to cycle back across the road.

'I don't know how you ride this thing,' Teddy said, getting off the bicycle. 'The chain needs oiling.'

'Yes, I suppose it is looking a little rusty,' Harry replied. Holding on to the handlebars, he bent down to inspect it.

'Can we go now?' I asked, feeling a little impatient. 'Harry's just given me sixpence. I'm so lucky, aren't I? I'm going to buy lots of things, are you, Eric?'

'Y-Y-Yes, I'm g-going to buy lots of things, too,' he replied, patting his hand on the outside of his trouser pocket to check that his money was still there.

Eric and I began to climb the steps. They were very steep and we held on to each other's hands as tightly as we could.

'Not far to go, now. Another five minutes and we'll be there,' Teddy reassured us.

'Aren't graveyards horrible, Teddy,' I said, feeling a little shiver as we walked slowly past. 'But the church is pretty, isn't it, Eric?'

'The w-windows are beautiful,' he replied, pointing at them.

'Yes, they are,' I whispered, standing still for a second to get a better look.

'I thought you wanted to be first in the queue,' Teddy shouted, striding out in front of us.

'Yes, we do,' I called back. 'We'll have to walk a little faster, Eric, or we'll never catch up to him. We're coming,' I called.

'Run,' Teddy yelled.

'We can't. Eric will start to cough and then he'll lose his breath. I can see the Church Hall, can you, Eric? That means that we're nearly there.'

'You're a couple of slow coaches,' Teddy said as we finally caught up to him. 'Now remember what I've told you, look first and don't spend your money all at once.'

'I won't, Teddy,' I replied as we stepped on to the drive.

'What a wonderful smell. It'll be the hotpot, won't it Teddy? Can you smell it, Eric?' I asked, watching him sniff into the air.

'Wouldn't mind some of that myself,' I heard Teddy say. 'I wonder how much the entrance fee is,' he said, looking curious as he climbed up the two oblong steps to read the notice pinned to the door.

'Aren't we lucky being the first in the queue, Eric? Susie should be here soon.'

'Yes, I'll have some of that,' Teddy said, jumping down from the steps.

'What does it say, Teddy?' I asked as I watched him root through his pockets.

'Well, it's two shillings just to get through the door, but they'll give you a plate of hotpot free.'

Oh no, I won't have enough, I thought, feeling full of gloom as I climbed the steps to read the notice myself.

'No, it doesn't say that,' I said out loud, reading it once more to double check.

'Only kidding,' he said, looking up at me with a grin.

'It's only a halfpenny to get in including one plate of hotpot, and orange juice is free. That's what it says, Teddy. That's really horrible what you just did,' I shouted.

'Yes, I suppose it was,' he replied. 'You don't have to keep reading it,' Teddy called.

'Anyway, your friend Susie's just arrived.'

'I don't believe you,' I told him, reading the notice once more.

'Can't lend you that shilling,' I heard her say. I quickly turned around.

'See, I told you she was here.'

'Wow, I like your hair like that.'

'Do you, Susie?'

'Definitely.'

'Does it make me look older?'

'I'll say; it's put three years on you at least.'

'They'll be opening the doors soon,' Teddy said, checking his watch.

'She found out he's married.'

'Who did?' Teddy asked.

'Maggie, my oldest sister. Not only that, he's got six kids. She really liked him, too. In fact she probably loved him. She's never stopped crying since she found out. Have you got those matches? I'm dying for a fag.'

'Good afternoon, children.'

'Christ, it's the bloody vicar,' Susie whispered as he cycled towards the steps.

'It's a bit nippy, but a nice afternoon, don't you think?' he said as he got off his bike and leaned it against the wall. 'Eric, it's nice to see you here. In fact it's nice to see you all. It makes me realise what a wonderful community we live in.'

'Like hell it's wonderful.'

'Now, now, Mrs Grindle. Things are never as bad as they seem,' he told her as she joined the queue.

'You want to live with my two lads then, lazy idle pigs.'

'Well, I must go and check that my ladies have set up their stalls,' he said, coughing twice with embarrassment.

'She's horrible, isn't she, Susie?'

'Sshh, don't let her hear you. She'll think nothing about giving you a good hiding.'

'But look at the backs of her feet. They're all hard and cracked, and she always wears that dirty headscarf.'

'Don't keep staring or she'll go for you. Did you get me those matches?'

'That's why I clipped my hair back, so I'd look older, and then they would sell me some at the Post Office, but I didn't have time.'

'Lend us a match,' she asked Mrs Grindle, watching her pull out a box from her bag.

'Tha can sod off,' she grunted as she placed a cigarette in between her lips.

'Ooh, look at her teeth,' I whispered.

'Pretty black, aren't they?' Susie replied.

'I've brought Eric with me. You don't mind, do you?'

'Where is he?' she asked, looking around curiously.

'He's over there, leaning against that tree.'

'Hi, Eric,' she shouted, waving over to him.

'He's tired because we had to walk fast so we could be first in the queue. Eric, it's nearly time for the doors to open,' I called, beckoning him over.

'It's about time they were,' Teddy said, rubbing his stomach. 'I'm starving.'

'There's not very many people here, is there, Susie?'
'There will be. Just look at that crowd coming in now. He never says very much, does he?'
'Who?' I asked.
'Eric.'
'He does to me.'
'Why you?'
'Because I talk to him. Eric, come here and I'll hold your hand. We'll be going in any minute.'
'What on earth are you going to buy, Eric?' Susie asked. 'Your shopping bag is huge.'
'Cakes,' he answered.
'They're for Mrs Crowswick, aren't they, Eric? She likes cakes, doesn't she?'
'Tha'd better leave some for me for those lads of mine,' I heard Mrs Grindle say.
'For her, more likely,' Susie whispered.
'How do you know?'
'Look at the size of her.'
'She is rather big, isn't she?'
'You mean fat,' Susie said. 'Anyway, she smells. Let's move closer to the door.'
I jumped a little at the sudden sound of the bolt being slid back. Within a second the doors were flung open to reveal the vicar standing just inside the doorway. I wonder if his bicycle clips are still fastened around the bottom of his trousers, I thought, as he stood there in his gown.
'I now announce this fayre open,' he called out.
'Quick, Eric, you can be the first one in and I'll be right behind you. Look at all those stalls,' I gasped.

'That's a halfpenny each,' Mrs Haseldine said as Eric and I felt inside our pockets.

'Can you change a penny?' I asked, pulling it out.

'Will you all stop pushing?' I heard Susie say to the crowd.

'Will you soddin' well hurry up?' Mrs Grindle shouted over.

'Isn't she so very rude, Eric?' I said as I watched him put the correct money into Mrs Haseldine's pot bowl. 'Look, she's trying to push her way to the front of the queue.'

'If she hadn't have nudged me I'd have let her go before me, but she can get stuffed,' Susie told me.

'Dear me, dear me, such terrible language,' Mrs Haseldine said.

'Are you all right, Mrs Haseldine?' I asked, noticing her face turning bright red.

'Next,' she shouted, passing me my change.

'Can we have a bit of calm,' the vicar called in a raised voice. 'After all, it's only a jumble sale.'

'Here, here!' Susie said, looking directly at him. 'It's like having a load of buffalo behind me.'

'Aren't you going to have some hotpot?' Teddy shouted as he picked up a paper plate.

'Eric, come and get some, it's piping hot. Doesn't it look delicious, Eric?' I said as Molly filled the ladle and poured it onto Teddy's plate. 'Look, there's even red cabbage. Hurry before it all goes. Are you hungry, Eric?' I asked.

'Yes, very,' he replied.

'So am I, but I want to see if I can find a pretty dress to buy for my holidays.'

'Look at them all stampeding past us,' Susie said with a disgusted look on her face.

'Will you look after Eric whilst I go and look for a dress,' I called over to Teddy.

'Sure,' he replied. 'This is so good I'm going to get a second helping,' he said, scraping up the last remains of hotpot on his spoon.

'There are so many stalls, Susie, I don't know which one to go to first.'

'Follow me,' she answered, pushing her way through the crowds.

'That looks like a good one over there,' she said.

'Wow, just look at all those clothes, Susie!'

'Will someone budge up,' she said, as we reached the stall.

'Grab, grab, grab, that's all they think about,' said Mrs Hart, a nice lady from the village come to pick up bargains at the jumble sale, as we squeezed in next to her.

'Well, if you can't beat 'em, join 'em, I say,' Susie told her. 'How about this one? It's got lots of checks on it, and you'll suit lemon,' Susie said, holding up a dress.

'It's too big, Susie.'

'Hmm, I suppose it is,' she replied, throwing it back onto the pile. 'This one would fit you but there's no zip on the back of it.'

'Can't we fix it, Susie? It's got nice puffy sleeves.'

'It's not worth it, and anyway, there's a stain on it.'

'Oh, this is nice,' Mrs Hart said, holding up a jacket. 'I like tweed and the lining is in perfect condition. I thought you'd be busy perming hair,' she said to Ruby, the village hairdresser, who was serving.

'No point opening, they're all here,' she replied snottily.

'Oh well, how much for this?' Mrs Hart asked, passing her the jacket.

'Threepence,' she said, holding out her hand immediately for the money.

'I wish Ruby wasn't serving. I don't like her, do you, Susie?'

'I wouldn't take any notice of her. The only reason she thinks she's better than anyone else is because she's the only hairdresser in the village. She thinks all the men fancy her, you know.'

'Does she, Susie? I don't think she's pretty, do you?'

'No, but she does. Just look at the size of her nose, it's like an eagle's, and her nails are false, too.'

'That reminds me,' Mrs Hart said as Ruby passed her back the jacket, 'I need to make an appointment for a colour.'

'Well, it certainly can't be for at least another couple of weeks. I'm fully booked. Did you give me the threepence?' she asked abruptly.

'Yes, you put it in your pot,' Mrs Hart replied.

'You'll look nice in that jacket,' I told her, searching through the pile of clothes. 'I'm looking for a dress for my holidays.'

'I think I've found one,' Susie said.

'Oh, I hope so, Susie.'

'What do you think?'

'That used to be mine,' Monica said, slowly walking past. 'It won't fit you, you're far too skinny.'

'You're probably right, Monica,' Susie said. 'You are rather fat.'

'She asked for that,' Mrs Hart said as Monica walked away with her nose in the air. 'Let's see if I can help. Have you any pretty dresses that would fit this little girl?' Mrs Hart asked.

'I've not a clue,' Ruby replied.

'Oh well, we'll just have to keep searching until we find one. I'm sure we will. Where are you going for a holiday?' she asked.

'Wales.'

'Oh, how nice! There are lots of beautiful mountains there. Some of them still have snow on top of them even in the middle of summer.'

'Do they really? I'm so excited.'

'Let's move further to the end of the stall. Maybe we'll find that dress in one of the piles over there,' Mrs Hart said with a kind smile.

'If anyone else stands on my foot, I'll scream,' Susie shouted. 'Oh no, look who we're stood near.'

'Who?'

'Don't look, she's moving closer.'

'Who?' I asked again.

'Mrs Grindle. That's all I need, her germs all over me. She's buying another pinny. She wears them over her skirts to hide the dirt.'

'Sshh,' Mrs Hart said, 'she might hear you.'

'Look, she's taking her old one off and putting on the one she's just bought,' Susie continued.

'What are you friggin' staring at?' she said to Susie.

'I'm just admiring the pinny you've just bought,' Susie replied.

'Aye, it'll do,' she said, pressing her hands over it.

'What are tha looking for?' she asked as we carried on searching through the pile of clothes.

'A dress for Lorne,' Mrs Hart replied, 'But we haven't had much luck so far.'

'Let's have a look at you,' she said, shuffling towards me. My body froze as she placed her leathery looking hands on the tops of my shoulders. 'I should imagine there's not a lot of meat on you with that coat off,' I heard her say as she spun me around to have a better look. 'Get out of my way,' she told Susie. 'Smoking at thy age.'

'Look at her throwing all those clothes around,' Susie said as she stood back allowing Mrs Grindle to take her place.

'She must be getting angry, Susie. Can you hear those grunting noises she's making?'

'Eric, I'm over here,' I shouted as I noticed him wandering around with a cake in his hand. 'You've got cream on the corner of your mouth,' I told him as he came towards me, taking another bite.

'Found you,' Mrs Grindle shouted, making us all jump.

'Oh, Mrs Grindle, that's beautiful,' I heard Mrs Hart say.

'It's probably another pinny,' Susie whispered.

'Get over here, lass, I've found something for you.'

'Me?' I asked.

'Aye, tha wants a dress, don't tha? Straighten your shoulders,' she told me as she held it next to me. I stared straight ahead, not daring to move. 'Now, in't that some dress, and it looks like it fits you, too.'

'It certainly does,' I heard Mrs Hart say.

'It's just lovely,' Susie whispered.

'Well, it's yours if you want it,' Mrs Grindle told me, stepping back and holding it out. 'That's if tha's any money to pay for it.'

'Oh, Mrs Grindle, only princesses wear dresses like this.'

'Tha's best not have bought all those cakes,' she shouted to Eric as he took another from his bag.

'Will tha make thi mind up, I haven't got all friggin' day.'

'I'll take it,' I quickly said. 'Thank you, Mrs Grindle. It feels like it's made of satin. It's quite heavy, isn't it?'

'That's because it's got a net underskirt sewn on the inside,' Susie said, inspecting it.

'I hope I have enough money to buy it.'

'We'll soon find out. How much?' she called, holding up the dress to show Ruby.

'Can't you see I'm serving?' Ruby replied harshly.

'You'll need a bag to put it in,' Mrs Hart said as she carefully felt the material. 'White dresses mark so easily.'

'A penny,' Ruby called to Susie.

'We'll take it,' Susie called back.

'Have you got a penny?' Susie asked me.

'I've got two,' I replied.

'Will you put it in a bag?' Mrs Hart asked.

'If I've got one. Here, pass it over. It's one of the old walking day dresses,' Ruby said, folding it.

'Don't look now, but Mrs Grindle's making her way towards us,' Susie whispered.

'I should have charged you a little more, but I doubt anyone else will buy it.'

'Why's that?' Mrs Hart asked.

'Well, it's fussy, don't you think? It's not something you could wear every day, and it smells of mothballs.'

'In that case you should have given it the lass for nowt,' said Mrs Grindle.

'I can't possibly do that, this is a charity event.'

'Tha bloody well will, you pissing snob.'

'I'll report you to the vicar if I hear any more language like that,' Ruby told Mrs Grindle.

'Put your penny back in your pocket, lass. You're paying for no dress.'

I don't care if it smells of mothballs, I thought, it's still the prettiest dress I've ever seen.

'Here, take it,' Ruby said, passing the plastic bag with the dress in it to Mrs Grindle. 'I'm leaving. I've never been spoken to like that in all my life.'

'Well, tha 'as now,' Mrs Grindle told her as Ruby picked up her coat and bag.

'I'd better let the vicar know that there's no one to run the stall,' Mrs Hart said as Ruby ran along the hall and out of the door.

'Well, I might as well be off, too,' Mrs Grindle said. 'I've got me pinny and me cakes for my lads. Don't need owt else.'

'Thank you, Mrs Grindle,' I said.

'Tha'll look like a princess in that dress. Wish tha were my lass.'

'Isn't it sad, Susie?' I said, watching Mrs Grindle walk along the hall towards the door.

'What's sad?'

'Mrs Grindle, she doesn't have any friends.'

'Are you surprised?' Susie replied. 'Everyone's frightened of her.'

'Are you, Susie?'

'No, not me. Well, maybe just a little if I was to tell the truth.'

'Susie, Susie, quick, look over there!'

'Where?'

'There, look. It's just what I've always wanted.'

'Wait for me,' Susie called as I ran straight over to the stall.

'Are you serious?' Susie asked.

'Yes, very,' I replied.

'But it's only got three wheels.'

'I don't care, Susie, I've always wanted one.'

'And it's full of rust. Besides, you don't even have a doll. You'd just be wasting your money. You'd be better spending it on a box of matches, then we can both have a smoke.'

'How much is this pram?' I asked Mr Drake the verger, who was running the stall.

'Well, with a lick of paint and a new wheel it would be worth quite a bit,' Mr Drake replied.

'Don't listen to him, Lorne,' Susie whispered. 'He's been digging those graves for far too long. It's sent him a bit silly.'

'Have you got a doll that I could put in it?'

'There are a few over there next to the crockery, but they're in a bit of a bad way.'

'Come on, we're wasting our time,' Susie said. 'His stall is full of old junk.'

'But I really want that pram, Susie. I've always dreamt that one day I'd have one.'

'It looks as though you're determined to have it,' Susie

replied. 'I'll give you a halfpenny for it,' she told him. I stood there holding my breath.

'Not on your nelly.'

'Well, it's not worth any more.'

'Give us a penny for it then, and it's yours.'

I quickly felt inside my pocket.

'Are you sure about this?' Susie asked as I handed him the money.

'Why are his hands so crooked?' I whispered to Susie as I watched him lift the pram off the stall.

'It's all that digging he does in all weathers.'

'Doesn't he wear any gloves?'

'Not with those twisted fingers,' Susie told me. 'He'd never be able to get them on.'

'It needs a good dusting,' Mr Drake said, passing it over.

'It needs more than a good dusting,' Susie replied.

'Well, I wouldn't complain. It's still a bargain for a penny,' he insisted.

'It'll look nice when it's painted, Susie.'

'You won't even be able to push it with that wheel missing.'

'You're making me feel miserable, now,' I said, feeling a lump in my throat.

'You're not going to cry, are you?' Susie asked. 'Come on, let's find a doll, and we'll need some blankets for when you take her for a walk.'

'Lorne,' I heard Teddy shout. I turned around quickly. 'Lorne,' he shouted again, waving his hands in the air.

'Are you in trouble?' I asked, running towards him.

'No, not at all,' he said, trying to catch his breath. 'Patrick is home. He's brought a friend back, too.'

'Susie, Eric, my brother's come home. Will you guard my pram? I must go and see him.'

'You might as well stay until the jumble sale finishes.'

'Why?' I asked.

'They've gone to the Old Dragon Inn for a couple of pints. Well deserved, too, after fighting in that jungle. I might join the army when I'm older.'

'Instead of fixing tyres, Teddy?'

'Maybe, I'm not sure yet. You should see them in their uniforms. They're even wearing berets.'

'Are you going to choose that doll?' Mr Drake called, 'Only I'm about to pack up.'

'Well, I'm off,' Teddy said. 'It's not been a good day for business with all this going on. He's as black as coal, you know.'

'Who?'

'Patrick. And so's his mate. Anyway, I'll catch up with you lot later.'

'What's all that commotion about?' Mr Drake asked, sounding curious.

'Lorne's brother. He's just come back from fighting in the jungle,' Susie told him.

'I'll have this doll. What do you think, Eric?' I asked as I pulled her from the pile. 'She's very pretty, isn't she?'

'Yes, she is pretty,' Eric replied.

'Will you hold her while I check how much money I have left?' I asked, listening to him chuckle as I placed her in his arms.

'How much is this doll?' I asked. 'Eric, will you hold her up for Mr Drake to see.'

'Her face is cracked,' Susie said, looking at it closely.

'Only a little, Susie. Anyway, Eric and I think that she's very pretty.'

'A farthing,' Mr Drake replied.

'I'll have her,' I said. 'I'd like those plates, too, the ones with the flowers painted around them.'

'Hmm, a lot of good people have eaten from these plates,' he said, holding them up and wiping the dust off them with his sleeve. 'I know for sure t'deacon 'as. Eeh, I remember as a lad, just startin' my trainin'; I didn't even know how to 'old a spade properly, never mind dig a grave, but I were invited into t'vicarage to be introduced to t'vicar, and there was Betty layin' t'table with them very same plates. Dead now, more's the pity. Fancied her, you know.'

'Was she the vicar's wife?' I asked.

'Heavens above, no. Mind you, she might as well 'ave been the way she cleaned for him. She would always bring me t'sandwiches that were left from those important people that used to call and see t'vicar. She was a bit on the stocky side, but a face as pretty as you'll ever see. Cursed myself for never asking her to come out with me.'

'Why didn't you?' Susie asked.

'Frightened she'd say no, I suppose. Let's 'ave a look 'ow much money you've got,' Mr Drake said. I quickly opened the palm of my hand. 'You can have them for that shiny sixpence,' he said, taking it from me. 'Anyway, why's a young lass like you buyin' plates? Pass me that old sheet, lad,' he told Eric. 'They'll 'ave to be wrapped up in something, and that's as good as owt.'

'They're for my mother,' I told him.

'She's a bonny woman that ma of yours. Heard many a man whistle at her. Mind you, I'm not surprised with those tight skirts she wears. Now you be a gentleman,' he told Eric, 'and carry these plates for this lass.'

'I'll be chain smoking by the time we get out of this place,' Susie said. 'It's ages since I've had a fag. What are you going to call her?' she asked.

'Lilian,' I replied.

'Are you serious?'

'Yes, why?'

'Well, if you don't mind me saying, it's a bit old-fashioned, especially for a doll. They'll take the mickey out of you if you tell anyone.'

'I'm naming her after my grandmother. I think she has a disease in her legs.'

'Come to think of it, I suppose Lilian is a nice name.'

'Do you think so, Susie?'

'Yes, especially if it's the same name as your grandmother.'

'Edna,' I heard Molly call into the kitchen. 'These pans are ready to be taken to the kitchen for washing.' Dear Molly, whose kindness was to save my soul.

'The hotpot, Susie. I'd forgotten all about it.'

'There might still be some left. Come on. Told you that pram would be hard to push.'

'I'll manage,' I told her, trying to balance it on its three wheels.

'Hey, Edna, is there any left?' she shouted.

'You're a bit late,' Molly told us as we reached her stall. 'There's just a little bit but it's stuck to the bottom of the pan.'

'Can't you scrape it with a spoon?' Susie asked.

'I suppose so, but I wouldn't recommend it. It's probably slightly burnt underneath.'

'Won't bother me,' Susie replied, picking up two paper plates and holding them out.

'Edna, you carry on with your work,' Molly told her.

'Why's Edna's face all shrivelled up on one side?' I whispered to Susie.

'Sshh, I'll tell you later.'

'Oh, I'm quite surprised just how much hotpot I've managed to scrape,' Molly told us.

'Slap it on the plates then,' I heard Susie say. I wondered why Molly was frowning at Susie as she served it. 'It's rather cold, now,' Molly said.

'As long as it fills my belly that's all that matters,' Susie replied.

'The forks are in that tray,' Molly said, rather abruptly.

'Christ, the vicar's here again. Better make sure I eat with my mouth closed. I'm starving as well.'

'This has certainly been a success,' he said to Molly, looking down into the empty pans.

'Shall I ask him if he'll christen my doll?' I asked Susie. I jumped slightly as she started to cough. 'Your eyes are watering, are you all right?'

'You nearly made me choke then,' she replied, finally swallowing her food.

'Vicars don't christen dolls,' she whispered to me, filling her fork with what hotpot was left on her plate and placing it into her mouth.

'Well, who does then?'

'Don't know. No one's ever asked me that question before. Anyway, she's not real, you know.'

'She is to me, Susie. Mmm, that was just delicious.

Would you like what I've left?' I asked. 'I'm too excited to eat any more.'

'No wonder you're skinny,' she said, burping quietly before taking the plate from me.

'Now children, what interesting things have you bought today?'

'I wish he'd beggar off calling me a child,' Susie muttered. 'I've been wearing a bra for the last year and I'll be buying myself stockings soon. Well, as soon as I can get more babysitting jobs.'

'Well, Eric bought some cakes, but I think you've eaten most of them, haven't you, Eric?' He nodded as he opened his bag to look inside. 'Susie hasn't bought anything, have you, Susie?'

I felt her nudge me on my side. 'Don't tell him why,' she whispered.

'Why?' I whispered back.

'Because it's for ten fags, isn't it? Didn't get paid for babysitting last night. That's why I haven't bought anything,' she told him.

'Show the vicar my dress, Susie. Oh, it is pretty, it's beautiful,' I told him, watching Susie take it out of the bag.

'You nearly dropped me in the shit then,' she muttered, 'telling I haven't bought anything.'

'Sorry, Susie.'

'You're absolutely right, it is beautiful,' he told me.

'And I've bought a doll and a pram. It's only got three wheels, but I can still push it. Where can I take her to be christened?' I asked.

'Who?' the vicar asked.

'My doll. Her name's Lilian. It's the first doll I've ever had. Do you like her name?'

'It's a splendid name. I've a sister called Lilian. Come to think of it I must write her a letter. We don't keep in contact that much. Well, not since she's moved to Cornwall.'

'I've told Lorne that vicars don't christen dolls,' Susie said, looking embarrassed.

'Well, there's always a first time for everything,' the vicar told her. 'Edna, bring me a cup of water,' he called.

'Hot or cold?' she asked.

'Cold, cold,' he quickly answered.

'Looks like he's going to do it,' Susie said, giving me another nudge.

'What, Susie?'

'Christen your doll.'

'Now pass Lilian to me,' he asked, taking the cup of water from Edna. My hands started to shake with excitement as I picked her up and passed her to him.

'I name you Lilian,' he said, holding her. 'Lilian...' he said again, looking over his spectacles at me.

'What's her surname?' Susie asked. 'That's what he wants to know.

'Clarke,' I quickly told him.

'Look,' Susie said, 'he's sticking his fingers into the cup of water.'

'Now I name you Lilian Clarke,' he said, making the sign of the cross with his wet finger on her forehead. 'In the name of the Father and of the Son and of the Holy Ghost. Amen.'

'Amen,' Eric said in a loud voice.

'Amen,' I whispered.

'Right, let's go,' Susie quietly told us. 'It's fag time.'

'Thank you very much.'

'You're most welcome,' the vicar said as he passed my doll back to me.

'I need a pee as well. Are we ready?'

'Oh, just a minute, I've seen something else.'

'What now?' asked Susie.

'It's for Grandfather.'

'A goldfish bowl?'

'Yes, to put his teeth in. Mummy complains when he soaks them in his old pint glass with his spit foaming on top.'

'Now I've heard everything,' she said as I ran quickly to the stall and bought the gleaming glass bowl.

'Sure you'll be able to push this pram all the way home?'

'I'm sure,' I told her, placing the bowl on top as we made our way towards the door.

'Here, hold this bag with your dress in,' Susie said as we stepped onto the drive. 'I'll only be a minute.'

'Why's she gone behind that hedge?' Eric asked with a bewildered look on his face.

'She needs to use the toilet, Eric. It's been wonderful, hasn't it? Did you enjoy your cakes?'

'Yes,' he replied, patting his stomach.

'Did you save one for Mrs Crowswick?'

'Two,' he told me, opening his bag for me to have a look.

Oh, Eric, they're all squashed and your bag's full of cream, I thought to myself as I peeped inside.

Chapter 12

'I'm back,' Susie said, waving her hands as she walked towards us. 'Right, we'll go to the shop next to Brindle's Bakery. It's the nearest one. Do you all agree?'

'Yes, we all agree, don't we, Eric?'

'Yes,' he replied, holding the plates tightly against his chest in order not to drop them.

'Can't you push it a bit faster?' Susie asked. 'I'm desperate.'

'I'll be able to when I get a new wheel. It's harder than I thought,' I said, stopping for a second to rest.

'Told you so. Look, I'll knock at some of my neighbours' doors later on,' she told me. 'Their gardens are full of junk. Someone's bound to have a spare one.'

'Let me just check what money I've got before we go in,' Susie said as we stopped outside the door of Mrs Brindle's sweet shop. 'Yeah, got enough.'

'Those batteries are going to run out if that bell rings any longer. Hurry up and close the door,' Mrs Brindle snapped as I struggled to lift my pram over the step.

'A ha'penny worth of that rainbow kali,' Susie said.

'Archie, there's three of them together, come and help,' Mrs Brindle shouted.

'Aren't they both tiny, Susie?' I whispered as Mr Brindle appeared from behind the curtain.

'Yes, they're nearly as tiny as the midgets that live near you,' she told me.

'And I'll have ten of those Woodbines up on the shelf there.'

'How old are you?' Mrs Brindle asked, looking at Susie suspiciously.

'Old enough to be sent to the shop by my dad to buy them.'

'Archie, get those stepladders and pass me ten Woodbines down.'

'Don't forget the matches, Susie,' I whispered.

'Oh, and I'll have a box of those Swan matches.'

'And a box of matches as well,' Mrs Brindle told him.

'What's happened to your pram?' she asked, stretching over the counter to have a look.

'Let's have your money then,' Mr Brindle told Susie before passing her the cigarettes and matches.

'Oh, it's only got a wheel missing. I've just bought it.'

'Where on earth from?'

'Don't get her nattering,' Susie whispered, 'or we'll be here all day.'

'From the jumble sale,' I replied.

'You kids will buy anything these days. Where on earth you get all your money from, God only knows.'

'Come on, let's go,' Susie told us.

'Mind you don't scrape my floor with it on the way out. I don't usually allow prams in the shop. Leave it outside next time.'

'Battleaxe,' Susie said as we closed the door behind us. 'She's an ugly cow, don't you think?'

'Who, Susie?'

'Mrs Brindle – and he's not much better. Did you see him staring at my bust when he handed me the Woodbines? My sister, Maggie, calls him a dirty old man.'

'Does he never have a wash?' I asked.

'No, it's a saying. Want some kali, Eric? I only bought it so she wouldn't think that the cigarettes were for me. Here, take the whole bag. Let's walk down to the football pitch, then I can light up. Shame the team aren't playing today. I fancy a couple of them, you know.'

'Do we have to, Susie? I'm a bit scared.'

'Of what?' she asked, opening the seal on the cigarette packet.

'Well, it's near that big house, isn't it?'

'What big house?' she said with a puzzled look on her face.

'Where all those strange men live. Look, it's over there,' I said, pointing in its direction as we turned the corner.

'You mean Lisieux Hall.'

'I don't know its name, but it's pretty scary. Can you see it, Eric?' I asked, slowly walking down the lane. 'It's just behind those trees.'

'It's a lunatic asylum,' Eric told me.

'You mean a loony bin,' Susie said.

'Can we turn back?'

'You're not really scared, are you?'

'Yes.'

'They won't attack you. They're too stupid, and anyway, they're all locked up, unless one of them escapes through an open window.'

'Please can we go back?'

'I'm only teasing you, aren't I, Eric? So stop looking so

nervous. You can have a Woodbine if you like. That should calm you down.'

'No thank you, Susie. Anyway, I've heard it stunts your growth.'

'What does?'

'Smoking cigarettes.'

'Who told you that one?'

'I don't remember, but someone did.'

'Well, it's not stunted the Grindles', and they've been smoking for years, and I'm not exactly what you'd call small, am I?'

'You're not, Susie.'

'We'll sit over there,' Susie said, pointing to a large stone that lay on the grass. 'Not much of a football pitch, is it? What do you say, Eric?'

'Don't leave me alone,' I said as they started to walk over the field. 'I'm stuck. I can't get my pram through the gap.'

'Leave it there then,' Susie told me as I caught up to her.

'You were just scared, weren't you? Scared that one of those loonies might have been walking along the lane and grabbed hold of you.'

'Well, just a little. I nearly dropped Lilian running over all those bumps. You won't leave me on my own again, will you?' I asked as Susie lit her cigarette.

'Want a drag?'

'No thank you.'

'Do you, Eric?'

'No, no,' he replied before sitting himself down on the edge of the stone.

'I wish he'd stop doing that,' Susie whispered to me as we sat down next to him.

'Doing what?'

'Picking his nose.'

'He'll have a handkerchief in his pocket.'

'How do you know?' Susie asked.

'Because Mrs Crowswick puts a clean one inside his pocket every single day. He's probably forgotten.'

'Well, will you remind him,' she asked, 'before he wipes it on his sleeve? It's making me feel sick.'

'Let me get your handkerchief, Eric. It should be in this pocket,' I told him, putting my hand inside and pulling it out. 'Here, wipe it on this.'

'Does it not put you off?'

'Off what?'

'You know, Eric, doing that.'

'Hey, you lot over there … you lot. Is there a match?'

'Oh Christ, it's Fellwick, that's all we need,' Susie muttered as she saw the young man limping painfully towards us. 'Yes, I've got a box full,' she shouted, shaking it in the air.

'Why has he got those iron bars around his leg?' I asked as he limped slowly towards us.

'Caught polio, didn't he?

'What's that?'

'I meant a bloody football match,' he shouted back.

'I'll tell you later,' she whispered.

'Takin' piss out of me again, are you?'

'Can't you take a joke nowadays?' Susie asked.

'Don't suppose I can.'

'Come on, things can't be that bad. Here, have one of my fags.'

'I'm sick of wandering around this bloody village,' he told us, snatching the matches from Susie's hand to light his cigarette. 'Can't even get a job.'

'Why not?'

'Why not?' he said. 'You bloody well know why not. They only have to take one look at this calliper around this useless leg of mine and I'm back out through the door. In fact, I didn't even get to sit down on t'last job I went for. It isn't worth it.'

'At least you try,' Susie said.

'Aye, and a fat lot of good it does,' he replied. 'I sometimes touch me face to see if it's still there. They never even look at me.'

'Who never looks at you?' Susie asked.

'Geezers that interview me. They talk to this,' he said, pointing down at his leg. 'Can't keep their eyes off it. Fancy a pint, Eric? Ain't seen you in ages. Come on,' he said. 'Just collected me dole money so I'll stand thi one.'

'I d-don't drink,' Eric stuttered.

'You'd get pissed off a pint of lemonade, never mind beer, wouldn't you, Eric? Only joking,' Susie added, reaching over and patting him on his knees.

'Fellwick,' I said, watching him throw the end of his cigarette as far as he could.

'What?' he quickly replied.

'Would you work for me?'

'Is this another piss take?' he said, staring at me with a hard and tired look on his face.

'Here, look,' I said, standing up and pulling out a penny from the inside of my coat pocket.

'What am I supposed to do for that?'

'Find me a wheel and fix it onto my pram. It's only got three and it needs four. I can still push it though so it doesn't matter if you don't want to.'

'Well, it's a job, Fellwick,' Susie told him. 'Here, have another fag and think about it.'

'It's not that piece of junk I nearly tripped over, is it?'

'What piece of junk?' I quickly asked.

'That's leaning against the hedge over there. It needs a lick of paint if you ask me. It's covered in rust.'

'I'd pay you more but this is all I've got left,' I told him.

'Come on, Fellwick, give the girl an answer.'

'I'm thinking, I'm thinking. It'll take me a couple of days.'

'What for?' Susie asked.

'To search around the tip. That's the only place they'll 'ave one. Might be lucky and find some old paint there as well. Does it matter what colour?'

'White would be nice, or pink, but it doesn't matter, Fellwick. I don't really mind what colour it's painted.'

'Give us your penny, then. I'll start tomorrow, though I can't guarantee anything. Should imagine it'll be pretty treacherous searching through all that rubbish, especially with this bloody leg of mine. I sometimes curse the day I was born. If tha changes thi mind about that pint, Eric, I'll be in t'Horse and Hound tap room.'

'Poor Fellwick. Will his leg get better, Susie?'

'Doubt it. You wouldn't think he was only nineteen. It's made him into an old man, you know.'

'What has?'

'That calliper. He's never come to terms with it. Well, that's what I heard Mrs Fellwick telling my mum.'

'Look, Susie. He's stopped to have a look at my pram.'

'Well, you've done him a favour, haven't you?'

'Have I?'

'I reckon you've made him feel really important asking him to fix that pram of yours. Poor sod.'

'Yes, it is a shame for him, isn't it, Susie?'

'You'd have thought so a couple of months ago. He tried to play football with some of the lads that live at our end. Had to be picked up off the ground – nearly collapsed.'

'How sad, Susie.'

'You're telling me. Heard he smashed most of his bedroom up he was that frustrated.'

'I'll be knocking at your door in the next few days,' he called over before disappearing out of view.

'Christ, look at the time!' Susie said looking at her watch. 'It's my turn to go to the chippy. It'll be packed, too. Always is on a Friday. Fancy some?'

'Not after all that hotpot, Susie. Wasn't it delicious?'

'It'll take more than a plate of hotpot to fill me up. It's steak pudding and chips for me with lashings of gravy.'

'Will you look after Lilian for me?' I asked as we all stood up to leave.

'You're not tired of holding her already are you? Mind you don't step in that dog dirt,' she said, steering me to one side.

'I don't want to leave her on her own when I go on holiday. Will you, Susie?'

'I told you, she's not real.'

'It's only for a week.'

'I'm going to look a right sissy if I do. What if I took

my boyfriend up to the bedroom for a snog and Lilian's sat there?'

'You haven't got a boyfriend.'

'Well, what's that then?' she said, pulling the collar of her blouse down.

'Oh, Susie, does it hurt?'

'It's only a love bite. Gave it to me last week. That's what boys do when they fancy you. Maggie's got them all over her bust.'

'Did she have to go to the doctor?'

'Okay, I'll look after Lilian for you,' she said with a frustrated sigh. 'But she'll have to be kept in the bottom of my wardrobe until you come home. I'll miss you, you know.'

'Will you, Susie?'

'Yes, we both will, won't we, Eric? Why does he never reply when you ask him something?' Susie asked.

'It's because he's in a day-dream. He always day-dreams, especially when he's tired.'

'Don't you regret buying that pram?' she said. 'You're struggling with it.'

'No, I'm not. It's just that this hill's steep and it's harder to push. Do you think Fellwick will really find me a wheel at the tip?'

'He'll probably have to have a good root round with all that shit that's dumped there. Anyway, he'll have spent your penny by now so he'll have to.'

'Are you coming to say hello to my brother?' I asked.

'Wouldn't mind. Need to paint my nails first just in case I fancy his mate.'

'Won't he be too old for you?'

'How old is he?'

'I don't know, Susie.'

'Well, I'm fourteen and I've a body just like an eighteen-year-old, so Chris down the road tells me. He keeps trying to put his hand up my skirt. Does it with everyone. He's a pervert, you know.'

'What's a pervert?'

'Someone who likes to touch women in rude places,' she whispered.

'You mean on their bottoms,' I whispered back.

'Worse than that. They call him shag the lad.'

'Why?'

Well, that's his nickname, isn't it? What's he staring at?' Susie said as we stood on the kerb waiting for a break in the traffic.

'Who?'

'That bloke who's just driven past. Should concentrate more on his driving instead of looking at young girls like us.'

'Was it shag the lad?' I asked.

'Sshh, you mustn't say that word to anyone.'

'Why?'

'Because it's rude. Anyway, he can't drive. Jesus Christ, she frightened the life out of me,' Susie said as we slowly walked past Mrs Patterson's house. 'That window's going to fall out if she knocks any harder.'

'Doesn't her face look horrible, Susie?'

'Yes, she looks like she should be in one of those fun houses. You know, like they have at Blackpool. Ugh, I can see the hairs up her nose,' Susie said.

'I wonder why she's squashing her face so hard up against that glass. It's dangerous.'

'Lorne, Lorne,' I heard her shout. 'Your Patrick's home.'
'I know, Mrs Patterson, Teddy told me.'
'Tell your mum I'll be down at Rose Cottage later.'
'I will,' I replied, giving her a little wave.
'She's nothing but a tart.'
'Who is, Susie?'
'Mrs Patterson. She'll fancy them you know.'
'Who?'
'Your brother and his mate. I bet she put those rollers in her hair the second she found out that they were home.'
'Will she want to kiss them?'
'Uhm, a lot more than that if you ask me. Did you notice her cheeks sinking in a little on each side of her face?'
'That's because she's taken her teeth out, Susie. Didn't you know her teeth were false? I've seen them with my own eyes.'
'What?' Susie asked.
'Mrs Patterson's teeth.'
'When?'
'When mother gave me a note to give to her. I had to stand outside her back door while she read it. That's when I noticed them. They were floating around in a glass on top of the kitchen sink. They were all yellow and stained.'
'Don't feel like going to the chippy now. You've put me off.'
'Sorry, Susie. Do you think my mother will like the plates I've bought for her?'
'Don't see why not. My mum would. They'll need a

good washing before you eat off them. Didn't you notice Mr Drake scratching his backside?'

'No, Susie.'

'Well, he did, quite a few times just before he wrapped them in that blanket he asked Eric for.'

'Ugh, how horrible.'

'He's another one who never washes.'

'How do you know?'

'Never noticed all those blackheads on his face?'

'No, I haven't.'

'Well, he has got them. You bloody prat,' Susie shouted as Harry pressed on his brakes, stopping his bike from skidding just inches behind us.

'Your brother's home.'

'I know, Harry,' I answered.

'It's history, we knew hours ago. You'll kill someone on that bike one day,' Susie told him.

'Well, that might be history but I bet you don't know that Lorne's Grandfather's arrived, too.'

'Has he, oh, has he Harry?'

'Pissed as a newt, mind you. Found him in a café on Preston railway station. Not me, one of the porters that works there. When the taxi stopped outside Rose Cottage he nearly fell out of the thing. Legless he was. Had to get off me bike and help him to the door. Stunk as well.'

'It will only be of whisky, Harry,' I told him. 'He always smells of it.'

'Wanted a fight with me, couldn't believe it. And the language – thought I could swear. What's that tha's bought?'

'It's a pram, Harry.'

'I can see that, but just look at it. Looks like it's been out in the rain for years. You've lost a wheel off it, too.'

'Fellwick's going to find me one and fix it for me.'

'Is that a joke? Fellwick don't do owt for anyone. Not with that chip he's got on his shoulder. I don't believe you. Anyway, if it's the truth, where will he find one? Ain't got no brains, you know.'

'At the tip. He's even going to find me some paint.'

'That doesn't surprise me. He's always rooting through yon tip. Have you seen their back yard?' It's full to the brim with old junk. He's there every day collecting it. His ma daren't say a thing to him about all the scrap he keeps in the yard.'

'Why?' Susie asked.

'She's frightened he'll lash out at her again. No wonder his old man left.'

'Did he, Harry? When?'

'Been gone years now. Pissed off, didn't he? Not sure who with. Think it was with one o' t'neighbour's daughters.'

'Just two more weeks to go and they'll be nice and ripe,' Harry said, pushing his bicycle as he walked alongside us.

'What will?' Susie asked.

'Dobson's apples,' Harry replied, pointing over to them. 'Going to nick the lot.'

'Ooh, it's a long drop,' Susie told him, stopping for a second to look over the orchard wall. 'He'll kick your arse if he catches you.'

'Already has done, so I reckon I've nowt to lose.'

'We're nearly home now, Eric. Look, there's Rose Cottage. Can you see any fish, Eric?' I asked, standing next to him whilst he leaned over the bridge to look down at the stream.

'They'll only be tiddlers if he can. It's too shallow for owt else. Not even worth throwing a rod in,' Harry said, glancing over. 'Is that what the goldfish bowl's for?'

'Don't ask,' said Susie. 'Right, I'm off,' Susie said, passing me the bag with my dress in.

'Aye, me too. Feel like jacking it in.'

'What, Harry?'

'Paper round. Mind you, suppose I wouldn't be able to keep me pigeons if I did.'

'Why not?' I asked.

'Seen t'price of pellets nowadays? Don't have much choice.'

'Don't forget to find out which pub your kid's going to tonight,' Susie shouted, half turning whilst walking up the hill.

'Wait for me,' Harry called to her. 'I'm going your way.' He jumped on his bicycle and pedalled as fast as he could after her.

'I'd like you to come and say hello to my Grandfather, Eric,' I said as we crossed the road and made our way towards the entry. 'But he's drunk today so he'll probably be asleep. Mrs Crowswick will be so excited when you give her the cakes, won't she, Eric?'

'Yes, she will,' he replied as he struggled to open his bag to check they were still there.

'Mrs Crowswick, we're back,' I said, giving her a wave as she stood at her door waiting for us.

'I can see that, my dear. Have you both enjoyed yourselves?'

'Look,' Eric said excitedly as he put the plates down onto the ground and opened his bag.

'My, my they look delicious. I'll make some tea. Would you like a cup?' she asked.

'I've got Lilian to look after now,' I told her, picking her up to show her. 'She hasn't any clothes on, Mrs Crowswick because I've only just bought her.'

'I've got just the thing,' she said. 'Step in whilst I find it.'

I wonder what it is, I thought, as I stood there with just the ticking of the clock to listen to. 'Shall I help you?' I asked, watching her struggle.

'This sideboard's always been temperamental,' she said before finally managing to open the drawer. 'I crocheted this when Mr Crowswick died. Don't know why I did. I've somehow never had the heart to wear it.'

'It's beautiful, Mrs Crowswick.'

'Here, take it, my dear.'

'But won't you need it one day to keep you warm?'

'Not at all. That was Mr Crowswick's favourite shawl,' she said, walking over and pulling it off the back of her chair to show me. 'If there was ever a little breeze he would always get up and drape it around my shoulders, wouldn't you Eddie?' I heard her say as she squeezed it to her chest.

'Eric, they do look lovely on that cake stand,' I told him as he appeared from the kitchen proudly carrying it over to the table.

'Are you sure you won't join us?' Mrs Crowswick said, passing me the shawl before sitting down next to Eric. 'Who on earth can that be?' she said, placing the teapot back on to the table as a loud knock came at the door.

'It's me, Teddy,' came the reply as he popped his head around the door which was slightly ajar.

'I nearly jumped out of my skin, young man. Don't knock so loudly next time.'

'Sorry, Mrs Crowswick, I didn't mean to make you jump. You'd better get home quick, Lorne, Mother's going up the wall.'

'What about?' I asked.

'You,' he replied.

'Am I in trouble?'

'You're telling me. Come on, you'd better hurry.'

I wonder if she's found out that one of her hairclips is missing, I thought, quickly taking it from my hair and placing it inside my pocket. 'See you tomorrow,' I said to Eric and gave them both a quick wave before hurrying from Mrs Crowswick's house and out into the garden.

'Will you help me with these plates, Teddy? Mr Drake wrapped them in a blanket for me so they wouldn't break.'

'I'll carry them down the entry for you, then I'm off,' he replied.

'Where are you going?'

'It's a bit of a joke, don't you think?' he said.

'What is?'

'That pram. You can't even push it properly. I think you got stung there.'

'It'll be as good as new when Fellwick's fixed it for me,' I replied, trying to balance it.

'Who are the plates for? They're pretty heavy.'

'They're for Mummy. Do you think she'll like them?'

'How do I know? I haven't seen them properly yet. You should see all the money Patrick has on him, wads of it.'

'Is he rich then?'

'Certainly looks like it. Gave me a £10 note to get everyone fish and chips. Mother said not to get any for you, though.'

'Why?'

'Don't know. I didn't ask. I'll ask Wilf if there are any scraps for you. There's always loads left in the bottom of his fryer. Christ, they're slipping. Quick, put that pram down and open the door.'

Chapter 13

I could hear the sound of laughter coming from the living room as I lifted up the catch allowing Teddy to brush past me.

'That was lucky,' he said, quickly placing them on top of the drainer next to the kitchen sink. 'Sounds like they've all had a few too many,' Teddy said, rubbing both his hands together.

'Too many what?' I asked.

'Beers, of course. Anyway, I'd better scoot before Wilf closes up.'

I thought how nice it was to hear everyone laughing as I carefully removed the blanket to admire the plates. Well, they are beautiful, I said to myself holding one up to have a closer look. That must be real gold painted around the edges, I thought, as it twinkled in the sun shining through the kitchen window. My heart skipped a beat as the living room door suddenly opened.

'Aahh, my little princess. Come here while I give you a hug.'

'Grandfather,' I called, running towards him.

'When are you going to get some meat on you?' he asked, lifting me up in his arms.

'What's happened to your eye?' I asked, with a sympathetic look on my face.

'The bastard accused me of not paying for my breakfast, so I threw my fried egg at him. Left in such a rage that I hit my bloody eye on the door handle on my way out. Threatened to phone the police.'

'Who did?'

'The bloke that runs the café on the railway station.'

'Does it hurt?'

'Nothing that a glass of whisky won't mend,' he whispered in my ear. 'You don't happen to know where there'd be a wee drop, do you?'

'Put her down, pops,' Mummy said in a stern tone as she appeared behind him.

'Better do as I'm told,' he said, giving me one last squeeze before lowering me to the ground.

'Go and sit down, you're staggering, pops,' Mummy told him.

Whoops, that was lucky, I thought, watching him take a step back whilst slowly making his way across the kitchen towards the living room. Watching him sway from one side of the kitchen to the other, I wondered how many lumps he would have had on his head if he had fallen over that chair.

'Shall I open the door for you, Grandfather?' I called as he stood there staring at it.

'He doesn't even know it's right in front of him. He can't even focus properly,' Mummy mumbled.

I hope he isn't going blind, I thought, running over to help him. I wonder what name he'll call his dog if he is.

'Get back over there,' Mummy shouted as she pushed in front of me. Confused and frightened, I quickly did as I was told. 'Where have you been all day, you little bitch?' she asked walking towards me. I felt a sting as she quickly raised her hand.

'Ouch,' I called out.

'You're lucky you didn't get a slap on the other side,' she told me as I immediately placed the palm of my hand over my cheek. 'Well, come on, give me an answer.'

'Yoo hoo, I'm here at last,' Mrs Patterson called, popping her head around the kitchen door. 'Must make an appointment with Ruby. I'll probably get it permed. What do you think, Jenny?' she asked, closing the door behind her and walking towards Mother.

I'm glad you're here, Mrs Patterson, I said to myself, holding back the tears. At least she looks a lot better with her teeth in, even if they are stained, I thought, as she turned around and smiled at me.

'Oh, these are lovely,' she said, standing on her tiptoes and looking over Mummy's shoulder towards the drainer.

'What are?' Mummy asked.

'Those plates, Jenny. Must have some. Where did you get them from?'

'I bought them for Mummy,' I whispered.

'Just look at the edging on them,' she said, picking one up and inspecting it.

'That's real gold,' I told her as she rubbed her fingers around it.

'Feels like it, too.'

I noticed her wink at Mummy as she placed it back on top of the pile. 'I bought them off Mr Drake at the jumble sale.'

'So that's where you've been,' Mummy said. 'Where the hell did you get the money from?'

'Harry gave me sixpence,' I told her.

'Liar,' she shouted. 'She's a thief, you know,' she said to Mrs Patterson, pointing towards me. 'She'll have had her dirty little fingers in my purse, you know.' I looked down at my fingers and saw they weren't dirty at all.

'Go and get him here now,' she told me.

'Who?'

'Harry. We'll soon see if he gave you sixpence.'

'But I won't be able to find him now. He'll be delivering his newspapers.'

'Seek and you will find, young lady,' Mrs Patterson replied, adjusting her hair.

'Were you given any change?' Mummy asked. 'Come here while I check inside your coat pockets.'

Oh no, the hairgrip. I felt my stomach turn over with fright as I slowly walked towards her. She'll probably slap my face again when she finds it. I'll close my eyes this time, it might not hurt as much.

'Jesus Christ, who the hell's that?' Mummy said, as we all jumped with the sudden banging on the back door.

'Would you believe it?' Mrs Patterson said, peeping through the tiny kitchen window. 'He'll have run out of money. I've already given him a fiver today. Stop banging on that door, you fat bastard,' she shouted, rushing over to open it. 'Suppose you've come for some more money,' I heard her say. 'Probably spent that last lot on that fancy woman of yours, 'aven't you? That's where your dole money goes, on her, doesn't it?'

'I've got no fancy woman,' he replied.

'You bloody well 'ave. She doesn't want you under her feet, otherwise you'd 'ave moved in with her, wouldn't you, you dirty bastard?'

He looks clean to me, I thought, as I caught a glimpse of him. His shirt's really white.

'Lend us a ten bob note, Jenny,' Mrs Patterson called.

'You'll be lucky,' Mummy replied.

'I'll go and find Harry,' I whispered.

'This is my prince,' Mrs Patterson told me as I tried to squeeze past her. 'Look at the bloody state of him.'

I hope his trousers don't fall down, I thought, noticing that most of the elastic had frayed on the snake belt he wore around his waist.

'Have a good look at him, lass. That's what happens when you marry them.'

'You're no oil painting yourself,' he told her.

I bowed my head slightly with embarrassment. His pumps are rather dirty, I thought. He must be getting angry; that's why he's moving his toes up and down inside them.

'Any luck, Jenny?' Mrs Patterson shouted. 'Go in, lass, and see if your mother's found that money,' she told me.

'But I've got to go and find Harry or I'll be in trouble,' I replied.

'Bugger off, then, in fact you can both bugger off.'

'Slag,' Mr Patterson mumbled as she slammed the door.

I could smell the strong aroma of his Brylcreem as a gentle breeze blew in the air.

'Don't need no money off that one,' Mr Patterson told me as I followed behind him.

Poor Mr Patterson. He'd look much nicer if he wore a wig instead of trying to cover his bald patch with the thin strands of hair left on his head.

'She's a bitter woman if ever there was one. Stopped fancying her years ago.'

'Have you seen Harry?' I asked.

'Ain't been looking. Caught her with a bloke half her age, but it ain't for your ears, young lass. It'll be the last time she tells me to bugger off.'

'If you see him, will you tell him I'm looking for him and that it's a matter of life or death.'

'Nowt's that urgent.'

'It is to me, Mr Patterson.'

'Might as well go home to my bed. There's nowt else to do. Ain't no fine lady waiting for me there, lass. Might find myself one though. It's a long time since I've had a bit of the old slap and tickle.'

I don't think she'll like you when you find her, I said to myself. It's not nice when you get slapped. Maybe he tickles her afterwards to make her feel better, I thought.

'Well, I'll be off,' he told me.

'Yes, so will I, Mr Patterson. Do you think you'll feel happier tomorrow?' I asked.

'Chance would be a fine thing,' he replied.

'My grandfather always says tomorrow's another day.'

'Yes, well he would, wouldn't he.'

'What do you mean?' I asked.

'Well, it's because he's always drunk. You don't remember the day before if you drink as much as he does.'

'He only forgets where he's hidden his whisky,' I told him. 'But I always find it for him. It's usually in one of the cupboards hidden underneath everything. He only hides it because Daddy says he's going to throw it down the sink if he has another.'

'Not that I've never had a skinful myself. Don't do no

harm to enjoy yourself now and again, but not every day like he does,' he told me. 'He's o'er yonder, lass.'

'Who?' I asked.

'Lad you were looking for.' He pointed to him across the street. 'See, he's just shoving a newspaper through the pub door of all places.'

'Harry, oh, Harry,' I called, waving my hands in the air. I stepped off the pavement and ran across the road towards him. 'Harry,' I called again.

'What's up?' he asked.

'Mummy wants to see you, Harry.'

'Does she want me to start delivering her a newspaper?'

'She might do if you ask her,' I said, 'but it's about the sixpence you gave me to spend at the jumble sale.'

'What about it?'

'She doesn't believe you gave it to me, Harry.'

'Well, I did,' he replied.

'I know, but will you come with me?'

'What for?'

'To tell her that I was telling her the truth.'

'Haven't got time yet. Still got the rest of these to deliver,' he told me, opening his haversack to show me.

'Please, please, Harry. It will only take a minute.'

'Can't,' he replied.

'Then I can't go back home ever again,' I told him, looking up at him hoping to see a sympathetic look on his face.

'Course you can.'

'I can't, Harry. I'll get locked in my bedroom again if you don't come back with me. It's cold up there, and I get frightened.'

'Of what?' he asked.

'Ghosts,' I replied.

'There's no such things.'

'There are, Harry.'

'Why, have you seen one?'

'No.'

'Well, there you are then.'

'I haven't seen one because they're invisible. I felt one touch me on my shoulder one night.'

'It's just your imagination,' he told me.

'It isn't. Sometimes the curtains move, too.'

'That'll be the wind,' he said.

'I'll even help you raid Mr Dobson's orchard if you come back with me.'

'You're too tiny,' he said. 'Dobson would catch you in a second.'

'Please, Harry.'

'You owe me one if I do,' he told me.

'What's a fancy woman?' I asked as we walked along together towards Rose Cottage.

'Why do you ask?'

'Mrs Patterson told me that Mr Patterson had one.'

'It's called a bit on the side.'

'On the side of what, Harry?'

'Oh, never mind. Ask me in a few years time when you're a bit older. Can't explain it properly anyway.'

'You'd better stand in the yard,' I told him as we walked along the entry, 'and I'll go inside the house and tell Mummy that you're here. I'm a bit frightened, are you Harry?' I asked, lifting up the catch to open the back door.

'I'm frightened of nowt,' he replied.

'Jenny, she's back,' Mrs Patterson shouted, pausing for a second before continuing to apply her lipstick. 'You can stop making that racket,' she told Harry as he stood at the back door with his hands inside his pockets. 'Can't stand people whistling. Anyway, what have you been up to, giving money away like that?'

'Ain't been up to nowt,' he told her. 'Anyway, it's Lorne's ma I've come to see.'

'You're a cheeky bugger, always have been. Stop that bloody whistling, will you.'

'Is she coming?' Harry called. 'I'll be getting the sack if these papers aren't delivered.'

'Harry's in a hurry,' I told Mummy as she appeared in the kitchen.

'Don't give a damn how much of a hurry he's in,' she replied as she brushed past me.

'Step in,' she told Harry, opening the door wider for him. 'How much did you give her?' she asked.

'Who?'

'The cheek of him,' Mrs Patterson said, shaking her head.

Just tell her, Harry, I said to myself, noticing the angry expression on her face.

'That one over there,' she said, pointing to me.

'Sixpence,' he replied.

'Told you to lie, hasn't she?'

'You don't have to tell that one to lie,' Mrs Patterson butted in.

'I'd have given her more if I'd had it.'

'You must have a bloody good job if you can give that kind of money away,' Mrs Patterson told him.

‘I do. I do errands, don’t I, around the village. Anyway, it’s nowt to do with you.’

‘You’re never, ever to give her money again, do you hear me?’ Mummy said.

‘Jesus Christ, I only gave it the poor girl to spend at the jumble sale. That ain’t no crime, is it?’

‘She shouldn’t have been going there in the first place, sneaking off when my back’s turned,’ Mummy told Harry.

‘But you gave me permission to go,’ I reminded her.

‘Keep that mouth of yours shut. I’ve told you time and time again you can only speak when you’re spoken to. I don’t want to see you in his company again. He’s a bad influence.’

‘I agree,’ Mrs Patterson said. ‘Anyway, he shouldn’t be going around giving young girls money. Only perverts do that sort of thing.’

‘Do I look like I’m a pervert?’ Harry asked, looking straight at me.

‘I don’t know what one is, Harry. I know that you’re the paperboy.’

‘They are dirty men who give young girls like you money,’ Mrs Patterson told me. ‘Then they take them away and play with them.’

‘I don’t think Harry would like to play with me. He’d look funny playing hopscotch,’ I told her.

‘You’ve a lot to learn, lass. Hanging around with his type won’t help you,’ she said, looking over at Harry.

‘I’ll be off then,’ Harry told me.

‘You ought to spend more time looking after those pigeons of yours instead of wandering the streets,’ Mrs Patterson told him.

'There's nowt wrong with me pigeons, and I'll wander wherever I want. It's a free world, ain't it?'

'Not if you're hanging around lasses like this one,' she replied.

'I'm off,' Harry said, banging the door behind him.

Poor Harry, I thought, as I stood watching Mrs Patterson inspect the plates once more. I'll write a letter to him and ask him if he'll still be my friend.

'You can have them,' Mummy told her.

'What these?' Mrs Patterson replied. 'Are you serious?'

'Well, I'll definitely not use them; not when they've been bought with someone else's money, especially his,' Mummy said.

'I don't blame you, Jenny. I've told you before that he's a cheeky bugger. I'll take them. Get some newspaper, lass, and help me wrap them.'

'Can I use this?' I asked Mummy, feeling a lump in my throat as I bent down to pick one up from a pile on the floor in the corner of the kitchen.

'Check the date first,' she told me. 'Your father might not have read it.'

'Hurry up, lass, I can't stand here all day,' Mrs Patterson told me, whilst stretching out her arms for me to pass it to her. Her bright red polished nails looked like the claws of an eagle as I stood silently watching her begin to wrap the plates. 'Well, come and help,' she told me.

'Mr Drake said that the deacon had eaten off one of these,' I told her, reluctantly picking one up.

'He'll tell you owt, that man. Mind you, it wouldn't surprise me with the quality of them.'

'You're as bad as she is,' Mummy told her, 'if you believe that.'

'If the Queen comes to visit you, will you be giving her something to eat off one of them?' I asked.

'There'll be no bloody Queen coming to visit me, lass, not with that dirty bastard of mine, sitting stinking in his chair all day.'

'Go away,' Mummy told me. 'You do nothing but irritate me.'

I don't care if you've given Mrs Patterson those plates, I thought, taking one last look at them as I made my way towards the living room. Anyway, they'd only get smashed like all the others do. Patrick, you're home, I whispered to myself as I crouched down and crept towards the back of the chair that he was sitting on. 'Guess who's behind your chair?' I said, putting on a strange voice.

'Couldn't be that favourite little sister of mine,' he replied.

'Boo,' I shouted, quickly standing up behind him. 'You're good at guessing,' I told him. 'Did I scare you?' I asked as I rushed around and sat on his knee.

'You certainly did.'

I could smell the beer he had been drinking as he kissed me on my cheek. 'I like your uniform,' I told him, touching his lapel to feel the material. 'Do you remember Susie, my friend?'

'Can't recall her.'

'She told me that her sister, Maggie, likes men in uniform.'

'Did she now?'

'Have you come back here for ever?' I asked, excitedly.

'Get that piece of junk removed from the yard immediately,' Mummy shouted as she stamped into the living room.

'But it's my doll's pram,' I told her, jumping off Patrick's knee.

'It's a piece of junk. Get it moved now.'

I quickly looked at Patrick for support. 'Fellwick's going to fix it for me.' I told him.

'Let's have a look,' Patrick said, standing up and straightening his trousers before walking over towards the living room window. 'It's not doing any harm out there,' he told Mummy as he looked out on to the yard.

'She's defiant, that one. I told her that I won't have any other people's junk here.'

'Oh, let her keep it,' Patrick told Mummy. 'God, is that the time?' he said, lifting up his arm to look at his watch. 'Better wake Stuart up.'

'You'll have to keep it in the shit-house,' Mummy told me as soon as Patrick had left the room. 'And that doll as well. I'm not having any more clutter in this house. Do you hear me?' Mummy said.

'Yes, Mummy, I'll go and do it now.'

'And check if there's enough newspaper in there while you're at it.'

I didn't hesitate and quickly made my way along the kitchen and into the yard.

'Mummy's told me that you have to stay in the outside toilet,' I told Lilian as I lifted the handle of my pram and pushed it along the yard. 'It's a bit smelly in there because there isn't any chain to pull. You have to wipe your bottom with newspaper and it makes it very sore, but I'll come back and check on you as many times as I can. We would all have had to run away if she hadn't let me keep you, to a strange land where we could never be found.'

'It was packed out in that chippy,' I heard Teddy say as he appeared at the bottom of the entry. 'Had to wait ages. Here,' he said, rooting through the plastic shopping bag, 'Got him to make a cone for you out of the paper he wraps the fish and chips in. There's not many though,' he told me as he peered inside it before passing it to me.

'Thank you, Teddy.'

'They're only scraps,' he told me. 'Don't have to thank me for scraps. When did she arrive?' he asked as we listened to Mrs Patterson roar with laughter from inside the house.

'Ages ago, Teddy. She's been putting on her lipstick in the kitchen, but it's all smudged because she keeps talking whilst she's doing it. Susie told me that she was a man-eater, but I don't believe her at all. They'd lock her away for ever if she was, wouldn't they?' I asked.

'Never mind standing there yapping,' Mummy called, knocking on the window to get Teddy's attention.

'Don't let her see that cone.'

'I won't, Teddy. I'll hide it inside my pram.'

'They'd better not be cold, and you hurry up and get the piece of junk shifted,' Mummy shouted.

'Nag, nag, nag,' Teddy whispered as he walked past me.

It's not very nice in there, I said to myself, feeling a little frightened as I approached the semi-derelict brick building. I stood for a while and stared at the weathered door that was hanging off its hinges. I don't know why Daddy doesn't knock it down completely, I thought, resting my pram back on the ground.

I felt a strange sensation on the tips of my fingers as I lifted up the rusty latch. The sound of the creaking door made me feel anxious as I carefully pulled it open. I felt a little shiver go down my spine as I stepped inside. The overcrowded cobwebs hanging from the walls gave it a ghostly feeling. I wish I didn't have to leave Lilian here, I thought, noticing the soggy newspapers lying on the floor. I could hear the sound of footsteps coming from behind me. I quickly turned around. 'Susie, you scared me.'

'Well, did you find out then?' she asked.

'Find out what?'

'Which pub your kid will be going to. What's his mate like?'

'I haven't seen him yet.'

'God, it stinks in here,' she said, stepping in. 'She looks like a real hooker in that dress she's wearing. She'll definitely pull tonight.'

'What's a hooker?' I asked.

'God, I'm going to choke if I stay in here any longer,' she told me, placing her hand over her mouth. 'Are you off out then?' she shouted as we stepped back into the fresh air. 'God they're bloody gorgeous. Just look at their uniforms. I'm going to follow them,' she told me as Patrick and Stuart made their way along the yard towards the entry.

'I see that she made it then,' Susie muttered as Mrs Patterson waved from behind the kitchen window. 'Old cow,' Susie said as she waved back to her.

'She's had her hair done and put her teeth back in especially to meet Patrick and his friend,' I whispered.

'Frightening,' Susie muttered once again, giving her a false smile. 'I'm off before I lose track of them.'

'I wish I could come with you.'

'You can't, you'd give the game away.'

'Why would I do that?' I asked.

'Well, they'd recognize you straight away, wouldn't they.'

'I could always go in disguise.'

'Too risky. Anyway, we've not got the time for all of that. Pinch us a few of your dad's dog-ends when you come,' she told me as she walked away. 'Can't afford to keep buying fags all the time. I'll have to start rolling a few. Catch up with you later,' she called.

I stood at the bottom of the entry and watched her run as fast as she could. I wish I still had you here for company, I thought, giving a sigh as she disappeared out of view.

'You're wanted in there,' Teddy told me, giving a burp whilst rubbing his tummy as he walked past me.

I walked towards the back door, dreading every step I took as I got closer to it. 'Here goes,' I said out loud, pressing my thumb down on the catch.

To my surprise, the kitchen held an air of silence as I stepped in. The stale smell of fish and chips lingering made me feel quite hungry as I tiptoed along the bare asphalt floor towards the living room. 'Did you want me, Mummy?' I asked, glancing over to her as she stood with her back against the fire holding her skirt up to warm her bottom.

'Clear those dishes,' she told me, pointing over towards the table.

'Nowt better than having a quiet ten minutes,' Mrs Patterson told Mummy as she sat back in the armchair. 'Wish I could get rid of these bloody varicose veins,' she said, stretching out her legs to have a closer look. 'Spend too much time on me feet if you ask me. Worked most of me bloody life feeding that bugger's habits. Wouldn't mind but he's not even good in bed.'

I wonder why Mr Patterson misbehaves when he should be sleeping, I thought. No wonder Mrs Patterson sometimes looks tired.

'Come and stay with me for a few days, lass,' she told me as I walked past her towards the table. 'That house of mine hasn't had a good clean for months. What with that bugger flicking his fag ash wherever he likes, you can't blame me. Don't have no heart.'

'I wouldn't recommend that,' Mummy said as I stacked the dishes. 'She pisses in her bed.'

I quickly gathered the knives and forks, holding them tightly in the palms of my hand. My head bowed with embarrassment, I walked as fast as I could towards the kitchen. I couldn't stop the tears as I leaned over the sink to rest the cutlery in the basin. I could feel them running down my face as I struggled to turn on the taps.

'What's that wailing for?' I heard Mummy shout. 'Get up into your bedroom until you've stopped,' she snapped.

I didn't look at anyone as I quickly walked through the living room. I ran as fast as I could up the stairs and threw myself onto the bed.

'Dear God, please help me,' I cried, burying my head in the pillow. *'Can I come to heaven and stay with you, just for a little while? I know that you should really have to die before*

you can do that, but I promise you that I won't get in your way. You see, things aren't getting any better here. I'd ask one of the neighbours if I could stay with them,' I told him, pausing to take a deep breath, *'but Mummy would only tell them that I wet the bed and they wouldn't want me, would they? I know that you forgive people who make mistakes, so that's why I'm asking you. Aren't I lucky to always have you around? I'll stop crying now, now that I've spoken to you,'* I told him, lifting my head off the pillow. *'I'm not allowed to go to Sunday school, otherwise I could have met you there. Would you send one of your angels down to let me know when I can come? I could always meet you inside St Paul's Church, couldn't I?'* I jumped a little as the bedroom door suddenly opened.

'Wipe that snot off your face, otherwise you won't get it,' Frieda told me with a sly grin. Recognizing the bag she was carrying, I quickly jumped off the bed, lifted up my pillow and picked up one of the rags that Teddy had given me.

'I had to wash the damn dishes because of you crying,' I heard her say as I blew on it. 'Next time you leave anything in that yard, it goes in the bin,' she told me, stretching out her arm for me to take it. 'Don't come anywhere near me when you wear it, it stinks,' she said as I took it from her hand.

'Only of mothballs,' I replied, opening the bag and sniffing inside.

'You'll be the laughing stock when you put that on.'

'Why?' I asked.

'Everyone will think you're a damn fairy, won't they? Look at the state of it,' she said as I took the dress out of the bag and laid it on top of the bed.

'Aren't fairies supposed to be very beautiful?' I asked curiously.

'I'm off,' she told me, slamming the door behind me.

I tried to pull the most horrible face that I possibly could at her from behind the door. 'Witch,' I whispered as I listened to her footsteps walking away.

I undid the buttons on my coat as quickly as possible, feeling excited as I stepped into the most beautiful dress that I've ever had. 'Please fit me,' I said out loud, pulling it up and placing my arms one after the other into the short puffed sleeves. My tiny hands struggled whilst placing them behind my back to feel for the zip. At last I was hold of it. With one quick pull it was fastened. It's rather big, I thought, looking down at myself, but I don't mind; I'll soon grow. I couldn't believe how happy I felt, bending my knees slightly to hold up the bottom of my dress. I twizzed around and around with joy.

I jumped with fear and then delight as Grandfather staggered into the room. He held out his arms before slumping down onto the bed.

'Ach, you look just like a princess,' he told me. 'Twirl around, twirl around.'

'Oh, Grandfather, do you really like it?'

'I've never seen anything so pretty,' he replied wiping a tear from his eye.

'I've got you a present, Grandfather. It's in my pram. When you go to the toilet outside you'll find it. It's for your teeth, but don't tell Mummy I bought it or she'll give it away.'

'The auld shrew,' he mumbled.

'How did you lose your teeth, Grandfather?' He thought for a while.

'Bloody pirate. I curse the day I chased him up the rope ladder on-board me ship. Had a patch over one eye, didn't he. And the sun did its worst glaring into the other with its bright dazzle. Didn't save me teeth, though, as he let out a right hook sending me hurtling overboard. Wicked he was.'

'Pops...' Mummy's voice called out from the bottom of the stairs and we both sat stark still.

'Better go, princess. See you in the morning,' he said hugging me tightly before staggering to his feet and creeping away.

Poor Grandfather. I wonder what happened to the pirate, I thought as I lay down on the bed feeling the tickle of the net underskirt on my legs.

Chapter 14

My brothers stood in line whilst Daddy placed a blob of Brylcreem on top of their heads. Daddy didn't make a good job of cutting their hair last night, I thought, as I sat down on the wooden armchair to watch him. I wonder if he really did put a basin on their heads before he started cutting; it certainly looks like it. I giggled at Teddy as he turned around and looked down at me, his hair stuck to his head and combed into a middle parting. He smiled showing off his crooked teeth, which made me giggle even more.

'Lily's here,' Teddy shouted, spotting her walking past the window along the yard before pulling his tongue out at me.

I jumped off my chair and ran through into the kitchen to greet her. 'Lily,' I called, jumping up and down with excitement as the latch was lifted. 'Are you coming with us?' I asked, swinging my arms around her waist and leaning my head against her stomach as she stepped into the kitchen.

'Maybe next time,' she replied, stroking my head. 'Where's Mother?'

'She's gone to Ruby's to have her hair done.'

'In that case I'll stay and have a cigarette.' I moved my head away and held on to her hand. 'I have a little present for you,' she told me as we walked through into the living room. 'Hello, Father,' she said, letting go of my hand to open her shopping bag. Daddy waved his hand in the air, leaving his cigarette firmly between his lips as he pulled out the strands of hair from the teeth of the steel comb he'd been using.

'A present for me?' I asked, looking up at her, quizzically. She handed over a small package wrapped in crisp, white tissue paper. 'Thank you,' I said, holding it tightly in my hand.

'Aren't you going to open it?' Lily asked, taking a cigarette out of the box and lighting it.

'Can I?' I asked, feeling my heart beat a little faster with excitement. With permission given, I knelt down on the lino and carefully peeled the tiny piece of Sellotape that held it together. I glanced at her before unwrapping it. 'Lily, I've never had a bag before,' I gasped, pulling the long crocheted strap up. I quickly opened the cream button that fastened it to look inside.

'Stand up,' she said, looking around for an ashtray to rest her cigarette on. 'I crocheted this myself especially for you to take on holiday,' Lily told me, pulling my cardigan down to straighten it. 'It's only the size of a purse,' she said, crossing the strap over my shoulder allowing the bag to rest on my side, 'but it suits you. You're heavier than I thought.'

'Am I, Lily?' I said as she lifted me up towards the mirror over the fireplace so that I could have a look.

'What do you think?' she asked as I looked at my reflection.

'How do you do?' a voice shouted from the kitchen.

'It's Mrs Patterson,' I whispered to Lily as she quickly put me down.

'Bloody hell, fancy you being here,' she said, walking into the living room.

'Haven't seen you in ages. Looks like you've sorted that rift out between you and your mother. It lasted long enough,' Mrs Patterson said. 'Mind if I make a brew?' Without waiting for a reply, she bustled her way back into the kitchen to put the kettle on.

'Isn't she a battleaxe?' I whispered to Lily.

'Lend us a fag, Lily,' she called over.

'She's always asking for cigarettes,' I told Lily. 'She even pinches some from Grandfather's pockets when he's asleep.'

'Go and give it to her,' Lily told me, taking one out of her packet.

I took it from her and carefully opened my bag and placed it inside. 'Mrs Patterson,' I said, standing on the step leading into the kitchen.

'What, pet?,' she answered as she concentrated on removing the leaves that floated on top of the mug of tea she had just made.

'Lily's sent you this.' I opened my bag once again, gently picking up the cigarette and taking it out.

'Special delivery,' she said, holding her mug in one hand and reaching out to take it from me with the other. 'That's a fancy bag you've got. Can't fit much in it though.'

'Lily crocheted it for me.'

'She's always had a soft spot for you, lass. Spoils you if you ask me.' I fastened the button of my bag inside the loop as she struck a match against a crack on the wall above the kitchen sink. 'I'd give you something to put in it, but I ain't got much myself,' she told me, shaking the match up and down to put it out. 'I'm down to ten fags a day now. Not my doing, it's that lazy bastard of mine swilling his wages down his throat every week. I can't imagine any other poor bugger putting up with him. Mind you, there's plenty of slags out there that probably would.'

'Sounds like nothing's changed,' Lily said, standing behind me resting her hands on either side of my shoulders.

'Well, I'm not as pretty as you,' she replied, turning and smiling at herself through the tiny mirror that was nailed onto the wall, 'otherwise I'd have a line of fancy men. Want a brew, love?' she asked Lily. 'The kettle's still steaming.'

'No thanks, I'm going,' Lily replied. 'I only called in to see Lorne. Don't look so sad,' she told me as I turned to look up at her. 'Anyway, I've got something in my shopping bag for you.'

'Something else for me, Lily?'

'Told you, you're spoilt, you are,' Mrs Patterson said as Lily left the kitchen to collect it. I stood to attention waiting for her to return.

'Are you all packed up, then?' Mrs Patterson asked.

'I'm not sure,' I replied, looking sideways to see where Lily was.

'You never know, if I win the jackpot at bingo this week I'll be following you down.'

That would be just awful, I thought, as I stared at her.

'What's that look for?' she asked. 'Here, pass me that plate; I've nowt to flick me ash in,' she said, pointing towards the kitchen shelf.

'I thought I'd left it at home for a minute,' Lily said, giving a sigh as she walked towards me.

'That's fancy,' Mrs Patterson said as Lily passed the thin, round bottle over to me.

'Don't look so shocked, love,' she said as I stood with my mouth wide open.

'I used to have that cologne. By gum, fancy a kid like you having a bottle of 4711. Give us a dabble,' Mrs Patterson said, stretching out her neck and looking once more into the tiny mirror.

'Put it away immediately,' Lily told me, taking it off me. 'There's only half a bottle left, and you'll need that for your holiday.' She undid the button on my bag and placed it inside. 'You'll be given some spending money, won't you?'

'Wouldn't bank on that,' Mrs Patterson butted in. 'It's cost your ma a fortune this holiday. You should see all the beautiful dresses she's got.'

'Lucky you,' Lily said to me, patting me on my back.

'Not her, for God's sake, your ma.'

'That doesn't surprise me,' Lily replied.

'I've got my walking day dress that I bought from the jumble sale,' I told Lily, standing on my tiptoes and stretching up to whisper in her ear. 'Susie's mother washed it for me.'

'Well, enjoy your holiday,' Lily told me, hugging me as tightly as she could.

I wish she could stay with me, I thought, as she walked towards the door.

'Bye, Lily,' I called. She blew me a kiss before closing the door behind her.

'Make us another brew,' Mrs Patterson asked, passing me her mug.

'Look at the damn time,' Mummy said as she opened the door and rushed into the kitchen. 'Yap, yap, yap, Ruby never stops. My hair could have been done in half the time.'

'It looks very nice,' I told her, emptying the tea leaves down the sink and rinsing Mrs Patterson's mug out. I blinked as she walked closely past me.

'You'll have a brew with me, won't you, then I'll be on my way.'

'A quick one,' Mummy replied.

I quickly walked over and reached up for another mug from the row of nails that Daddy had knocked into the wall to hang them on.

'Get that fire set,' Mummy told me as she peered into the living room.

'Quite right. It'll be bloody cold in this place after a week away. Don't want to be messing about with things like that as soon as you get back,' Mrs Patterson said, placing her hand behind her back and scratching her bottom. She noticed me watching her and quickly stopped.

'Your tea's ready.'

'Pass it over, love,' she replied as she reached out and took it from my hand. 'Ouch!' she shouted as the heat from the mug went through her fingertips. Her smile turned to a snarl, showing off her heavily stained teeth, as she thanked me.

'I'll leave Mummy's on here,' I said, placing the mug on the kitchen shelf before bending down to collect the bundle of old newspapers that lay in the corner of the kitchen floor.

'Jenny, your tea's ready,' she bellowed, making me jump with fright.

I gave a little scream as a spider ran out from underneath the pile of newspapers.

'That'll make your hair curl. Go on, stand on it lass. Don't want it coming near me.'

'I can't, Mrs Patterson, it's running too fast.'

'There's no such thing as can't. Stand on the bloody thing.'

'I'm too frightened,' I told her as we watched it run underneath the cooker.

'You're a useless article if you ask me. No wonder your mother can't stand the sight of you.'

You're a horrible woman, I thought, as I wrestled with the newspapers, trying not to drop any. I listened to her slurp down the remainder of her tea as I made my way towards the living room. Susie always told me to stick two fingers up if someone was horrible to me but I'll stick three up instead, which I did as soon as I was out of view. That will teach you to be so rude to me, Mrs Patterson, I said to myself.

Chapter 15

'Stop wriggling,' little brother Charlie complained as I tossed and turned on top of the broken spring mattress we lay on.

'She's too excited about the holiday,' Teddy whispered over from the single bed he slept on near to us. 'Look, the sooner you close your eyes the quicker you'll get there. You've only until the morning to wait.'

I stared through the gap where they wouldn't quite meet in the frayed linen curtains that hung down from a thin piece of wire. I lay as still as I could and gazed out towards the stars in the dark, clear sky, imagining the journey we would take as I let my eye travel from one bright star to another until I stopped at the one that twinkled much brighter than the others. That's where we would start our holiday if we lived up there in space, I thought, before finally falling fast asleep.

The dawn was just peeping through and Daddy's bells on his alarm clock rang, echoing around the tiny landing from the open door inside his bedroom. I nudged Charlie a couple of times before he made me jump by suddenly shooting up from the hard pillow we shared and rooting for his brown spectacles from underneath.

'Charlie, this is the day we go on holiday.' Charlie lifted his wrist up towards his face, checking the imaginary watch he wore for the correct time. 'Charlie,' I asked, 'is it the first of August?' Charlie sat there very still checking through his memory. 'Well, is it?' I asked again before he agreed that it was.

My eyes flickered as I looked out through the open door of my bedroom on to the landing and up towards the bare bulb hanging down from the ceiling that suddenly lit up the stairwell. Charlie jumped down off the bed and ran towards the chamber. I quickly peeped out from the bedroom window into the dusky morning to see if Mr Ramsbottom, the milkman, just might be there so I could wave goodbye to him for a whole week.

Charlie and I dressed as quickly as we could and I ran down the narrow stairs to sit and guard the packed luggage in Mummy's best room until Charlie appeared. 'Will you take guard,' I asked, 'when you've finished?' before he disappeared through into the living room towards the kitchen to brush his teeth over the sink with the toothbrush we shared. I crossed my legs and waited. Hurry, Charlie, I'm dying to go to the toilet, I said to myself whilst slipping the long strap of my bag that Lily had crocheted for me over my shoulder.

'Looks like she wants to be first out,' I heard Frieda say, drawing Mummy's attention to where I sat.

Mummy pulled me up towards her by the tip of my ear. 'Get that kettle filled and make some tea, you ungrateful little bitch, sitting next to the door thinking you'll be first in the queue. You should be staying behind with one of the neighbours; that's if they'd have you. Then you'd probably appreciate the next holiday you might have, instead of getting me in debt to pay for you to come along with us.'

So scared of being left behind, I let Mummy drag me along showing no pain as she squeezed my arm, digging her red painted nails into my flesh until she broke the skin, leaving tiny round bubbles of blood to surface.

Charlie panicked and spat out immediately over the sink, leaving a froth of toothpaste around his mouth as I was hurled into the kitchen. My hands shook as I scooped the loose tea from the caddy into the hollow cracked base of the plump teapot.

'Why are you crying?' Teddy asked, wandering through.

I didn't answer, trying to catch my breath as Teddy wiped my face with the smelly old dishcloth after squeezing it out from the running tap of ice cold water.

'Don't look so sad,' he told me before I ran out in tears towards the dark, brick building to use the toilet. I jumped off the seat as the squeak of the hooting horn was heard from outside.

'The driver's here to take us,' I told Teddy, rushing back in whilst struggling to pull down the ruffle on my skirt before wiping my hands across my face. Teddy led me through, with Frieda at the head, to board the minibus.

'Now our holiday really does begin,' he told me, guiding me up over the two iron steps to make sure I got a view by the window before sitting back against the head of the cushioned seat next to me.

'All on board,' Daddy called as he hopped on the bus after Mummy and Frieda had taken their seats. Teddy saluted after turning to check. 'Let the steam engines roll then,' Daddy told the driver.

With the click of the door closed and locked, I stared with my face pressed up against the window just in case

Eric and Mrs Crowswick were waving me off. I probably couldn't see them, not through Mrs Crowswick's net curtains, so I waved and waved over to the window where they might have been standing until the minibus roared up its engine and took me completely out of view.

'Do you think we've travelled to the other end of the world?' I asked Teddy whilst staring through the window towards the high mountains.

'Doubt it,' he replied, yawning quite heavily as the long journey continued over the bumpy road.

'Well, we're passing through Africa right now,' I said, nudging him with urgency to look through the window with me at the sheep that wore long, curly tusks on top of their heads. 'We could... We just might see some elephants.'

'You and your geography. You're not going to see one no matter how long you keep your face glued to that window. Elephants don't live in Wales.'

'Why?' I asked him.

'Because it's not hot enough.'

I still carried on with my search just in case.

The minibus finally stopped and we all left in single file to a spray of smiling faces wearing bright red jackets with golden badges pinned on their pockets, each with a different name.

'I hope you've brought the sunny weather with you,' a tall thin man, wearing the same, leant down to ask.

'We haven't,' I whispered to Teddy, nudging him. 'Will you tell him there wasn't enough room in our suitcases?'

'For what?' Teddy asked annoyingly.

'To bring the weather,' I whispered.

Daddy handed us the long iron key with the label dangling from the ring. 'Well, off you go, you two.'

'Looks like we're sharing.'

'Chalet two-one-two,' Daddy called as Teddy checked that the straps of the haversack he had packed were still firmly fastened around his narrow shoulders.

The excitement took my breath away, stepping out into the magical world of the holiday camp, with a brass band playing jolly music against the crash of cymbals as Teddy and I walked along to the beat in search of chalet 212. 'My heart's fluttering,' I told Teddy with excitement.

'Well, in that case, take a deep breath, cos there's so many more exciting things for you to see.'

'What?' I asked, peering up towards the numbers along every row.

'Well, there's the children's theatre,' he replied whilst checking we were still heading in the right direction. 'It's a place where you sit on chairs that slant down in rows towards the stage.'

'Will I fall out?' I asked.

'No, but you'll laugh. There'll be Punch and Judy and a magician waving a magic wand.'

I stopped and thought, 'Like the ones the fairies hold?' I asked.

'It's a black and white stick. You tap it on top of a hat and the magic things appear from underneath. Look, as soon as we've found our chalet, I'll show you the programme I was given when we arrived. I'll take you there myself.'

'Where?'

'To the children's theatre. And no, I'm not going to

leave you – if that's what that look's for. We'll both laugh together. Look, there it is ... chalet two-one-two. Hurry!'

Teddy opened the lock on the red-painted door and we both stepped inside. 'Just look, Teddy, our own bunk beds and a sink where we can wash,' I said, standing in wonder.

'Can I cadge the top bunk?' he asked as he stared up towards it whilst slipping the straps of his haversack down from over his shoulders. It was agreed with a nod. 'Aren't you excited?' he called out after throwing his rucksack on top and climbing up the ladder as I perched myself on the edge of the bunk below.

'Yes, I'm just waiting for my luggage so that I can wear my pretty dress.'

'What pretty dress?'

'The one I bought at the jumble sale, Teddy. Have you forgotten?'

'What colour is it?'

'White, Teddy with a net underskirt underneath. See, you have.'

'Have what?' he asked as I listened to him rustle through his belongings.

'Forgotten.'

'We're in the chalet next door. Charlie's sharing with me,' Frieda told Teddy, peeping her head around the door before throwing a bundle of clothes on the floor next to my feet, then disappearing.

'What's that sigh for?' Teddy asked.

'Will you go and ask Frieda if she's forgotten?'

'What?'

'To give me my dress.'

'Didn't you pack it yourself?'

'No, Mummy said that Frieda had to do all the packing because she's the sensible one. I'll check once again,' I called, feeling a huge lump inside my throat. 'It's not here, Teddy, in this bundle. There's two vests, a t-shirt, a blouse and my pleated skirt I wear for school, but no dress,' I whispered, feeling a tear roll down my cheek. I felt confused, yet desperately happy as Teddy leapt down over the last two steps of the ladder and handed me my dream, the prettiest dress I had ever seen.

'Frieda must have forgotten to put it inside the suitcase,' I told Teddy.

'Yes, I found it lying on the floor in her bedroom when I checked that all the windows were shut before we set off. It still smells of mothballs but only a little. Well, come on then, hurry,' Teddy told me as he turned his back.

I quickly got changed, and then coughed a little. 'I'm ready,' I called.

Teddy whizzed around in a flash. 'Lorne, you look beautiful, just like a princess.'

'But I haven't got a crown, have I?' I asked, feeling the top of my head just in case a fairy had surprised me and placed one there.

'See, everyone's looking at just how pretty you are in that dress.'

I stopped and stepped back to look at my image through the shiny glass shop window we had passed to see if Teddy was telling the truth.

'We'll be late for tea,' he said, guiding me by the hand along the narrow pavement that took us through a magical world.

I held on to him tightly as we reached the long queue. We were eventually shown to our table, passing the hustle and bustle of waiters and waitresses that rushed up and down the aisle wearing white uniforms with pinnies tied around their waists and cloth caps, frilly ones and plain, placed on top of their heads.

After eating in silence at the same table as Mummy and Daddy in the huge dining hall, with Frieda sitting opposite, her eyes peering towards me, Teddy guided Charlie and me out into the fresh air. He asked Charlie to remind him of the number of his chalet. 'It's only so I know that you've remembered should we lose you in a crowd.'

'Two-one-three,' Charlie replied sharply, adjusting his round spectacles that always slipped down the length of his straight nose. I gripped on to Charlie's hand tightly as Teddy told us we were off to the theatre.

Charlie and I sat still in wonder after climbing step after step to take a seat that sprung upright if you didn't catch hold of it in time. I thought of Lily as the huge velvet curtains opened to a cheer of clapping hands, and wished she was sitting next to me to hear the gasp of excitement as the magician appeared holding a magic wand through glove covered fingers.

'Abracadabra,' he called out in a husky voice. 'Repeat after me,' the tall, well rounded magician called out to everyone.

'Abracadabra,' everyone screamed, including Charlie.

Suddenly, the magician's tall, black, silk hat, after tapping it with his stick, started to move right there on top of his head. I looked towards Teddy in fear.

'You'll miss it,' he said, nudging me to look forward, down towards the stage.

A rabbit as white as snow appeared from inside the hollow as the magician lifted his hat. The seat of Charlie's chair sprang back as he jumped up and stared down in amazement. The sudden excitement died down and Charlie sat back in his chair. If only Eric could be here too, wouldn't he have a wonderful time, just like me, I thought. Charlie and I smiled at each other with excitement, wondering what would come next. I felt sorry for the two girls who sat in the row in front after they sneezed and then turned their heads and looked directly at me. They must be twins, I thought, both with the same freckled faces and long red hair, tied into pony tails with bright tartan ribbons fastened in bows. They turned and stared at me again, gathering together closely and whispering in each other's ear. They must be admiring my dress, I thought, conscious of their stares. I was sure they wished that they could look like princesses too. I wanted to give them the address of the road where the jumble sale was held so they could go to the next one to find a dress as pretty as mine. I would keep my fingers crossed for them if they did.

A juggler appeared on stage, missing his catch more than once to the hiss of his audience. Charlie still clapped and so did Teddy, and I clapped too. The two girls bowed their heads and sneezed again. One of them turned and wrinkled her flat nose towards me. They both stood suddenly, with a loud slap from the seat of their chairs, squeezed their fingers around their nostrils and turned once again, glaring at me through the flicker of their ginger lashes before leaving for a seat further below to the roar of excitement and the clapping of hands as the juggler threw the skittles in the air once again, catching them as they twirled down towards him. My face turned bright red with embarrassment. I felt a huge lump stuck inside my throat and tears instantly filled my eyes.

'Come on, Lorne, get some spirit in you,' Teddy called, applauding along with the others.

My hands tingled and felt weak from clapping them together. I glanced towards Charlie and then Teddy who was sitting in amazement enjoying the show. 'Do I smell?' I asked Teddy. 'Well, do I?' I asked, sniffing up in the air as the applause died down.

'Only of mothballs,' he told me.

I wanted to run all the way back to Rose Cottage where I could wave to my friends through the bedroom window and see Eric and Mrs Crowswick, and my special sister, Lily.

'Why are you crying?' Teddy asked as the people on stage scurried around preparing for the next act.

'I'm homesick,' I whispered, skipping a breath.

'You'll make it worse,' Teddy said as I unclipped my bag and lifted a tiny bottle of cologne out.

'Lily gave it to me.'

'I know she did, Lorne, but it won't take that smell away.'

'What smell?'

'Mothballs,' Teddy whispered taking the cologne and placing it back into my bag. 'Lorne, whatever's wrong?'

I didn't answer but buried my head in my hands.

'You're tired. Come on, Charlie, let's head off. Anyway,

it's time you were both in your beds. It's been a long day.'

I buried my head in shame as we walked down the steps, passing the row of seats where the twins sat, before Charlie, Teddy and I left through the theatre door.

'You're probably wondering why my heart's broken.' Teddy didn't answer as we walked in between crowds of people. 'Well, it is.'

'Lorne will you please tell me why it is?' he asked, pulling Charlie away from the attractions in the brightly lit amusement arcade as a gang of drunken youths staggered by.

We walked slowly that evening back along the row of chalets. I didn't look up to the sky for the magical star that had shone so bright, but gripped hold of Charlie's hand tight until we came to the light that burned in chalet 213. Teddy tapped on the door. Frieda opened it, her long fingers curled over a paperback book. It's probably about witches, I thought, holding back the tears in my eyes as tightly as I could. She welcomed Charlie in before suddenly shutting the door and closing it tightly behind her.

'What's the matter, Lorne?' Teddy asked as he placed the key into the lock of chalet 212 whilst I sniffed up the tears that now flowed. 'You can't keep breaking your heart all the time. It's not good.'

'But I'm not the one that's breaking it.'

'Well, who is then?'

I didn't want to tell him about the twins who looked at me scornfully before they moved away just in case it would spoil his holiday too.

'Look, I've got to be back here for ten. Mind if I have a wander around? The door's locked,' he shouted from outside. 'Don't open it to anyone.'

I listened with my ear pressed to the door as Teddy's footsteps slowly faded away into the night. I tried to wrinkle my nose at the smell, the smell of mothballs. 'I'll never be able to wear you again,' I cried out, pitifully, reaching behind and undoing the zip. 'Do you want to know why? Because everybody thinks that you smell and we don't want anyone to pull faces at us while I'm wearing you, do we?' I shivered with goose pimples as I rolled my dress that had gently fallen down on to the floor into a tight bundle. My stubbornness told me to open the chalet door and throw it outside so the wind might come and blow it away, but my heart wouldn't let me.

The long strip of fluorescent light fixed to the ceiling shone brightly as I lay in bed with my dress tucked in beside me, trying to plan in my mind how many postcards I would send to all my friends. The robin who hops around in the yard at Rose Cottage would be sent one – one with snowy capped mountains so he can dream about winter and the snow that will fall at Christmas time. I smiled a little at the thought of him while holding my hands together to say a prayer.

'Dear God, I'm going to go to sleep now, only because my eyes keep closing and I keep on yawning. I'm wondering if you know that I'm on holiday and if you have looked down from heaven. Did you see those twins pulling a face at me? That's because my dress smelled of mothballs. I felt very, very sorry for myself tonight, and my dress. I don't think I will be able to find the courage to wear it again whilst I'm here on holiday

but I have thought about saving it to wear when I get home, when I'm with Eric in his garden, that's if he recognizes me when I knock on his door. You see, he might think I'm a princess but I'll tell him it's only me when he opens it. I'm trying very hard to forgive the twins but they squeezed their noses at me too. I suppose I will, though, forgive them. Do you know why? Because they don't know how important it is to be kind to others do they, God? But I still feel sad. I don't feel any more pain now, now that I'm speaking to you. Well, just a little. I have tucked myself into bed with my dress beside me. There's even a nice, clean woolly blanket that covers my toes to keep them warm. Excuse me, God, for yawning again. I'm going to fall asleep now. You will get a postcard too. I'll try and find one with clouds floating around in the sky with the sun that shines through. Your son, Jesus, makes us all feel warm.'

I don't remember falling to sleep and waking up early that morning to the sound of Teddy snoring. I quickly dressed into my grey pleated skirt before fastening the loose buttons on my white blouse. Don't fall off, I whispered to the top one that dangled from a brown thread of cotton as I slipped my feet inside my red plastic sandals. My bare toes squeaked inside them as I stepped over the rug on to the solid bare floor. I reached to turn the latch, waiting as I locked it, in between Teddy's snores, before I quietly left to go on an adventure all on my own.

Chapter 16

The door banged shut. I turned anxiously. The curtain inside chalet 213 moved like a ghost. Frieda must have spotted me. I ran as fast as I could with a beating heart down the long row of chalets into the gentle atmosphere of the holiday camp. Seagulls squawked overhead as I calmly walked along the pathway.

Old men with coughs queued up for newspapers whilst I stood on tiptoe admiring the postcards stacked above one another on racks in the open air. The queue got longer with puffs of cigarette smoke whirling up into the damp morning air. I quickly decided to move on.

A podgy boy was hit on the back of his head, forcing him to spit his chewing gum out on the ground. He threw a tantrum, screaming and stamping his short pale legs up and down to the annoyance of his stern looking parents as I passed by.

'Not open yet, lovely,' the grey-haired old lady with rags stuffed inside her overall pockets and a mop in her hand said, as I stood staring through the open door at all the prizes stacked high on the shelves. 'Anyway, kids aren't allowed to play bingo,' I was told as she carried on mopping the dark red tiles around the worn, matted carpet covering the floor.

'It's very colourful in here, isn't it?'

'More colourful if you win a game,' she replied, laughing to herself before coughing up phlegm from the back of her throat and spitting it out on a screwed up paper towel that she pulled out from underneath her sleeve.

I imagined Mrs Patterson sitting there, around the circle where the bingo caller would stand, with her hair stiffly in place, chipped bright red nail polish on her long fingers, closing the tiny shutters on the board game in front, anxiously waiting to win. I shuddered at the thought of her sitting there and ran as fast as I could along the pavement in front away from my imagination.

I took a step back from ducks clucking from hunger as they floated around the oasis on top of the rippling waves underneath the dark, cloudy water of the lake. My knees shook with the fear of water. I stepped back a little further and watched from afar. That was when my heart sank, when I saw a girl, someone as tiny as me, holding on to her Mummy's hand, jumping with joy as bread was ripped and thrown with care to the quack of open beaks. I saw other parents with their children and watched as they kissed and cuddled with arms stretched around, giving comfort and love to their crying children when the last crumb had gone. I sighed as I stood there, catching my breath and sighed once more at the love that I saw in this moment in time that I could only dream of.

Leaving the hustle and bustle behind, with the key gripped tightly inside the palm of my hand, I walked along the quiet pathway, passing sweet-scented flowers that grew in clusters along the borders.

There were no passers by, just bees and bugs hovering over scented flowers scattered along the narrow borders.

My toes, squashed together inside my red plastic sandals, began to ache. I shivered at the thought of blisters. I thought about my best friend, Eric. Oh, Eric, if only you were here with me right now, I wouldn't feel lost and alone. I tried to tell the lump inside my throat, as I limped further along, to go away, that I would soon find my way back to my holiday chalet, but it wouldn't. Then it was too late, I started to cry.

'You're there,' Teddy called in a panic, running towards me. 'Lorne, what is it?'

'My heart's broken.'

'Lorne, you can't keep breaking it; haven't I told you that? Look, you've to go back to the chalet and smarten up. Mother's instructions. We've to be in the ballroom in half an hour.'

'But I can't dance.'

'It's nothing to do with dancing, Lorne, it's a competition.'

'A quiz?' I asked. 'But I won't know any answers.'

'You can stop guessing, Lorne. It's a competition to find the happiest family on camp. "Family Album", I think it's called. Piggy back?' he asked. 'Don't be scared, just hold tight around my neck. You won't fall, promise. Not that tight, Lorne,' Teddy told me, coughing as he spoke.

'Who do you think will win?' I asked as Teddy lowered me on to the ground before searching inside the pocket of my long coat and taking the key out from inside.

'Anyone's guess, isn't it? Come on, Lorne, instead of standing there thinking.' Teddy opened the chalet door, allowing me to be first to step inside. 'Reckon you'd better wear that white lacy dress of yours. Stop sniffing at it, Lorne. You can't go dressed as you are.' I screwed my face every time Teddy dragged the fine toothed comb through my hair.

'Keep still, Lorne, and stop shouting ouch. You'll soon be able to put it up into a pony tail when it's grown a little longer.'

'With a ribbon fastened around it?' I asked 'Ouch,' I shouted again

'Where's your slide?' I quickly pulled it out. 'You store everything in those coat pockets of yours. Keep still, Lorne.' Teddy clipped my fringe back before he rushed me through the open door, slamming it tightly behind him. 'Give me your hand, Lorne,' he said, dragging at my arm as he strolled along. He wouldn't slow down, ignoring my complaints and nearly tripping over my own two feet.

The stairs were bare and wide. Teddy pulled at my hand as I sighed on each step I climbed up the long staircase. The ballroom was packed with seated crowds. Teddy stopped in his tracks for a moment then tugged at my hand once more. The centre floor looked shiny and slippery. I jumped as we walked across.

'It's only the microphone whistling,' he told me, pointing towards the stage before pulling me along further. I pulled back and looked up. Teddy stopped. 'They're called chandeliers, Lorne.'

'They're diamonds, aren't they, Teddy?' I said, looking up towards the sparkle of glittering stones reflecting down underneath clusters of brightly lit bulbs. I felt a little dizzy and spots appeared in front of my eyes. 'I can't see,' I complained as Teddy continued to pull me along.

'You've been dazzled, Lorne; and stop limping. You've

worn those sandals long enough to be used to them.' I pulled my hand back from his. 'Lorne.'

Refusing to speak to him any more, I followed behind.

'Will all contestants form a queue,' a quivering voice spoke over the crackly microphone.

Teddy grabbed back hold, gripping my hand much tighter. 'He's the commentator,' I was told as I turned my head slightly towards the stage to where the stocky, elderly, grey-haired man in a dark pinstripe suit stood.

The ballroom rumbled and seats to chairs flapped as people stood. Droves of families moved around, creating a queue that reached the far corners of the ballroom floor.

'We're over here, my boy.' With the melody of an Irish accent, I knew then that that was my Daddy's call.

Teddy raised his arm and saluted. 'Stick hold tight, Lorne.'

Bewildered amongst the hum of voices and people's faces, I tried to spot where Daddy could be. Teddy was soon to loosen my grip and stood me right by the side of Mummy. Daddy leant his head forward and winked. I winked back. Mummy wore white lace gloves and a polka dot suit. I gasped at how beautiful she looked. Daddy moved along, checking we were all in line, whilst straightening his dark blue tie underneath the stiff paper collar on his white shirt. His moustache had been neatly trimmed and his hair, with a tint of grey, Brylcreemed back from the frown lines on his forehead. Mummy checked her French pleat was clipped firmly into place before we, as family number five, were called on to the stage. A photographer grouped us closely together. Charlie stood in front and I was placed behind.

'You stink in that dress,' Frieda told me when she was asked to stand next to me. I saw relief on her face when the photographer shuffled her further along. Mummy and Daddy were placed on either side. Charlie was told to save his smile whilst the photographer rolled on a film. Clear sharp whistles directed at Mummy floated through the air as she stood posing for the camera.

'Lorne, you're supposed to look happy,' Teddy whispered in my ear, nudging me before the bright flash of the camera struck. The padre, dressed in a long black gown, sat back, relaxed, on the wooden-backed chair, tapping a wooden pencil against his lips. Sitting shoulders apart, the matron, with her frilly starched cap clipped stiff upon her head, looked deep in thought. Her face looked grey and stern. She was sitting next to the Queen of Latin Dancing, who sat pondering with shoulders straight, a net of sequins glittering over a twist of shiny auburn hair that was pulled back and rolled over tightly into a bun on top of her head.

'They're the judges,' Teddy told me as they stared across towards us. 'So stop fidgeting Lorne,' as I reached out to see if my hair slide had melted under the glare of spotlights above. 'Stop standing pigeon-toed, and take that sad look from your face. We might have to smile once more.'

The photographer knelt down on one leg, squinting his eye against the lens of his camera. I was scared, really scared, standing there in full view for everyone to see. I stared beyond the table of judges. Films of patchy smoke from lit cigarettes floated through the air. The camera immediately flashed and the audience clapped as we were led down from the stage. Charlie sneezed in the line where we stood. 'Bless you,' I called, leaning my head forward. Frieda grabbed hold of my hair and pulled me back.

The commentator finally called down into the microphone that he was ready to announce the first, second and third in reverse order. Teddy ignored the puzzled look on my face. Mummy stood nervously holding a square white card with the number five printed in black. Daddy wiped the sweat from his brow. With roaring cheers from the crowd, the winner was at last called out. We were rushed up the steps and back on to the stage.

'We've won,' Charlie told me in excitement, looking at me through his round lop sided spectacles.

'Won what?' I asked, straightening them for him. Charlie shrugged his shoulders and so did I. We all smiled once more for the camera. Mummy's face beamed. She reached out her hand. No one took it. I hesitated before taking the few steps over to hold it. Mummy pushed me back, welcoming an onlooker, a short stocky man who had stepped up from behind on to the stage to congratulate her, clenching a thick round cigar in between the gap of his short stained teeth.

'You still stink,' Frieda told me whilst sniffing over my shoulder. 'We would never have won if the judges had smelled you.'

Teddy gripped me by the elbow. 'Come on, Lorne; let's get you back to the chalet so you can change.'

The crowd had started to dwindle. Teddy tugged at my elbow. Mummy gave me a scornful glance. Teddy used his weight and firmly led me towards the top of the steep stairs. I spat out in temper before taking my first step down. My body shivered, covered in angry goose pimples as Teddy pushed the key into the lock of the chalet door. 'I won't ever come out of here again,' I told him, stamping my bottom down on to the edge of the bed.

'Women,' Teddy muttered, closing the door behind him.

I felt another lump inside my throat and sang lullabies to make myself feel better, whilst struggling to undo the ragged zip on the side of my dress.

'Lorne, I'm not going anywhere without you,' Teddy shouted, knocking twice on the door.

'You scared me,' I called, finally stepping out of my dress, 'and anyway, I'm in a bad temper.'

'Then why are you singing "Go to sleep, my baby, close your sleepy eyes"?'

'Because I'm hiding my dress away for ever,' I shouted, rolling it up into a ball.

'Lorne, come on, let's go ice-skating.'

'I can't skate, especially on ice,' I called out, before crawling out from underneath the wire springs, leaving my dress to lie on the bare stone floor underneath the bed.

'Then let's go swimming.'

'I'm scared of water, and anyway, I can't swim and my throat's getting sore calling out to you.'

'So is mine,' Teddy replied, whilst I stood and dusted myself down.

'Well hurry and get changed. And give us a smile, then,' Teddy said, straightening the collar of my long red coat after I had found the courage to open the door. He gently took my hand and we walked in silence. 'Would you like to go boating on the lake?' I shook my head in fear.

'Then how about the funfair? Don't tell me, Lorne,' as I looked up towards him, 'you're scared of that, too. Come on, Lorne, let's give it a go, and stop lagging behind. I'm having to tug at you all the way. Your head's turning and twisting in all directions.'

Chapter 17

'Lorne, Lorne.' I recognised the voice and immediately turned around as Teddy ran across the narrow road towards me. 'Get this coat on ... wandering off. You know I'm in charge of you for the week. Lorne, stick your arms down through the sleeves. Aren't you cold? See, you're shivering.'

Teddy straightened my collar and waited until I had fastened all the buttons.

'Where are your socks?' he asked, looking down the length of my long red coat that stopped just above my ankles. 'Come on, it's time for breakfast.'

I quickly followed behind and queued up once more, stepping with one foot at a time until we reached the wide open doors that led us into the dining hall. I hesitated before sitting on the wooden seat on the vacant chair next to Frieda. She turned her head away in disgust as I sat myself down.

Charlie was sitting straight across, looking through his thick rimmed spectacles towards me. 'Take them off,' I told him as the steam from the bowl of porridge the waiter had placed in front of him covered his lenses with mist. 'Can you see me, Charlie?' I asked after he took them off. Charlie smiled towards me showing the gap in between his front teeth and I smiled back. Frieda abruptly left, calling over the table to Mummy that she would meet her in the coffee lounge. I passed the bacon she had left on her plate over to Teddy who stuffed it inside a bread roll and ate it at once.

'I'll have the porridge,' I whispered in Teddy's ear as the waiter stood waiting for our attention. Mummy stood up and left, with Daddy following behind. The chairs surrounding the table were soon deserted, leaving just Teddy, Charlie and me.

'Your teeth will rot, Lorne,' Teddy told me, lifting the glass sugar sprinkler from my hands after I had shaken the glistening grains over the thick bowl of porridge I was ready to eat.

Charlie looked over my shoulder, squinting, before slipping his glasses on and looking again, making me turn with curiosity. 'Doesn't she make you want to pull your tongue out at her, Charlie?' I asked as Frieda beckoned him over with an evil look in her cold, dark eyes. Charlie was too scared to answer and stood, leaving almost immediately.

'What's the number of our chalet?' Teddy asked, chewing on the last bit of bacon from his plate.

Surprised that he'd forgotten, I stopped blowing the steam from the porridge I'd scooped up on my spoon. 'Two-one-two,' I replied.

'You're blowing too hard, Lorne,' Teddy told me as I tried to save the porridge with my hands before it dropped back into the bowl. 'Look, now I know you've remembered I'll give you the key. You need to go and put some socks on. You can borrow my comb too, I've left it on the sink.' Teddy sat and waited until I couldn't eat any more and then I left with him. 'I'll be getting changed too but only after I've snooped around this place. There's so much to see,' he said as he slowly wandered off. 'What's the number of the chalet?' he called, leaving me standing there. 'Well?' shouting in the distance.

'Two-one-two,' I called. Teddy, with his back still turned lifted his arm, raising his thumb up into the air before disappearing out of view. I wandered off watching groups of families passing me by with cheerful looks on their faces, making me hope with all my heart that Mummy would enjoy her holiday, enjoy it so much that it would make her happy for ever and ever. I crossed my fingers and thought that if my wish came true I would never ever again feel the dread of going back home to Rose Cottage.

It was a humid afternoon. As I walked along the narrow pavement, trying to find my bearings, the aroma of food from the tiny café lingered in the air. I was relieved to discover that I was going in the right direction, noticing the oblong sign with a painted arrow and the word 'Amusements' printed next to it.

The atmosphere seemed to come alive as I got closer. I could hear a man's voice calling out numbers. Just look at all those lovely prizes, I said to myself as I walked past the bingo hall, stopping for a second to watch the coloured balls flying up and down in the air. This is so exciting, I thought, stepping into the amusement arcade where I could hear all the different sounds coming from the machines.

Wow, he's lucky! A young boy pulled the handle down before scooping up the pennies that had dropped into the tray beneath. I could hear the sound of laughter and wandered over in the direction it was coming from. I stood slightly back as a tall, gangly girl stood laughing at a puppet. I wondered why he was dressed as a policeman. He seemed to stare me straight in the eye as he stood in his glass box laughing repeatedly. 'Sorry,' I said, accidentally bumping into a mother carrying a young child as I moved away.

You'll never do it, I thought, watching two boys manoeuvre the tiny handle of a crane inside a tall plastic container as they tried to pick up one of the prizes that lay squashed in a pile. They squealed with excitement as the teeth of the little crane caught hold of a tiny plastic doll; then sighed as it dropped back on to the pile. They seemed somewhat embarrassed as they turned around and saw me watching. 'Don't waste your money on that thing,' they told me as they began to walk away. 'Anyway, the prizes are crap.' I stepped forward to take a closer look. They don't look crap to me, I thought, as I stared at all the fluffy toys.

'Excuse me, miss,' I heard a man's voice say. I stepped aside and he picked up the keys that were dangling from the loop around the waist of his trousers and walked over to the machine. 'Haven't you won anything?' he asked, looking at my empty hands before placing the key into the lock and turning it.

'I haven't had a go yet,' I replied as he emptied the tray full of pennies into the canvas bag.

'Well, don't leave it too long; they'll soon be gone,' he told me, patting me on my head before he left. I hesitated. If I put some money in, which way should I turn the handle to win a prize? What if I lose? But I wouldn't mind winning that tiny, pink teddy bear, I thought, once again peering through the clear plastic container to take a closer look.

'I'm first.'

'No you're not, I am,' said one to another as I was surrounded by a group of girls.

'Budge,' another said, pushing one of the girls to one side as she attempted to place her money in the narrow oblong slot. I felt slightly nervous and quietly slipped past them. I'll come again when it's not as busy, I thought, making my way back to the entrance.

My eyes squinted with the strong sun as I stepped back into daylight. The gentle music playing softly over the tannoy made me feel peaceful as I wandered again along the pathway. An odd-looking lady stood by a funny booth smiled, one leg crossed around the other as she leant against the open door. It reminded me of Christmas, the tiny coloured fairy lights flickering on and off pinned around the door.

'Hello,' she said as I came closer. 'Fancy having your fortune told?' She paused and took a drag of her cigarette.

'Do you tell the truth?' I asked, looking towards the open door.

'See that crystal ball?' she said, pointing towards the ball on the table. 'When I look through that I can tell you anything, but you have to cross my palm with silver.'

I looked up at her. She was quite a pretty lady, her colourful scarf wrapped around the top of her head allowing her long black hair to flow down on to her back. Her long, slender hands matched her body and her bright red painted fingernails glowed in the sunlight as she once again placed her cigarette in between her lips and inhaled the smoke.

'Could you tell me if I'm going to meet a prince?' I asked, looking into her eyes. 'But not one that wears any armour. He'll always feel hot and sticky underneath it all and he won't be able to bend down properly to pick me up and take me away with him.'

'Come on, my dear,' a plump man said, barging into the booth. 'Tell me what's in store for me then, and no bullshit.' He brushed by me and sat down inside the room. She quickly followed and I carried on along the pathway.

'Hey,' I heard a voice call, followed by two whistles. I turned around and there was Teddy running towards me. 'I'm on my way to the fairground. Fancy coming?' he asked, slightly out of breath.

'You look nice in the new t-shirt and shorts,' I told him.

'Suppose I do. Well, do you fancy it or not?'

'I'm not going on any rides. I'd be too scared.'

'Follow me,' he said, walking briskly ahead of me. 'Well, what do you think?'

'Of what?'

'This place.'

'It's wonderful, Teddy.'

'Going swimming later on. Coming for a dip?'

'You're walking too fast,' I called. 'Slow down. You know I can't swim,' I told him as I caught up to him. 'And anyway, I've already told you how frightened I am of water.'

'Look over there. Fancy a ride on that?'

I didn't answer as I turned and watched the huge wheel from a distance go around and around.

'Can't you move a little faster?' he asked.

'I'll try, Teddy,' I replied, hastening my step. I could hear the roar from the rides as we got closer. The man in uniform nodded to me as I reluctantly walked through the gates. 'I can't hear you,' I shouted, listening to all the different sounds crashing through the air as Teddy began talking to me.

'Fancy the waltzer?' he shouted.

He grabbed my hand and marched me alongside him. 'Why is everyone screaming?' I asked as he pulled me up the three wooden steps.

I almost lost my breath as the oval chairs turned around and around underneath the dazzle of flashing lights. 'I'm going dizzy,' I told him, slipping my hand from his. The steps felt unsteady as I climbed back down.

'It's not as bad as it looks. Come back,' he called. I turned around and shook my head. 'Where are you going?' he asked, jumping down the steps.

'I don't know. I'm just going to follow the signs,' I replied, making my way back towards the gates. 'Nearly spent up; have you, Teddy?'

'Well, just today's spending money. Anyway, it's a good job nearly everything's free. Won't change your mind, then?'

'No,' I replied, quite sternly, feeling a little scared in case he insisted.

'Catch up with you later, then,' he said, giving me a little pat on my shoulder.

* * *

I'll never catch her attention, I thought, watching her turn over the pages of the heavily bound book as she read on, moving her fingers along every line. All of a sudden she rested her finger at a certain point, and without taking her eyes off it, searched around the table for a pen. It looks as though she's underlining something, I thought, as she rested the tip of the pen on to the page and moved it straight along. She lifted her head slightly with a look of satisfaction. Then she looked directly at me, smiling, before beckoning me to step inside.

'I've just come to say goodbye,' I told her as I held the door partly open before stepping inside.

'I'll miss seeing you walk past my window,' she told me as she stood up and reached for my hand.

'Can you really see into the future?'

'Past as well,' she smiled, pulling out a stool for me to sit on.

I gave a little shiver. I'd never been so near to a crystal ball before. I couldn't take my eyes off it. 'Do you scare people?' I asked, moving my bottom around on top of the stool to find a comfortable position.

'Not deliberately,' she replied, before sitting herself down. I noticed she had a slight Irish accent. 'The crystal ball sees many things,' she said, placing her hands over the top of it. 'It's getting very warm. You must cross my palm with silver to bring you luck or the story can't be told.'

'But I haven't enough,' I told her, lifting up my bag that hung down from my shoulder. I shook it and heard the jingling of the small amount of money I had saved. I quickly undid the buckle and searched around inside. 'There's only ha'pennies,' lifting some out to show her.

'The feelings I had are slowly going away,' she said, looking straight at me.

'Hold on, I'll get some silver from the amusement arcade,' I told her, jumping off my stool and running out of the door. Soon I was ducking and weaving through all the people that were strolling along the street.

I ignored the usual jingle of bells and the sound of money that echoed as it dropped into the machines. 'Can you give me some silver for this?' I asked, standing on my tiptoes and stretching my legs so that I could reach the counter.

'How much have you got?' said the man, looking disgruntled at me as I tipped it all out. 'Could do without these fiddly things,' he mumbled, quickly sliding the coins up into his hands and dropping them into the drawer that he was leaning against.

He didn't look up as he slid a sixpence in my direction. I picked it up and thanked him before quickly turning around and running as fast as I could through the arcade and back out on to the street that led me to the fortune teller.

'I'm back,' I called, pushing open the door. 'It's not very shiny,' I said, lifting myself back on to the stool. I gave it a rub against my coat before placing it on to the palm of her hand.

'My name is Rose,' she said, bending her shoulder down.

I heard the tinkle of the sixpence as she let it drop against the rest of the silver coins that lay in a floral painted bowl on the stone flagged floor next to where she was sitting. She looked at me as if waiting for a reply. 'My name's Lorne,' I told her. 'I live in a house that has the same name as you. It's called Rose Cottage.'

'That sounds nice,' she replied.

'It isn't really. The walls are damp and the wallpaper keeps hanging down. Daddy sticks it together, but after a few days it starts to hang down again. Daddy says a very rude word when it happens. He threw his shoe at it one day and it landed on the table breaking Mummy's glass vase. Then they had another fight. He twisted Mummy's arm around her back. She started to scream and I kicked him as hard as I could on his leg. I yelled at him to let go because I thought that Mummy's arm might drop off. But they've had a nice holiday. Mummy's won all the fashion and beauty competitions this week.'

'Yes, I saw her. She's a very beautiful woman,' Rose whispered.

'Yes, she is, isn't she?' She beckoned me to stretch out my arm. I felt slightly nervous allowing her to touch my hand. She slowly turned it, inspecting very closely the lines on my palm. Her unvarnished nails looked old and discoloured as she guided them along. Maybe she didn't have time to polish them today, I thought. I gazed at her with a curious look on my face.

'Keep still, my child,' she said as I fiddled around in my seat yet again. She didn't move when she spoke to me. She must be concentrating very hard, I thought, noticing the frown that had suddenly appeared on her forehead. 'You've lived in a very dark past.'

'Have I?'

'Yes, very dark.'

'Only in winter,' I told her. 'I'm not allowed to switch my light on in the bedroom, and I get scared. You're very clever aren't you?' I told her, feeling excited at what she might say next.

'You have a very special friend who you love dearly. It could be a man or a woman.'

'It's God,' I quickly told her. 'I've written him a postcard and I'm going to leave it in the church. Eric as well. I love him too. And Susie and Harry.'

'You do a lot of crying.'

'Yes, but I'm going to try not to any more. It makes my eyes and lips swell and there's never any toilet paper there so I can't wipe my nose.'

'Your hands feel weak, you must find more strength.' She lifted up her head and looked me straight in the face. 'There's someone very mean to you in your life.'

'Yes, it's Frieda, my sister. She picks on me all the time. Mummy doesn't like me either. Well, that's what Mrs Patterson says, but I think she does or she wouldn't have brought me on this holiday, would she?'

Rose gently released my hand from hers and stared deeply into the top of the crystal ball. 'I can see flowers, lots of them.'

'That'll be the daisies in the field,' I told her. 'They're my friends, too. Can you see a stream as well with lots of clay on the bank?'

'Shush. I need to concentrate. I can see a lot of black clouds swimming around, but behind there's a bright sun that's making its way to you, but not for quite some time. That's why you have to be strong and stick up for yourself.'

'Can you tell me if Mr Dobson will catch Harry this time when he raids his orchard?'

She lifted one finger in the air and took a deeper look

inside her crystal ball. 'The clouds are fading; there's mist falling down. I see him. He's holding a ring. Beware,' she said, 'Beware, as you get older, of a very handsome man. He's dangerous. He hides a very deep secret.'

'Who is he?'

'Someone who will cross your path. I can see him laughing as he's fading out of view.'

I nearly jumped out of my seat with the sudden knock on the door. 'Get your skates on,' Teddy told me, slightly out of breath. 'I've been searching all over for you; should have guessed you'd be here. Mother's going mad. You've not even packed your things and the minibus is here to take us home.'

I jumped down from my seat, checking that the strap of my bag was firmly across my shoulder.

'Hurry, will you?' Teddy said.

'Thank you, Rose. I'll write to you when I get home.'

'I'll look forward to that,' she replied as she covered the crystal ball with a silk cloth.

Chapter 18

Was it five or seven days since I last saw Eric, I wondered, patting my finger against my lips? As the minibus passed a housing estate, I stared at all the beautiful flowers growing in their gardens and hoped he'd remembered to water the plants.

I wonder if Eric likes liquorice. I think he does, I said to myself as I peeked inside my plastic bag and looked at the stripes that swirled around the bar of rock I had bought him.

'Stop fidgeting,' Mummy said as I quickly turned around to have a last look at all the sheep wandering high up on the snowy mountains. I felt her finger poke me in my back. 'Turn around and sit still properly.'

'Do you want to read my comic?' Teddy asked, turning over the last page.

'*Beano*'s only for boys.'

'I suppose it is, but there are a few jokes in here that might make you laugh.'

'What, with Mummy sitting right behind me?' I whispered. 'You know what she's like if I get the giggles. Stop pulling funny faces at me,' I said, giving him a nudge.

'Well, at least you're laughing.'

'Stop it,' I begged as he twisted his face again. I felt a kick from behind my feet where Mummy was sitting. 'See,'

I told him as he pulled another. I closed my eyes and held my hand as tightly as I could against my mouth. I wanted to laugh even more when Mummy ordered Teddy to the back of the bus. Within seconds he was gone, and I knew that I had to take control quickly.

'Sit down there,' Daddy told Charlie, letting go of his hand before holding on to the very edge of the seats as he passed to get to the driver. I quickly removed Teddy's comic as Charlie took his place.

'Would you like to read it?' I asked. I wonder why his glasses look like the bottom of Mr Ramsbottom's milk bottles, I thought, as he sat staring at me. 'Take it. Teddy won't mind,' I told him, placing it on his knee. 'Wasn't our holiday lovely, Charlie?' I asked as he sat engrossed in the cartoon pictures. He didn't reply.

'We're stopping in five minutes,' Daddy called out, 'for anyone who wants to use the toilet.' Immediately Charlie raised his hand.

'You can put your hand down now,' I said, reaching over and pulling it down for him. 'We won't be there for a few more minutes and it will start to ache. You're cute, aren't you?' I said, whilst rubbing his short spiky hair. I must pay him more attention. I'll start to cuddle him a lot more, especially when Mummy leaves him to cry for hours and hours. I placed my hand inside my pocket to feel how much spending money I had left. Yes, I'll buy a box of tissues especially to wipe his tears, I thought, as I held on to the coins.

I gripped the seat in front of me as the driver quickly turned. I wonder what that sign says, I thought, as he drove us down the narrow cobbled road.

'Everyone out,' Daddy called as the bus came to a halt.

'I think I'll stretch my legs,' the driver said as we all scrambled out.

'Everyone in line,' we were told as Daddy led us towards a tiny brick building that stood at the end of the cobbled path. 'After you've finished, meet us in there,' he said, pointing to the house adjoining it.

Obeying instructions, I quickly allowed Charlie to stand in front of me.

'Stop jumping up and down,' Frieda shouted at Charlie with her usual sulky face.

'Can he go first?' I asked her. 'He can't hold on any longer. Well, can he?' She didn't reply. 'Come on, Charlie,' I said, getting hold of his hand. 'He'll have to go first,' I told Daddy as we both walked to the front of the queue.

'We're all in the same need,' Frieda said as we stood in front of her.

I took the pleasure of taking no notice of her as I watched Daddy lift up the latch. 'Go on,' I told Charlie, giving him a gentle push forward. 'What's the matter?' I asked, watching him still jumping up and down.

'It's dark in there. I'm frightened.'

I peered over to try and see inside the building. 'Yes, you're right, it is pretty dark. Shall I stay with you?'

'Yes please,' he said without hesitation. We both stepped in, cautiously.

'Don't forget to lift up the seat,' I told him.

'Too late,' he said as I heard a trickling sound. 'Don't look.'

'I'm not. I'm just guarding the door for you,' I replied, holding it slightly ajar to let in some light.

'Finished,' he said. I could hear him fiddling around with his shorts until he managed to pull them up.

The sound of the wooden chairs being pulled out one by one on the flagged floors seemed to irritate the plump old lady who was putting out the tea. 'Her cap's crooked,' I told Teddy, nudging him to have a look as she carried the large stainless steel teapot over to where we were sitting.

'It's because she's got hardly any hair to clip it on,' he whispered. 'How clumsy of her,' Teddy said as she leaned over and rested the teapot with an unsteady hand on to the table, allowing some of the tea to spill from the spout.

'I'm getting too old for this job,' she mumbled, wiping up the spillage with her sleeve.

'Why does she have a moustache?' I asked Teddy, noticing the hairs above her top lip.

'Don't ask me,' he replied as we watched her shuffling her way back to the counter, only to return within minutes holding a tray of well-used cups. 'Look at her fat stomach bouncing up and down with each step that she takes,' Teddy whispered to me.

I thought she had heard what he'd said as suddenly she stopped and stared at us all. 'We're in trouble now, Teddy.'

'Don't be silly. Do you really think we are?' he asked with a nervous look on his face.

'Yes,' I replied, sitting as still as I could. 'Why is she moving her head like a chicken?' I whispered, before realizing that she was counting the cups.

'It looks like she's just double-checking there's enough for us,' he answered.

'So we're not in trouble after all?'

'Doesn't look like it.'

I didn't feel the need to jump as she shuffled her way forward towards our table. 'We'll not say anything more about her, shall we, Teddy?'

'No,' he replied, watching her pick the cups off the tray one by one. 'She should pick them up by the handle. I'd sack her if she worked for me,' Teddy said.

'Sshh,' I quickly told him as she leaned her tray against her side before walking away.

'Anyone for tea?' Daddy asked as he poured Mummy a cup and then himself.

Yuck, I'm not having any of that, I thought, as the pot was passed around the table. 'No thank you,' I said as Teddy handed it to me.

'I'd have a little bit if I was you. It's going to be a couple of hours before we get home,' he told me, reaching over and placing a cup in front of me.

'How do you know?'

'Well, I read all the road signs, don't I?'

'Ugh, it looks like dishwater,' I told him, leaning over and watching him scoop the sugar on to the spoon and stir it into his tea.

'Oh, please yourself,' he said, pushing the empty cup to one side.

'Are we still in Wales?' I asked.

'We sure are. I've learned to speak a lot of Welsh since we've been here,' he told me.

'Have you really?'

'Yes, it's easy.'

'I don't believe you.'

'It's true, I swear.'

'Well, what does that sign say?'

'Which sign?'

'The one chained to the wall, just outside.'

'Oh that. I'll go and have a look when I've finished my tea.'

I gave him a look of disbelief as he took a sip of it, wiping his chin with his hand as a little dribbled. 'Do you think the woman who served our tea is called Gwyneth?' I asked, turning around to have another look at her.

'How should I know?'

'Well, nearly all the ladies in Wales have that name, don't they?'

'Not necessarily,' I was told, watching him turn to look at her. 'Anyway, she isn't a lady is she? So probably not.'

The only excitement I felt as the bus pulled up in front of Rose Cottage was thinking about giving Eric his bar of rock. I sat and stared at the white-washed cottage, my eyes glancing up to my bedroom window. One day I won't have to come back here, I thought, whilst bending down and lifting up my plastic bag from the floor. I held on to the handles as tightly as I could, sitting patiently whilst everyone tried to get out at the same time. 'I wouldn't go yet,' I told Charlie as he jumped up from his seat. 'You'll get squashed,' I smiled as I watched him worm his way through everyone, waving to me as he jumped from the step on to the pavement.

'Aren't you coming?' Teddy asked, leaning over to collect his comic. All of a sudden there was a knock on the window. There was Mrs White with a big smile on her face.

'Did you have a nice holiday?' she asked. I nodded to say yes.

'Nosy bitch,' Mummy said as she stepped off the bus.

Mrs White's long floral dress blew against her slim legs as I turned to watch her walk away. 'Do you think that I'd suit blonde hair like Mrs White's?' I asked Teddy.

'You'd look stupid; you're too dark. You'd have to have a fair complexion like she has and the same blue eyes.'

I wonder if Mummy's jealous of her, I thought. After all, she is a pretty lady.

'Well, are you coming? We're the last on,' Teddy said as he started to walk away.

'Wait for me,' I called, keeping my eye on the driver as I stood up.

'He's not going to set off with you still on,' Teddy assured me before holding my hand to help me down the steps.

'I feel dizzy,' I told him as we stood on the pavement.

'Here, follow me. You'll be okay.'

Oh, Eric, you've forgotten to water the plants, I said to myself, peering over the garden wall before making my way down towards the entry. I sniffed at the damp smell that hit me as I followed everyone through the open door into the kitchen.

'Put the kettle on,' Mummy shouted at me as she shuffled through a pile of unopened mail.

'The luggage can go in the front room,' Daddy told the driver as he struggled in with the cases.

'Are there any letters for me?' I asked as Mummy ripped open the envelopes.

'Who the hell would want to write to you?'

'Quite right,' Frieda said, holding a pen and pad whilst she checked the larder.

'What's that bag in your hand?' Mummy asked, looking down at it.

'It's a present for Eric,' I replied.

'What are you doing spending what little money we have on halfwits like him?'

'Here, here!' Frieda said, butting in, half turning her head to show a slimy grin on her face.

'It's a bar of rock and it's got stripes of liquorice around it. Would you like me to show you?' I asked, placing my hand inside the bag.

'I've better things to do than look at silly bars of rock,' she said as she continued to rip open the mail.

I quickly pulled out my hand and left the rock where it lay.

'You'd better go and give it to him. I don't want it lying around this house,' she told me.

I turned around and walked as fast as I could through the kitchen and out of the back door. I do hope he likes it, I thought, as the bag gently banged against my leg with every skip I took along the entry. 'Here goes,' I said out loud as I reached Mrs Crowswick's door and knocked loudly. I wonder what a halfwit is, I thought. The Grindles call me a half-caste because I'm brown. At least that's what Susie tells me. Maybe Eric's a halfwit because he's so white, I thought, shrugging my shoulders before reaching up and knocking again.

Oh, Eric, why haven't you watered them? I said to myself as I wandered along the tiny flagged pathway to the patch where all our plants were. I thought I heard Mrs Crowswick's door open as I bent down to have a closer look at them. 'I'm back, Eric,' I called, standing up and looking towards the door. Hmmm, it must have been my imagination, as the door stood firmly closed. Eric and I will come back and water you, I told the plants, as soon as I've given him his rock. 'Eric, Eric, where are you?' I called, knocking on the door again. 'Please, please, Mrs Crowswick, no matter how long it takes you, please open the door,' I whispered to myself.

I reached up again to give it one last try. I could feel a slight pain on my knuckles as I banged as hard as I could. 'I'll come back and knock on you later,' I told the door, 'otherwise I'll be in trouble if I stay out any longer.' Well, it's a nice afternoon, I thought, looking up at the clear blue sky. Maybe Eric's taken Mrs Crowswick for a walk. There was a gentle breeze in the air, and I hoped she'd remembered her shawl.

'I'll have to call back later,' I told Mummy on my return home. I didn't mind being ignored as she lifted the lid off the caddy to check what tea was left. At least then she couldn't say no. What are you staring at, Mummy's girl? I wanted to say to Frieda who was standing behind her, still wearing that same slimy grin. I followed them into the living room. I'll buy those tissues for Charlie at the same time, I thought, listening to him cry.

'He's lost his glasses again,' Teddy said as he brushed past me, 'so Mother's given him a slap.'

'I'll help you find them,' I told him. I walked towards the chair he was curled up on and placed my hand inside my pocket to check that my money was still there.

'What's that jingling?' Mummy asked.

'It's the change from my spending money,' I replied.

'Hand it over. You're not on holiday any more,' she demanded. I felt angry as I gathered the coins together.

'Hurry up, I haven't got all day,' she snapped.

I looked directly into her cold eyes as I passed it over.

'Put it in the tin,' Frieda was told. 'It will be more use in there than in her pocket.'

I watched Frieda grin again as she picked up the old rusty tin. At least I won't have an empty baked-beans can to save my money in when I grow up, I thought, listening to the coins drop into the bottom as she threw them in.

'Ah, look what I've found,' Frieda spoke with a glint in her eye whilst leaning down and plucking up Charlie's glasses that peeped out from underneath the settee. She held them out proudly for Mummy to see. 'He's stood on them; that's why he told you he'd lost them,' moving them in her hand from side to side.

'Come here,' she said, bending her pointed finger up and down, beckoning Charlie over.

Don't hit him, I said to myself, as he pulled himself off the chair. His tiny eyes looked tired as he reluctantly walked towards her. Immediately she raised her hand and I saw him squirm as she moved it towards him. Then with such force he was slapped across his face.

'That's for being clumsy,' she said as he screamed out.

'Ouch,' I said out loud as she repeated it.

'And that's for lying to me.' His face was burning bright red. He had no control over the tears and just stood there allowing them to flow. 'Now here,' she said, snatching the glasses off Frieda. Charlie pulled back a little whilst she clumsily put them onto his face. He struggled as she placed the arms behind his ears. I watched as his eyes blinked through the cracked lenses. 'You'll wear these glasses until your eyes ache,' Mummy told him. His tiny body was shaking as he remained standing in front of her, pausing in between his tears to catch his breath.

I couldn't help myself as I pushed her out of the way. I nearly fell over myself as I felt the sting of her hand hit the back of my neck.

'Insolent bitch,' she shouted as I quickly removed his glasses. 'Get them off her,' Frieda was told.

I held on to them as tightly as I could, watching her approach me. Immediately, my bag with Eric's present was snatched from me.

'Let them go,' Frieda demanded, whilst trying to pull my fingers apart. 'She's not letting go,' she called to Mummy. 'Look how white her knuckles are.'

'Ouch,' I called again. This time it was I who felt the pain. 'Stop twisting my arm, you're going to break it,' I told her, raising my voice. With another firm twist my hand opened and the glasses fell to the floor. I quickly jumped on them, digging my feet into the tiny lenses to make sure that there wasn't much left of them.

'Get her to the bedroom,' Frieda was instructed. 'And you get up too,' she told Charlie.

Well, at least you won't be made to wear them now, I thought, finding a second to look down at them before being hurled through the living room and thrown on to the stairs. 'Give me Eric's rock back,' I shouted.

'Chop it up,' Mummy told Frieda in a loud voice, 'and share it out.'

I kicked my heels up and down on the stairs with

frustration as Frieda dragged me up, purposely digging her long fingernails into my skin before hurling me into the bedroom. I gathered as much saliva as I could whilst stumbling over myself, and spat it out in her direction.

'Missed,' she said with her usual slimy grin before closing the door behind her.

I immediately buried my face into the palms of my hands and sobbed. The tears spilled uncontrollably between my fingers. All of a sudden I felt a little tug on my arm. 'Is that you, Charlie?'

'Please don't cry,' he told me, tugging me once more.

'I'll stop in a minute when all the pain has gone.'

'Shall I get the ballerina to dance for you? She won't find out.'

'No,' I said, pulling my hands away from my face. 'You'd never be forgiven, and we'd be punished for ever. Have they chopped up Eric's rock yet?' I asked, wiping the tears on the sleeve of my coat.

'Don't know,' he replied, climbing on to the bed and resting his head on the pillow.

'I wonder if there's such a thing as glue made out of toffee.'

'Probably,' he said as I sat on the edge of his bed.

'Would you help me stick it back together if there is, then Eric can still eat it?' He didn't reply.

'I don't know,' Teddy said, walking into the room.

'Will you find me a pencil and paper?' I asked, still catching my breath between sobs. 'I want to write a letter.'

'Give me a minute,' he said, leaving the room.

I tiptoed along the floor towards the bedroom window and gazed out. Harry looked up and winked at me as he pushed his bicycle along the pavement. My arm felt weak as I lifted it up and slowly moved my fingers up and down to wave.

'Who are you going to write to?' Teddy asked on his return.

'Maybe to God,' I replied.

'Not again,' he said, passing over the pencil and paper to me.

'I've written him a postcard,' I told him.

'Right, I'm off,' Teddy said, hastily walking out of the room.

I knelt down on the bare wooden floorboards and rested the paper on the narrow window ledge. I know, I'll write to Eric and Mrs Crowswick. I'm sure they must think that I'm still on holiday.

Dear Eric and Mrs Crowswick,

How are you? I am well and am writing this letter to let you know that I have come back from my holidays. I did buy you a present but I haven't got it any more. I hope you don't mind. Shall I tell you what it was? It was a bar of rock with liquorice stripes that spun all around, that's if you twirled it. I'm wondering if you might have lost your memory and forgot that I was due home on Saturday. Did you receive my postcard? Sorry that I didn't put a stamp on it, you see I didn't know how to work the machine and everyone was queuing up behind me, so I ran back to my chalet and drew one on the side of it with the pen Mrs White gave to me. I've written so many postcards it's nearly run out of ink. I've got

> one here that I've written to God, but I'll go and leave that in the church myself. Will you come with me Eric when I do?
>
> There was a lot of lovely food to eat on holiday and I had real porridge every morning for breakfast with as much sugar on it as I liked. I suppose that I'm making you feel hungry Eric whilst you're reading this, but it was good. I miss Butlins, but I miss you too, so will you please open the door next time I knock. I'll knock three times and then you'll know it's me. Lots of love, your friend. Lorne.

I quickly folded the letter as many times as I could to make it as tiny as possible, and pushed it down as far as it would go inside the ankle of my sock. I crept across the narrow landing, standing for a second at the top of the stairs to listen if all was clear. It's too risky, I thought, as I placed my foot down on to the top stair, listening to the sudden bang of the door. I hesitated and stepped back. The corner of the letter scratched against my ankle bone as I quickly tiptoed back towards my room. 'Move up,' I whispered to Charlie, gently turning him around to make enough room on the bed so that I could lie down. I placed my head on the shared pillow next to his. 'It's only me,' I whispered as he partly opened his eyes. 'Go back to sleep.'

The days passed slowly; I, once again, shut away from the world inside the gloom of Rose Cottage. I was sure I would spot Eric and waited patiently, kneeling against the ledge making patterns with the tip of my finger against the dusty film that had settled on the glass of my bedroom window.

I yearned for Lily to walk over the humped bridge directly facing me. I'll give her a big wave if she does, feeling the excitement at the thought of seeing her. I sighed and sighed each time I looked down towards Eric's garden. 'Hurry, please, Eric,' I said out loud before lying on my bed, wrapping the brown fluffy blanket around me to keep myself warm.

I took my time choosing a dream as I lay there staring up towards the bare bulb hanging down from the wire on the ceiling. The picture in my mind was of me sitting with Lily and Eric on the wooden bench in his garden, handing them each a present which I had hidden under one side of my cardigan. I had chosen a gold Alice band for Lily's shiny black hair and a bar of rock for Eric. I smiled to myself, imagining seeing their faces as they opened them. There, I imagined, Eric would sit, and I would help him unwrap the twisted cellophane before he held the rock tightly in his hand, slavering with every lick from his tongue, his sticky fingers clasped around the stick giving no one the chance to snatch it away. Lily, dazzled by the sun as it reflected against her band, then resting it neatly with excitement on top of her head. I closed my eyes to try and make the dream come true.

Chapter 19

The sudden bellowing of voices from downstairs rose up from the cracks between the floorboards. I listened to see if Charlie was in trouble again.

'You bloody whore,' Daddy shouted. I curled up in a ball beneath the blanket and didn't move in the hope that the shouting would stop. Lily, please come and take me away from Rose Cottage, I whispered, as the arguing got louder and louder.

I jumped with fright at the sound of a large crack against the glass on the outside of my bedroom window. Stepping down from my bed on tiptoe, I cautiously crept along the floor and peeped through. 'Susie,' I gasped, pushing up against the window, opening it this time with ease. 'I was going to buy you some chocolate cigarettes whilst I was on holiday,' I called down to her. 'I saw them in the sweet shop but they would have melted when you lit them.'

'I'm not worried about any fags, I'm worried about you. What's all the racket going on in there? I knocked on the door but with all that bawling and shouting I couldn't get anyone to hear. How do you stand it?'

'Never mind, Susie, I'll be in heaven soon. I don't think God realizes how urgent it is for me to be with Him. I've written lots of letters to Him but I haven't had any reply.'

'I knew you'd take it bad – told my ma. She suggested

I come and see you. Not that I wouldn't have, you know, come on my own accord.'

'I forgive Him though, Susie. God, that is. He must be very, very busy, mustn't He?'

'Just because Eric's up there with Him now, doesn't mean you should want to go. You'll meet up with Him again when it's your time.'

'I meet Him every day. Well, in my mind,' I told her. 'And I leave letters for Him in church.'

'Who, Eric?' Susie asked, looking puzzled.

'No, Susie, God. I've got a letter here for Eric and Mrs Crowswick. It's inside my sock. What time is it, Susie?'

'Don't know exactly. I've just had my lunch. Bloody awful. Ma threw everything she could get hold of from the larder into a pan big enough to feed an army. It's been simmering all morning. The house stinks of it, some sort of stew. So do these bloody clothes I'm wearing.' She sniffed at the pink cotton blouse that hung loosely over a baggy pair of jeans.

'Hold on,' I called, leaning out of the window. 'Here, it's a bit crumpled because I kept it safe. Would you post it through Mrs Crowswick's letterbox?' I reached out and threw the letter down to her. 'I don't think they know that I'm back from my holiday, so I've written to tell them that I am. Good catch,' I called as she caught it with one hand.

'Are you all right, Susie?' I asked as she looked up at me with a terrible frown on her face. 'It's probably that stew that your mother made. You look like you're going to be sick. Sit down on the wall.' I leaned out further from the open window. 'Is it, is it the stew?' I asked feeling concerned. Another crash from below made me jump. 'Mummy must be throwing plates at Daddy again.'

'You poor thing,' Susie said.

'Never mind, Susie, I'll try and glue them all together when they've stopped fighting, or Mummy won't have anything to put the pies on when she comes home from work.'

'No, it isn't that. You don't know, do you? You don't know, otherwise you wouldn't look so puzzled. Eric's dead. He died two days into your holiday.'

'Will you post that letter, Susie? They'll be so excited to know that I'm home. Be careful, though. Mrs Crowswick's letter box is hard to open so make sure that you push it in hard.'

'Mrs Crowswick's been sent into a home. They'll take care of her there, now that Eric's...'

'Hurry, Susie, will you post it now?' I shouted. 'Don't look at me like that,' I screamed. 'Eric's not dead. He's not dead, he's not,' I called out to myself as I ran along the landing, picking up my long red coat from the hook behind the door at the bottom of the stairs, sticking my arms inside the sleeves as I hurriedly made my way towards the front door. My hands were shaking as I reached up and lifted the latch, leaving the bellowing that was going on behind the closed door of the living room. Outside I came face to face with Susie. 'Don't touch me,' I told her as she attempted to straighten the collar of my coat.

'Look, I'm sorry; I thought you knew.'

I snatched the letter from her hand and ran towards Mrs Crowswick's front door. 'Mrs Crowswick, I'm home,' I called again whilst stretching my legs as far as they would go to try and peep through her letterbox. I glanced towards Susie who immediately turned her back and looked up towards the cloudy sky. 'I'll knock on her window,' I told her, tapping on it several times before trying to peer through the pattern in the net curtains that hung against the window.

'There isn't anyone there,' Susie whispered.

'Mrs Crowswick ... Eric,' I screamed, kicking furiously at the closed door. 'Is he dead?' I cried, looking at Susie. 'Has Eric really died?' With her acknowledgement I buried my head in my hands, fell on to my knees and howled. I felt the warmth of Susie's hand on my shoulder. There was nothing to say as my tears flowed with sadness. Eventually, the collar of my coat was straightened by her gentle touch, and I was coaxed to stand up as she wiped the tears that streamed down my face.

She took my hand and guided me on to the pavement. We walked a short while, my head bowed, before sitting on a chunk of old stone that was embedded into the soil at the gateway to a farmer's field. Susie struck a match against the stone and puffed away on her cigarette in silence. I stared down at the ground. A spider crawled past my feet. My fear of them had suddenly left me. It crawled towards Susie and, with one bump and a twist, she squashed it underneath the sole of her shoe.

Susie aimed for the open grid on the opposite side of the road, whirling the end of her cigarette up in the air before rubbing her hands together in the satisfaction of a direct hit. 'I'm going to ask your ma if you can spend the afternoon with me,' Susie nudged me to say. I looked towards her in fright. 'I'll handle it,' she said, standing up and straightening her blouse over her thick waist. 'You wait here,' she told me as she headed back along the pavement towards Rose Cottage.

My tears stung the sides of my burning cheeks as they streamed down my face.

'Knew you'd be crying somewhere or other. Want to go and see the vicar?' Harry asked. He spit the gum he was chewing out of his mouth and stepped off his bicycle. 'Just passed your mate, Susie. She reckons you've only just found out. Budge up,' he told me as he sat down next to me, leaning forward to rip a thick blade of grass from its roots. 'Can't think of owt to say,' he said. 'Look at those little hands of yours trembling.'

'He would have missed me, Harry, when I went on holiday.' I paused for a moment to wipe my nose. 'Do you think he died of a broken heart because I'd left him behind?'

'Stop blaming yourself. Blimey, you're only a kid. It ain't your fault.'

'Harry,' I said, taking a deep breath, 'I don't ever want to go back to Rose Cottage, especially with Eric not being close by me.'

'Hey, lass, come on.' He placed his arm around my shoulder as my tears flowed. 'Look, you'll soon be grown up,' he said, taking the tightly squeezed handkerchief from my hand.

'Ouch,' I called out.

'Sorry, I forgot how tiny that nose of yours is,' he said after he had finished wiping it. 'Then you'll be able to do owt you want.'

'Can you do owt you want?' I asked.

'Always have done,' he laughed, 'besides kiss a girl, that is, but there's still plenty of time for owt like that.'

'Tha's put weight on,' he called to Susie as she came into view.

'Piss off, Harry,' she answered, lifting her thumb and swaying it outwards for him to move. Harry quickly jumped off the stone slab and Susie puffed as she took his place. 'They're having a right old barney.'

'Who?' Harry asked, balancing his feet against the floor as he sat on the seat of his bicycle.

'Her ma and dad.'

'Is Daddy shouting too?' I asked with a quiver in my voice.

'She says she doesn't ever want to go back to Rose Cottage,' Harry explained. Susie frowned at him. 'All right, tell me it's nowt to do with me,' he told her.

Susie threw a cigarette over to him and the tension was lifted between them as they puffed away.

'Where have they taken Eric?' I asked.

'Want to go? The grave is packed out with flowers.'

Susie reached out and kicked Harry's foot.

'Will you take me?' I asked, standing up and fastening the buttons of my coat.

'Stick your hanky in your pocket and hold on to the handlebars.'

'Bloody well wait for me,' Susie moaned, taking one last puff at her cigarette before throwing it down. We both stopped and waited for her to catch up. She swore to herself whilst slipping her foot back into her sandal.

'Shouldn't wear such fancy shoes if tha wants to keep up with me,' Harry called.

'They are pretty though, Harry. Look at all those twinkling sequins.'

'Aye, I suppose they are.'

'They're our kid's,' Susie called back. 'I borrowed them without her knowing,' she said as she caught up to us. 'Never know who I might meet on my travels. Got to look right, ain't I.'

I left them to their banter on the slow journey over the bridge. Harry used all his strength pushing his bicycle up the steep hill where the dark clouds left a shadow over the long blades of swaying grass that faced either side.

'Good afternoon,' Harry said as Mrs Patterson appeared, trying to walk steadily down the slope in her high-heeled shoes that clicked with each step.

'Where are you lot off to?' she asked, stopping for a second and feeling that her bouffant hairstyle was still in place.

'Taking her to pay her respects,' Harry said, looking towards me.

'But I haven't any money,' I whispered to Susie, searching inside the pockets of my coat.

'Dear God, don't they teach you anything at that school of yours?' Mrs Patterson said, peering down at me. 'And whispering is rude. Anyway, young man, glad to see you're not on your own with her. You know what your ma said about being in his company,' she told me.

'We'd best be off,' Harry told her. 'It's too cold to stand talking.'

'Aye, and I've not got the time to stand around either. I've a bus to catch. Give us a light before you go,' she asked Harry, unzipping the top of her white plastic handbag and rooting through until she found her cigarettes.

'You don't need no money to pay your respects,' Susie informed me, 'so take that worried look off your face.'

Mrs Patterson's cigarette burned brightly as she puffed hard on it. 'If you see that drunken bastard of mine,' she said, blowing smoke down through her nostrils, 'don't tell him you've seen me. I'm off for a session at the bingo hall. Don't want him lurking around in the background waiting to see if I've won owt.' Harry passed wind and pardoned himself. 'I should think so in front of a lady. Right, I'm off,' she added, wiggling her hips from side to side as she walked down the hill towards the village.

'She's got a mouth like a horse,' Susie said.

'And teeth too, Susie. I've seen them floating in fizzy water.'

'You haven't!'

'I have. She'd left them inside Mr Patterson's pint glass on top of the drainer next to the kitchen sink.'

'Don't want to hear no more. I feel sick,' Harry said as we approached the main road.

The church dominated the stretch of road, or so it seemed, as Susie squeezed my hand tightly whilst we waited for our chance to cross over and head for the short distance towards the churchyard. I had often looked down, taking only a fleeting glance, at the gravestones neatly in line facing east towards the woodland, but would always ignore their presence on my swift visits to leave my letters inside the vestibule of the church. I always admired the grey stone vicarage that stood back magnificently in its own grounds, before my regular attendance at the school of St Paul's, built next to it. I looked ahead in the direction of the church hall, beyond a row of Victorian houses, their tall chimneys blocking its view, and my heart ached with the recent memory of the fun Eric and I had had at the jumble sale.

I had released my hand from the grip of Susie's and snuggled them down into the warmth of my coat pockets. Harry's bike ground to a halt and he propped it against the spiky iron gates which were left open to welcome any visitors. I pretended I had grown up and, with my head held high, shoulders stiff and straight, I walked in silence behind Harry and Susie around the narrow windy path.

'Will it thunder and lighten?' I asked as we walked down as far as the churchyard could take you.

'Shouldn't think so,' Harry replied, looking up at the grey cloudy sky.

'It would be bloody spooky if it did,' Susie said.

I almost bumped into them as Susie and Harry suddenly stopped. There, near a willow tree, its branches swaying low, was Eric's grave. I looked up at Harry and Susie. The solemn expression on their faces told me that Eric had really and truly died. A dreadful smell hung in the air from the rotting flowers, sweating inside wrapped polythene tied with stiff ribbons that rattled in the breeze, strewn across a mound of recently dug soil where Eric had been laid to rest. I began to sneeze violently.

'Stinks, don't it?' Harry said. Susie nudged him hard with her elbow before blessing me.

I could feel Susie's warm breath against my neck as she stood behind me, leaning both her hands on my shoulders. Harry coughed a couple of times within the silence. I looked down and stared, my eyes blurred with each tear that flowed, stinging with emotion. Susie gripped my shoulders tightly.

'Here, pass her this,' Harry said, pulling a crumpled hanky out of his jeans pocket. 'It ain't clean, but it's better than nowt,' he told Susie in a disgruntled tone as she reluctantly reached over and took it from him.

'Let's go into church and say a prayer for the poor sod whilst we're all together,' Harry said as the clock on the church steeple chimed. 'Got to get off to deliver the evening papers soon.'

'Could do with a fag before we go,' Susie replied. 'We'll leave you to pay your respects. Don't worry,' she said as I gave an anxious look, 'we're not going far.'

'Lend us one,' Harry asked as Susie pulled out a packet of cigarettes from her pocket and counted how many she had left as she walked the short distance to lean against the stone wall. Susie pulled her face at his request, lifted one out and threw it over.

'Cheers,' Harry said, catching hold of it.

'I've come to pay my respects, Eric. I haven't any money. Susie said I didn't need any, but I'm sure I do,' I said, inspecting the insides of my pockets once more just in case there could have been some loose change lying at the bottom. An unexpected trickle ran down my face and I quickly wiped it on the sleeve of my coat before turning to Susie. 'Can he hear me?'

'Of course he can.'

I quickly turned back. 'I know that you're down there somewhere. It seems strange talking to you like this, but if you're not really dead, will you cough or make a noise? Any noise will do.' I stood and listened as hard as I could. 'Mr Drake won't mind digging you out, although he might complain a little, only because of the arthritis he had in his hands.' I stood again and listened.

'Come on,' Susie said, taking hold of my hand and pulling me gently until we walked side by side.

'Let's go into the church,' Harry suggested, throwing the end of his cigarette down towards the ground and striding towards us. 'I'll take the place of Eric – well, until you stop grieving.' I looked at him questioningly. 'Well, what I mean is,' he said as we carried on walking, 'if you want owt digging, like those fancy plants you and Eric dug 'oles in the ground for, I'll do it.'

'What does grieving mean?' I whispered to Susie as Harry rubbed the soles of his shoes hard onto the bristle mat before we entered the church. Susie opened the arched door, lifting the ring and turning the latch gently as if we were going to disturb a full congregation. We all crept quietly along the aisle, yet the empty church echoed our presence.

'Let's grab t'front pew,' Harry said as if, by some chance, the flow of worshippers were about to invade. Susie tutted as Harry pushed past and sat down, immediately taking the lead. 'Dear God, we've lost one o' t'gang.' Then he stopped for a second. 'Sorry, forgot you had to kneel to pray to you.' He slid a tiny footstool covered in a deep red velvet towards him and pointed his finger down towards the dark-stained floorboards for Susie and me to do the same before kneeling down and resting his head in between his hands.

He waited for Susie and me to settle, and as soon as the shuffling had stopped he continued his prayer. 'Suppose tha knows he's been dead for a week.'

'Nearly two,' Susie said, nudging him once more.

'Sorry, God, it's been as close as two as can get it. Well, you will know won't you? Cos he'll be standing with you up there in heaven.'

I immediately looked up towards the arched ceiling before lowering my head once again as Harry continued to pray.

'There's only one of t'Grindle lads or Edward who could take his place, but they're not up to much cop. In fact t'Grindle lads don't do owt.'

'Except spit and fart,' Susie whispered.

'Yeah, except for spitting and farting,' Harry said. 'And Edward, well, should have ribbons in his hair he's so soft.'

'Get on with it,' Susie muttered, keeping her head down.

'Well, He needs to know to give us some guidance,' he snapped at Susie.

'Will you ask God to check that Eric has got the right buttons fastened if he's wearing his pyjamas? You see he gets the buttonholes on his jacket all in a mix when he's trying to fasten them. That's if he's wearing his striped ones that Mrs Crowswick made for him on her sewing machine,' I asked in a whisper as I leaned over towards Harry.

'He'll be wearing a gown,' Susie said.

'That's twice you've butted in,' Harry told her. 'Just keep your gob shut while I finish t'prayer. Don't matter what t'lad's dressed in, God, but just in case he's wearing striped pyjamas, would one of th'angels check if he's fastened t'jacket properly, only I've got his best friend here and she don't want no one to laugh at him.'

'Me neither,' Susie whispered.

'Aye, and me too,' Harry told God.

'Getting cramp in me legs kneeling here,' Harry told Susie, struggling to stand.

'Is that it?' she asked as he stamped his feet up and down against the floor. 'I think the prayer's over with,' Susie told me, giving me a helping hand as we both stood whilst Harry continued to dance up and down.

'Wouldn't like that again in a hurry,' he said as the pain died down. 'Might as well say amen now. Ain't kneeling down there no more.'

Susie and I said it together, leaving Harry saying his in a snappy manner. 'It's not God's fault you've got cramp,' remarked Susie.

'Didn't say it was, did I?' Harry blurted as we left the pew in single file and made our way back along the aisle in silence.

'Being a gentleman, are you?' Susie asked, wiggling past him as Harry stood against the open door to let us through. The tension was lifted with Susie's offer of another cigarette.

'Will Eric have wings?' I asked as we grouped together.

Harry cupped his hands around the match he had just struck as the breeze blew in our direction, his thin lips sucking heavily on the tip of his cigarette. 'Aye, of course he will,' he mumbled, balancing the cigarette on the tip of his mouth as he spoke.

'Will he heck,' Susie said as we made our way through the open gate.

'Look, they don't know and I don't know, so let's presume he 'as,' Harry argued, gripping on to the handlebars of his bike as we walked back along the busy road. 'That's all I need. Don't start yapping to her,' Harry told us. 'Don't want to hear her tales of woe, been through enough today,' he added as Mrs Patterson made her way back up the steep hill on our journey down. She tied her blue chiffon headscarf that was blowing in the wind firmly underneath her round chin, before lifting up the cream collar of her shiny plastic mac and pulling it across her open neck. As she walked swiftly past, she buried her head into her collar, acknowledging us with a grunt.

'Must have lost at bingo,' Harry whispered.

'It'll be more than that if I know her,' Susie remarked as we continued down the slope past Mr Dobson's orchard. Harry, unable to resist, stopped for a second and looked down over the stone wall, choosing which trees he would climb as soon as Mr Dobson's apples grew ripe enough to be picked in one of Harry's usual summer raids.

'I was right,' Susie said. There was Mr Patterson leaning over the bridge as we walked towards it, still wearing the same old dirty trousers with the frayed elastic belt keeping them fixed tightly around his slim waist.

'Bloody bingo caller ain't he? Won't forgive her this time,' he said, spitting with force over the wall of the bridge into the stream below. 'Pretending she fancies me so that she can go out leaving me sat in t'chair while she's canoodling with that.'

'Who, Tommy?' Harry asked. 'It's probably your imagination.'

'Well, how come he stunk of her perfume and had the print of her lipstick stuck on his cheek? What does that tell you, hey? Bastard. Nearly got me arms around his bloody neck, except she went hysterical and stormed out of t'place.'

'If it's Tommy you're talking about, he's only got one eye. T'other's glass.'

'That's all he needs to fancy a bit on t'side.'

'Can't see him making off with your wife. Ain't got it in him,' Harry remarked. 'Anyway, judging by talk in t'village, he's queer.'

'Must be,' Mr Patterson said, 'to fancy 'er. Anyway, I'm standing 'ere till pub opens.'

'Nowt stopping you getting a fancy piece yourself,' Harry told him.

'Aye, tha right. Anyway it's nowt to do wi' you.'

Leaving them to their chit-chat, I stared across towards the tiny cottage. It never had a name. It was just the house next door where my best friend, Eric, lived. Susie enjoyed a bit of gossip and gave Mr Patterson her full attention, leaving me with my sorrowful thoughts. I imagined that through the netted curtains which hung down in a disorderly manner against Mrs Crowswick's window, she and Eric would be sitting at the table having afternoon tea. It would be the main part of Eric's day. Mrs Crowswick baked every morning, and enjoyed surprising Eric with a freshly baked teacake. I'll never again smell that delicious aroma that rose from the inside of her oven and lingered in the air, leaving my mouth watering with the thought of how delicious the cakes would taste.

Susie turned her attention towards me, placing her arm heavily against my shoulder.

'Mrs Crowswick would never leave her curtains like that,' I said. Susie looked at me curiously. 'She would always gather them neatly each morning, before giving her usual wave to me, and I would wave back until I disappeared over the bridge on my way to school. But maybe, maybe she's still in her cottage. She might be,' I said, looking up towards Susie hopefully.

'She ain't. The shock of Eric dying … well, she couldn't cope, could she. Not on her own. Reckons she'll be next. Pretty soon, too. She lived for that lad. Harry, couldn't you have found a more gentle way?' He looked puzzled. 'You're too blunt,' Susie told him.

'Can't do owt right these days,' he complained, shrugging his shoulders. 'We're off,' he told Mr Patterson, leaving him resting his elbows on the parapet with his head bowed low staring down over the bridge into the stream. 'He'll soon be drowning his sorrows,' Harry said, taking an extra stride to catch up with us.

'Can't he swim?' I asked, feeling concerned as I turned my head to take a quick glance.

'I'm not even going to answer that one. Feel the piss has been taken out of me all day long.'

Susie tutted and I swallowed deeply as we crossed the narrow road. 'Don't,' Susie called as I left her side and suddenly burst into tears.

Ignoring the presence of Rose Cottage, I ran over the loose flags down to Mrs Crowswick's door. Chips of dull paint, cracked and dry, fell down against my knuckles as I banged and banged hard with my fist.

'Leave her be,' Harry shouted as Susie made an attempt to drag me away.

'Mrs Crowswick, you don't have to go into a home,' I cried. 'Please open the door. I won't let the wheels of your chair get stuck when I take you out for a walk. And anyway … can you hear me, Mrs Crowswick? I'm strong enough now to push you in it. I'm going to leave Rose Cottage for good to come and look after you. Can you hear me?' I quickly wiped my nose once more on the sleeve on my coat whilst standing closer on a cluster of wild daffodils before pressing my ear against the door to listen for an answer. 'I know that your heart's broken. Mine is, too,' I wept.

Before I knew it, Harry had whisked me up in his arms. 'There's not an ounce of strength in you,' he said, hoisting me up slightly until my head rested against his chest. 'I'm taking thee to see me prize pigeon. He's under lock and key in one o' t'pigeon holes.'

'Hey, wait for me,' Susie called, clicking her heels against the hard surface of the road until she eventually caught up.

'No more tears,' Harry whispered against my ear. 'Don't want to frighten them do we?' He lifted a piece of string from his jeans pocket that held the key before leaning to one side and stretching his arm down to open the gate. 'This fence ain't that strong,' he told me as it shook whilst he was opening the gate.

'Whoa,' Susie called as she nearly lost her balance over the lump of soil that lay disguised underneath the blades of thick grass.

'Should be wearing your clogs. They'd suit you better

than those fancy sandals,' Harry told her, winking at me with his sparkling blue eyes. Susie mumbled under her breath that she was trying to be a lady as she struggled to walk, lifting her jeans above her ankles whilst keeping a conscious eye on each step she took.

Harry quickly closed the gate after her and we all grouped together, with instructions from Harry in a whisper that we all remain silent. 'They're making more noise than us,' Susie told him as we stepped closer.

'Aye, well it's natural, ain't it, for 'em to coo?' Harry lowered me down and held on to me until I had steadied myself firmly on the ground. 'I'm sending that one o'er t'channel soon,' he told us, pointing up towards a red-eyed pigeon that peered down at us through the pigeon hole.

'Looks evil, if you ask me. Look at its bulging eyes,' Susie said.

'Got to be a pigeon fancier. Wouldn't look at them the way you do if tha were,' Harry said bluntly.

'Can think of other things to fancy than pigeons,'

'Aye, thy would,' Harry said, moving along.

'Eh, you,' a voice called.

We immediately turned in its direction.

'Stop shaking the bloody fence,' Harry told Mrs Grindle as she held on to it with both hands, gripping her grubby fingers around the wire.

'Get that bloody loft cleaned out,' she shouted, squashing her face up against the fence, 'before I report thee to th'authorities. Can't open me own kitchen window with t'stink.'

'Sending one over t'channel soon,' Harry called, 'so tha'll have to wait. Don't want no disturbance.'

'They'll all be sent over t'bloody channel if tha doesn't heed what I say,' she grunted before walking away.

'There's more than me pigeons stink around here,' Harry shouted.

Susie and I waited in fright for her to turn around and march back towards us. 'Lucky she's wearing that thick headscarf,' Susie whispered.

'Nowt to do with that. She can't hear owt anyway wi' muck she'll have inside her ears.'

'Cheer up, Harry, it's just been a bad day. You've probably built it too close … your loft … you know, too close to her home.'

'Me dad owns this plot of land. Only bit around 'ere. Nowt I can do if me pigeons loosen their droppings over t'roof of her house. Where there's muck they'll find it.'

'Come on, cheer up. Old battleaxe will never change,' she told Harry, passing him another cigarette. 'I'll regret it later when I've no fags left,' stuffing the box back deep inside the pocket of her jeans.

'My Mummy's going to have a shock when she finds out,' I said. Harry looked down towards me. 'About Eric dying,' I explained.

'Thanks a lot, Harry,' Susie said as he threw the lit match down on the ground.

'Sorry, Susie,' said Harry, passing the box of matches over to her, 'but that Grindle woman's made me feel so angry.'

'Couldn't explain to your ma that you were with me,' Susie said, blowing a ring of smoke from her cigarette up into the air. 'Only knocked once, then gave up expecting any answer. Should have heard the racket that was going on.'

I suddenly spotted clusters of daisies growing under the shade against the wooden stilts that supported Harry's loft.

'Where are you going? You'll bang your head,' Susie called, stooping down to have a look as I crawled underneath.

'I'm picking these for Mummy,' I told her. 'I'll have to ask her to sit down before I give her the bad news.'

'What bad news?' Susie asked.

'Eric dying.'

'Watch the nettles,' Susie warned as I squatted, picking each tiny stem with care before clutching the bunch of daisies tightly in the palm of my hand.

'She didn't like Eric very much. Well, she might have done a little bit,' I added, pausing as I stretched out further to pick the remaining ones.

'Keep still,' Susie told me as I crawled back out. She brushed her hand lightly over the top of my head as I struggled to stand. 'Cobwebs.' I shuddered at the thought.

'Chip van's here,' she said, ruffling my hair before grabbing hold of my hand. 'Come on, Harry, we'll all share a bag.'

''Ere,' rooting inside his pocket, 'some coppers. Ask him to throw in some extra.'

'Stole this from me ma's purse,' Susie said, pulling out a shiny sixpence 'Don't look so shocked,' she told me. 'She's not wi'out.'

The smoke swirled through the spout of the miniature

chimney pot of the mobile van which was parked in its regular spot beside the old village pub. We ran over the gravel towards it.

'You'll have to wait a minute or two,' Mr Grundy told us, checking the temperature before hurling a bucket of peeled chipped potatoes that hissed against the hot fat as they were dropped inside. Susie admired her reflection in the stainless steel fryer as we waited patiently with watering mouths.

'Put a fish in,' Mrs Grindle asked, appearing from nowhere.

'Stand back,' Susie whispered as Mrs Grindle pushed in between us.

'Aye, keep out of me road. Ain't even room to splash on t'vinegar with you two stood there as if you've never seen food in your life.'

'Shouldn't be so buxom,' Susie muttered.

'Looks like a fish, don't he? No wonder he's in that trade,' Harry said, pacing up and down, conscious of Mrs Grindle's presence as she tapped a three-penny bit on top of the counter.

'Aye, he does,' Susie whispered, 'with those goggly eyes popping out of his face.'

'Leave it open,' Mrs Grindle told him as the steaming fish was lifted and placed on a sheet of greaseproof paper. 'I'll eat it on me way 'ome. And give us a fork.'

Mr Grundy looked like he was ready to smile but had a change of heart when she pushed a huge piece of fish inside her slavery mouth, grabbed the change from his hand and slowly walked off.

'Got a job yet?' Mr Grundy asked Harry,

'No, I ain't. Why do you ask?' Harry replied in an abrupt manner.

'Nowt changes in this village,' Mr Grundy said.

'Only his bloody chips,' Susie muttered as he lifted them out, banging the spatula twice against the fryer before tipping them into the heated grill. 'They're all soggy,' she complained to me.

Harry walked off in a huff. 'Wait for you over there,' he told us. He walked over to the wall of the village pub and squatted with his back leaning against its rough stone surface.

'He'll be okay,' Susie said as I looked over feeling anxious. 'He often sits there watching all t'drunks come out.'

'What, from that pub?' I asked.

'There's more goes on in there than meets the eye,' Susie said. I looked up at Susie with a confused expression on my face. 'Don't ask me to explain,' she said. 'Don't know the meaning of it myself.'

'Good God, the heavens have opened,' Mr Grundy remarked as the rain lashed down.

Eric's coming home, I said to myself, immediately looking up at the grey cloudy sky. I clapped my hand over my eyes to try and stop the rain blurring my vision.

'A large bag of chips,' Susie shouted. 'It's coming down in buckets.'

My stomach turned with excitement.

'Taking shelter,' Harry shouted, 'in the telephone box over there.'

'Oh,' I gasped as my head was thrown back forcefully. I dropped the bunch of daisies I held in my hand in panic. With a tug of my hair and a constant jerk, I was turned, in agonizing pain, towards the direction of Rose Cottage. Falling over my own two feet, my head went down, and I was given a sudden jerk upwards. The familiar smell of dampness as I was dragged down the dark entry filled me with fear, knowing it would only be seconds before I was behind the closed door of Rose Cottage.

'Please don't,' I whimpered as I was thrown down on to the bare asphalt floor inside the kitchen, shrivelling up in a bundle whilst being taunted by the long handle of the sweeping brush. I immediately covered my cold hands over my face for protection. I heard the swish in the air of the swift movement as the handle came down towards me. Having no time to think, I wriggled over on to my side, not knowing in those split seconds if I had moved in the right direction, before it hit the hard floor and snapped in two. Dragging myself up with help from the greasy rail fixed against the front of the cooker whilst Mummy screamed in frustration, I clambered towards the door. My hands trembled against the latch before it loosened, enabling me to lift up the lever from the rusty catch and run out through the door. I cried out loud, stumbling against the wall of the dark, gloomy entry as I ran in panic to get away.

The raindrops bounced up from the pavement as the rain lashed down. There was no sign of Mr Grundy's van, or Susie and Harry. I stopped for a second. The grids bubbled with waves of grey water, choked with the heavy rain. I felt unsteady as I stepped down, ankle deep, and waded through until I reached the bridge. I could hear the strong current of water flowing with rage along the stream below.

I quickly looked back. A light mist had formed leaving Rose Cottage barely visible. Not daring to look below I stepped cautiously up and over the hump. Then, leaving the bridge behind, I ran with squelching feet as fast as I could up the hill. The burning lights from the tall street lamps shimmered under the downpour of tumbling rain as I reached the almost deserted road ahead. I stuck to the pathway, aware of the odd vehicle driving slowly past with beaming headlights and creaky windscreen wipers flapping from side to side. I walked quite quickly, trying to show no signs of distress, in the hope of finding Mrs Crowswick. Glancing quickly towards the church as I made my way past, I peered through windows and rhymed off every name of each house as I walked by their front doors. The road seemed endless, the houses big and old with dark gloomy chimneys that pointed up into the grey skies. I tried in vain, sometimes stretching on to my tiptoes, daring as I crept closer to peep through the windows inside each dimly lit room, desperately hoping that Mrs Crowswick would be there, sitting in a chair with her favourite shawl wrapped around her shoulders.

The tall houses were nearing an end. I sneezed furiously but, not wanting to catch anyone's attention, I quickly crouched down under the dripping ledge of a window before moving on along that stretch at my last attempt to find her.

'It's not called that,' poor, polio-crippled Fellwick said, creeping up behind me as I called out the name. 'Name of that house. Big ain't it. Sorry I scared thee,' he added as I turned to him with a frightened expression on my face before turning back and checking the name once again on the oval wooden plaque. 'It's Willows,' he told me. 'W fell off, didn't it. Pass 'ere every day and they've still not got a hammer and nail out to fix it. It's not often I see thee wandering up and down 'ere. Could wring you out tha's that wet.'

'Are you going to get drunk?' I asked with a shiver in my voice as he pulled a bottle of cider from the ragged pocket of his oversized jacket. He unscrewed the top and began to drink the strong smelling liquid, gulping as he swallowed it down.

'Already am,' he said, hiccupping in between his words. 'You're in trouble, aren't ya?' wiping his hand over his mouth. 'Want a swig?' Fellwick waited for my refusal before screwing the top back on and sticking the bottle of cider into his pocket.

'Promise you won't tell, Fellwick? I've run away from home,' I whispered.

'That don't surprise me.'

'I've something terrible to tell you, Fellwick.'

'Aye?' he said as we wandered back along the same stretch of road. 'You've got the shivers, ain't you?' noticing my teeth chattering as I tried to speak. 'Well, go on then.'

'Eric's dead.' There was silence for a while as we continued to walk.

'Aye, I know. Biggest shock of my life. Wanna know why? Cos if any of us lot were going to die, well, thought I'd be first. Poor sod. He's had the piss taken out of him all his rotten life. Just like me with this calliper. Should have been me, not him, cos there ain't nowt in my life, no hopes, no dreams, no owt, state of me. Didn't go to t'funeral cos I only found out after they'd buried him. Bet there were hardly a soul there.'

'Where are ya going?' Fellwick called as I left his side. 'Wait for me, will you?' I clenched my hand around the shiny brass ring whilst he struggled to walk as fast as he could with the burden of his limp, towards me. ''Ere,' he said, taking hold himself and lifting the latch.

Fellwick burped and asked God to pardon him, whilst I followed slowly behind as we made our way along the aisle. 'Plonk yourself down,' I was told as he chose a pew at random. 'Never prayed before,' he told me in a loud voice.

'Shush,' I said, holding the palms of my hands together.

'Blamed Him all me life,' he said, looking towards a figure of Jesus that was fixed on a tiny wooden cross.

'It's not His fault, Fellwick.'

'What, that I'm a cripple? Well, tell me this. If He's supposed to be able to 'eal, why am I still like this?'

'It's probably because you haven't asked Him.'

'Me ma has loads of times. 'Eard her in her own bedroom, but nowt's 'appened. And t'disciples were just as bad and there were ten of them.'

'Twelve,' I whispered as we both sat shivering.

'Aye,' thinking to himself. 'Well, that just makes it worse, don't it?'

A sudden gust of wind swept through the church. Fellwick and I turned as the arched door quickly closed. 'Christ, thought it was t'bloody Lord then,' Fellwick shouted.

'Teddy,' I called as he pulled the hood down from his head, rubbing his cold hands together. The drops of rain rolled down from the shoulders of his plastic mac along his sleeves.

'The river's burst its banks,' he told us as he walked towards us along the aisle. 'We have to get home. Flood warnings. The road's going to be blocked off. It's two inches deep already. You're not safe out here. Anyway, Mother's told me to find you and bring you back. Somehow I guessed you'd be here.'

'I feel safe inside the church, Teddy.'

'If it wasn't for Fellwick, you'd be all alone.'

'But at least no one's going to hurt me. Do you know why? Because this house belongs to God.'

'It's spooky if you ask me,' Fellwick said. 'Want a swig?' he asked Teddy, pulling out the bottle of cider with difficulty as it stuck against the inside lining of his damp jacket pocket. Teddy shook his head as Fellwick unscrewed the top and gulped the remainder down.

'I'll be glad when you're grown up,' Teddy said, in between Fellwick's burps. 'I'm sick of worrying about you. Look, don't get me into trouble as well. I've been told I have to find you and take you home.'

'Well, I'm not coming. I'm going to sit here and wait for God,' I told him, looking straight ahead towards the altar.

'If God can do anything in His power, He will,' Teddy told me, reaching out his hand towards me, 'but right now He can't and you're drenched with the rain. He might make you wait an awful long time before He's ready to take you up there.'

'Where?' Fellwick asked.

'Heaven,' Teddy answered, reaching out and gripping my hand.

'Aye, well let's get off then,' Fellwick said, struggling to stand. 'Anyway, I'm pissed wet through.'

Reluctantly, I allowed myself to be guided by Teddy's hand. 'Come on, Fellwick,' I called, turning around halfway along the aisle to see where he was.

'Think I'll take meself off to me bed for t'rest o' t'day,' Fellwick said, limping towards us as he counted his money. 'Only a few coppers left. Can't do much with that.'

The wind took my breath away as I was led from the church. 'It's chucking it down,' Fellwick shouted. 'Oh aye, I've found t'right wheel. Might be bigger than t'other three. I'll fix that pram of yours before t'week's out. Half a tub of paint, too. It's black, though, but should do the job,' he called, shouting louder through the stormy weather as he pulled the collar of his jacket up around his neck. Fellwick bent his head low before wandering off in the opposite direction.

Teddy hurried me along as I fought to catch my breath against the gusts of wind that blew towards us. He picked me up and cradled me in his arms, wading his feet heavily against the current of water as we left the bridge and headed for Rose Cottage.

Daddy was ripping up the lino that had covered the living room into strips. The drop leaf table had been pulled out, making room for the wooden chairs that were stacked high on top of its worn surface The rusty springs of the settee propped up against the wall faced us as Teddy hurried me through and let me down on the bottom stair.

'Go to your room,' he whispered, encouraging me to take each step up the dark, narrow staircase. My wet hands slipped against the bannister. 'Hurry,' he called. I turned, barely catching sight of him as he quickly disappeared.

The buckle on my sandal had come loose making the sound of my foot squelching inside them more apparent with each step I took along the narrow landing. I brushed my hand along the inner wall feeling for the light switch. The bare bulb hanging from the ceiling barely lit the room as I crept along the creaky floorboards towards my bed. The rain pelted against the window leaving no view.

Chapter 20

A tremor of voices could be heard and I sensed the panic below. I quickly undressed and removed the stained feather pillow from inside the worn cotton pillow case and tried to rub myself dry. My nightwear consisted of a rather short set of pyjamas that I snatched quickly from underneath Charlie's pillow. I'm sure he won't mind, I thought, as I stood shivering and covered in goose pimples whilst stumbling in my rush to slip them on. I could smell the soggy warmth of my red coat as it lay with my clothes in a bundle on the bare floor.

Numb with cold, I pulled off the shabby blanket that covered the bed and wrapped it around my body several times. My jaw ached from my teeth clicking in a constant chatter, whilst twiddling my bare toes up and down to ease the cold sting as I walked in circles around the room.

'Hello, it's only me, Molly,' she called with a warm voice whilst tapping on the door. I took a gulp and ran straight over, perching myself on the edge of the bed.

'May I come in?' she asked.

My teeth continued to chatter giving me no time to reply as the door was slowly opened. She stood for a second, a plump, gentle lady of medium height. I didn't know what age she was. She wasn't young and neither old.

‘I volunteered to help,’ she quietly told me, ‘whilst Rose Cottage isn’t functional at the moment.’ I gave her an inquisitive look. ‘You know, with the floods. It’s going to take days to get back to normal, there’s been so much damage, and Teddy suggested that you should, only if you wish, come and stay with me.’

Feeling comfortable with her presence as she walked towards me, I nodded in agreement. Her rosy cheeks filled out against her fair complexion. She smiled warmly towards me. ‘I’m not so sure about these wellingtons,’ she said as we both looked down towards her feet. ‘I look like a farmer’s wife, don’t I?’ she smiled. ‘Your clothes?’ she asked, looking around the room.

I knelt down and stretched my arm reaching out for the plastic shopping bag, sneezing hard, disturbing a layer of dust that had settled against the floor underneath the bed. Molly knelt down next to me, her tartan pleated skirt spread out against the floor as she offered her help before I finally got hold of it and dragged it out.

‘I think we ought to take more than this,’ she said, standing whilst feeling the light weight of the bag.

‘They’re wet with the rain,’ I told her, leaning down and picking my coat up from the floor with my clothes wrapped inside. ‘There’s a bolero in there that Lily knitted for me.’

‘It’s so beautiful,’ she said as she took it out of the bag.

‘Those vests are mine too,’ I added as she rummaged through, lifting them out and inspecting them. ‘They don’t look very clean, Molly. That’s because Daddy’s black sock got mixed in with the washing and the colour ran.’

'That leaves a skirt and one pair of grey socks.'

'That's right,' I told her, slipping the vest over my head.

'Haven't you any more underwear?'

'They're wet from the storm,' I said in a muffled voice, pulling the vest down from over my face and slipping my arms through the sleeves.

I sensed Molly had spotted strange marks on my back the way she sighed. 'They're from the thorns, Daddy's roses,' I explained, rushing to bury my head through the open neck of the vest I was going to wear.

Molly struggled with her plump fingers, undoing the button which was to fasten my skirt at the waist. 'Good job my nails aren't long,' I was told before she held it out. 'Hold on to my arm,' she said as I nearly lost my balance whilst stepping into it. Molly looked towards me and smiled as she squeezed the oversized button back into place. 'We're nearly there,' she said, holding out the bolero and encouraging me to slip my arms through the short fluffy sleeves before passing me my long grey woollen socks.

'They've shrunk,' I told Molly as she watched whilst I squeezed my feet inside them.

'Found them at last,' Teddy called out in a fluster as he appeared in the room with a pair of clogs in his hand. I pushed as hard as I could until my feet slipped inside them.

'Right,' Molly said, 'We'll soon have these dry,' pushing the bundle of clothes I had worn that day down into the empty plastic bag.

Teddy took off his jacket and draped it over my shoulders. 'You snuggle into that,' Molly told me before I was hoisted up in his arms, Molly following behind making the plastic bag she carried rustle as it clicked against her broad hips with every step she took down the dark narrow staircase.

'I thank my lucky stars Primrose Cottage was built on a sloping hill,' Molly said, pausing as she quickly took another step. 'I lit the fire early on this afternoon,' she continued, pausing once more as she stepped down further. 'I knew by the darkness of the sky that crept in over us. Oh dear, and what a storm that followed. So you see Primrose Cottage will be lovely and warm by now.'

'Be careful, Molly,' Teddy told her. 'The carpet's loose on this one.' Everything went silent as she took her time stepping down. 'Only one more now, Molly.'

'Thank heavens,' she said, 'What a terrible mess. I knew these old wellies would come to some use,' she said, lifting her long skirt up a little as she waded through the flood of water which had forced its way in through the gap underneath the front door.

Teddy headed towards it and Molly rushed past and lifted up the latch. I felt myself slipping and Teddy hoisted me up once more whilst Molly stepped to one side to let us through, holding on to her hat. 'Would you believe it?' she called, catching her breath as we faced the oncoming wind which caused her mac to flap throughout the short journey. 'The sooner we arrive at Primrose Cottage, the better,' she called.

'Only a few more yards and we're there,' Teddy called back.

'Thank goodness,' she said, rooting through the pocket of her mac, pulling out a large copper coloured key as they both walked along the cobbled path towards the door that was no taller than Molly herself. Molly placed the key in the lock. 'It always sticks,' she complained as her shivering hands finally turned the key.

'I can't linger,' Teddy told her as we were welcomed in.

The fuzzy pattern made me feel dizzy as I looked directly down at the mosaic tiled floor whilst Teddy eased me lower until my feet touched the ground.

'I've got to go back and help,' he explained.

'Come on then, let's go inside,' Molly said as she calmly opened the stained glass door that led me into the living room. 'Right, let's get tucked into biscuits and a hot cup of cocoa,' she said, immediately taking off her mac.

The door suddenly opened. 'Sorry, Molly, should have knocked,' Teddy said whilst taking his jacket from my shoulders before disappearing.

'You can sit down, you know. There's plenty of empty chairs,' she called, making her way into the kitchen.

'Thank you,' I whispered, carefully sitting on the edge of a floral covered armchair.

'Don't worry about Arthur,' she called. 'I named him after my father. He's a fluffy old thing.'

I realized that Molly was referring to the long-haired tom cat that was sprawled in a lazy fashion on top of a frayed woven rug which rested, like him, close to the warmth of the fire. His pitch black eyes stared towards me.

'He likes the heat,' she called as I listened to her shake her rain-soaked mac vigorously in the air. 'So we can expect him to lie there for the rest of the day,' she added, popping her head around the door, 'can't we, Arthur?' she mimicked before disappearing back into the kitchen.

'I'm hanging your coat up with mine,' she called out again. 'The heat from the boiler will soon get them dry.'

Fragments of ash from the red-flamed coal fell suddenly through the grate, leaving particles of white dust scattered over the dull marble stone that surrounded the fireplace. Arthur didn't move but lay still staring directly towards me. I tried to stare him out to make him think that I wasn't scared.

'Oh dear,' Molly shouted as I heard a sudden burst of water hit the bottom of the kettle. 'This tap's playing up again,' she called from the kitchen. Arthur continued to lie there staring at me and I stared back. Not even the sound of the pilot light clicking, and then a roar of burning gas interfered with our game.

'The kettle won't be long now,' Molly said. 'I'll have a minute sitting next to the fire, with you and Arthur of course.' His eyelids closed up and down with each stroke of Molly's hand, spoiling the game, before she sat down in a matching chair opposite me. I yawned, to my surprise quite loudly and shook slightly in a shiver.

'Maybe that's the last,' Molly said in between yawning herself and shivering with the sound of the howling wind outside. She leant over and rubbed my hands together. 'You'll be warm soon,' I was told as she glanced towards the fire. 'A good night's sleep will help,' she said, looking closely into my eyes. 'Those dark rings around them should be gone by the morning. Anyway, there's the kettle boiling.' The sharp whistle blew louder and louder disturbing Molly from the comfort of her chair.

Arthur lay there, spreading himself out and stretching the width of Molly's rug. 'Tea time,' Molly called from the kitchen. I hesitated. Was she calling me, I wondered, listening to her rooting through the cutlery? Arthur lay there quite snug and then instinctively shot up with the familiar sound of Molly turning the tin opener until the tinkle of the lid was heard to drop off. 'There's usually only you and me,' I heard her say. 'Now eat up,' she told him as I heard the clutter of a pot dish scrape across the hard floor. 'It's so exciting, isn't it, Arthur, that we have company? Why don't you come into the kitchen?' she called. 'Now that you've warmed up. We'll eat at the table next to the window, even though we can't see out,' she complained.

'Oh,' she said in surprise. 'Can't see who'd want to come out in this weather,' she added, slowly making her way out from the kitchen and walking casually towards the door as the door knocker rapped several times.

'Is me best friend here?' I recognized the voice and stood immediately. 'Only her brother says that she's come to live with you.' I peered out through the open door.

'Come in, my dear. Another coat to dry,' she told Susie, slipping it from her shoulders. 'You can leave your wellingtons next to mine. It's only tiny this porch but it certainly comes in handy.' By that time I had wandered back into the living room. 'I'll leave you both to have a chat,' Molly said, 'whilst I go and hang this up.'

'She's a good old stick,' Susie said, making herself immediately at home.

'How come you're here?' Susie whispered, leaning towards me as she took over the chair that Molly had sat on. 'She'll be Bible bashing your brain. Religious teachers always do. Jesus Christ, frittened me to death!' Susie said, jumping slightly whilst lifting her feet up off the floor.

'That's Arthur,' I whispered, 'Molly's cat.' He slowly made his way in between the chairs we were sitting on.

'Ugly brute if you ask me,' Susie whispered, relaxing a little as Arthur took his rightful place next to the fire. 'Never liked tom cats. It's like a doll's house inside here,' she said, looking around the room. 'Nice though. Even t'curtains hanging down on that tiny window match chairs we're sat on. Just admiring the room,' Susie said, sitting up much straighter as Molly walked in.

'Cocoa?' she asked.

'Wouldn't mind,' Susie replied. 'She always wears those loose long-pleated skirts and white blouses with that fancy embroidery around the collars,' Susie whispered as Molly left the room. 'No one's ever seen her in a pair of high heels. Not that there's no harm in that, I suppose. Can't get shoes any flatter than the ones she wears. Mind you, she has to wear them come to think of it, and long skirts too. Reckon she's got trouble with varicose veins in her legs, painful too, so I've heard from the women that gossip at the end of our street. She doesn't have owt to do with anyone, Molly, I mean,' Susie whispered, 'unless it's for a Christian matter.'

'Like saving me from the flood at Rose Cottage?' I asked.

'Yeah, yeah, that's what I mean,' Susie said, looking around the room. 'Wish I lived in a place like this, but me dad would keep banging his head with those low beams. Anyway, I was really worried about you. Did you get a good pasting?'

I looked at her questioningly.

'When your ma dragged you across the road?'

'Guess what? I ran away!'

'What, you ran away from Rose Cottage?'

'Yes, Susie, I did.'

'Well you couldn't have got very far cos you're here now.'

'Well I wouldn't be if Teddy hadn't come into the church.'

'See, knew you wouldn't have got very far. Anyway, what difference does that make?'

'What?'

'Your brother in church.'

'I was with Fellwick.' I leaned over and whispered, 'He was drunk. Well, that's what he told me. He was hiccupping like Grandfather does so he must have been.'

'What, drinking in church?'

'Shush,' I told Susie, not wanting Molly to overhear. 'Anyway, Susie, God might have taken me if Teddy hadn't walked in and frightened us.'

'Don't start that again, and don't mention this to Molly or she'll go on for ever.'

'About what?' I asked.

'Religion, you know. Holy Ghost and all that sort of stuff. I knew it,' Susie whispered. 'There, over there on t'sideboard,' she said, slightly raising her voice. 'There's got to be eight at least,' as she counted quietly to herself.

'What?'

'Bibles. You're in t'right place if you want to be near God.'

We both turned around facing the glow of the fire as we heard Molly stirring the cups from inside the kitchen with a metal spoon.

The pendulum of the clock sitting on top of the mantel noticeably ticked from side to side in our silence. 'Don't suppose I can have a fag in here,' Susie whispered, breaking the silence after a while. 'Can't see no ashtrays, can you?' She moved the packet of cigarettes from the side pocket of her jeans and slipped them into the other. 'He don't look happy neither,' she said, turning to the black and white picture of an old thin-faced bearded man that hung down on a loop of string inside a dark wooden frame on Molly's whitewashed wall. 'And Harry can piss off when I see him, too,' she said as I sat staring across towards the picture and the sad expression that was shown through the wide eyes of the man framed inside. 'He scoffed most of t'chips after I'd stood all that time in t'pouring rain waiting to be served.'

The room went into an uncomfortable silence and Susie sat looking quite disgruntled. 'To tell you t'truth, why I feel angry,' she said, staring into the fire, 'is that me ma and pa fell out again.'

'Did they hurt you, Susie?'

'What, just because they were angry? Nowt to do with me if they scream at each other, is it? But it's getting to be a regular habit. I've a feeling that me pa's got another woman.'

'As well as your mother?' I asked.

'Ma never dresses smart any more. She ends up looking like some washer woman, and me pa's gone the opposite. Hardly ever comes home either. Chucked in me boyfriend because of all t'stress. God, I wish I could light one up,' she said, patting the outside of her pocket where her cigarettes lay.

'Susie, I want to go home,' I whispered.

'Well, that's a shock if there ever was one. Why the hell do you wanna go home?'

'Sshh,' I said, reminding her to keep her voice down so Molly wouldn't hear. 'Because Molly hasn't taken me into her home because she loves me.'

'What's that got to do wi' it? It's because your 'ouse is flooded. Look, you're gonna have to stay t'night at least.'

'But, Susie,' I whispered, 'I might wet the bed.'

'Well, try and wake up when you want a pee,' she whispered back.

'Not much of a selection,' Molly said out loud, arriving with a huge tray. 'I forgot to fill the biscuit barrel. That's with Mrs Grindle stopping me on my shopping trip with a bombardment of words. She told me that the vicar should do more for the community instead of rubbing his hands every time the collection box is filled.'

'Good gracious,' Molly said as Susie stood and took the tray from her hands. 'It's the way she said it; as if the vicar was pilfering.'

'That means stealing,' Susie turned to tell me.

'But that really disturbs me,' Molly said. 'That money goes to the upkeep of the church and most certainly not in the vicar's pocket as I'm sure she was trying to suggest.' Molly shuddered at the thought.

'The dreaded Mrs Grindle,' Susie said.

'Well, yes, I suppose she has to be dreaded,' was Molly's reply as she took Susie's place in the chair.

Susie, anxious not to spill a drop, served the cups of steaming hot cocoa.

'Aren't you hungry?' Molly asked as I refused the offer of a biscuit. 'Have you something you want to say?' Molly asked again.

I was unable to speak as I listened to Susie crunching away, and a sudden burst of tears followed.

'Oh dear,' Molly said, standing immediately.

'It'll be over Eric. He was her best friend,' Susie said. 'I had to break the news to her that he'd died.'

'Here, take this,' Molly told Susie as she took the cup of cocoa from my hand.

'I wouldn't like that job again. She wouldn't believe me. Well, not at first, not until we took her ... that's Harry and me ... to t'grave.'

Molly moved her arms away as I rejected any kind of comfort. 'You're so alone in your own little world,' she said, kneeling down on to the woven carpet next to where I sat.

'Don't look so disturbed; she's not used to it, Molly ... affection ... well, she ain't, is she?'

'Well, it's time she learnt how much she's loved in this tiny village.'

'Molly,' I said looking towards her as I wiped the tears that flowed with the palm of my hand.

'I know what you want to ask me. I can see with the look in your eye. I can't, my dear, he's gone. He's gone up to heaven, in peace at last. He won't be alone; God will be by his side.'

I stared into her eyes, bewildered.

'Do you know his spirit will always be with you?'

I shook my head in anger. 'But what about our shopping trips together?' I asked, my voice faltering. 'I won't be running over the bridge with excitement again,' I told Molly. 'Do you want to know why? Because he won't be there, sitting on the wooden bench in his garden waiting for me at the end of each day for me to tell him about what I'd done at school. We'll never have that picnic that I'd promised because I told him when I'd grown up...' I paused for a second to try and catch my breath, 'grown up into a lady, I would take him to the seaside. He was so excited ... so was I. Oh, Eric, please, please come back.' I buried my head against my knees and sobbed.

'Shall I call t'doctor?' Susie asked.

'Why on earth do that?' Molly replied.

'Well ... well, cos she's in so much pain.'

'There isn't any doctor that can heal this sort of pain,' Molly replied. 'Oh dear,' she said, lifting my head up gently before walking the short distance to the sideboard.

'I'll have one, too,' Susie said as Molly rummaged through a box of tissues, picking a handful out before wiping her eyes.

'We're all crying now,' she whispered, passing one over to me. A sudden patter against the window caught Molly by surprise.

'It's me,' Teddy called.

Molly blew into her tissue and unlocked the cottage door.

'I'm not stopping,' he said as the wind blew in behind him. 'Brought this; it's rather creased. She'd hid it underneath her mattress.' Teddy popped his head around the stained glass door. 'Lucky you being able to stay here with Molly,' he told me before saying hello to Susie.

'Yes, and she can stay as long as she likes. We're going to listen to the radio after supper,' she told him.

Susie pulled a face at me and quickly wiped her tears. 'Bet it's t'bloody Archers,' she whispered whilst Molly saw Teddy out through the door.

'Hey, my dear,' Molly said, shaking the white lace dress I had bought from the jumble sale and holding it out.

'Still stinks of mothballs, and that's after me ma washed it and pegged it out on t'line,' Susie told her.

'Well, it's Sunday school tomorrow,' Molly said. 'A good wash and a spray of starch will just do the job. We'll go to church in the morning and Sunday school in the afternoon. Then the dress can be worn in full glory.'

'Don't include me,' Susie told her. 'Catch up with you in the week,' she added, grabbing her coat from the kitchen and slipping into her wellington boots before rushing through the door.

Chapter 21

Molly had taught me a lot in the five days I had stayed with her. I wore my white dress and attended Sunday school for the first time. The bed-wetting, to my surprise, only happened once. Molly made no fuss.

Evenings consisted mainly of me being allowed to sit by the fire in Molly's ancient old armchair. I would be given a book to read. Molly thought *The Famous Five* by Enid Blyton would give me an exciting read. She had no knowledge that I could barely spell and, to save my embarrassment, I kept my head down, going over the tiny lines of words, slowly turning page by page in pretence that I was enjoying the story, whilst Molly softly played, with sentiment, on the upright piano.

Deep in my heart, I dreaded each time there was a knock on her door. Sometimes I heard it in my imagination, so Molly would tell me, but I knew the day would come when someone would be there, waiting for me, to take me back to Rose Cottage.

We were constant visitors to the graveyard, Molly and I. Molly talked me through the pain I felt.

I remembered my first day at Sunday school. There was Molly rooting through the charity box after lifting it down from the top of the dusty shelf inside the church hall, opening it up and holding out knickers and vests for my approval on the size. A bundle of white ankle socks were thrown into a plastic shopping bag before Molly lifted down another box. The cardboard sagged underneath with the weight. She lifted out several pairs of shoes and lined them together against the stone floor. I held on to Molly's arm, balancing myself whilst I slipped my feet inside them until at last the right size was found.

'And these can go in for good measure,' she told me, noticing my constant glance down towards a white pair of open-toed leather sandals. I smiled towards her and she smiled back.

The following day, Molly purchased a pink slide. She thanked the hunched old man behind the chemist counter before brushing my fringe back with her fingers and clipping it in my hair.

The rattle of the foot pedal and the wheel going round and round kept me awake part of the night and I wondered what Molly could possibly be sewing. To my great surprise, the following morning, after I had washed in hot soapy water, a dress, short sleeved, made in gingham that flared slightly from the waist, was given to me.

'Now you've got exactly the same dress to wear as every other girl in your class has at school.' I felt sick with excitement that it actually fitted, twizzing around in it whilst Molly looked on with glee.

Molly dusted and I cleaned the brasses. I cracked the eggs into a bowl; Molly baked the cakes. Bulbs of tulips were planted in the miniature greenhouse. Molly filled a pot with compost and handed it to me. She passed me two bulbs and I planted them with care. It was agreed that after they had blossomed they were going to be placed on top of Eric's grave.

Arthur and I became friends and I took over the role of feeding him. Molly ticked the homework books that spread the width of the table. I sat next to her and placed them neatly in a pile. That day had turned into night and we both yawned together. The oil lamp was put out. Arthur curled up in his basket before the creaky wooden door leading us from the kitchen was gently closed. Molly wished me sweet dreams as I reached the top of the stairs. I wished her goodnight.

Molly looked flustered the following day when I flew in from the garden to give her the bad news that the tulips hadn't blossomed. 'Well, we only planted them yesterday, my child,' she told me with a slight falter in her voice.

I sensed there was something wrong and closed the door quietly before undoing the buckle of the brown leather shoes Molly had given me. 'They're a bit muddy,' I told her on my inspection as I slipped them off.

'Leave them over there on the floor,' she said.

I tiptoed over and placed them neatly underneath the shadow of Molly's long mac that hung down from the hook on the wall. Maybe Molly's working too hard, I thought, whilst peering inside the living room to see if Arthur was lying there waiting for me. She is, I told myself as the steam lifted and rose up into the air from my clothes that Molly had washed and put to dry on a wooden maiden in front of the fire.

'Arthur'll have gone wandering again,' Molly said. I looked back towards her. Molly slipped out after dabbing her nose with a white embroidered hanky she held in her hand. I sensed something was wrong. 'Oh dear,' she said, pulling a chair out from the kitchen table and sitting down immediately. 'I will miss you.' She blew into her handkerchief.

'He's back,' I told Molly, listening to Arthur's cries whilst running over towards the kitchen door and lifting up the latch. Arthur moved in swiftly, squeezing himself through the narrow gap before I had any chance of opening it wider. I rushed behind him, stopping in front of Molly as he leapt into the living room.

'You go, dear, and enjoy each other's company,' Molly told me as I looked with sadness towards her. 'I'm all right. I'm going to dry these silly eyes of mine.'

I stood and waited until the last tear had been wiped, and then scrambled as quickly as I could through into the living room.

'Is she in?' I heard a masculine voice ask. I looked at him with a puzzled expression on my face. 'Molly?' he added, whilst tapping on the door as he walked in. I stumbled for a second on my reply and it was only by the sound of his well-to-do voice that I recognized him without his cloak and collar as he stood there in a well-worn, light grey, baggy suit. The finely knitted rib of his crew-necked sweater sagged slightly at the neck showing his prominent Adam's apple that moved up and down as he swallowed nervously. Black didn't suit him, what with his fair complexion. He was too tall for me to look any further. His shoes, laced and tied, appeared quite shabby as I looked down with a feeling of considerable shyness.

'I'll go and tell Molly that you're here,' I told him. He

nodded and turned towards the window, stooping a little as he stared out before I rushed towards the kitchen. 'Molly,' I whispered as she sat concentrating on her search through an old shoe box that was filled with photographs. 'Molly,' I whispered again, 'the vicar's here.'

'Who, Edward Applehurst?' she whispered, looking straight at me before shooting up off her chair as soon as I had confirmed it.

'I'll put the kettle on,' I told her.

'Those fancy cups and saucers, up there with the pattern around the edges. We'll use those,' she said with a slight panic in her voice. She turned and rushed over to root through her handbag that stood upright on top of the kitchen shelf, before pulling out the compact mirror and applying a quick coat of pale pink lipstick around her plump lips. She checked her blouse was neatly tucked in and straightened her long skirt that stopped just above her ankles.

'Oh, Molly,' the vicar called in a rather loud voice as she stepped into the living room.

'Well, this is a surprise,' I heard Molly tell him.

I wonder if they've embraced each other, I thought, as well-to-do people usually do, so Susie once told me. I dragged the footstool from underneath the kitchen table along the stone floor, enabling me to reach the narrow shelf that was built high upon the wall.

'I don't know, Molly,' he said as she asked him if he would like to sit. 'After these floods…' he started to say. 'Well, let's put it this way. Some of the villagers expect me to put things right. I know a lot of damage has been done but there's very little I can do only offer hot cups of tea and a snack in the church hall for those who have been badly hit. Mrs Grindle told me to get off my backside... Well, rather worse than that,' he muttered, 'as we passed by each other in the street. I told her I wasn't a saint and was doing my best.'

'Quite right,' Molly said.

'Yes, but, Molly, she told me if I stopped filling my pockets from other people's kindness that I probably would be, doing my best, that is, and I simply don't know how to take that,' he told her.

'Are you all right?' I heard Molly say as he began to cough.

'Just a tickle in my throat,' he replied.

'I wouldn't take any notice, Edward. Mrs Grindle's quite rude to practically everyone. She's got the devil in her.'

I'd better warn Susie when I see her, I thought, whilst pouring the milk from the glass bottle into Molly's china jug. Warn her about how dangerous Mrs Grindle is.

'I know, I know that, Molly,' I heard the vicar say. 'I have prayed, Molly, prayed that she'll rid herself of the anger that lives inside her.'

I felt quite frightened by then and crept over to bolt the back door that led out to Molly's garden, just in case Mrs Grindle was lurking around.

I carried the wooden tray into the living room as steadily as I could. The vicar immediately stood and lifted it from my unsteady hands. 'Where are you going?' he asked as I quickly turned.

'Please join us,' Molly said.

I refused the invitation with grace and scurried my way back into Molly's kitchen.

'She brings joy to you, Molly,' I heard him say. 'That smile on your face, with her presence, tells me all.'

'Well, as you have angels that surround you with your task, Edward, so have I with this little girl.'

Was Molly ... was she really talking and telling the vicar about me? The thought of being an angel filled me with excitement. Turning my head to one side, I peered down over my shoulder in case I had grown wings. I must have been mistaken, I thought. Molly must have meant another little girl. Disappointed, I sat on the edge of the spindle legged chair, resting my elbows on top of the wooden surface of Molly's kitchen table. I wish the oil lamp was lit, I thought, with little light shining through the window as I sat and looked out. It left Molly's grey painted kitchen looking cold without it.

The room became considerably dimmer as the grey clouds circled above. There was a sudden crack of lightning, followed a few seconds later by a crash of thunder.

'Oh dear, Molly,' I heard the vicar say, leaving me imagining Mrs Grindle's face, her bulbous nose squashed against the outside window whilst tapping on the glass, begging me to let her in to shelter from the storm. I jumped off my chair in fright.

'May I go to my room?' I asked, looking into the living room where Molly and the vicar sat in silence across from one another.

'Don't you want to sit with us?' Molly asked.

'Yes,' the vicar said, 'and we'll pray this storm won't last.'

'Of course you can go, my dear, if that's what you want. If you're not down before supper, I'll give you a call.'

'Shall I stay and help?' I asked, holding on to the latch of the green-painted door that led up each tiny step of the narrow staircase. 'I'd like to.'

'I don't see why not,' was Molly's reply. 'We'll give it another half an hour,' I was told as she looked up towards the clock that ticked away on the mantel. 'So you go and have a little time to yourself,' she said, sending me off with her warm smile. 'You're staying, aren't you, Edward, for supper?'

'Well, if you...'

'Yes, I do insist.'

I left them to chatter and ran up the stairs. Lying fully stretched on top of the bed, I was curious as I nestled my head back against the pillow, about how the tiny light bulb found its way inside the frosted glass lampshade that hung from the ceiling above me. Its cupped figure with tiny petals moulded tightly inwards reminded me of a tulip in spring that was waiting to bloom. I squinted several times as I stared up towards it and I was reminded of Charlie, wondering how long the punishment would last until he was allowed to wear another pair of spectacles. A single tear flowed down on to my face, knowing how hard it would be for him to see without them, remembering all too clearly that awful day when Charlie stood, shaking, his bright red burning ears ringing from the severe slap Mummy had given him, his broken spectacles being forced against his face, leaving a look of fear in his bloodshot eyes. I knew, though, deep in my heart that the humiliation he suffered would be made to last for a long, long time.

I thought I heard the sound of Molly's light-hearted voice as I lay there feeling quite solemn. 'Harry's here to see you,' she called. I was right and jumped from the bed, pulling my socks above my ankles before running down the stairs. 'You know, the cheeky lad, but kind,' she told me as she waited at the bottom.

'Lorne's never forgotten me, has she, Molly?'

'No, no, of course not.'

'Hey, you're posh, aren't tha?' Harry said as I passed through the door at the bottom of the stairs that Molly held open for me.

'Molly chose them from the charity box,' I replied.

'Well, not all; we made the skirt didn't we?'

'Posh, if you ask me. Look at t'shoes, too.'

'I shine them every day,' I told Harry.

''Ere, I've brought you sommat.' He rooted down deep inside his jacket pocket.

'A speckled egg,' Molly said.

'It's so tiny.'

''Ere, don't be frittened,' Harry told me, placing it with his fingertips into the palm of my hand.

'You'll stay for tea, won't you, Harry?' Molly asked. Harry hesitated on a reply. 'Yes, you will,' Molly told him. 'I'm sure you're hungry.'

'Aye, I've been out in t'cowd all afternoon. Ain't gonna be fancy is it?' Harry whispered, leaning over to Molly's ear, 'Cos 'e's here, t'vicar. Chip butty would do me.'

'Young chap, you don't fancy lending a hand and helping Mr Drake?' the vicar called over, sitting with his legs crossed and holding the palms of his hands together close up to his mouth.

'No, I don't, sir. Ain't helping dig no graves.'

'No, no,' the vicar replied. 'It's just ... well, the graveyard

… it looks somewhat like a battlefield with flowers strewn all over the place with the horrid weather.'

Harry looked at Molly. 'He means that some of the flowers from the top of the graves have been blown all over with the wind,' she explained.

Harry grunted and groaned to himself. 'Alreet,' he said, after some thought.

'Good lad,' the vicar told him. 'As early in the morning as you can. Mr Drake likes an early start.'

'The pigeon laid it,' Harry told me as I gazed down at the tiny egg. 'You can keep it.'

'Will it break if I drop it, Harry?'

'Course it will, but don't be frittened of it or you will.'

'I'm quite fond of pigeons, myself,' the vicar said, peering over to have a look.

'Why don't you get some?' Harry asked. 'You could stick a loft on that lawn behind t'vicarage; it's big enough. In fact, I've a couple to spare. They breed like hell.'

'Thank you but no, Harry. There's enough complaints from … well, that Mrs Grindle.'

'You know, old Mrs Grindle will always find something to complain about but, unfortunately, it's always … well, the smell, Harry. She says she wouldn't make a pigeon pie from any you keep. Mind you, that's between you and me.'

'Well, she can't say me loft stinks now. I've spent all afternoon cleaning it. There's more dirt inside her fingernails than there is on me pigeons.' Harry told him in a huff.

'You must feel sorry for her and help her along. She obviously thinks that the world's not been very kind to her.'

'Wouldn't have no sympathy,' Harry told the vicar. 'She's called you a name or two.'

'Why don't you go and pour Harry a glass of lemonade?' Molly asked, walking across to her chair.

Harry followed slowly behind me as I carefully watched the egg from rolling with each step I took, before gently placing it on the top of Molly's kitchen table.

'T'fun and games that go on in this village,' Harry said.

'I haven't seen any, Harry,' I replied, turning to make sure the egg hadn't rolled whilst leaning down and picking the tall glass bottle of fizzy lemonade up from the stone floor.

'What?' Harry asked.

'Any fun and games,' I replied. 'Have you ever won one?'

''Ere, I'll open it,' he said as I screwed up my face in an effort to unscrew the top.

'Will it hatch, Harry,' I asked, holding up two cups with both hands, 'the egg that you gave me?'

'Doubt it,' Harry replied, pouring the lemonade into the cups. 'Might do,' he said on reflection, 'if you keep it warm.'

'How does shepherd's pie sound on a wintry day like this?' Molly called through.

'Sounds good to me,' Harry called before downing the lemonade in one. 'Want any 'elp?' he asked as I dragged the stool along the floor towards the sink. 'Anyway, what are tha up to?'

'I'm going to cook the potatoes.'

'I'm impressed,' Harry said. 'Didn't know you'd got t'strength.'

'Well, it's only a saucepan, Harry.'

'Aye, I know,' he said, rushing towards me and taking over as I reached up towards it. She's got some owd stuff hangin' up here. Must be hundreds of years old,' Harry said, brushing away a cobweb as he lifted the handle of the copper pan from the iron hook that dangled down from a wooden rod along the frame of Molly's window.

'I think they were her mother's before she died.'

'What, all these pans hung up 'ere in a row? Anyway, 'ow do you know that?'

'Because she gazes up to them sometimes saying "Ah, Mildred"; then she sighs and Mildred, Harry, was her mother's name.'

'You ain't been nowhere in your life, 'ave you?' Harry said as he placed the saucepan down on to the base of the sink.

I rolled up the sleeves of my woolly cardigan that Molly had told me to keep quiet about when she grabbed it from the charity box inside the church hall. I peered down to see if the motif knitted in the pattern on the side pocket was still there. 'It's a butterfly,' I told Harry.

'Aye, anyone would think by the way you're looking at it that it's going to fly away. Well, it ain't,' Harry said, admiring the stitching.

'The potatoes,' I whispered.

'I'll get 'em,' I was told on my attempt to step down from the stool. 'It's dark in 'ere,' he said, leaning against the open door that led into Molly's larder. 'Found 'em,' he called as he disappeared inside.

I listened to him stumble before he appeared looking a little distraught.

'They're all loose,' he said, struggling towards me with a handful of potatoes in all shapes and sizes.

'We'll need more than that,' I told him as he tipped them down into the base of the sink, brushing at the fragments of clay that had rubbed off against the rather shabby sweater he wore underneath his open jacket.

'All this trouble for t'sake of a shepherd's pie,' he muttered before going back to collect some more. 'Betcha,' he said, returning this time much quicker, 'we'll 'ave to say grace cos vicar's 'ere. I'll feel a right idiot. Don't know t'words.' Harry emptied his hands and the rest of the potatoes rolled into the sink. 'Ain't got no knife, 'ave you?'

'It's that tiny one there,' I pointed to Harry as he rooted through the top drawer of Molly's kitchenette. 'Just say amen then, Harry.'

'When?' he asked, passing the knife over to me.

'At the end of grace.'

'How the 'ell will I know when it's th'end.'

'Because I'll nudge you, Harry.'

'Anyway, he'll like that, will t'vicar.'

'What?' I asked.

'What we're 'aving for tea, shepherd's pie. Ya know, wi' t'shepherds and all that stuff. It's in t'Bible ain't it.'

'Harry,' I said, turning my head towards him as he picked up an apple from a bowl on the table, 'I'd better warn you…'

'Don't worry. Gonna ask Molly first if I can eat it,' he said, holding it up in his hand.

'No, Harry, I need to warn you of the danger.' Harry looked puzzled. 'Mrs Grindle's got the devil in her,' I whispered whilst quickly turning to the window just in case her face was squashed against it. 'She has, Harry; I've heard it with my own ears,' I added, turning my head back towards him to see his reaction.

''Ave you only just found out?' he replied. 'She's always had t'devil in 'er.'

I'll never go near her again, I thought, giving out a little shiver whilst Harry threw the apple up into the air several times showing no expression of fear about the news I'd just told him.

'Anyway, as I was saying, you ain't been anywhere except t'jumble sale and t'church and t'church hall, 'ave you?'

'I have, Harry.'

'Where, then?' he asked, throwing the apple up in the air once more.

'I've been to some scary places,' I told him.

'Yeah, sure, name one.'

'I went back to India.'

'Well, tha's never been there in t'first place. Come on then, tell me more.'

'And I've crossed the sea to Ireland and fed the canary. Nana can't walk, Harry, so I went over to help her feed it.'

'Can't 'ave. I'd 'ave known wi t'village gossips.'

'Harry,' I said in a whisper as he stepped closer. 'I tell my Nana lots of things whilst she sits in her wheelchair crocheting. I trust her Harry, do you want to know why? Because she's old and wise. Nana's taking a secret with her to the grave, well that's where she told me it would go.'

'Eh,' Harry asked, 'whose?'

'Mine,' I whispered looking over my shoulder.

'Who else were there when ya told your Nana?'

'Nobody, Harry, just Nana, me and a yellow canary.'

'Tell us,' lending an ear, 'ain't that important then if tha can't share.'

'No one besides Nana knows, not even Lily, because of the cones...'

'Consequence,' Harry urged me on to say.

'Won't tell a living soul, promise, even swear on t'Holy Bible if I 'ave to.'

'My Daddy isn't real.'

'Eh, just seen him t'other day, looks real to me.'

There was silence, Harry heard me swallow the lump inside my throat and huffed.

'I told Nana about Mummy prodding me in the back when I look out for Daddy coming back over the bridge from work. It really hurts, Harry. Mummy reminds me every time she digs her fingers into my skin that I'm a bastard, another man's child, and if Daddy gets to know that I'm a fake, Mummy says I would be suffocated by the pillow I sleep on by his very own hands.'

'Blimey,' Harry muttered, 'when did ya get back then, from Ireland?' he asked.

'When I woke up during the night, Harry.'

'Eh?'

'I went there in my dreams.'

'All this I've just 'eard, it were 'ard to belive in't first place.'

'Well, it's true what I told Nana, that's why I dreamt about it. I'll never know, will I, if my Daddy is, well,' my words choked inside.

'Course, tha will, tha instinct will tell thee. Ey, there'll be no 'eartache 'ere, not in Molly's house,' as my lip drooped, 'your Pa is your Pa, after all's said and done. Surprised your Ma named you Lorne in first place, taunting ya like this. Don't know what it means neither,' as I looked with question. 'All I know it's a cruel word. If it were only a dream,' Harry said, scratching his head in thought, 'there'll be nowt to worry about, anyway, dreams don't come true.'

'This one did, Harry.'

'Blimey, don't be stripping.'

'I can only see them when I peep over my shoulder.'

'Bleedin' 'ell, your back's full of scabs, few mattering too.'

'They'll be better soon, Harry, but when they are, Mummy starts all over again.'

'Ya don't have to sound angry to me. I believe ya. After all that I were only gonna suggest a trip to t'seaside in t'first place cos you've never been. I'll go and ask Molly if I can eat it,' I was told as he finished rubbing the apple against his jacket, 'now that it looks nice and shiny.'

My eyes caught a glimpse through Molly's kitchen window of daisies swaying in clusters on the miniature lawn outside, a sign of summer that seemed a million miles away with the freak storms and gushing winds that lingered. I was suddenly filled with haunting memories. I begged myself to let them go. I didn't want to remember where they swayed with the buttercups on that one particular morning but I still felt the ache from his grip, as my mind wandered back, where he lifted me from underneath my shoulders. I listened to the squelch from the soles of my plastic sandals as I was lowered down over the stile on to the dewy grass and left there alone; the slam from the door, the engine humming, before the white van was driven away with Mummy inside. I shuddered hearing his deep voice call out my name on their return, which echoed across the hilly field whilst I sat moulding the clay from the banks of the stream, making Minnie a vase and Daddy an ashtray.

'Oh,' I screamed out, feeling a hand on my shoulder whilst moving my head to one side in case I was going to get slapped.

'What's up?' Harry asked.

'I think I startled her,' Molly replied, gently turning me around on the stool.

'My dear child,' she whispered, hugging me closely against her. 'I'm so sorry if I alarmed you.'

'You haven't, Molly,' I sighed. 'It's just that I was thinking, that's all.'

'Well, seeing as you're all gathering here,' the vicar said, 'I might as well join in with the fun and roll my sleeves up. I'm quite good in the kitchen,' he told Molly, taking off his jacket and hanging it over the back of the kitchen chair.

'Edward, there's no need.'

'Come on, Molly, if I can't chop an onion... Well, at my age it's a bit of a bad do.' Molly looked embarrassed, but pleased by the smile on her face, whilst he took over.

Harry lifted me off the stool, dried my hands with a thin, worn tea towel whilst Molly and the vicar chatted away. 'Follow me,' Harry said in a whisper as he led me towards the living room. 'See t'sparkle 'e had in his eyes?'

'I didn't, Harry.'

'Well, I did and it could only 'ave been for Molly. Reckon 'e loves her.'

'Couldn't it have been the onion he was peeling?' I asked.

'Could 'ave been,' Harry replied, 'but tell me this, why 'as 'e spent so much time wi' 'er? And 'elping to prepare tea of all things.' Harry and I sat in silence and thought. 'Towd ya. Listen to 'er laugh,' he whispered.

'Do you think he's tickling her?' I whispered back.

'Wouldn't 'ave time, would 'e?' Harry said, sniffing up into the air. 'I can smell th'onions frying. She's nice ain't she, Molly? Do her good to fancy 'im,' he said, lending an ear towards the kitchen. 'Shush,' I was told as I was about to reply. 'Towd ye. He's just offered 'is 'and.'

'What does that mean?'

'Marriage.'

I looked with eyes wide open towards Harry, who now got down from his chair and crawled the short distance around to the open door that led into the kitchen.

'Harry, are you all right?' I heard Molly call.

Harry quickly stood. 'Aye, Molly, I am.'

'Only Edward's offered a hand so there's no need for you to help if that's what you wanted to know.'

'Could 'ave meant owt,' Harry said, looking quite red in the face. 'This business of 'e lives on his own and so does she, so I were just 'oping that 'e were asking 'er to be his wife.'

'Don't look disappointed,' I told him as he huffed while sitting down on the chair.

'Feel stupid, don't I?'

'Anyway, Harry, I might marry you. That's when I've grown up of course.'

'I'll be an owd man by then; too weak to pick you up any more.'

'Don't worry then, Harry. I'll probably marry someone else. That's if they ask me.'

'Aye, and don't be saying yes to t'first one. Anyway, tha's a lot of growing to do before that 'appens.'

'Mummy says she's going to throw me out on to the streets as soon as I'm old enough. I suppose that means she doesn't want me any more. I don't mind though, Harry,' I said as he sat and tutted. 'Although I'll miss Charlie and Teddy.'

'Blimey,' Harry said, standing quickly and digging deep down inside his jacket pockets. 'Th'only reason I came 'ere in t'first place was to give you this. It's a letter,' Harry told me, pulling a crumpled envelope out. 'It's for thee.'

'Me?' I asked.

'I ain't sent it to you. It was sent to me ma, asking 'er to pass it on to you when it was safe. You'd think it were t'bloody war, me pa said, but soon shut up when me ma gave 'im one of 'er looks. Tha can open it now. It's got tha name on t'front o' th'envelope. Well go on then.'

'I've never had a letter before, Harry.'

'Aye, I can tell, time it's taking ya to open it. Hurry up. Caught it,' Harry said as a pink petal floated down from inside the letter as I pulled it out from the envelope and opened it up.

'Read it out then,' Harry said, leaning down over me whilst I silently read the opening words. ''Ere, I'll read it out with ye.'

My little Princess,

I can picture you in my mind as I write these words to you to make into a letter for you to read, picture you stood holding up the paper in your tiny hands, still, so still, going through every word I have written.

Posting this letter out to you and addressing it to Rose Cottage would have left me in turmoil,

'Don't ask me what that means,' Harry said out loud as I looked up towards him.

knowing that if it wasn't collected in safe hands ... that you would never have had the chance of ripping open the envelope and reading it.

Remember you and I making that beautiful perfume from every petal that dropped from the roses Father grows in the garden?

'That's why she sent you this,' Harry said, reminding me of the petal he held in his hand.

I have just lit my second cigarette whilst I'm writing this letter to you. Not that it will give me the comfort that I need from giving you one big hug. Leaving you behind at Rose Cottage was the hardest thing to do and sometimes it is extremely difficult to get on with my own life. I fear the constant sadness you have to endure.

'Blimey, you need a dictionary to understand these words,' Harry said.

'It's from Lily, Harry,' I told him, turning on to the

next page and staring down at her signature scrawled at the bottom.

'Aye, we knew that cos of t'petal.'

> But one day, just like me, you will be able to walk away and leave Rose Cottage far, far behind you.

Harry read out loud before stopping and scratching his head. 'Where the 'ell will you go?'

'Lily's only worried about me, Harry. Only because Mummy's always pretending that she doesn't like me. But she must do, Harry, deep down, because I'm one of her children.'

'Come on, let's read on,' he told me, holding on to the edge of the paper.

> I know you have a good friend in Eric and Susie...

'Lily mustn't know Eric's dead, Harry,' I whispered.

'Aye, she don't know that I'm your friend too. Ain't got a mention.'

> Anyway, I have decided to be strong and try to cope with the horrible misery I see and feel at Rose Cottage and not to be discouraged from coming to visit you more often. Then who knows, Mother might, in time, allow you to come and stay with me.

'It's like a flippin' book this wi' t'length o' t'pages, and all this writing,' Harry told me. 'Well, come on, let's read on,' he said after a silent pause.

> The news on me is that I have found an excellent elocution teacher. My final exam's soon and I'm nervous.

'Flippin' 'eck, why's she using all these big words? Can't even pronounce 'alf of what she's written.'

> But now I feel confident on getting the job of telephonist. The pay's good which means lots of ribbons for your hair.

'It's all smudged,' Harry said, 't'last bit o' writing, as if teardrops 'ave fallen on it.'

'Maybe she was writing it outside and it started to rain.'

'Aye, but 'er name's still clear on th'end o' letter.'

'Tea's practically ready if you would like to wash your hands,' Molly said, popping her head around the kitchen door.

'She's been crying, Molly 'as. I bet 'e's jilted 'er. You know, given 'er th'elbow. Well, told 'er he don't love 'er.'

'Who?' I asked.

'T'vicar, who do ya think? Look, I'll stuff t'letter back in me pocket wi' t'petal and we'll walk in there pretending nowt's 'appened. So whatever they do, don't stare at 'er, cos if it's true she'll be embarrassed. Stop fidgeting wi' your skirt, will ya. There's nowt to be worried about, you look fine. Reet, let's move. I'll try and make small talk when we go in,' Harry told me, pulling me back after I'd taken the first step.

'Do you have to say lots of tiny words, Harry?' I whispered as he smoothed out his hair with his hands.

'It means talking while pretending that nowt's 'appened, in case 'e's finished wi' 'er,' he explained. 'First thing we do is to tell Molly what a wonderful smell, reet, on her cooking. It'll make 'im think, won't it, about changing 'is mind?'

'About what, Harry?'

'Marrying 'er. Are ya ready?'

I nodded and with a slight cough from Harry, we both took the few steps towards the kitchen. The kitchen was humid and stuffy with a flare of gas hissing wickedly inside the stove.

'Molly and myself have had an extremely long chat about things,' the vicar told us.

Harry looked at me, and I at him, before he dipped my hands and splashed them under the cold running water over Molly's pot sink. 'Ow's everyone doin' in t'village?' Harry asked him whilst we both walked over and pulled our chairs out.

'Not good, Harry, not good at all.' Another glance passed between Harry and me as we sat down on opposite sides. 'Oh, I feel quite depressed. This terrible storm has done me no favours. Everything's breaking up,' the vicar told us.

Harry winked over to me and I winked back.

'Hey come on all of you. It's nature that's made these awful things happen,' Molly said. 'Everything will soon get back to normal, you'll see.'

Harry and I stared into each other's eyes across the table as the vicar rushed to Molly's aid. 'It is rather hot,' he told Molly, grabbing a towel and taking over. 'Gracious me, it looks delicious.'

'Edward!'

'Well, it does, Molly,' he called, rushing over towards the table and placing the earthenware pot down in the middle.

'Beetroot?' Molly asked as the vicar did the serving.

Harry stuck his fork inside the jar and thanked her. 'Ouch,' he said as I stretched my leg out underneath the table and kicked him, stopping any attempt to place what he had scooped up on his fork from entering his mouth.

I placed the palm of my hands together after Molly and the vicar had done the same. Harry put his fork down with a clatter whilst the vicar said grace. Another kick was given, this time more gentle, reminding Harry that grace was over as we all sat there waiting for him to open his eyes. 'Amen,' I repeated again.

'Yes, amen,' Harry shouted, making me jump.

The salt from the pot was sprinkled and passed around the table. Harry, in his hunger, refused and rapidly devoured most of the meal on his plate.

Molly intervened during the vicar's conversation, standing slightly over and reaching for the ladle, ensuring another dollop of the pie she had cooked landed on Harry's plate. Harry nodded with thanks and then turned his head slightly pretending to listen with interest at the vicar's continuing concern about the church. Points of importance were raised in a loud voice, simmering down to a lower level when he talked about particular people that joined his congregation who had little respect.

'I need say no more,' he told us.

'Don't tha ever feel like swearing?' Harry asked.

'Well, I suppose I'm only human,' he laughed half-heartedly. 'But goodness, no, Harry.'

'On the other hand, Edward, you can't have the likes of Mrs Grindle demanding to join the church choir,' Molly told him.

'She ain't, is she?' Harry butted in whilst I sat looking horrified. 'She's takin' t'piss,' Harry said. He was given another kick from underneath the table, then apologised for his rude language.

The vicar leant his head down burying it in his hands. The strands of his hair fell loosely over his forehead as he nodded his head from side to side. 'I'll be accused of snobbery, you know that don't you, Molly?'

'Well, Edward, communicate with her.'

'About what?' he asked, releasing his hands and looking up.

'I suppose you'll have to tell her the truth.'

'Aye, 'e'll 'ave to,' Harry chirped in.

'That she's not suitable for the job,' Molly continued.

The vicar took his glasses off and rubbed his small tired eyes.

'Not in that manner, of course,' Molly said. 'A more subtle approach will be needed.'

'Th'only vocal chords Mrs Grindle uses is to tell everyone to piss off,' Harry said. 'Ouch,' he called as I swiftly kicked my foot against his shin once more.

'Well, when matters like this are sorted, I have suggested to Molly that a trip to Scotland will do us both a power of good. Just a couple of days mind you. I couldn't possibly leave the parish for any longer.'

'Things aren't as bad as they seem,' Harry whispered

to me over the table, 'between Molly and 'im,' he explained before turning his attention back to the vicar. 'Gretna Green?' Harry asked.

'Pardon?' the vicar replied.

'No, it's nowt really. Just thought it were worth taking Molly up there.'

The vicar immediately pulled a hanky out from his trouser pocket and blew hard into it. Molly sat there, bright red in the face.

'We'll clear the plates,' I told Molly, sensing an uncomfortable silence. 'Won't we, Harry?' giving him a signal with my eyes. He responded by standing and taking the vicar's empty plate first.

'Edward, why don't you go and sit down in the living room?' Molly asked. 'You're looking rather pale.'

'You'll join me, won't you, Molly?'

'Yes, yes, right away,' Molly replied as he stood uneasily on his feet.

'I'll make a brew,' Harry called. 'Sugar?'

'No, no, not for me, young man,' the vicar turned to say as Molly linked her arm with his to steady his walk.

'One for me,' Molly told Harry, leaving us behind.

'Get the kettle on quick,' Harry told me. 'Vicar looks like 'e's just seen a ghost 'e's so pale. Mind you, e'll be used to it, won't 'e?'

'What?' I asked as I held the spout of the kettle underneath the cold running tap.

'Ghosts, wi' t'graveyard at t'bottom of 'is garden. Well, sommat's upset 'im,' Harry said, trying to figure out what it could be as he stood in thought.

'It's probably because you swore at the table,' I told

Harry before he took the kettle off me and placed it on the stove.

'That's not clean,' he said pushing the stool I was standing on closer up, enabling me to reach further down into the sink. Harry passed the china plate I had just washed back to me. 'Could be though, me swearing,' he said, passing the tea towel before the plate was passed back. 'It's t'thought of that Mrs Grindle that makes me do it.'

'What, Harry?'

'Swear. Anyway, only swore once.'

'Twice, Harry.'

'Well, twice then. Ain't end o' t'world.'

'What's in Gretna Green?' I asked. Harry looked confused. 'Where you told the vicar to take Molly.' The whistle from the kettle began to blow, hissing steam from the spout before Harry ran to its aid.

'It's a place where they can go to get married,' he called whilst turning the gas down. 'They don't ask no questions. Give 'em a fiver and that's it; they're husband and wife.'

'What's wrong with the church where the vicar lives?' I asked.

'Nowt,' Harry replied as he emptied the loose tea from the scoop inside the caddy into Molly's teapot. 'Anyway, by look on 'is face, didn't think 'e thought it were a good idea. It was just that, in me 'eart, I felt that they wouldn't get no peace 'ere. That's if 'e were thinking of marrying 'er, especially wi' t'likes o' Mrs Grindle waiting outside t'church to catch Molly's bouquet. Anyway, sorry I said owt. Find us two mugs,' Harry asked. 'Tea'll be stewed if it's not poured soon.'

'Anyway, Harry, they're probably not in love because he hasn't kissed her yet,' I told him, stepping off the stool to help.

'But they must 'ave. 'E's not waiting till t'shepherds pie's cooked for t'sake of it. There's more to th'eye than we can see. Will tha stop blinking and staring at nowt?' he told me in a harsh manner. 'It's just a saying ain't it.'

The cups of tea were stirred and Harry lifted the remaining leaves that floated on the top, discarding them from the spoon into the basin of the sink.

'I'll carry one for you.'

'Aye, frittened of spilling it if I 'eld 'em both. Steady,' Harry said as the tea swirled around with each step I took. 'Don't want it dripping on Molly's lino.'

Slowly, we made our way into the living room. As we entered, I sensed something was wrong. Molly held her hanky in her hand and wiped away a tear. We didn't linger. Thanked generously, we quickly turned away.

'Either she's crying wi' 'appiness, or she's crying wi' sadness,' Harry whispered on our way back into the kitchen.

'She's probably crying with happiness, Harry,' I whispered back. 'Molly's never sad.'

Harry grumbled away to himself whilst I stepped back on to the stool to wash the remainder of the dishes. 'Do you think I will marry a prince, Harry?' I asked with my hands embedded deep into the water.

'Aye, most probably,' Harry replied. I turned to him as he stood with the tea towel in his hands. 'Will I, Harry?'

'Just told you, ain't I?' he said, gripping hold of the cutlery that had just been washed from the top of the drainer.

'Will he be wearing his shiny armour or just a crown?' I asked.

'Don't matter, does it? If he's the prince, don't 'ave to wear any armour or a crown on 'is 'ead, does 'e? Anyway, 'e'll 'ave met 'is match if 'e does,' he said as I lifted the plug out with all my strength, watching the water being sucked down into the drain. I turned then to look at him. 'It means that tha already wear one.'

'What?' I asked.

'A crown,' he replied. 'There's nowt there,' he said as I lifted my hands up immediately to touch the top of my head. 'Don't have to see it to wear one. Come on,' he said, lifting me up from the stool before letting me go once my feet had firmly touched the ground. 'Anyway, I ain't had a bird yet. What's that look for?' Harry asked whilst he dried the soap suds that lay in between my fingers with a towel he had just used.

'What about your pigeons?'

'Well, there's two sorts of birds ain't there? Ones that fly, reet, and ones that walk. Look, sit 'ere, back o' t'kitchen table,' Harry said, pulling out two chairs.

Molly's quiet approach made us both jump. Harry and I glanced at each other and sat silent as she rested the two empty mugs beside us.

'Well, I'll be off now,' the vicar said, wandering in and slipping on his jacket. 'How about a trip up the hill and along to the parish?' he asked Harry. And then I can show you the dreadful mess the storm's created in the church yard before my congregation settles for evensong,' he told us, pulling out a watch from his jacket pocket and checking the time.

'Mmm,' Harry replied.

'Well, come on, young chap whilst the night's still young as the saying goes.'

'You've never taken that off since you arrived,' Molly told Harry as he fastened the buttons on his rather warm-looking jacket, lifting the collar up as high as it would go.

Molly was thanked by them both to the sound of the whistling wind that crept through the open door as they made their way out. I peeped through into the living room to see if Arthur was lying there waiting for me.

'Come on, let's go and sit down,' Molly said with a shiver.

I curled up on the rug next to Arthur, and Molly with a huge sigh sat down in her chair. The clock on the mantelpiece ticked noticeably from side to side in the silence of the room. 'Shall I tell you a story?' I whispered to Arthur as he lay fully stretched, enjoying the warmth from the fire. Molly looked so sad, I thought, glancing towards her as she sat silently in her chair.

'Oh, I was daydreaming,' she said, noticing my stare.

'Once upon a time there was a tom cat called Arthur who had no friends of his own and wandered aimlessly around the village scaring away, through no fault of his own, the other cats who lived there too. He was big, bold and black but unknown to everybody except his mistress, Arthur had a heart of gold.'

'Good old Arthur, aren't you?' Molly told him, leaning over to stroke his furry head as I continued.

'The old creaky wardrobe, that rattled against the

floorboards if you should dare enter the room upstairs, was home to a house full of mice.'

'Arthur will be licking his lips soon with the story that you are telling him.'

'I'm only making it up, Molly, the story.'

'Well, I wonder if Arthur knows that. He'll never be as lucky as to find a wardrobe crammed with mice.'

'But Arthur was lucky,' I continued. 'Molly, Arthur's mistress had fallen in love with the vicar and the vicar with her.'

'Oh my goodness,' Molly said out loud.

'And to avoid village gossip,' I told Arthur, 'she had crept out one dark, stormy evening to secretly meet him. Arthur knew he was alone with the sound of the latch pulled down before a bang, as Molly closed the door behind her, and then the twist of the key inside the lock.

'Arthur knew he was now free to make the challenge. After all, there was only one master and that was Arthur. He slowly stretched and leaped from his rug, sneakily placing one paw at a time up the narrow staircase to the room with the wardrobe.'

Molly listened sharply as the story continued. 'The thunder rumbled outside behind the thick, cloudy sky. A flash of lightning struck the window, throwing a glimpse of light on a tired looking wardrobe, standing limply on its two rounded legs, whilst Arthur crept through the narrow gap of the partly open door and lay there in wait. The rain lashed down on the roof of the house. Another blast of thunder and the wardrobe that the mice had clambered into and made their home, finally fell down, crashing into tiny pieces on to the bare wooden floor.'

'My oh my,' Molly said, stretching her legs and curling her toes up and down inside her fluffy slippers, sitting contentedly as the story continued.

'There was panic all around. Dozens of lady mice scrambled out over the rubble, searching frantically to the sound of tiny screeches to collect their first born. Arthur didn't move. He just lay there and stared, satisfied at the fear they held as he stared towards them with his hungry eyes. Arthur knew what he was doing, and lay with patience waiting for the king of mice, who boldly walked out wearing a silver crown on his head.

'The king mouse, with his sharp pointed ears and tiny red eyes, waited to hear what was to be said as they finally came face to face. Arthur stared straight into his eyes and licked his long pink tongue around his mouth. "Meeow," Arthur said, his long whiskers moving up and down to his voice that was loud and deep on his introduction.

'The king of mice took one step back, stumbled, then straightened his crown. "You're deafening me with your voice," the king squeaked.

'Temptation nearly struck with the sweet smell of a certain grey haired mouse. Arthur's mouth watered as he strolled by and stepped up towards the king. Arthur lay in wait as the king acknowledged what he had whispered in his ear before he took a step forward. Arthur admired his bravery. After all, he could have eaten the king whole in one swift move.

'"You've just been invited to the christening before you eat us all up," the king of mice squeaked to Arthur. Arthur's long whiskers brushed along the floor causing chaos as he shook his head. "But you can't say no," the king squeaked.

'Arthur's eyes moved slowly, looking towards the corner of the room. Groups of mice stood trembling.

'"They've asked you to celebrate with them the birth of their young ones. Not a lot to ask before you eat them for supper."'

'He looks like he already has,' Molly said as Arthur lay there fast asleep.

'I dream about lots of things,' I told her.

'Do you, Lorne?' Molly asked.

'Yes, lots of things, Molly, but most of them I hope will never come true.' The room went into silence except for the old clock ticking. Molly sighed once more and rested her head against the back of the chair whilst Arthur slept contentedly next to the gentle glow of the fire.

Molly suddenly jolted, lifting herself swiftly up from the chair. 'I was drifting,' she said, 'thinking that everything will be all right and nothing would ever change.'

Confused at her statement and the dither in her voice, I lay and snuggled next to Arthur. 'I can hear his heart beat,' I whispered to Molly as she rushed over to the sideboard. We both jumped at the sudden burst from the radio.

'Sorry,' she called, her hands trembling whilst tuning it in. The beeps from the radio signalling the time caused Molly to look across the room towards the clock. The time was checked before the grim, deep voice of a man began to announce the news.

'Oh, what nonsense,' Molly said. 'All these strikes, that's all you hear about these days.' The round dial was turned and the radio switched off.

'The church bells are ringing,' I told her, listening to the faint chimes that echoed from outside.

Molly stood still and leant an ear. 'So they are,' she said.

'One day, Molly, when I'm old enough and Mummy doesn't lock me in my bedroom any more, I'm going to ring those bells. Don't look worried, Molly, there isn't a key to the room I sleep in at Rose Cottage. The door's only made of plywood; that's what Mummy says, otherwise, I was told that if she could she would lock me away for ever. So I pretend she has, and I never attempt to open it, to make Mummy feel better. One day I'll buy her some proper doors. That's when I've grown up and can bring a wage home to her like Daddy does. And I'll get some keys made for her and put them on a ring.'

Molly rushed out into the kitchen, and then rushed back in with the iron in her hand before resting it down on the hearth. 'Oh dear,' she said 'Ah, there it is.' She walked over and lifted my clothes from the maiden which she must have moved to the corner of the room earlier that day to accommodate the vicar to a seat near the fire.

Molly touched each garment to see if it was dry, and then wrapped them in a bundle. I stood. Arthur sat and licked his paws. Molly poked at the fire before lifting the iron, her knuckles white with the weight of it, and placed it on top of the embers that glowed inside the grate. Her back partly turned towards the fireplace, she quietly wiped a tear that had rolled down over her face.

'Molly, are you all right?' I asked. I sighed when there was no reply.

'Oh sorry, my dear,' she said with a slight quake in her

voice. 'It's just that I'm feeling a little sad.' She walked over once more to where the sideboard stood and pulled open a tiny drawer. Her fingers fumbled through its contents. 'Now where's … ah there,' she said out loud. 'Come here, my dear,' she called, closing the drawer with a rush.

I walked the few steps over as she turned towards me holding a little black box. 'This is for you,' she told me clasping her fingers around it. I looked at her.

'It's for you,' she said, releasing it from her hand and passing it over.

I lifted open the plastic cover. 'It's a diary,' I whispered.

'And an old one at that,' Molly said. 'It's stayed unused in this drawer for years. You can write anything you want inside there, your thoughts, your tears, your laughter. Just pencil in the date on each page you do and one day in years to come, you'll open it and remember, whether good or bad, your memories.'

I sniffed the cover up against my nose before looking up towards Molly to thank her. Her eyes looked like glass, swimming in tears that hadn't flowed. Molly tried to smile. 'I've to go home haven't I?'

'Yes,' she replied. 'Not now,' I was told as I walked towards the porch to collect the sandals Molly had given me. I stopped and looked towards her. 'In the morning,' she said with a faint heart.

'I'll go and feed Arthur then,' I told her, feeling a lump in my throat as I called over to him. I heard Molly sigh as Arthur followed behind. I had tasted a life in a loving, content atmosphere whilst staying with Molly. Although I missed Teddy and Charlie, it would have been my dream to live at Primrose Cottage for ever. Molly followed me in saying nothing. I placed my diary down onto the table and began to root through the kitchen cupboard drawer. My hands shook at the touch of the old rusty can opener.

'Do you know how much I'm going to miss you?' Molly said, blowing into her hanky.

'I'll be able to see you at Sunday school,' I reminded her, trying to hide my feelings. 'Now that my name's down on the register.' The lump felt bigger in my throat. Arthur followed me towards the pantry, brushing himself against my legs. I opened the grey painted door, leaning my shoulder against its weight. Little light filtered through and I felt frightened of the dark that loomed inside. Leaning down on one knee, I moved in slightly and searched with the touch of my fingertips. Molly always leaves Arthur's food right here near the door, I thought as I leant in a little further feeling anxious about being trapped inside. Arthur didn't help with his persistent stroke as he brushed himself sideways against me.

'Got it,' I called, hoisting the can in one hand and stepping back quickly in a rush to leave the darkness behind. The pantry door slammed, closing by itself, leaving an eerie silence. I looked sharply to the side where Molly was perched, not sitting back on her chair in the comfort of her kitchen as she should have been, but perched on the edge with a look of great sadness on her face. I felt concerned, tripping over Arthur's feet on my way over to the far corner of the kitchen. Arthur followed me, step by step, towards his bowl which lay next to Molly's dull, black wellington boots. I took one more glance towards her before I knelt down on the floor with Arthur beside me.

Molly blew once more into her hanky. I heard her. My hands clenched, I screwed my face up with every turn. It was hard with that old rusty tin opener. Arthur purred, knowing full well that his dinner was in sight. 'Won't be long now,' I whispered, feeling a huge lump right there inside my throat. I didn't want Molly to be sad. I was sad, very sad, but I didn't want her to bear the same feelings. A tear trickled down my face. It was wiped quickly away as I knew it would only make Molly worse if she should see me.

I buried my head low and used all my strength whilst forcing the old rusty opener to stay gripped to the edge of the can. Arthur purred as the seal began to open, sending a fishy aroma up into the air. There was a sudden clink from the lid as it fell and hit against the floor. I peeped up towards Molly who noticed immediately.

'It's a knife that you'll need,' she said, shoving her hanky tightly underneath the long sleeves of the cardigan she'd previously slipped on when complaining of the cold. Molly rooted through the drawer making quite a clatter before she took the few steps and passed over the knife. The bone on the handle was cracked and dry on my touch, the blade tarnished and blunt. 'That's Arthur's special knife, isn't it Arthur?' she told him as I thanked her. I looked towards her, just quickly, hiding the pain I felt inside and smiled. Molly smiled back.

This was a simple ending. Molly had never pried; there were no questions and answers to give during my stay and I felt humble, but I had been privileged at feeling so genuinely wanted by such a wonderful lady. And at least, if nothing else, for once in my life I could carry the love that Molly gave so freely and hold it inside my heart for ever more. My voice started to crack with emotion. 'Come on, Arthur, eat it all up.' I had to stop, I couldn't speak another word as Arthur buried his head deeper into the bowl and ate with contentment. I was no longer to be his companion. My world was different from the world I had shared with those at Primrose Cottage.

The can had been emptied and Arthur's old knife placed inside. My voluntary need to help in the small things I did had come to an end. I knew the truth deep inside, that once sent back to Rose Cottage, there was little hope of ever returning here for a long, long time. Tears flooded my eyes and rolled down over my burning cheeks, falling in drops on to Molly's kitchen floor. Arthur's knife shook fiercely inside the can as I clung hold of my last memory. Molly took it from my hand and put her arms around me.

'I know, my child,' she whispered, stroking the top of my head. The scent of her body smelled of summer roses as I leant against her. 'At last I'm able to comfort you,' she whispered.

'Do I have to go back to Rose Cottage, do I?' I asked, looking up at her.

Molly nodded with tears in her eyes. I cried too. 'Arthur's going to miss you,' Molly said, skipping a breath whilst squeezing me much tighter. I could feel the fast beat of her heart. Mine was beating fast too, leaving no more words left to be said.

Chapter 22

Another morning to another day, but a very special day to me. It was my thirteenth birthday.

'Dear God,' I whispered, kneeling down on to the bare floorboards and praying over my bed. 'It's 5th August, the sun is shining through the gap in the curtains and the birds outside are singing, and it's my birthday. I just want to ask you a really big favour. Will you help Mummy to realize that now that I've turned thirteen, I won't be a burden to her any more? You see, I will be able to do more jobs around the house for her, more responsible ones, now that I'm a teenager. There won't be any more wet beds and I'll sweep the dust from the stairs much harder. Could you please just help her to stop getting so cross with me? Dear God, I don't want to be locked away in this room any more.'

'What's all this doom and gloom?' Teddy said, lifting me up off the floor.

'I'm just asking a favour, that's all.'

'A tug for each year, that's what I say.' Teddy tugged at my hair, stopping on the twelfth count.

'I'm thirteen,' I told him, looking up at him in shock just in case I wasn't.

'I know you are.' He winked with a smile on the final count. 'Happy birthday, Lorne.'

'I've hid it under here for days,' Charlie called from underneath the bed, holding a brown paper card. 'What do you reckon?' he asked, passing it over. 'It says happy birthday inside if you open it, but you can't,' Charlie said. 'I glued a daisy and a buttercup inside your card too but when I closed it, it all stuck together.'

'Thank you, Charlie.' He looked slightly embarrassed and started to shake the blanket that covered the bed we shared.

'Lost your spectacles again?' Teddy called, leaving me to dress. 'Here, grab a biscuit. Go on, no one will know. They're all broken anyway,' Teddy said, noticing me look towards the table as we passed through the living room into the kitchen, just in case there was a present waiting. 'Charlie, get your skates on,' he called again. 'I've to lock this place up. We're the last to leave and you'll both be late for school.' I believed in my heart that from that day there would be no more heartache.

'What are you thinking about?' Teddy asked as we walked briskly to school with Charlie lagging behind.

'My birthday.' I turned to him and smiled. He, with a light squeeze of my hand, smiled back.

'Well, what did you get?' Susie asked lining up alongside me for assembly.

'A book, Susie.'

'What, you were bought a book?'

'Well, no. I wasn't really,' I whispered, 'so it will have to be an imaginary one that I will leave underneath my pillow and read each night before I go to sleep.'

'How the hell can you read in t'dark? It's pitch black in your bedroom.'

'It isn't, Susie, when the moon shines through the window.'

'Blimey, nowt's simple in your life is it? Anyway, 'appy birthday. Let's get on t'back row before bloody Edward sits next to us again,' Susie said as the creaky door opened. 'Mind you, just cos he's a sissy don't make him all that bad,' I was told as she scrambled towards a seat.

'I like him, Susie,' I said, sitting down next to her.

'Aye, well, you would say that. Wait until you're my age. You'll soon change thi mind. I knew I had sommat to tell you. My ma's got me a job in t'bakery down t'road. I'll be leaving here in a couple of weeks.'

''Ere he is. He'll be preaching again how important love is. Wouldn't mind but he's never found any except a secret one and that didn't last,' Susie said as we stood to welcome Mr Applehurst, the local vicar. I would listen intensely to Mr Applehurst as he preached kindness and love.

'How much does it cost?' I asked Susie.

'What?'

'Kindness and love.'

'It's bloody free, ain't it?' she whispered with a nudge as the vicar coughed for silence.

Although I had imagined a plan to steal the money to buy it, I sighed with relief, sitting shoulders straight and head held high, counting on hope.

'Hey, you wi' th'oles in yer socks, budge up.'

'Not on your Nelly,' Susie called in a rather loud voice.

'Who's Nelly?' I asked.

'Shut up and sit right where you are,' I was told.

'Crook by name, crook by bloody nature. That's him, scruffy get, wi' t'bleeding spots all o'er his face.'

The vicar coughed again for silence. 'You're a teenager now, Lorne. As from today, you're not going to put up with any more name-calling. You'd better grow up quick from now on, because if you don't, you'll get trampled on,' Susie told me.

With a rumble of chairs, we all stood. Mr Applehurst walked back along the centre aisle limping. I looked up at Susie. 'Well he walked in wi' one so he's bound to walk out wi' one too. Nowt to worry about,' she told me. 'It were a windy day and his bicycle clip got stuck in between the flapping gown he wore over his trousers. Neighbours said serves him reet that he fell off. He'd have had a drink or two while out cycling on that rusty old bike of his.'

Bottles of milk clinked from plastic crates stacked high on the tarmac playground after the bell had rung for morning break. Susie always glugged hers down before passing me her empty glass bottle, swapping it behind my back in exchange for mine. 'It's just so horrible, Susie.'

'What?' holding the bottle away from her mouth.

'That awful milk we have to drink.'

'Don't know what tha has to complain about,' she said swallowing the remainder and wiping her hand across her mouth. 'If it weren't for me drinking t'bleeding stuff for you, you'd have been reported by now for not getting any calcium down you by that owd battleaxe o'er there that's got nowt else to do but spy. If you ask me, a couple o' fights in t'playground, she'd be dead scared; probably collapse wi' a heart attack. Mind you, come to think about it, wi' t'muscles she's got I'd imagine she'd join in.'

'Who, Mrs Stanley? The dinner lady?'

'Aye,' Susie said whilst placing the empty bottles back into the crate. 'Never mind her being guardian for all us lot. Only job she can get after t'shame Mr Stanley put her through is her wandering around this playground like some detective. Her 'usband were t'local bobby and when I say local, I mean local. Get what I'm saying?' Susie said, nudging me. 'After he'd jumped in and out of every bed in t'village ... well, nearly. She thinks she's taken over his position. Got sacked, didn't he? Pay won't be much either, so she can stop looking over wi' those piercing pea eyes of hers. Finally ran off wi t'local barmaid.'

'Who?'

'Mr Stanley. And she were nowt to look at either. Anyway, kid, it's your birthday and guess who's o'er theer?'

'Where?'

'O'er theer,' Susie said, pointing towards the iron railings.

'Lily,' I whispered, running towards her, unaware of crossing the path of wild playing boys who ran at full speed.

'Stop,' Susie called.

I was instantly knocked down to the ground. 'They've burst your bloody nose,' Susie said in anger whilst trying to tilt my head back. I could see Lily running through the gates towards me before she took hold of me and held me in her arms.

'She's my sister,' Lily told Mrs Stanley who marched over. 'It's her thirteenth birthday today. I didn't mean to startle her.'

'Unlucky for some,' Mrs Stanley replied. 'Anyway, how's that gallivanting ma of yours? Not seen her parading through t'village. Well, not recently.'

'Piss off,' Lily told her in well spoken English.

'Aye, piss off,' Susie said.

'You're on report,' Mrs Stanley pointed out to Susie.

'Tha'll regret it if tha does wi' t'report I have on you and your hubby.'

'I beg your pardon.' Mrs Stanley immediately turned and blew hard into the short whistle. 'Everyone line up,' she called. Her short fat legs rubbed against each other as she walked, stepping into the centre of the playground, blowing hard on the whistle once more.

'Your forehead's grazed,' Lily told me.

'So's her knee,' Susie said.

'I'm all right, Lily, I really am.'

Lily kissed the side of my cheek and held on to me until I felt steady on my feet. I put on a brave face, not wanting Lily to know I was hurt, and smiled. Lily smiled too, passing me, from inside the deep pocket of her loose cream coat, a square box wrapped in bright gold paper with a tag hanging loosely down by its side.

'They're chocolates,' Lily told me as I shook the box trying to guess what was inside.

'Chocolates, Lily, in a box,' I gasped.

'Happy birthday, Lorne,' Lily whispered in my ear. 'I love you so much.'

'Do you, Lily? You can't cry; not on my birthday,' I told her as her dark shimmering eyes filled with tears.

'You're thirteen now, Lorne,' Lily told me whilst straightening the back of my cardigan so it sat neatly on my shoulders. 'Don't let anyone bully you.'

'I won't, Lily,' I whispered. She blew me two kisses and I blew her five before she made her exit. 'I will go with you to Paris where we will dance all night,' I whispered through the wispy morning air over to Lily before she disappeared from view.

'What's all that about?' Susie asked.

'An evening in Paris, Susie.'

'Blimey, got to be rich, really rich, to be going there. Stop patrolling up and down like some police woman will thee? We're all in t'queue, Mrs Stanley. We're at t'back specially to read out t'message.'

'What message, Susie?'

'Well, if she'll stop peering over me shoulder, I'll read it out to thee. Here, pass me t'box.'

Mrs Stanley shuffled further along with the tip of her whistle dangling in between her chapped lips, blowing hard into it warning the group of boys that were scuffling to immediately stop.

'Blimey, just look at t'message she's written.'

I stood there with my mouth wide open, waiting to hear what Susie was going to read.

'Come on, you two,' Mrs Stanley called in a squeaky voice as everyone entered in single file.

'Owd on,' Susie called back to her.

'Lily's already told me she loves me, Susie.'

'I know that, but listen. Her handwriting's pretty smart. Written in ink, too. Listen, says here on t'card: "I wish all these chocolates inside here were diamonds made especially for you." Blimey, speaking proper English is really 'ard,' Susie said. 'Aye, well I wish they were too; then we could piss off to some island,' Susie said, grinning widely at Mrs Stanley who stood looking irritated as we quickly stepped up to join the remainder of the queue.

'I love you too. Might not have any fancy present in me 'and … well, not yet … but I've two fags, and matches too. So after we've listened to Gogglegook teaching about geography he knows nowt about, except that t'world is round…'

'Mr Galway,' I reminded her.

'Aye, well Gogglegook to me. We'll leet one up down t'lane. Buy you a cigarette holder when you're older. You know, like t'film stars have. I should be earning a decent wage by then. Might as well have left weeks ago; having to sit in t'classrooms wi' you lot.'

'Don't you want to learn, Susie?' I asked as she manoeuvred me through the open door by my shoulders.

'Afternoon,' she said to Mr Galway who stood tall and thin with a long neck that stretched as high as a giraffe's. 'Due to leave, aren't I? Anyway, been taught all there is to know. Edward's just picked his nose and wiped his bogey under t'wooden bench he's sat on, so carry on walking.'

Mr Galway tapped a ruler hard against the top of his desk. 'This'll do,' Susie said, pulling me in and sitting down almost immediately.

'I feel the impatience of a young woman,' he called in a vicious deep voice as Susie shuffled her bottom from side to side.

'Aye, well how would he feel having to wear a sanitary towel once a month,' she whispered.

'She might think there's nothing to learn about in this world,' he called down, 'but believe me,' he said, 'there's much more to see and learn than sitting there smelling of stale tobacco.' Mr Galway made it his intention then of looking directly towards Susie before wiping his goofy stained teeth with the tip of his long pointed tongue.

'Don't let him con you when I've finally left this place,' Susie whispered. 'Pretending he's travelled t'world. He's too tight even to pay for t'fare on t'bus. Walks everywhere, that's how far he's been. Anyway, there's t'bell. Last trip to t'last lesson.' Susie stopped and folded the creased time table from her shabby blazer pocket. 'Yep, last lesson to Mrs Bake-a-cake.'

'Who's she?' I asked.

'Grumpy Mrs Fondant, cookery teacher.'

'Mrs Flander,' I reminded Susie.

'Look, shouldn't tell you this but we're holding a special party for you after I've been home and helped me ma wi' tea. It's in t'car park next to t'Dragon Inn.'

'Susie,' I gasped.

'Aye, so stick hold of those chocolates. We'll all fancy one when t'party begins.'

'I know it's late in the day for breakfast,' Mrs Flander called out whilst grappling at the string that held her glasses close against her chest, as we clambered through the open door and sat down on our seats. 'Elbows off the tables, girls,' she called with a harsh tone in her voice whilst placing her glasses over her button eyes. She was a short, stocky, elderly woman with a mottled complexion and blue-rinsed curls covering her balding head. 'What are you doing here?' she asked Susie, preoccupying herself by tying a floral pinny around her thick waist.

'Asking meself that,' Susie whispered.

'Well?' Mrs Flander asked looking up sternly towards Susie.

'Leaving in two weeks, sat me exams so there's nowt else left for me to do except sit in here wi' t'classes.'

'Well, going back to what I was saying,' Mrs Flander said, 'no matter what time of the day it is, it's important that you all learn how to scramble.'

I looked up towards Susie. 'Eggs, should imagine,' as the girls opened their satchels, lifting one each from the cardboard cartons.

'Where's yours?' Mrs Flander asked peering over her nose towards me.

I looked up towards Susie. 'She ain't got one.'

Mrs Flander expressed a look of disgust. 'Lorne, go and stand out in the corridor until the lesson is over. You're for ever coming in here for cookery lessons empty-handed. We don't run a charity you know.'

'Look here,' Susie told her, 'her ma's from India. Wouldn't even know where a bleeding egg comes from.'

'She does, Susie, because sometimes she boils them in a pan.'

'Shut up,' Susie told me. 'And her dad's Irish and doesn't even have time to get pissed in t'local pub working so hard trying to feed her. So if you're a bleeding egg short, change t'menu. Suggest wi' all eggs t'rest of class has brought, you can bake her a cake instead. It's her thirteenth birthday today. Look at you all staring wi' your pinnies that your ma's have all ironed and starched, mardy gets t'lot of you, looking down on t'kid all t'time.'

'And you can also stand out in the corridor,' Susie was told.

'Who me? Come on, Lorne, and don't forget the chocolates. There's thicker thieves in here than me. Stop shivering. You're a bag of nerves. No one's gonna hurt you because you've not got a bleeding egg. Anyway, you could have dropped it on t'way to school and it cracked open on t'pathway. Well you could; owt's possible. I'll be glad to get out of this place for good,' Susie told me whilst slithering her back against the grey-plastered wall of the corridor until she rested with knees bent against the hard floor. 'What wi' her in there thinking she's Fanny Craddock. And my science teacher, owd Mr Twinkle...

'Mr Twindle, it's Mr Twindle, Susie.'

'Seen how his hairs stick out on his legs over his dirty socks in between half-mast flared trousers he wears. He thinks he's gonna make his own rocket and fly to t'moon. Well good luck to him if he does. Just hope he shoves Mrs Fondant in t'rocket with him when it blows off t'ground.'

'Mrs Flander, it's Mrs Flander, Susie.'

'Just don't want your heart to be broken when I finally leave.'

'It won't, Susie.'

'God knows why they named this place St Paul's,' Susie said, looking up and down the corridor. 'Ain't no saints in here. Well, will thee not miss me?'

I nodded with tears in my eyes at the very thought.

'Hey, hey, I'll never be that far away. Anyway, bakery's only at t'back,' Susie said, giving a huge sigh. Susie shot up from where she knelt on the sudden opening of the classroom door. It banged quite hard behind Mrs Flander before she stomped down the corridor stretching her short plump arms behind her back, undoing the bow to her pinny along the way.

'Blimey, look who's coming back with her. Bleeding headmaster,' Susie said, breaking the silence between us. 'He's quite handsome don't you think? Tall, broad shouldered and a good head of hair on him. There's hardly a wrinkle around those big brown eyes of his considering he must be fifty at least. Mind you, still lives with his ma. Mollycoddles him; that's why he always looks so smart.' Susie gave out a nervous cough as the sound of their footsteps came closer, and so did I.

'Well, young lady,' Mr Wilde stopped to say, looking directly towards Susie before giving a sharp short nod to Mrs Flander who then quickly disappeared back into the classroom. 'It's unfortunate for me to say, but giving considerable thought on this matter, I would like you to leave the premises immediately.'

'For good?' Susie asked.

'Sadly, you have no certificates to take with you.'

'Me 'ands are me certificates. Can't roll dough and make it into bread holding on to bleeding certificates can I? Anyway, only you and t'doctor in t'village have things like that.'

The school bell rang out echoing inside the walls of the narrow corridor. 'Come on, we're off,' Susie said, gripping on to my hand and pulling me along.

Dark patchy clouds formed in the sky and it drizzled with rain as Susie continued to pull with a tight grip around my hand. 'Reet, that's it. Out of these school gates for ever,' Susie said, leaning her back against the outer railings.

I noticed a teardrop rolling down her rosy plump cheeks. She wiped it away with her hands and then another appeared. 'Make sure you're there for t'party,' she told me whilst swallowing hard before criss-crossing her way amongst passers-by on her route for home.

'Dear God,' I whispered after the lollipop lady halted the traffic and beckoned me to cross the road. 'Please watch over Susie when she starts work at the bakery. It's hot inside there because there's always steam pouring out from the chimney. She really wanted a certificate, just one so she could run home with it and show it off to her Mummy, especially one for art; she's good at drawing, God, really good. She drew a man and a woman before painting them. They were lying down on top of thick blades of green grass. Don't mind me saying, God,' I whispered, 'they were naked. Susie told me that the reason she drew the woman sitting up looking startled in the painting as the man reached up and touched her breast, is because the blades of grass were too sharp. But Mrs Florence, the art teacher, screwed Susie's painting up in front of the whole class. That's what Susie told me. Please, please, God. Please send Susie a certificate down from heaven. Could you leave it in the church? She always sits on the third pew from the top. You see, God, I saw tears in her eyes today.'

'Tha'll be going mad soon, talking to thiself.' Mrs Grindle made me jump, suddenly appearing from behind. 'Liver and onions for tea toneet. Those lads of mine better eat it. I've not trailed all t'way to t'butchers for nowt. Why are thi limping? And look at your forehead.'

'Just fell,' I told her.

'Stick some Germolene on t'grazes when you get home. I swear by it. Mind you, it's not done any good for t'pimple that's growing inside me ear. I'm off to t'doctor's to complain.'

'Does it hurt?' I asked.

'Aye, well, a lot more when those lads of mine give me grief.'

The sun beamed down from the broken clouds, lighting up Mrs Grindle's short hairy beard. 'Come for tea if tha likes. I've bought enough liver.' Mrs Grindle stopped for a moment and searched through the hard cracked plastic bag she carried, lifting out by the tips of her black fingernails, a bag that wobbled with floating blood inside. 'Aye, there's enough. Bloody hell, nearly missed t'place,' she said turning back before disappearing through the open door of the doctor's house.

Instant fear struck. Would Mrs Grindle catch up with me with the gruesome bag of liver she carried deep down inside her shopping bag? I constantly looked over my shoulder before turning down into the brow where Rose Cottage stood in view. I shook the box that Lily had given me just to make sure that all the chocolates were still inside, before stopping for a second over the humpbacked bridge, checking that Mr Patterson wasn't floating in the stream below. 'Harry, you scared me,' I said as he stopped with a screech from the tyres on the bicycle he rode.

'What's down there?' he asked, leaning over on to the side of his bicycle and peering over the narrow brick wall.

'I was just checking to see if Mr Patterson had jumped off the bridge.'

'Look, he ain't gonna do it. He's always leaning over here and threatening to jump. It's only cos he's had a skin full and found t'wife's gallivanted off again. He'll be hanging over this bridge till t'day he dies feeling sorry for himself.'

'Oh, Harry.'

'Aye, well, he won't stop drinking, will he? And she'll never stop fancying all t'men. So stop looking for his body floating in t'stream below every time you walk over t'bridge. Should have opened their own theatre company those two wi' drama they cause in this village. Anyway, can't hang around. Rest of t'evening papers to deliver. Happy birthday, Lorne,' Harry called, spinning the pedals of his bicycle whilst cursing the rusty chain as he rode off.

I checked once more, peering over down at the stream, just in case Mr Patterson's snake belt he always wore around the waist of his trousers might have got tangled in between the algae that swayed from side to side underneath the flowing water. If it was, then he'd definitely jumped over the bridge and drowned.

'Mind thi don't fall over. Mind you a tadpole couldn't even drown wi' t'water that's left down theer. Did I scare you, lass?' Mrs Grindle asked, standing close by.

'A little,' I replied.

'Aye, well, tha too young to be a bag of nerves. Just seen that rascal of a paper lad ride by. Stuck me fist up in t'air at him. Tell him if you see him before me that if he doesn't shovel t'shit out of that pigeon loft of his ... stench that comes from it ... get it reet in me kitchen ... well, tell him I'll shovel it out myself and leave it on his bloody doorstep.'

'Complained to Parish Council, through cooing this

time. Those bloody pigeons ne'er stop. They're at it all bleeding day.'

I wondered if the war between Mrs Grindle and Harry would ever end.

'What's that sigh for?'

'It's a growing up sigh,' I replied.

'Eh?'

'Just wishing, Mrs Grindle, that's all.'

'Aye, well, wishes don't come true, lass, not round here anyway. Well, I'm off.'

'I'm off too, Mrs Grindle.'

'Aye, well watch t'road when tha crosses. Better things coming in life to you than living around here.'

'Are there, Mrs Grindle?'

'Better had be. Go on lass, I'll watch thee until tha's safely over.'

I looked back towards her.

'Look straight ahead when you're crossing t'bleeding road,' she shouted in a gruff voice.

Mrs Grindle had shown me kindness with her watchful eye, knowing that as soon as my foot touched the pavement on the other side she would make her way up the sloping hill for home.

The scent of Daddy's colourful roses made me sneeze. I stopped still in my tracks staring over towards the silent home I had secretly named Daffodil Cottage. That's after Eric died and Mrs Crowswick was sent away. The tiny garden, now choked with weeds, left no sign of the happy times when once upon a time bulbs were planted, silly conversation made, and smiles were given freely. Would I dare step over the narrow stone step and peep through the window if it were there? Bluebottle flies hung lifeless, caught in the mesh on the droopy lace curtains that once were frilly white.

Mrs Crowswick's cottage must feel very lonely, I thought, with just memories left inside. 'I wish you would come back, Eric,' I called before looking over my shoulder as I made my way down into the dark entry, frightened of his ghost.

The rusty latch squeaked as I carefully let myself in. The kitchen was deserted and everything was deadly quiet. Mummy was sitting on the high backed armchair in the tiny square living room. Her head was buried in between her hands and both feet rested on the hearth near to the grate that was spilled with grey ashes from burnt out coal. Only the ticking from the wooden clock on the mantelpiece was to be heard.

'Would you like a chocolate?' I asked, creeping closer and shaking the box in my hand. 'Would you, Mummy?'

Her head rose slowly. I stood still and stared at her bruised swollen face. She looked at me with evil in her dark eyes. 'Are you poorly?' I asked. She kicked her foot out catching my ankle bone with the point of her shoes. 'Ouch,' I called. The box in my hand fell on to the floor. 'Ouch,' I called again as Mummy kicked me once more as I leant down to pick it up.

'Hand it over. Who gave you them?' Mummy asked rattling the box. 'Well, girl?'

'Lily gave them to me.'

'So she's sneaking behind my back to win you over.'

'It's the 5th August,' I whispered, my legs in a tremble.

'Meaning?' Mummy asked.

'Lily gave them to me because it's my thirteenth birthday,' I whispered.

'Should have remembered,' Mummy said. 'You've been a burden to me ever since.' Mummy threw Lily's present back to me. 'Now get out of my sight.'

My heart filled with sadness, I looked at her and wondered why she was so cruel and, for once, her beauty had disappeared.

The door to the best room suddenly opened. 'Hurry,' Teddy mouthed, ushering me through. It was always cold in there, shivering cold. 'Look, Lorne, sit down … just sit down. I need you to listen.'

'Is Mummy going to die?' I asked as I sat down on the edge of grandfather's favourite chair.

'Of course not.'

'Well, what?' I asked.

'Father came home from work today, earlier than usual.'

'It's because it's my birthday, Teddy.'

'Listen, Lorne. Considering you're now thirteen,' he whispered, 'there's things that go on in here that sometimes aren't nice to hear.'

'I hear everything, Teddy.'

'Well, you certainly haven't heard about this,' Teddy told me pacing up and down. 'Father's caught Mother with another man.'

'Did he chase them?'

'No, Lorne, he didn't have to. He caught them in his very own bedroom.'

'Where Daddy sleeps with Mummy?'

'Yes, Lorne.'

'Can I go to my bedroom? You see, I'm feeling really

sad and unhappy and I'm going to have to practise wearing a smile. That's if Mummy will let me go to my party. Do you think she will? It's on the gravel across the road. Where's Daddy?'

'He's getting drunk in the Dragon Inn.'

'On whisky?' I whispered. Teddy nodded. He chewed the corner of his lip in thought and so did I.

'On my head be it. I'll give you permission to go to your party,' Teddy said, inspecting the time from the round face of his watch strapped around his narrow wrist, 'but only for an hour. When does it begin?'

'Now,' I replied, shooting up from the chair. Teddy walked over and looked through the window. 'Is Susie there?' I asked.

'Shush, Lorne. I can't see her,' he whispered. 'Anyway, Daddy's roses don't help, they're blocking my view. Look, creep up to your bedroom and watch through the window. Let me know when Susie arrives, but only in a whisper, Lorne. Go,' Teddy said.

I didn't hesitate, and carried Lily's present tightly in my hand up the narrow staircase. If I had a wish, just one, then I would wish for Fellwick to walk without the calliper stuck to his leg, I thought, as I watched him limp over the humpbacked bridge carrying a fat white candle in one hand and holding a bottle of cider in the other.

'Fellwick,' I called whilst pushing the window open in excitement. 'Fellwick,' I called out again.

Fellwick stopped, took a large swig of cider, and then raised the bottle up in the air. ''appy birthday,' he called before tumbling over.

'Bloody prat,' Susie shouted, running to his aid from

behind. 'He's pinched t'candle from t'church to leet it for you cos it's your birthday. Don't know where the 'ell he's got t'cider from ... probably pinched that too. No dole money till t'end o'week. Anyway, give over staring at us through that bedroom window of yours and get yoursel' down here. Party's just about to begin.'

'Teddy,' I whispered from the top of the landing. 'They're all gathering for my party and Fellwick's just fallen.'

'Shush. Creep down quietly, and stop rattling those chocolates,' he whispered before reaching out for my hand as I neared the bottom stair.

We crept over the lino in the best front room. Teddy opened the catch, looking over his shoulder with caution and ushered me quickly out. I ran across the road towards my friends who cheered me on all the way.

Fellwick sat leaning his back against the stub of the old tree trunk with his legs stretched straight out in front. 'I only tripped,' he told me as I leant down towards him, 'so take that look off your face.' Splinters from the dried-out bark fell loosely upon his head. 'Jesus Christ, thought it were him patting me on th'ead then,' he called out, ruffling his short stubby fingers through the dullness of his wispy brown hair. His complexion was pale, very pale. He half heartedly smiled showing the gaps in between his neglected teeth. ''Appy birthday, Lorne,' he said between taking another swig of cider.

'Get t'cake out, Harry,' Susie told him on his arrival. Harry pulled out a jam roll from inside the deep pocket of his jacket.

Susie ripped off the cellophane cover. 'It's stale, Harry.'

'Aye, well I didn't bake t'thing, did I.'

'Will someone get a bleeding leet for this candle?'

'God'll send me to 'ell if I don't put it back next to t'altar in t'church,' Fellwick called. 'Eh up,' he said.

The bright red balloon tied with a long piece of string flapped in the air as Edward, with lengthening stride and under his mother's watchful eye, crossed the road towards me.

'Balloon matches t'colour of his hair,' Harry said.

'He's tall and lanky, ain't he,' Fellwick remarked.

'Has to be to ring t'church bells. Ever been up in t'belfry?'

'Cold and spooky if you ask me,' Susie said.

'He's brave,' I whispered.

'What, just because he's crossing t'road with a balloon in his hand?'

'Lorne's right, Fellwick. Grindle boys always make a beeline for him if they catch him out on his own. In fact,' Susie said, 'it weren't that long ago when Edward went out in t'storm to practise in t'belfry. Grindle boys caught sight of him and beat him up, so his ma told mine, just cos Edward hadn't heeded t'warning they gave him. Edward were ringing t'bells at St Paul's too loud, so t'Grindle boys told him. They complained that Mrs Grindle gets bad headaches wi' sound of 'em. So, Edward's ma said, they pushed him down on t'ground calling him a freckly-faced gingernut and wearing a dress would be more fitting than t'trousers he wears. And then,' Susie said, raising her voice slightly, 'when Edward were lying on t'ground, one o' t'Grindle boys sat on his head and you know what.'

‘Farted?’ Fellwick asked.

‘Shush,’ Susie said. ‘’Ere he comes.’

‘Happy birthday, Lorne,’ Edward whispered, looking shyly away whilst passing over the balloon. The string slipped through my fingers. We all stood in silence and watched as it floated slowly up towards the sky.

‘Look, mate, don’t look so sad,’ Fellwick said whilst clambering on to his feet.

Harry gently patted Edward on his shoulder. ‘Our friend, Eric’s, up there in heaven,’ Harry said as we all watched the balloon fade into a tiny dot. ‘So maybe it’s floating up to him, lad, so he can share in t’party we’re having.’

‘I’d take it as some gesture,’ Fellwick said. ‘Don’t look at me like that, Susie.’

‘Can’t help it wi’ big word you’ve just come out wi’. Bet tha don’t even know what it means.’

‘Well, I ain’t gonna carry a dictionary round wi’ me to find out, am I,’ Fellwick snapped.

‘Thank you, Edward,’ I called as he strode back looking up towards the sky.

‘Edward!’ his mother screeched. ‘Look where you’re going.’

‘She’s wrapped him up in cotton wool all his life, poor kid,’ Susie said as Edward was led back down his garden path to a door that closed behind him.

‘Would Eric have got my present?’ I asked, shielding my eyes as I stared up towards the sky.

‘Don’t look no more up there,’ Harry told me. ‘It’ll have reached heaven by now. Anyway, let’s eet t’cake.’

‘Cake’s all crumbled and t’candle’s too bloody big,’ Susie said.

'Can someone leet t'candle?' Fellwick asked. 'God'll have me guts for garters if I don't get it back.'

Harry struck a short match. 'Bleeding hell!' he shouted, shaking his scorched fingers. 'Bloody breeze,' he cursed before striking another.

'Hurry up, will thee – I'll have to scoot.'

The clapping finished and Fellwick burped as the last drop of cider was drunk.

'Good job yer not in t'bleeding choir,' Susie told him. 'Never heard you sing a word.'

'Well, at least I've getten her a bleeding present.' Fellwick felt inside the ripped pocket of his half-mast trousers and pulled out a tiny bunch of clover. ''Ere, they're for thee.'

'For me, Fellwick?'

'Aye, don't come in any fancy wrapping but t'thought's there,' Fellwick said looking towards Susie quite pleased with himself.

'Half dead anyway,' Susie said.

'Well, if thy gets any fatter, thy'll be too.'

'Well, let's cut t'cake,' Susie said. 'No bleeding knife, have we? I'll have to tear what's left into pieces.'

'Aye, and make sure tha doesn't get biggest slice.'

'Piss off, Fellwick.'

'I would if it weren't for Lorne's birthday. Can't do t'job Jesus Christ did,' Fellwick muttered.

'And what's that?' Susie asked.

'Feeding o' five thousand wi' just a loaf in his hand.'

'Christ, yer pa's there. Never seen him like that before,' Harry whispered as Daddy staggered out from behind the doors of the Old Dragon Inn. 'Don't look like he cares that much either. Never even looked for t'traffic while he crossed t'road.'

Susie pulled me back. 'Sometimes some things are better left, Lorne.'

'Trouble at t'mill if tha asks me,' Harry whispered. 'Eh, kid, stop crying. Your pa's gonna be all reet. Why don't you open t'present in yer 'and. Here, I'll 'elp you.'

'Don't screw t'wrapping up,' Susie told him. 'There's a special message from Lily hanging from it.'

I gasped as Harry opened the lid. 'Aye, that's reet, wipe t'bleeding tears from your eyes. Can't see in t'box properly if tha doesn't.'

'They're wrapped in gold and silver,' I told him whilst skipping a breath. 'Are we rich?'

'Aye, we are,' Fellwick said, 'wi' all these to choose from.'

'Keep thi bleeding hand off ... scoffin' t'lot ... there's more here than you,' Susie snapped.

'God help t'man that marries her,' Fellwick told me.

'Aye, well that'll be pretty soon. Pregnant, aren't I?'

'Fellwick,' I whispered, 'you can have as many chocolates as you like.'

'I know that, Lorne. But I ain't greedy. Mind if I stuff a few in me pocket? Always seem to get hungry late at neet.'

Chapter 23

Time had gone so slowly over the years, such wasted years. The pain and broken heart, listening for footsteps – Mummy's footsteps, stepping down the creaky staircase – me, holding on to fragments of hope for a last chance of being loved, yet the ticking from the old wooden clock that sat on the mantel was the only sound to be heard. The pet mice that once played inside the glass arena of their cage were well dead and gone. Grandfather had been buried alongside Nana in some cemetery in North Belfast, so I had heard. The old armchair with the broken spring smelled no more of whisky. It was a long night, sitting there with the moonlight glowing through the tiny cottage window around the room, the best room in the house.

Beside the open fireplace where no wood crackled except on Christmas Day, I glanced into the bare alcove where a tree would slot in before it glistened with frosty sprayed leaves, and a fairy then stood on top holding a wand above the decorations that hung motionless on branches, wishing silently in between the sparkling glow for us all to have a Merry Christmas.

The milk bottles clinked. The dawn broke through. The clock struck five. I stood, picked up the worn canvas suitcase, clenched the strap tightly in between the palm of my hand and walked over to the door before shutting it gently behind me, leaving Rose Cottage for good. Dewdrops, like tiny crystal balls, lay on the pink petals of Daddy's roses.

Charlie and Teddy knew I was leaving just before the Saturday in August of my seventeenth birthday, leaving the misery behind. The tips of my high heels clinked along the pathway as I tried to walk like a lady, finally reaching the humpbacked bridge. Daddy, oh Daddy, I cried inside as I walked as steadily as I could up the brow. I didn't really want to leave you. It's just that I can't stay here, expected to clean and cook for everyone, hoping that one day Mummy will treat me like her daughter. I now know that to have her love would be too much to ask.

The five thirty bus had already arrived, parked along the quiet stretch of road. The smell of diesel and the hum of the engine left me in a panic.

'Hurry up, love,' the conductor called, leaning out through the open door whilst throwing out the tip of his burnt cigarette on to the pavement. 'It's those fancy shoes you're wearing slowing you down,' he called.

'Lily gave them to me,' I told him, slightly out of breath.

'Not to worry, we're a few minutes early. Come on, I'll help you up t'steps. Where are you off to at this early hour o' t'morning? Right, Joe, no one else around,' he called to the driver.

'The train station,' I replied, sitting down on the seat and rummaging through the pockets of Lily's cream plastic mac that she'd left for me to wear. I handed over a threepenny bit. He rolled out a ticket with his short stubby fingers and then passed me the change.

Teddy knew of my plan to send money home once it was earned, and so did Charlie who promised not to cry, just like I'm doing now.

'Now, now, just look at all those tears rolling over those pretty cheeks of yours.' A gentle voice as if carried on the breeze invaded my thoughts through flickering lashes.

'Molly,' I whispered.

'My name's Brenda. I'm the staff nurse,' she said, carefully lifting my head. 'Here, sip this,' feeling the strength of a plastic straw touch my lips. 'You've had me weeping, sitting here with you, listening to your ramblings. It's all right now,' she murmured as I felt the flood of silent tears drop below my chin. 'You let it all out.'